NECESSARY SINS

Book One of the Lazare Family Saga

ELIZABETH BELL

Claire-Voie Books

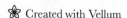 Created with Vellum

In memory of Colleen McCullough

CONTENTS

PROLOGUE

The characteristics of a saint are: deep humility, blind obedience, dove-like simplicity and a complete detachment from things of Earth. These virtues, however, are not incompatible in living saints with some defects and lingering imperfections.

— Bishop William Stang, *Pastoral Theology* (1897)

J oseph knew he was committing a terrible, terrible sin, but he could only draw closer. He'd been alive ten whole years, and he'd never seen anything so beautiful. It occupied the very center of the painting. Soft and round, smooth and *crowned*—there, between the lips of the Christ Child, unmistakable: the perfect pink nipple of the Mother of God.

Joseph should be imitating his patron saint, who stood at the edge of the canvas. White-haired and lumpy-faced, Mary's husband seemed oblivious to his wife and Son, peering at a book through the spectacles on his nose. Much as Joseph himself liked to read, he could not imagine concentrating on lifeless pages in such company.

Draped in rich robes and her own golden hair, the Blessed Virgin gazed down serenely at her divine Son. The Christ Child's arms encircled Mary's right breast possessively, His green eyes pointing out of the painting as if He sensed Joseph's unholy stare.

"Joseph!"

He jumped and closed his eyes. Only then did he realize his mouth was open too.

His sister Cathy continued behind him, from the threshold: "Haven't you found it yet?"

Joseph turned quickly, to distract her from the painting. He'd completely forgotten why he'd come into Papa's office. Mama, Cathy, and Hélène were knitting something for the children at the Orphan House, only their scissors had broken. Joseph had been seated nearby at the piano-forte, and he'd offered to fetch another pair from Papa's office.

Huffing with impatience, Cathy strode to his desk. Joseph tried the drawers of Papa's medical cabinet and found scissors. On their way out of the office, he and Cathy passed the painting of headless Saint Denis, the one their father had had for years. Joseph had never seen the portrait of the Holy Family before. Papa must have brought it back from Paris.

In the parlor, Mama signed her thanks for the scissors by touching her fingertips to her mouth and then gesturing toward Joseph. She would not be smiling if she knew why he had lingered in Papa's office. Mama snipped whatever needed snipping, then returned her attention to her work.

Joseph sat down again at the piano, but as he stared at the pages in front of him, the notes became fuzzy. He dropped his eyes to the keys, but all he could see was that breast, that nipple. Were all women so beautiful?

Were all boys as wicked as he was?

Joseph closed his eyes tightly, and still the vision lingered. He tried desperately to pray, but the words would not come.

Fortunately, before too long Papa returned from visiting patients. Hélène ran to show him the mess of wool she claimed would soon be a mitten. Papa praised it and kissed the top of her head.

Joseph ventured: "Papa?"

"Yes, son?" he answered as Hélène scampered back to Mama.

"May I go to church before supper?"

"Is the choir practicing today?" Papa sounded confused, though Joseph didn't see his expression because he couldn't meet his eyes.

"No, sir."

"Joseph? What's troubling you, son?"

His sisters stopped chattering to each other, and Joseph felt their stares. Mama must be watching too.

Papa moved a chair next to the piano stool and sat facing Joseph. When Papa spoke, he sounded very grave. "You want to go to Confession, don't you?"

Joseph nodded miserably. He'd committed a mortal sin. His soul was in peril. What if the negroes tried to rebel again and weren't caught as Denmark Vesey had been? What if they killed Joseph in his sleep tonight? He would go straight to Hell. He deserved it.

"Whatever it is you think you've done, Joseph, you know you can talk to *me* about it?"

Again he nodded. But his earthly father couldn't grant him Absolution, couldn't make his soul clean again.

"You do realize that most people confess only once a year?"

"Father Laroche says he confesses every week," Joseph murmured, "and that we should too." What a Priest had to confess, Joseph still didn't understand.

He heard Papa draw in a breath to respond; but then, from the other side of the room, came the familiar, insistent-yet-polite finger-snap Mama used to attract their attention. Cathy must have been translating for her. Mama made Papa's sign name, and the expression on her face turned it into a plea. 'Let him go,' she said with her hands.

Papa turned to her. 'In the three years since he began, our son—our *perfect* son—has made more Confessions than most people do their entire *lives*.'

Mama frowned. Papa was criticizing her too: she took Joseph every Saturday. Cathy would go with them only once a month. None of her friends confessed more often than that, she said. At the church, Mama always went first, clutching her little notebook till she passed it to Father Laroche. He would read her transgressions and then write down her Penance. Afterward, as Joseph watched Mama burning the pages, he would wonder what she had to confess every week. Apart from her deafness, Mama was perfect, as sinless as a Priest.

Unlike him.

'None of us is perfect yet,' Mama argued with her hands and expression. 'It is only through union with Our Lord—through the Sacraments—that we can become perfect. We are *blessed* to receive Absolution every week. Have you forgotten Bastien already?'

'Of course not,' Papa signed impatiently.

'He is lucky if he sees a Priest once a year.' Joseph knew his mother's brother lived somewhere in North Carolina, surrounded by Protestants. 'Here, we even have a Priest who knows our language!'

'Father Laroche does *not* know your language,' Papa insisted, emphasizing the sign. 'He knows *French*. Your English is just as good, Anne. It's certainly better than his. I wish you'd confess to one of the Irishmen instead.'

Mama tensed. 'Father Laroche—'

'Father Laroche makes you do Penance for'—Papa's hands hesitated—'for being a woman!'

Mama drew in a sharp breath, and crimson flooded her cheeks. Her eyes darted nervously to Joseph and his sisters. They were still watching, though Joseph didn't understand what Papa had meant or why it should make Mama blush. 'We were talking about Joseph. Please don't discourage him.'

Papa sighed, glanced away, then finally signed his consent. But he added aloud: "If it's Father Laroche, son—promise me you won't believe *everything* that French bull-dog says."

Joseph worried about Papa's soul, too. At Mass, he always looked bored or angry. Now, Papa was acting as though a Priest could be wrong. That was like saying God could be wrong.

. . .

ILLUMINATED BY SEPTEMBER SUNLIGHT, two fine churches stood directly across Archdale Street from their house. Joseph turned away from them. They were Protestant. He hurried past the shops and houses on Beaufain till he reached Hasell Street and the Catholic church, which had no steeple.

Joseph climbed the steps, pulled open the heavy door, and genuflected to the Body of Christ in the Tabernacle. He peered into the sacristy, but he saw only Mr. Doré polishing the sacred vessels. "Is Father Laroche or Father Gallagher here?"

"I think Father Laroche is saying his breviary in the cemetery. Do you need him?"

Joseph nodded. "For Confession."

The sacristan frowned. "On a Wednesday?" But he agreed to fetch the Priest.

Joseph knelt in the stifling darkness of the confessional. This was the first time he'd truly dreaded putting his sins into words. Till now, his most serious faults had involved his great-grandmother Marguerite. So many times, he'd felt anger toward her and broken the Fourth Commandment, which included adults beyond your parents. Joseph knew it was wrong to blame Great-Grandmother Marguerite for his own sins; but with her buried, he'd thought the narrow path of righteousness would be easier.

Now he had no excuse, and he understood how wicked he was. Surely no one had ever stared at the Blessed Virgin as he had. Was Absolution possible for such a sin? Even if it was, how could Joseph ever face Father Laroche again?

At last, the Priest entered the other side of the confessional.

"Bless me, Father, for I have sinned." Joseph could scarcely breathe. He knew how this would begin, but he was terrified about how it would end. "I confess to almighty God, to blessed Mary ever Virgin"—the words felt sharp in his throat—"to all the saints, and to you, Father, that I have sinned exceedingly...through my fault, through my fault, through my most grievous fault." *His* fault, no one else's, Joseph reminded himself each time he struck his chest. "Since my last Confession, which was four days ago, I accuse myself of impure thoughts. For this and all my other sins which I cannot now remember, I am heartily sorry and humbly ask pardon of God, and Penance and Absolution of you, Father."

The Priest sighed. "How old are you?"

"Ten."

"Did you entertain impure thoughts about women generally, or about someone specific? *Don't* give me a name."

"I-I *have* to, Father."

"Now you're being disobedient!" Father Laroche barked.

Joseph started. He hoped no one else had entered the sanctuary, or at least that they didn't understand French.

"I don't need the foul details, boy; I just need to determine the gravity of your sin."

"But—my impure thoughts were…about Our Lady."

"*What?*"

"There's a new painting in my father's office of the Holy Family. Our Lady, she's nursing her Son, and you can see…"

"You looked upon the Blessed Virgin, the Queen of Heaven— the pure, undefiled Mother of Christ and the Church, the *only* woman who never sinned—and instead of falling on your knees and praising her, you *sinned* against her?!"

Joseph had wanted to fall on his knees and praise her too. He'd wanted to *worship* her. "Yes," he managed aloud. "And I—I envied Our Lord."

"Do you envy His sufferings, too? Do you understand that every time you sin, you make Christ suffer more? You're driving another nail into His precious body, flaying His back open again and again with the scourge. Can you imagine the agonies He suffers when you look at His *Mother* with lust?"

Joseph squeezed his eyes shut, but the tears seeped out anyway.

"Because of what you've done, what you've thought, your soul is *filthy*, boy. Black as pitch. Black as a *negro*. You're hideous! If you could see your soul in a mirror, you would vomit. Do you *want* to be white? Do you want to be beautiful in God's eyes?"

"Yes, Father."

"You must discipline yourself to avoid occasions of sin. If this painting is in your father's office, you must never set foot there again. If you might see it from the hall, then walk past quickly and do not even raise your eyes. Do you know of Saint Aloysius Gonzaga?"

"No, Father."

"You should. He is the patron of young people for a reason. He kept his eyes *always* downcast. He did not dare look at any woman— even his own mother—because he knew she might be a temptation for him. You would do well to follow his example."

But Joseph *had* to look at his mother, or he couldn't obey her, because he couldn't see what she was signing.

"You are entering a very dangerous period of your life. These next few years will determine what kind of man you'll be. As Saint Jerome reminds us: 'The Devil only wishes us to begin.' If you open the door but a crack, he will gain possession of your soul."

Finally Father Laroche instructed Joseph to say the Act of Contrition: "I am heartily sorry for having offended Thee, and I detest all my sins... I firmly resolve, with the help of Thy grace, to sin no more and avoid proximate occasions of sin."

The Priest gave Joseph Absolution and his Penance. He concluded: "And say a prayer for me."

"Y-Yes, Father."

"Don't sound so reluctant, boy."

"I'm sorry, Father," Joseph answered quickly. "I will; I have been. Mama tells me to pray for you and Father Gallagher and Bishop England too. It's only...you're Priests. I don't understand why you *need*—"

"Priests need prayer more than anyone! Whose souls do you think Satan covets most? Think how valuable each Priest is, how many souls he saves in his lifetime! For every one of us lost, Satan can claim thousands of you. It is your responsibility to protect us. When Priests sin, it's because their parishioners haven't prayed for them. That's why there are so many bad Priests in America— because there are so many bad parishioners. Don't be one of them. Do you hear me?"

· · ·

JOSEPH TRIED VERY HARD to obey Father Laroche and keep his eyes always lowered, at least when no one was signing. For a few days, he was successful. Then they went to visit Mama's sister. Her son Frederic was five years older than Joseph.

The moment they were alone, Frederic started chuckling. "Am I so very ugly, cousin?"

"No," Joseph stammered without looking up.

Frederic stooped over sideways till his head was lower than Joseph's. "Then why are you keeping your eyes cast down like a negro?"

It was *pride* that made Joseph raise his eyes then—another sin. He shouldn't be ashamed if someone mistook him for a negro. Not all of them were like Denmark Vesey. Many negroes were as humble and docile as saints. They obeyed their superiors without question and took correction when they deserved it. They knew they were nothing.

PART I
ABATTOIR

1789-1822

SAINT-DOMINGUE, FRENCH WEST INDIES;
PARIS, FRANCE;
AND CHARLESTON, SOUTH CAROLINA

You will see all my blood flow before I consent to your freedom, because your slavery, my fortune, and my happiness are inseparable.

— Saint-Domingue planter Prudent Boisgerard, 1793 letter

CHAPTER 1

THIRTY-THREE YEARS EARLIER
APRIL 1789
SAINT-DOMINGUE, FRENCH WEST INDIES

There are physical needs that make themselves felt more urgently in hot countries. The need to love there degenerates into a furor, and it is fortunate that in a colony like Saint-Domingue black women are found to satisfy a passion that without them could cause great devastation.

— Michel René Hilliard d'Auberteuil, *Considérations sur l'état présent de la colonie française de Saint-Domingue* (1776)

Marguerite watched in her mirror as her maid vomited into her chamber pot. She clenched the muslin on her dressing table till her fingernails scored her palms, as though anything could dull the pang in her empty womb. Marguerite wanted one more child, just one—there must be a way to convince Matthieu before it was too late. She'd do better this time, nurse it herself…

Instead, God gave a child to this little *mulâtresse*, who surely did not even want it. As soon as her baby was born, she would probably stick a needle into its brain, so its soul could fly back to Africa.

There could be no doubt now: the girl was pregnant. This was not the first morning she'd run for the chamber pot. Marguerite had felt a difference when the girl brushed against her to retrieve her wig or a hatpin. For too long, Marguerite had told herself the girl was simply developing—she was what, fourteen?

"Well?" Marguerite inquired. "Who is the father?"

The *mulâtresse* wiped her face with her apron, still looking green in spite of her dark skin. Not as dark as the pure Africans—a sort of chestnut. "I do not know, *Madâme*."

"What do you mean, you do not—" When the truth hit her, Marguerite almost laughed. "You mean there is more than one possibility?"

"Yes, *Madâme*."

The expression was true: *"The mulatto's only master is pleasure."*

The girl wobbled to her feet, bringing the chamber pot with her. She carried the noxious basin to the other end of the belvedere.

Marguerite turned her attention to her powder box and plucked off its silver lid. "I want their names," she called, twirling the swan's-down puff in the powder. "You *do* know their names?"

"Of course, *Madâme*." Her words grew louder as she returned. "Their names are Gabriel and Narcisse."

Marguerite dropped the puff. Powder bloomed like a burst mushroom. She whirled around on the stool, as fast as she could fully dressed, and gaped at the girl; but such impertinence stole her voice as surely as a voodoo curse. The idea that Marguerite's sons would fancy this little brown bitch…

The girl smirked.

Marguerite struck her hard enough to leave her palm on fire, as if she'd been stung by one of Matthieu's bees. Marguerite flung open the window and shouted his name. If the girl did not respect her mistress, she *would* respect her master. But everyone else had risen hours ago; the hot flashes had robbed Marguerite of sleep.

Over the shingled roof of the gallery, past the plumeria trees,

Marguerite saw blue parasols, and below them, male legs. "Matthieu!"

No one answered.

Marguerite didn't have the strength to drag the girl with her bodily, so she hurried alone through the children's bedchambers to the other end of the belvedere—and nearly tripped over the chamber pot. The clinging billows of her peignoir slowed her pace down the stairs, so she tore it off. The motion pooled perspiration at the small of her back, reminding her to snatch a straw hat from the rack. She reached the back gallery—empty, though she heard voices through the jalousies.

Without pausing to peer between the slats, she hurried down the steps into the cloying fragrance of the plumeria. Gabriel and Narcisse stood with their backs to her in the scant shade of the parasols held aloft by their valets. From this distance, her sons looked like half-grown cherubs, their golden curls tapering into queues.

Under her breath, Marguerite cursed the little whore, for making her come out here like this, for interrupting her toilette. Her face was utterly naked, and in her slippers she felt as if she were wading through the thick grass. She tied the hat's ribbon awkwardly. The girl's accusation was so ridiculous, Marguerite refused to sully her sons by addressing it; but she damn well intended to tell Matthieu and ensure a just punishment.

Another slave approached her sons and their valets, a woman past her prime with skin as black as pitch. The negress carried a basketful of lemons in her only hand. Her right sleeve was pinned and empty. The boys seemed to be waiting for her: as she neared, Gabriel called an order in Creole and pointed west.

Narcisse's valet noticed Marguerite and shifted his parasol. Narcisse glared at the man, saw her, and laughed. "You're redder than cochineal, *Maman.*"

She would address his manners later. "Where is your father?"

Gabriel glanced toward the citrus hedge. "I think he took Étienne to the apiary."

How many times had Marguerite told Matthieu she did not

want their sons anywhere near his bees! Especially an eleven-year-old! She picked up her skirts, consigned her slippers to ruin, and plowed toward the hives. What need did they have for honey, amidst a hundred acres of sugarcane? Why couldn't Matthieu keep birds like their neighbor? Marguerite would not lie awake at night fearing parakeets might turn on their master.

Ahead, she heard Matthieu whistling. He thought it calmed his little monsters. He'd read that continence calmed them too, as if the bees could smell her on him. He'd slept on the gallery for months now. He preferred *insects* to her. Was *she* one of his experiments? Was he testing how long it would take before he drove her mad?

Behind her, Narcisse yelled: "Farther!"

She knew perfectly well where the apiary was! Marguerite did not stop but glowered over her shoulder.

She realized her son was shouting at the one-armed negress. With her basket of lemons, the slave trudged closer to the cane nearly three times her height. "She must think we are terrible shots," Narcisse complained to Gabriel, who peered into a wooden case another slave had brought them.

Marguerite gritted her teeth and kept striding toward Matthieu's whistle. Fifteen was too young to be playing with pistols. Seventeen, too—but she had lost that debate months ago. At least her sons had found a use for the cripple.

That negress must be the latest mill worker to fall asleep feeding cane into the machine. The cast iron grinders had crushed most of her arm along with the stalks, ruining the entire batch of juice. Dr. Arthaud had been their guest that night. Matthieu had urged his friend to return to his bed and not to bother with the woman— they'd just buy another—but Arthaud had revelled in the opportunity.

Marguerite halted well away from the citrus hedge, where dark bees assaulted white blossoms to Matthieu's whistled tune. No matter how he went on about queens and workers or the pastry scent of the hives, she would not venture any closer to that dangerous mass of life. Did he think fire wouldn't burn? "Matthieu Lazare!"

The whistling stopped at once. For a moment, only that unearthly buzzing filled her ears. Then Étienne giggled. Matthieu called from the other side of the foliage: "Coming, my queen!"

Apian humor. It made a mockery of her. If Marguerite were truly in charge of this household…

The report of a pistol made her start, twice when it echoed against the mountains. A whoop of pride drew her attention back to her eldest sons. White smoke hung over Gabriel, who held his gun aloft and beamed in victory. At a distance, the crippled negress stood with her eyes squeezed shut and her face turned away from her single extended palm. It was empty, the remains of a lemon presumably propelled somewhere behind her into the tall green sea of cane, where anything might hide.

They should all be in Le Cap right now. No fountain, convent, or theatre could make it Paris, but the city was more tolerable than this plantation, surrounded by wild animals and negroes. In Le Cap, Marguerite could take the children to the wax museum (how the proprietors kept the figures from melting, she'd never know) and pretend that she was back at court in the most civilized country in the world.

Finally, the beekeepers emerged from the citrus hedge, the first looking like an executioner and the second like a mourner: Matthieu in his masked hood and Étienne with his straw hat draped in black crape. Neither of them wore gloves. Marguerite rushed toward her son, who tucked his swollen thumb behind his back.

"I am all right, *Maman!*" Étienne kept on his path toward the house. "Papa got out the stinger. It was a warning; that's all. They don't attack unless you've done something wrong."

Marguerite cradled the boy's hand as they walked; and she remembered what waited for them back in that house. She narrowed her eyes at Matthieu. "I told you that girl would be trouble!"

"Pardon?" He doffed his hood to reveal a shaved head gleaming with sweat.

"That little"—Marguerite thought of Étienne and restrained

herself—"*mulâtresse* has gotten herself with child, and she had the audacity to accuse our sons!"

Ahead of them, another gunshot cracked. Marguerite's attention jumped from the negress, who stood quivering with an undamaged lemon on her head, to Narcisse in his cloud of smoke. Pistol arm limp, her son scowled at the ground and muttered, "*Merde.*"

Marguerite stamped her foot. "You know how I feel about cursing, Narcisse!"

Looking remarkably contrite for once, he mumbled, "I couldn't help it, *Maman.*"

Before Marguerite could argue, Matthieu cleared his throat as though he were about to speak; but in the end, he only stood there with the bee hood under his arm.

Instead, Gabriel spoke. "It was as if she bewitched us."

Suddenly, Marguerite couldn't breathe.

After a moment, Étienne leaned closer to her. "Does…this mean I am going to be an uncle?"

She gaped at Matthieu. "You *knew* of this?"

He only shrugged. "It was bound to happen eventually."

"How can you—" Marguerite sputtered. "After what she has done!"

Matthieu took her elbow to direct her away from the boys and lowered his voice. "I don't think Ève is the one to blame here."

Marguerite threw off his arm and planted her feet. "She seduced our children, Matthieu!"

He kept walking, up the glacis toward the east garden.

She was obliged to follow or lose his ear. "We should burn her at a stake!"

Matthieu glanced over his shoulder, frowning. "She is carrying our first grandchild."

Marguerite clenched her fists. "That baby is an abomination!" God's blood, would the thing have two heads? "I never want to set eyes on it!"

"You know what's expected, Marguerite. We owe that child its freedom."

"That is *custom*, Matthieu, not law!" She pursued him through the shade of the flamboyants. "Don't you *dare* give that little bitch—"

Marguerite heard a squeal. Their daughter Delphine sprang up from behind one of the rose bushes, giggling, her face the color of its petals.

Matthieu chuckled in return. *"Bon matin*, Guillaume."

"Good morning, sir." Their daughter's suitor stood up from the garden bench next, buttoning his waistcoat and not even attempting to conceal his grin.

Marguerite buried her face in her hands and groaned. This island was ruining her children. When she peeked between her fingers, Delphine was wearing one of those gauzy white chemises she called gowns, whose inadequate ruffles left no part of her to the imagination. Her unpowdered hair was bound up in a garish turban, as if she were a negress. *"This is how all my friends dress!"* she would argue.

Matthieu, meanwhile, chatted amiably with their daughter's corrupter. "I see you've returned from your Grand Tour."

"Last night." Guillaume glanced at Marguerite and added: "I do not mean I *spent* the night. I have been *here* not more than a quarter of an hour." And what a welcome Delphine had given him.

"Look what he brought me, *Maman!*" Her daughter bounded toward her, those unmistakably aroused nineteen-year-old breasts jouncing behind the sheer muslin. She thrust forward a dull grey pendant, a cameo of a nude Cupid playing a flute. "It's carved from *lava*," Delphine declared. "From Mount Vesuvius! And Guillaume got to watch it erupt! Can you imagine?"

"It wasn't like the eruption that buried Pompeii," the lecher shrugged, "only puffs of smoke."

What a pity, thought Marguerite. *We might have been rid of you.*

"But it's an active volcano, just waiting..."

Guillaume could have brought Delphine a rosary blessed by the Holy Father himself. Instead, their daughter's suitor had brought her a piece of God's wrath, His judgment on all those hedonist Romans.

Marguerite sank to one of the iron benches and let her eyes drift from her daughter's lack of clothing, across the road, beyond Guillaume's banana fields, to the clouds looming beneath the dark peaks in the distance.

Twenty years before, those emerald mountains had been her first sight of the island. After three months at sea, she'd clung to Matthieu and exulted as they inhaled the fragrance of the tropical blooms that carried all the way to the ship. Nestled between the mountains and the sea, the grand buildings and parks of Le Cap appeared like a heavenly city. She thought they'd found Paradise.

Saint-Domingue: the Pearl of the Antilles, the richest colony in the world, it promised them a new beginning, a shedding of their old lives. They wouldn't need to work or dress or build anything more than a hut; fruit would drop from the trees and the weather would always be perfect…

Then they'd stepped onto this American soil and seen, thick as locusts, twelve black faces for every white one. Their neighbors were the refuse of France. Even the Priests kept colored concubines.

The wrath of God took every form but volcanoes. Less than a year ago, a hurricane had decimated Port-au-Prince, when the city had barely recovered from its last earthquake; two years before that, not a single drop of rain had fallen on this Northern Plain. And in the jungles on those emerald mountains, bands of runaway negroes worshipped snakes, drank hogs' blood, and plotted how to murder them all.

Delphine and Guillaume's murmurings grew more distant. Marguerite supposed Matthieu had sent them away. She watched the pair go: swaying closer together as they walked, the shape of her daughter's posteriors clearly visible through the chemise.

"I know what my mother would say," Marguerite muttered. "'What else did you expect, from children conceived in sin? God is punishing you for your lust.' And I suppose she would be right. But it isn't only us, Matthieu. This island is cursed. It ruins everyone it touches."

His bee hood still tucked under one arm, Matthieu glanced quizzically at their retreating daughter. "How has living here harmed Delphine?"

Once, she had thought him intelligent. "Look what she's wearing!"

"*La chemise à la Reine*? What our Queen and her ladies are wearing?"

"Who introduced the fashion to that Austrian bitch? Creoles from this island."

"I imagine it's comfortable." Matthieu tugged at his own shirt, plastered to his skin with sweat.

"Look who she's ruining herself with!"

"They intend to marry, Marguerite. After all these years apart, that hasn't changed. Delphine might have wed a dozen other men while Guillaume was at university and travelling."

Precisely. Not that anyone on Saint-Domingue deserved her. Marguerite narrowed her eyes as her daughter tilted up her face for a kiss. "I had hoped the old proverb would prove true."

"'Far from the eyes, far from the heart'?" Matthieu offered with a smile.

Marguerite nodded gloomily.

"I prefer: 'Absence is to love as wind is to fire; it extinguishes little ones and feeds great ones.'"

Marguerite could only sigh in defeat as the lovers vanished around the corner of the house.

"Why is Guillaume so objectionable to you?"

"He's a *Creole*."

"Our children are Creoles too."

Yes, they had been born here—but Guillaume's family had been wallowing on this island for more than a century. "He is descended from pirates and whores."

"And I am the son of a barber! If it were not for those 'pirates and whores,' France would never have gained a foothold on Saint-Domingue. We owe them a great deal."

"Do we?" She forced her eyes to the four rose bushes surrounding them. White, pink, red, and variegated—a rose for each child they had lost. Marguerite remembered their birthdays, their death days, and every day in-between. Félicité would have been two years old today, if she had lived.

Soon they would be unable to visit any of their children's graves. So cramped was the cemetery in Le Cap, every three years, negroes turned over the soil to make room for more corpses. This was not the New World Matthieu had promised her. No one had warned them about the fevers, that they would "pay the clime's tribute" with half of their children.

Matthieu sat beside her on the bench. "We might have lost just as many in France."

That was no comfort. She knew it wasn't a child stopping her menses now. She was forty-six: she had reached the critical age. If Matthieu ignored her much longer, she would *never* have another child to love or to lose. She wasn't sure whether to lament or give thanks.

The *mulâtresse* came outside with a jar on her head and sauntered toward the well. Marguerite clenched her teeth.

"Do you really think any of it would have been different in France?" Matthieu asked. "It is hardly a bastion of morality, and there are servants there too."

This *was* different. Just look at her.

"If Ève bothers you so much, she will be gone by nightfall." Matthieu set the bee hood on the ground next to them. At the back of the house, they heard gunshots and whooping again. "I made certain Gabriel and Narcisse confessed before Holy Week. They are far from ruined. Remember Saint Augustine?"

Marguerite remained silent. She was waiting for the little whore to disappear.

"You cannot say the island has ruined Étienne."

"Not yet."

Matthieu took her hand, but she left it limp. "Are you ready to write to Denis?"

Marguerite closed her eyes. In his letters, her brother had mentioned the fine school in his parish. Even if the boys began their educations on Saint-Domingue, the island would never have a university—such a thing encouraged independence, as the British colonies had proved. She knew it would be best to surrender her sons to Denis's keeping, that they should have sent Gabriel and Narcisse to France years ago; but to lose them, too…

"Can't we go back with them, Matthieu?" She squeezed his hand in supplication. But when she opened her eyes, he was shaking his head. "Surely no one would recognize us now."

"You have only a convent to fear; I have a noose." His voice became strident. "I won't risk it—not while your husband is still alive."

"Matthieu! The children might hear you!" Her gaze leapt toward the sounds of their laughter.

Matthieu stood at once and cupped his hands around his mouth. "Gabriel! Narcisse! Étienne! Delphine!"

He'd always wanted to tell them—the lies were hers. Panic strangled Marguerite, and suddenly her limbs were useless—she couldn't stop him.

But the corner of Matthieu's mouth flickered with a grin, and not one of their children appeared. She realized he'd chanted each name loud enough to frighten her, but not loud enough to attract their attention. Still he motioned to the garden bench across from their own. "Sit down, please. Your mother and I have something very important to tell you." Matthieu paced before their imaginary audience with his hands clasped behind his back in mock gravity. "Remember the choleric baron we've told you about? My erstwhile employer? The reason we cannot return to France? He is not in fact your mother's father, but her husband. I tutored her stepson. You are all—"

Now her own threatening laughter lent her strength: Marguerite sprang to her feet and clamped her hand over his mouth so he wouldn't say *that word*.

Matthieu pulled it off and continued: "—indebted to the little demon for bringing me under your mother's roof. Where she and I made the beast with two backs until we made *you*, Delphine. Your mother was elated but terrified. She thought she was barren: ten years with her husband and not one child—until you. Until me. What were we to do but flee? We couldn't do that without money. Unfortunately the baron didn't see this as reclaiming your mother's dowry; he used it to convince the court that I deserved to hang." For the first time Matthieu's smile faded, and his steps faltered. "I was nineteen years old."

Even that would shock the children; she and Matthieu lied about their ages as well, to obscure the fact that he was seven years her junior. Too many questions would be raised: why had Marguerite still been unmarried at the age of twenty-six? Their name itself was false—Lazare belonged to his mother.

It would be exhilarating, after all these years, to tell the truth. But it would serve only themselves, not their children, blissful in their ignorance. The truth was a door that, once opened, they could never close. The children would see themselves differently, see her and Matthieu differently, and each of them would have their own decision to make. For all these reasons, they must remain in exile, or some police spy or gossip would make the decision for them. Matthieu was right.

But so was she. This place was destroying them all, and only the children could escape it. Marguerite stared at the blue pleats of her lustring skirt. "It's ruined us too, this island."

"What do you mean?"

She'd been deceiving herself, to think it would last forever. It was a wonder they'd lasted so long. He'd made no vows to her. "When we came here, we were like...*oxygen* to one another." Till the day she died, she would never forget Matthieu's countenance that first time, his gratitude and astonishment that *she* wanted *him*. "Now..." Fiercely she wiped away the tears that rose against her will. "You haven't touched me in months, Matthieu." It was like the baron all over again—she'd become more furniture than woman—except she and her husband had never loved each other, so it hadn't hurt like this. "I know I'm—shrivelling up..." She grimaced at her own breasts, concealed though they were beneath her fichu, elevated as they were by her stays. She knew the truth. "And you're still..." She raised her eyes miserably to his face: skin tanned and lined now; but he was as virile and handsome as he had ever been, those luminous blue eyes undimmed after all these years.

Yet that beloved face was crinkling to *laugh* at her. "Oh, *m'amour.*"

It was cruel, for him to call her "my love" now. She tried to pull away, but he grasped her hand.

"I haven't touched you because I am waiting till you are a little *more* shrivelled. Till we can be certain you won't..."

She made herself look at him.

"Three in succession, Marguerite. Félicité was *so hard* on you, even before she was born." With a sigh, Matthieu's eyes settled on the flowers beside them. "I decided we have enough rose bushes."

Marguerite stared at him. Every line of his body was taut. How could she have mistaken his own suffering? "It isn't because of the bees, then?"

Matthieu chuckled. "The bees are a welcome distraction; that is all." Yet he kept his gaze averted. "I would give them up tomorrow —if you would allow me to *prevent* another child."

How she wanted to say yes... But she could not let him commit such a sin.

It was only for her brother's sake that Marguerite felt any guilt about what she and Matthieu had done. Not for her tyrant of a husband; not for her terror of a stepson; not for her parents, who had chained her to a widower twice her age simply because he was a baron. Denis was the only member of her family who had not disowned her, he who might have the greatest reason to recoil; he was a Priest. *If you persist in this sin,* had come his first letter to Saint-Domingue, *do not compound it. Live faithfully as husband and wife and accept joyfully all the children God gives you. If you do anything to prevent them, you usurp a prerogative that is His alone...*

Surely it wouldn't be much longer till this women's hell passed, till there was no risk of conception. More than another child, she'd needed to know that Matthieu still wanted her. So she would not break her promise to Denis now. Slowly Marguerite shook her head, even as she met Matthieu's blue eyes. "You will wait for me?"

"I have been waiting for you for twenty years," he smiled, taking her face in his hands. "One day, *m'amour*, I *will* make you my wife. All we have to do is outlive your current husband."

CHAPTER 2

I felt a certain revulsion when I first saw what resembled the heads of four small children in the soup, but as soon as I tasted it, I easily moved beyond this consideration and continued to eat it with pleasure.

— Jean-Baptiste Labat, on consuming monkeys, *Nouveau voyage aux isles de l'Amérique* (1742)

H er son raised the skull like a Priest elevating the Host at Mass. "*Maman!*" Étienne cried. "Look!"

Even through the jalousies of the gallery, Marguerite could see that his fingers were as filthy as the bone. When he moved toward the steps, she scowled. "I don't want that thing in the house, Étienne."

"Yes, *Maman.*" Her son stopped and lowered his trophy, his shoulders sagging with it. The boy did not take his eyes from the dead sockets but turned toward the *ajoupa* he had fashioned for such artifacts. The collection in his hut was beginning to rival the

museum in Le Cap. Étienne would make a name for himself someday, if he ever escaped this island.

Narcisse, meanwhile, seemed to belong here. Snoring open-
mouthed beside her, he sprawled in one of their caned chairs with his
legs propped up on the extended rests. Marguerite worried about him.
He had inherited Matthieu's face, but little of his intelligence and none
of his good humor. Instead, Narcisse too often reminded her of the
parable about the Creole boy who wanted an egg. When he was told
there weren't any eggs, the boy responded: *"In that case, I want TWO!"*

With a sigh, Marguerite tried to resume her brother's letter, but
Gabriel emerged from the doorway behind her. In spite of the heat,
he retained his militia jacket, though he had undone its gold
buttons. Gabriel must know how fine he looked in it, how the indigo
dye matched his eyes. "Where have you been digging now, little
brother?" Gabriel called to Étienne as he leaned against the outer
doorway and sliced into a guava.

The boy returned breathlessly, still cradling the skull. *"I* wasn't
digging. The negroes found it in the latrine—what will be the new
latrine, when it's finished."

The monkey Gabriel had brought back from the market in Le
Cap shrieked in anticipation and skittered up the jalousies in pursuit
of the guava. The noise finally awoke Narcisse, who grumbled as he
stirred.

Gabriel flicked seeds between the slats, distracting the monkey,
then motioned to the skull with his knife. "How long has he been
dead?"

"At least three centuries! This was an Arawak."

"An Indian?" Gabriel asked around the pulp in his mouth. "The
ones who were here when Columbus landed?"

Étienne nodded. "See how the forehead is sloped? The Arawaks
did that on purpose."

"Whatever for?"

Étienne shrugged. "If the Spanish hadn't killed them all, maybe
we'd know."

"The Spanish didn't kill *all* the Indians," Narcisse interjected, letting his feet thump to the floor and startling the monkey. It retreated past the slave working the fan. "You think you know *every-thing*, but you don't. We had a half-breed right—" Narcisse caught himself, glancing at Marguerite.

Yes, she remembered: on one of Dr. Arthaud's visits, an entire dinner conversation had been dedicated to whether or not one of their servers had Indian blood—the little whore Marguerite managed to forget about most days, since Matthieu kept his promise and disposed of her.

"I've seen Indians in town," Narcisse amended. "Live ones."

"Slaves, you mean?" Étienne remained undaunted. "Those aren't Arawaks. They're from our colonies in Canada and Louisiana. We brought them here just the same as the Africans."

Narcisse mumbled something and consoled himself by lighting a cigar.

"The Arawaks were different." Étienne kept gazing in awe at the skull. "Maybe even better than us. The Spanish tried to enslave them; but the Arawaks were 'kindly and peaceable men,' so they didn't fight back. They only threw themselves off cliffs."

Marguerite scoffed. Suicide was a sign of merit? The negroes would kill themselves, too, if you didn't watch them.

Étienne continued as if he and the skull were alone in the world: "There were millions of Arawaks on this island—they called it Hayti—and in a couple of decades, they were extinct. Maybe that's why God gave us the best part of the island, because of what the Spanish did to the Arawaks. In his pamphlet, Dr. Arthaud says—"

Gabriel rolled his eyes. "You and Arthaud and Rousseau and your noble savages. Natural man is not noble, little brother; he is simply savage."

Étienne launched into some impassioned defense, but Marguerite stopped listening. The boys' conversations were usually abstract like this, with no bearing on their lives. For all their differences, Marguerite missed Delphine—only a palm avenue and a banana field away, and yet so far, over the rutted roads.

Marguerite returned to Denis's latest missive. These past two years, every letter brought fresh horrors. The King and his family were being treated like prisoners—pious, harmless Louis XVI and his innocent children! They were not to blame if their mother was a traitor.

This upstart National Assembly knew no limits. It had abolished not only noble titles but also religious orders and confiscated Church property. It had even granted suffrage to mulattos if their parents had been born free! France was mad, Denis warned. It was not safe. Planters were being attacked in the streets, despised for their wealth. Human heads had been paraded on pikes! This was why their sons remained with them on Saint-Domingue under Matthieu's tutelage, though Gabriel was nearly twenty.

Meanwhile, the former baron had celebrated his sixty-fifth birthday in perfect health, apart from his gout. Clearly her husband planned to live to one hundred simply out of spite. Marguerite had thought they'd be free of him years ago, that she and Matthieu could quietly, truly marry and legitimate their children before any of them came of age.

May God in his infinite mercy guard you from accidents, Denis had prayed from the beginning. *If you take ill, dear sister, and you feel death approaching, you know what you must do: send for a Priest immediately and repent. You must renounce Matthieu, or you will die in a state of mortal sin and be damned.*

Marguerite could not stop thinking about their last King. The year she was born, a grave sickness had struck Louis XV. Preparing for death, the King had repented of his mistress and sent her away. He had recovered and lived another thirty years, but that mistress could never share his bed again. No Priest would absolve even a King for the same mistress a second time: the first Confession would be proven insincere. Louis XV soon found himself new strumpets— but what if such a false alarm happened to Matthieu or herself? Even if death were certain, could Marguerite truly repent of her choice? And yet without that Confession...

On the back of her hand, Marguerite felt the familiar stab of a mosquito. She smacked at it but missed. *Merde.* Perhaps it had been Makandal, she thought wryly. A decade before she and Matthieu arrived on Saint-Domingue, the slave had conspired to poison all the whites on the island. He'd been caught and burned alive; but Makandal claimed he was immortal, that he would turn into a mosquito to escape the flames and return someday to finish what he'd started.

The bite itched fiercely. Marguerite glared at the little *griffe* who had abandoned the fan and was instead staring uselessly at Étienne's skull. "Did I tell you to stop?"

The slave jumped and stepped back toward the fan's cord. Narcisse, however, grabbed his arm. "Your mistress asked you a question, *crétin*: Did she tell you to stop?" He did not let go, though he knew full well the boy wouldn't answer. "Why do you *never* say anything?" Narcisse demanded. "Do you think you're better than us? Because your father went to university in Paris? If he was so smart, why didn't he know the penalty for aiding runaways? It's his fault you're here now. You know that, don't you? Your father put you here. He must really hate you." Narcisse's argument made no sense: the boy's father had forfeited his own freedom, too.

The *griffe* did not protest; he only kept his silence, even when Narcisse pressed the lit end of the cigar to his wrist. The boy squirmed and fat tears dropped from his eyes, but still he did not speak.

"Stop it, Narcisse," Marguerite ordered, scratching the back of her hand till she drew blood. "I want the fan."

"I will stop when *he* tells me to."

Fortunately Matthieu's return from the fields distracted Narcisse and allowed the boy to resume his duty. Étienne ran over to introduce his skull, but it elicited only a murmur of acknowledgement from his father. Marguerite frowned. Last week, Matthieu had been ecstatic about a rock their son had brought him. Now, he kept his eyes downcast and climbed the steps of the gallery as if each were a mountain.

"Is something the matter, Matthieu?"

"Hm?" He looked up like a man awaking from a dream. "Oh. The...crabs are eating the cane roots again." As if this drought were not enough. He paused at the inner doorway, then turned back. "What would you think, Marguerite, about going to Eaux de Boynes tomorrow?"

"Are you feeling ill?"

"No, not at all." His smile did not convince her. "I just think it would be good for all of us to get away from here for a while."

"But Gabriel just returned from Le Cap."

"Don't delay on my account, Papa—I can be ready at a moment's notice to view ladies in bathing attire."

Marguerite tried to ignore this remark and how Narcisse snorted when he laughed. "Should we invite Delphine and Guillaume? I don't know if she will want to travel…"

"Her confinement isn't for another month, is it? I think the waters will do her and the baby good." Matthieu turned to their youngest son, who stood on the steps still holding his trophy. "What do you think, Étienne? Can you tear yourself away from your skeletons?"

The boy frowned, considered the skull, and glanced in the direction of the latrine pit. Finally he looked back at his father and nodded. "I still have today!" he cried as he ran toward his *ajoupa*.

CHAPTER 3

Everything is disastrous under slavery; it renders the master cruel, vindictive, proud; it renders the slave sluggish, deceitful, hypocritical; sometimes it brings man to atrocities which, without it, he would never have been capable.

— Pierre-Paul-Nicholas Henrion de Pansey, *Mémoire pour un nègre qui réclame sa liberté* (1770)

In the humid oppression of August, sleep was a welcome release. Naturally, as soon as Marguerite achieved it, she felt a familiar hand on her shoulder and heard Matthieu's voice in her ear. Their year of continence had certainly fed the flames of *his* desire.

"It's too hot, Matthieu…" she moaned.

"*Please*, Marguerite." For heaven's sake, he sounded as frantic as he'd been at nineteen.

Something assaulted her nostrils then, at once pleasant and acrid, and she squinted open her eyes. "Do I smell…smoke?"

"The cane is on fire."

She still didn't understand why Matthieu was waking her. He had planned the plantation to protect them from such danger. Even in this drought, the flames shouldn't jump across the irrigation ditches. She rubbed her eyes. "A lightning strike?"

"I don't think so."

The silence began to worry her—not a single tree frog or insect drumming. Marguerite's bleary vision focused slowly on a pattern of blue and ivory stripes: Matthieu's banyan. He had said he wanted to finish reading the latest *Affiches Américaines* before retiring—yet beneath the robe, he still wore his breeches, as if he had never intended to come to bed.

When he turned his attention from her, Marguerite followed his gaze through the mosquito netting. Étienne stood in the doorway holding a rifle as tall as he was. She sat up at once.

"Pellé rode to warn us," Matthieu explained. For the first time, she saw the pistol butt sticking out of his banyan pocket. "There's a band of negroes coming up the road. They've got hoes and cane knives."

"*What?*" She stared at the window as though she could see them. Through the slats seeped only a strange orange glow. It couldn't be any of *their* slaves rebelling. Perhaps their family was not as lenient as the Gallifets, but neither were they like "Caradeux le cruel," burying negroes alive in the—

"You have to hide yourself, *Maman*." Étienne was offering her a pair of his own leather boots.

Matthieu caressed her cheek, but only for a moment. "You are still a beautiful woman, Marguerite."

What use did flattery have— Then she realized what he meant: Forty-nine years and eight childbirths would not deter the lusts of black men. Marguerite grabbed the boots from her son and did not bother with stockings, though she glanced longingly toward her wig. Somewhere on the lower floor, Gabriel's monkey began screeching.

"Pellé and the boys and I will try to scare them off," Matthieu promised. "But if we can't… You have to hide."

In nothing else but her chemise, she stood, and found that Étienne's boots almost fit her. "Hide where?" Apart from that road, beyond the outbuildings, they were surrounded by cane fields, and if those were on fire…

"Étienne suggested the new latrine. I can't think of a safer place."

"It hasn't been used yet, *Maman*," their son put in before she could protest. "It's not even finished." Fluidly he passed the rifle's sling over his head and under his right arm, then took the lantern from his father. In that moment, he looked so much older than thirteen.

Matthieu pressed the foreign weight of the pistol into her palm. "I've loaded it and put it at half-cock. Remember: you have only one shot." She opened her mouth to object, but he silenced it with his own, kissing her quickly—yet so fiercely it frightened her even more than the gun.

"Come on, *Maman*." Étienne seized her hand. Marguerite had only a moment to glance back at Matthieu, who tried to smile. Their son towed her past the other bedchambers and down the staircase without stopping. At the bottom, she tried to pull against him, to catch a glimpse of Narcisse and Gabriel; but Étienne was surprisingly strong. "There's no time, *Maman*."

She surrendered to his momentum. Through the back gallery and down the steps they raced, out into the night glaring orange and furious. They did not need the lantern. From the cane, knives of flame slashed at the sky. Black plumes of smoke surged all the way to the stars.

To the right, she was sure she heard the shrieking of their horses in the stable, and passing far above their heads, the angry hum of Matthieu's bees. Behind them, she thought Gabriel yelled a question and his father answered. Then the snap and roar of the fire in the cane filled her ears as the ghastly light filled her vision.

Étienne pulled her closer and closer to the flames, to the heat, until at last he halted at the edge of the new latrine. Marguerite doubled over, but she could not catch her breath; she inhaled only burning air.

Her son set the lantern near the pit and tapped the top rung of the ladder. "You go first, *Maman*."

She hesitated, still gasping, looking over her shoulder past the plumeria trees to the house. She heard a gunshot.

"We have to hurry," Étienne urged, taking the pistol from her.

She had no choice. She descended cautiously, keenly aware that she was nearly naked, with nothing beneath her chemise but Étienne's boots, without even a cap. At least the half-dug latrine was not as deep as she'd feared—not quite six feet. Inside, she could breathe more easily. Her son knelt at the edge and handed her back the pistol as well as the lantern. In the candlelight, she scanned the small floor of the pit for a flat spot. When she'd set down the lantern and the pistol, she looked up to find her son still above ground. He was pushing the ladder at an angle into the latrine, till its top sank below the surface of the earth.

"Étienne, what are you doing?"

He checked the flintlock mechanism of his rifle. "I have to help Papa."

From the direction of the house, shouts now—and more shots.

Étienne turned toward them as well. "I have to help Gabriel and Narcisse."

"No, Étienne!" She reached for his ankle, but he had only to step away from the pit, and in an instant he was lost to her. "Étienne!" She sucked in a terrified breath and tried to hoist herself above the earth. But the breath was all smoke; her lungs seized with coughing, and she collapsed into the latrine.

She did not know how much time passed before she recovered enough to move. Her eyes tearing, she groped for the ladder and dragged herself upwards into a ceiling of heat. She held her breath as best she could, but the stench of burning overwhelmed her and took on a new edge, harsher than the cane. She supposed *she* was roasting now. She dared not open her eyes any farther, but—

Her left foot slipped between the rungs, and she fell hard against the ladder. It wobbled sideways under her weight and dumped her back into the latrine. She coughed and moaned and extracted her leg, pulling it protectively against her. Bruised but not broken, she hoped. At least she could breathe again.

Still supine, she assessed her person. Her hands and forearms radiated heat, and the skin of her fingers was painfully stiff when she slid them into Étienne's boot to check her ankle. Her hair—her natural hair, cut close to the skull—was strangest of all: *unnatural* now. Clubbed. Brittle. Forlornly she stared upward through the rungs of the ladder. What could she do for Étienne that armed men could not do?

From this pit, she could see nothing but a few bright stars, and then smoke swallowed even those. There was no moon. She worried that the negroes might see the candlelight. Careful of her left ankle, she made herself sit up and crawl to the lantern. She grabbed the pistol, then blew out the flame. She heard no more gunshots, only cries that sounded like animals, or savages.

She retreated to a corner of the latrine, till something hard and bulbous jabbed her in the spine. Terror twisted her stomach. She scrambled away in a crouch, gritting her teeth at the sudden pain in her ankle and aiming the pistol wildly. She squinted hard but saw only shadows. She wished she had not extinguished the lantern. She had no way to relight it.

She backed away the few feet she could, under the ladder again. It must be Indian bones, she reasoned. She pulled her knees against her body, protected from the naked earth only by her son's boots and the muslin of her chemise, nearly as thin as netting.

Was Delphine hiding somewhere like this? How many plantations would these negroes attack before they were crushed? Surely even savages would spare a woman eight months with child.

Marguerite clutched the pistol and stared up at the lurid firelight above the pit. She knew that if a black face appeared, she would have the strength to shoot. *And then what?* The explosion would only draw more of them.

Perhaps Matthieu had intended her to use the shot on herself. But suicide was sin, mortal sin, whatever the reason… Then again, she was already damned.

Not if she made an Act of Perfect Contrition. God might still forgive her, if she was truly sorry, if she repented not from fear of Hell but love of Him. She closed her aching eyes. Why hadn't she remembered her rosary? If only the bones in this pit belonged to saints and not savages. She didn't care what Étienne said, they were all the same: red or black. How she wished he were here to argue with her…

New, precise pain seared into the flesh of her knee. Her eyes flew open to find an ember of cane perched on her chemise. She smacked at it and only burned her palm. She tossed aside the pistol and flipped the ember from her skirt, but the muslin had caught fire. She grabbed one fistful of dirt after another and threw them at her legs until the flames died.

Beside her, the ember pulsed dimmer and dimmer like an injured insect. *"The Virgin's chemise is full of fireflies."* Her lungs convulsed in a mad, noiseless laugh, that the Creole expression should come to her now. Marguerite had never understood it, but she knew it was some kind of blasphemy. Not even the Mother of God was sacred on Saint-Domingue. How could Marguerite expect her intercession? She doubted Saint Dominic would listen either; the colony was an insult and not an honor to him.

She recovered the pistol. She thought it was still at half-cock, but she wasn't sure. Gabriel had given her that shooting lesson almost a year ago, after the mulatto uprising. The danger had been over; she'd nodded indulgently, but she hadn't really—

A sound speared through her, worse than her twisted ankle, worse than her burns. She knew who made the sound, though there was no way she could know. She had heard Matthieu howling with laughter; she had heard him bellowing with anger; she had heard him groaning with pleasure; but in their twenty-three years together, she had never heard him scream. Now, he would not stop.

She clenched her eyes shut and tried to cover her ears without letting go of the pistol. Her own whimpers became desperate whispers, a prayer to drown out those screams: *"Pater noster, qui es in cælis…"*

Perhaps the sweet stench of the cane would simply suffocate her. "Thy kingdom come." She would welcome it, to be anywhere but this world where subjects imprisoned their King, where slaves raised their hands against their masters.

"Thy will be done…" The words choked her like the smoke. "Forgive us our trespasses, as we forgive those—who trespass…" She couldn't say the rest, but in her head, she chanted: *Deliver us from evil. Deliver us...*

If the Lord turned His face from anywhere, she knew it would be from here.

Have pity on me, Saint Margaret... Huddled in the dark, waiting for death or delivery—was this how her patroness had felt, after she had been swallowed by the Devil in the form of a dragon?

Was it morning yet, in France? Her brother would be saying Mass. *Offer it for us, Denis...* Unless he was in prison, awaiting his own executioners. When she came out of this pit, would there be anything left?

She should have gone back with Étienne. Why hadn't she gone back? *Saint Monica, Saint Anne, Blessed Mary, all you holy mothers—only spare my children; only spare my children...*

CHAPTER 4

[Blacks'] griefs are transient. Those numberless afflictions, which render it doubtful whether heaven has given life to us in mercy or in wrath, are less felt, and sooner forgotten with them.
— Thomas Jefferson, *Notes on the State of Virginia* (1787)

S he waited and prayed until silence fell thicker than the ashes, until her throbbing eyes found it easier to call shapes out of the shadows: the unfired pistol; her burned knee poking through the filthy muslin; the toes of Étienne's boots; the ladder. This must be morning: the sky was grey instead of black.

She could not remain in this pit forever. Marguerite crawled to the ladder and used it to drag herself upright, ignoring the pains in her left leg. She stared at her hands and saw the blisters for the first time. She tried to swallow, but her throat was dry as bone.

Cautiously she raised her eyes, sensitive to any trace of movement in the world above.

She found neither threat nor ally, only ravaged earth. To the east, their cane was still burning. Past the plumeria trees with their eerie white blossoms, she *should* be able to see the house. She set the pistol at the edge of the pit and pulled herself from the latrine rung by rung. Where the belvedere of bedchambers should have been hung only smoke—and below, charred boards, smoldering embers. Marguerite's heart seized. No one had been inside, surely...

She snatched up the pistol and tried to call Matthieu's name. It came out as a croak. Better that way; better not to make too much noise; what if one of *them* heard her? Still she needed water desperately. She reeled toward the well, grasped the crank, and drew back her hand. What if they'd poisoned it, as Makandal had planned?

Étienne's *ajoupa* stood relatively untouched, its palm fronds only singed. She sighed with relief and started running as best she could. He might have hidden here. "Étienne?" she whispered. Pistol first, she ducked beneath the leafy roof of his museum.

In the murky light, her eyes skimmed over the boards displaying Étienne's treasures: arrowheads; bits of pottery; little fetishes fashioned from conch shell (one of them clearly a penis, which she had insisted he throw back where he found it); ribs and limb bones from the latrine pit; the skull he'd brought her yesterday; another one; and—the head of her son.

Marguerite clapped a hand over her mouth to muffle the surfacing scream and nearly dropped the pistol. She stumbled backwards, trying to convince herself she hadn't seen it, but the shelf leaking blood drew her eyes irresistibly like metal to a lodestone, and it wasn't just Étienne, it was *all* of them, all her sons, set there amidst the bones.

She staggered only a few steps before the bile overtook her, before her knees gave out, and when she opened her eyes again her stomach convulsed again—it did not stop, because she was kneeling next to the body of one of the older boys, she couldn't even tell which. She wanted to squeeze his hand, as if it could comfort either of them now; she wanted to go back and close their eyes—she should, she was their mother, how could she be afraid of them?

She stroked the trigger of the pistol. But the sugar works on the rise pulled her attention away from her sons: the machine for crushing cane stalks, the channel for the juice, and below, the boiling shed with its row of vats. Under the roof, the form of a man leaned over the clarifier vat. Her legs shuddering beneath her, she made herself stand.

As she limped toward the boiling house, the man did not move; he only stared into the first vat as if it were a wishing well. Realization weighted her steps. The tilt of the man's body was too severe, too complete. His feet did not quite touch the ground. She halted just outside the roof. The man's face was submerged in the grey-green juice, his bald head boiled crimson. He had been drowned in the sugar, his blood streaking it as though some part of him had burst.

But the body was too short and stocky to be Matthieu—it was only their overseer, Pellé. She released a breath and leaned against one of the roof supports. To her left rose the channel for the juice, a neat narrow man-made river descending from the machine. The great geared wheel and the three iron grinders stood motionless now, no oxen to turn them. Marguerite frowned. Why was the channel stained with blood as well; it would have to run uphill from Pellé in the vat...

Her gaze followed the channel to the machine again, and she saw it. A ragged, white-cored, horribly branched red *thing* erupting from the grinders meant to crush cane. That *couldn't* be a...

The closer she came, the more she sank towards the ground, the more she began to crawl. Grass and dirt and ash ground into her burns, her ankle throbbed, yet she hardly felt it. She reached the machine but refused to look up at the grinders, to see any closer what she knew was there. Still gripping the pistol, she dragged herself around the side of the base. Her eyes groped ahead of her, saw—blue and ivory stripes. Matthieu's banyan.

The pistol dropped from Marguerite's hand. She reached out to grip the edge of his robe, to convince herself this was not some mirage of smoke and madness. Beneath her fingers, the silk was horribly smooth, horribly real. She sank into the ash and sobbed and did not care who heard.

The skirt of his banyan pooled on the ground, concealing most of Matthieu's legs. He must be kneeling. Among the folds of silk hung his pale left hand, white as marble. Above her, she could just see the back of his shaved head, sagging forward in death—so close to the still grinders, to the place where his right arm disappeared into the machine and the stripes of the banyan became blue and ivory and red.

She crawled to him, pulling herself upwards with the robe, wanting to pull him free of the grinders and yet dreading what she would reveal. Dear God, he was still warm, but she knew it must be only the heated air of this inferno. She wrapped her arms around his back; she buried her face in the open throat of his shirt; and she felt a shudder that was not her own.

Marguerite cried out, let go, and fell to the ground. She gaped up at the groaning corpse. "Matthieu?"

His eyelids fluttered. He was trying to say her name.

"I'm here! They didn't find me!" She ducked beneath his good arm and kissed his neck, his jaw, his cheek, whatever she could reach. "Thank God, Matthieu!" She fought to support his weight. She knew she mustn't put any more pressure on what remained of his right arm. Or…should she look for the machete they kept here to free the slaves? "I have to find a doctor!"

He answered in a murmur she couldn't understand.

"What?" She had to hold her breath so she could hear him.

"Too late…"

When she gripped his undamaged hand, his fingers felt like ice. She bit into her lower lip, tasting blood with the vomit. Too late for a doctor. Too far to go. For a Priest, as well. But there was still a chance Matthieu could die in a state of grace. "All right. All right. Do you remember the Act of Perfect Contrition?"

Matthieu only repeated hoarsely: "Too late."

"It's not! I'll help you—"

"Not sorry."

"You *must*, Matthieu! If you don't—"

"Only sorry— My fault. Our sons…"

Marguerite pressed her face into his neck, willing away the images. If he didn't know, she couldn't tell him.

"Safer in France," he muttered.

He *did* know. Merciful God—*merciless* God, had the fiends made Matthieu *watch* while they…

"Forgive me, *m'amour*."

"Of course I do; but—"

"Find Delphine," he whispered fiercely, "and our grandson."

Did he mean the child yet to be born?

"Please." He was shivering in the heat.

"I will; after—"

"His eyes—remarkable."

Whose eyes? But she stumbled then beneath Matthieu's weight; he felt heavier suddenly. She planted her feet, struggled, stood with him, admitted: "Matthieu, I don't understand." She held her breath, waited for him to reply. He must be gathering strength. "Matthieu?"

Nothing.

"I'll go to Delphine, but what did you mean, about…"

He was so still.

Gingerly Marguerite slid her fingertips over his lips, felt for breath. She felt nothing, but surely it was only weak, surely he'd only passed out again. She was trembling too much to tell. She closed her eyes and kissed him, clung to him.

Only their daughter remained. Almost Matthieu's last words: *"Find Delphine."*

"I love you," she whispered into his ear. She let go and turned without looking back. She only stooped to retrieve the pistol.

She glanced toward the stables, but they were blackened ruins. She would have to walk, in spite of her burned knee and her sore ankle. She was grateful for Étienne's boots.

In the ditch beside the road, tall grass grew wild, making the way more difficult but offering her shelter while she made sure no one was coming. Job's Tears, the grass was called. She almost laughed. Job had been lucky.

She darted across the road into the banana field on the back of Guillaume's land. The long leaves waved above her like thick green feathers, in welcome or in warning. She smelled burnt flesh but found only a wild pig collapsed in the dirt. Her empty stomach begged her to stop, but she went on.

Between the banana leaves appeared the orange tiles and blue shutters of Guillaume and Delphine's belvedere. Still intact. Thank God. Marguerite limped faster. At the center of the enclosed gallery, the front doors yawned wide, but they were left that way, night or day, for the breeze.

"Delphine?" Marguerite did not see the chairs till she entered the gallery, and her voice gave out. The caning of the seats had been stamped through. The negroes had been here after all. Marguerite gripped her pistol more tightly and swallowed, still tasting bile.

Inside, the sphere of Guillaume's globe greeted her first, loose from its base and upside down on the floor. Nearby, one of his model ships lay sunken in debris next to the dining table: shattered crystal and china, papayas oozing their shocking black seeds. On the walls, crooked portraits of Guillaume's mother and father were slashed through, decapitated.

Marguerite shuffled through the destruction to the side gallery and the foot of the staircase. Guillaume lay face down on the landing in his night-shirt, blood and brains dripping down the steps. No matter. Delphine was better off without him.

Marguerite waded back to the smashed papayas, knelt, and ate like a watchful animal. The soft pink flesh soon alleviated her hunger and her thirst. In the beginning, she used her fingernails to claw out the guts, the peppery seeds inside their gelatinous sacs. Then, she chewed a few purposefully and grimaced at the strength of their bitterness; but the taste of vomit remained in her mouth.

Delphine was young yet and beautiful. As a widow with a tragic story, she would have no trouble finding another husband, a superior husband. Marguerite would see to it. Their ties to this godless, godforsaken island had been severed completely. Together she and Delphine would leave this place; they would make a fresh start in— not France, not till that revolt had been quelled. Charleston; yes, Charleston, in one or other of the Carolinas. Matthieu had an uncle who was a merchant there.

Marguerite sucked her fingers clean and passed Guillaume's body as quickly as possible. She reached the spare bedchamber in the belvedere. Through the doorway of Delphine's room, Marguerite caught a glimpse of a black face.

She flung herself against the wall and clutched the pistol. "Come out of there right now!" Marguerite ordered in Creole, pleased some of the strength had returned to her voice. "I have a gun!"

No response.

"Did you hear me? There's nowhere for you to go!"

Still no reply. It had been only an aging *mulâtresse*, probably robbing her mistress.

Marguerite took a breath and strode forward, leading with the gun. In the dressing glass atop the small table on the other side of the bed, she met only her own reflection. Her own singed curls and haggard face, so smeared with dirt and ash that her skin was more black than white. Marguerite lowered the pistol and released her breath. She looked like a *zombi*.

Between her and the mirror, the great canopy bed stood violated. It had been her and Matthieu's gift to their daughter and son-in-law, with its beautiful mahogany posters carved like pineapples and its headboard like palm fronds. The rich wood had been shredded as if by the claws of a monster, the coconut husks of its mattress bulging out like intestines. At her feet, a smashed decanter filled the room with the tantalizing scent of rum, but it did not quite mask the reek of urine.

Across the soiled bed, that hideous reflection kept mocking her. Marguerite snatched up the decanter's crystal stopper and hurled it at the dressing glass. The stopper hit its lower half, giving a satisfying *crack* and tilting the broken mirror to reveal what waited on the other side of the bed.

Delphine. Eyes and mouth gaping. Dark hair spilling down the front of her white chemise, framing the blood that had spilled from her open throat.

Marguerite staggered closer. In the fragmented glass, between her daughter's limp arms where her great belly should have been, there was only more blood. Marguerite gripped the ravaged bedpost but slid to her knees.

This was God's punishment. There was no other explanation. To lose the man she loved and every one of their children in a single night...even their *grandchild* before it was born... In one terrible swath, the scythe had destroyed every fruit of her sin. These savage negroes were merely the instruments of God's wrath. Marguerite had been running from this judgment for half her life. She'd dishonored her parents and committed adultery for twenty-three years. *"The wages of sin is death."* And death, and death...

So be it. Nothing mattered now. Not even damnation. She refused to spend eternity praising the God who had done this. She preferred Hell with Matthieu.

The pistol was still in her hand. It felt as heavy as a millstone, but she raised it. Beneath her chin, the mouth of the barrel was one last caress, not so very different from the ones that had brought her here. She did not regret one of them. What else could she have done?

Before she could pull down the cock, a child's cry pierced through her labored breathing, coming from somewhere below. Still trembling, she let the pistol sag a few inches. Could—could Delphine's child have *survived?* Marguerite wobbled to her feet, to the window. A mule stood tethered to the star-apple tree beside Guillaume's office, where the unseen child was whimpering now.

Marguerite wheeled toward the stairs before she remembered she was nearly naked. She yanked open a drawer of Delphine's wardrobe and found a morning gown. Marguerite fastened it over her ruined chemise, covering black with white.

She found a large pocket as well, tied it around her waist, and tucked the pistol inside. She might need her hands for the baby. She hastened down the stairs, past Guillaume's body and into the yard. The mule did not look up from cropping grass. It was harnessed to a cart filled with calabashes, blankets, and sacks of supplies.

Marguerite crept up the steps of the office and peered through the open doorway. She saw a child seated on a skirted lap. Perhaps two years old, not a newborn. But he was beautiful, with a halo of dark curls. Something in his small face was familiar, though he looked Spanish. What would a Spanish child be doing on this side of the island? He wore only a dirty shift that ended above his knees. One of them was skinned.

A female voice was cooing to him. Broad lips bent to kiss his forehead, and a brown hand offered him a piece of succulent orange fruit—mango, perhaps. The boy accepted it, and the brown hands lifted him from her lap to stand on the floor. With her back to Marguerite, the *mulâtresse* strode toward Guillaume's desk.

Silently, Marguerite crossed the threshold. Mouth still full, the boy reached for another piece of mango from the wooden bowl on the chair beside him. He saw her and hesitated, as if she might scold him, gazing up at her with huge blue eyes, blue as indigo, blue as—

The *mulâtresse* turned then, as she wiped the knife on her skirt, and Marguerite's breath caught. It was the girl who'd seduced Gabriel and Narcisse. Matthieu had banished her *here*. For two years, he had lied, by omission, by concealment; Delphine and Guillaume too, every time Marguerite visited their plantation...

The girl looked her up and down, then smirked. *"Madâme."* Without another word, she leaned over Guillaume's closed fall-front desk, frowned at the lock, and poked it experimentally with the point of her blade.

"What do you think you're doing?"

"Getting our papers." The girl did not turn. She jammed her knife into the slit just above the fallboard. "If the *maréchaussée* catch us, I can show them we were going to be free." She was running away, taking this beautiful little boy into the jungle to live with the maroons.

"You can't read," was all Marguerite could stammer.

"I saw what the master signed, the day René was baptized."

"What who signed? Matthieu? Guillaume? They're dead!"

The girl paid no attention to her. She only grunted with the effort of using the knife as a lever.

"They're *all* dead!"

With a great splintering of wood, the fallboard dropped open.

"Étienne was thirteen! Thirteen!"

"Same age I was," the girl muttered, "when the other ones started pawing me."

Was she *bragging*? Marguerite strode forward and grabbed her wrist. "Did you cut my daughter's throat with this knife? Did you——"

The girl twisted free and thrust the blade so close to Marguerite's face, she nicked her cheek. Marguerite stumbled back and fumbled for the pistol.

"You whites started this, long ago," the girl hissed.

Inside the pocket, Marguerite cocked the pistol fully.

The girl didn't hear it. "This is only 'eye for eye,' as your precious Book says——for Makandal and Ogé and all the others you've killed and mutilated: 'burning for burning, stripe for stripe, hand for hand'——"

For a long moment, the memory of Matthieu caught in the machine blinded Marguerite. "Were you *there*? Did you tell them to——"

"I didn't do anything! I was hiding!"

"'Hiding'?" Marguerite scoffed. "What did *you* have to fear?"

"I wasn't afraid for me." The girl seized a pile of letters from the ruined desk and squinted at them. "I was afraid for René." She glanced at the child. "They were crazy for white blood. I didn't want them to think…"

Marguerite looked back to the boy, who was pouting at the now-empty bowl. René. Yes…someone might mistake him for white, with those eyes. Astounding, that such a fine child should have come from this brown bitch. His complexion was olive, at most. Marguerite had seen Frenchmen with darker skin. Away from this tropical climate, the shade would surely lighten.

Gingerly, Marguerite reached down to touch his black hair. The coils were softer than she'd expected. The width of his nose worried her, but perhaps age would improve it. He must be Gabriel's boy, with those eyes; that was in his favor.

This child was all that remained of Gabriel, of any of her children——of Matthieu. *He* had planned to free René. If the girl had been lying about the manumission papers, why would she have returned here? It was just like Matthieu. Marguerite could still carry out his wishes. This boy was what he'd meant: *Find our grandson with the remarkable eyes*.

Marguerite assessed the girl as coldly as she could, setting aside what the little whore had done to her sons to conceive this child. With the corner of her head kerchief sticking up like a feather and those high cheekbones, she did look part Indian. If Étienne's theories about their nobility had any merit, then that was in the boy's favor also. Indian blood would explain the girl's melancholy, and why her shade was more like a *griffonne* than a true *mulâtresse*.

Whether quarter or half, she clearly had *some* French blood, so altogether the child was more white than anything else. The best in him simply needed to be nurtured. To let this girl take him up into the mountains to be lost among the drumming and dancing of the negroes would be like tossing a pearl among swine.

Marguerite simply had to invent a new mother for him. She had lied to her children all their lives and they'd never suspected; she could lie to one grandchild with ease. Stiffly she knelt before the boy, who stared back at her with the curiosity of his uncle Étienne. Marguerite smiled. "*Bonjour*, René." *Re-né. Re-born*. She could not have chosen a better name.

The girl snatched up her knife again. "You get away from him," she ordered, as if she had the right.

Marguerite scooped the boy into her arms and backed outside. "I can take better care of him than you *ever* would."

"Let go of my son!" She was only a child herself. But as the girl stalked toward Marguerite, she looked more like a panther than a kitten, baring her single metal claw.

René began whining at once, but Marguerite *had* to clasp him tight in one arm in order to access the pistol. She wrested it from the pocket and pointed it between the girl's eyes.

They widened at once and she hesitated, so close to Marguerite that the end of the barrel nearly touched that chestnut skin.

Whining in her ear, René pushed against Marguerite's shoulder and chest, trying to twist around.

"Please don't take him," the girl whispered, obsequious at last.

Marguerite glanced down the steps to the animal waiting below.

A baroness riding in a mule-cart... She would do what she must. With her injured leg, Marguerite could never outrun this girl, and she needed those provisions. But how in the world would she untie the mule and keep the pistol steady, while holding a flailing child?

The girl guessed her thoughts. "Let me come with you! You sit in the cart, and I'll lead the mule."

She might be useful, it was true...

"There's food and water already, and I'll get more, whenever you want it!"

She would run off the first chance she got, and probably take the boy with her. He was fussing worse than his father ever had, blubbering nonsense in Creole. Marguerite would soon correct *that*.

The girl seemed to think Marguerite had agreed. She hurried down the steps ahead of them to spread a blanket on the seat of the mule-cart.

Without lowering the pistol, Marguerite followed and climbed inside with René. Before she'd even set him down, he crawled toward the girl. Marguerite gripped the neck of his shift to keep him from going too far, which only set him to wailing louder.

"I'm here, *trezò mwen!*" the girl babbled, swiping at his tears with the pale undersides of her thumbs. "It's all right."

This would never do. "Take off your kerchief," Marguerite ordered, motioning with the pistol barrel.

The girl pulled the cloth from around her neck and swabbed at René's snotty nose.

"The one on your head, then!" Marguerite clarified through her teeth. "Tie him to the rail."

She only stood there slack-jawed while the boy continued struggling, proving Marguerite's point.

"He'll fall out otherwise!"

Finally, the girl unwrapped the large green kerchief from her braided hair. She tethered one corner of the cloth to the rail on the side of the cart.

René slipped from Marguerite's grasp and stood on the seat to fling his chubby arms around the girl's neck, sobbing something that sounded like *"Maman! Maman!"* His paler skin against hers was a startling contrast, proof they did not belong together.

Great crocodile tears began to splash down the girl's cheeks as she disentangled him and bound his wrist to the cart. "It's only for a little while, *trezò mwen.*"

Marguerite swallowed and picked up the reins in her left hand. She did not let go of the pistol. "Now untie the mule."

The girl obeyed. René cried even louder, if that was possible. "I'm not leaving you!" she assured him. "I'll never leave you!" She looped the mule's tether around her wrist.

Marguerite waited till the girl had walked the rope's full length, till she was as far away from the animal as possible. The girl's back was to her. That made it easier. She had no chance to react or dodge. Marguerite knew she was a terrible shot, even at this range, and she couldn't be certain the pistol would still fire. But it did. The explosion startled Marguerite as well as the mule, making her drop the reins. The animal bolted and dragged the body of the girl several yards before the rope came loose and they were free of her.

Marguerite retrieved the reins, but she let the mule run. She did not look back.

She tried not to worry. Even if the girl lived, everyone knew negroes had minds like sieves. In a day or two, the girl would forget René entirely. She'd throw herself at other men and get more children. Marguerite never could.

Beside her, René strained against his binding, but he was only making it tighter. She wished he would stop screaming.

"Shhh," Marguerite soothed him. "Your grandmother's here now."

CHAPTER 5

Man is born free, and everywhere he is in chains.
— Jean-Jacques Rousseau, *Du Contrat social* (1762)

Marguerite had plenty of time to construct her grandson's new past, on the long journey by land to Le Cap and by sea to Charleston. Even her fellow refugees pitied her: to have lost all her family but this one grandchild, and him so ill-behaved. René had had a colored nurse, Marguerite explained, and he'd learned Creole from her.

Before they reached South Carolina, he stopped speaking altogether. He even stopped throwing tantrums and settled into mere sullenness. Marguerite was relieved.

She considered making him Delphine's son, then rejected the idea. If they survived the revolt, Guillaume's family must have no claims on René, no questions; the boy must be Marguerite's alone. His mother had been a *señorita* whom Gabriel had met at Fort Dauphin when he went to buy a horse. She was the daughter of a Spanish officer, a beautiful, pious, aristocratic, headstrong young woman who had died in childbirth but left behind this little angel… Marguerite chose the name Maria Dolores, after Our Lady of

Sorrows. She and Gabriel were far too young to wed, but they'd done it anyway, in secret, and her family had disowned her. Marguerite made their tale into a romantic tragedy.

Matthieu's uncle, Thierry Lazare, knew no better; he'd communicated only fitfully with his nephew. Marguerite knocked on the door of Thierry's brick house on Archdale Street with considerable trepidation.

The old bachelor greeted them coolly—until René looked up at him. Then, Thierry smiled. "You have her eyes," he declared, referring to his late sister, Matthieu's mother. "The very color of a blue Morpho!" This was, apparently, a butterfly from South America. Thierry showed them a specimen of the creature, for which he'd paid a ridiculous sum. If he could afford to throw away money on something like *that*...

"Aren't those wings the prettiest blue you've ever seen?" Thierry asked the child.

"Blue," René agreed solemnly. It was only a murmur—but it was the first word he'd spoken in weeks.

The old man was obsessed with butterflies—and their "caterpillars." They looked like worms to Marguerite. No wonder Thierry had never married. The reason he lived on the outskirts of Charleston was *insects*. Day in and day out, Thierry went traipsing about the nearby fields to collect his worms, which he brought home *alive*.

Outside his house, the society was hardly better. Directly across Archdale Street: not one but two Protestant churches. Directly behind them: a brewery, a poor house, and a jail, in that order. This was hardly the return to civilization Marguerite had hoped for. But as these English-Americans put it: "Beggars must not be choosers."

Besides, Charleston was only a sojourn before Marguerite and René returned to France. She wrote to her brother Denis, who was relieved Marguerite was alive and delighted to learn he had a grand-nephew. They were welcome to join him in his presbytery— as soon as France was safe again.

Then, the Terror began. It proved the commoners were a separate race from the nobility: while they claimed to worship Reason, they acted as savage as Africans. They rid Marguerite of her husband and parents, when it hardly mattered anymore. "Let us go to the foot of the great altar," one of the revolutionaries declared, "and attend the celebration of the red Mass" at the "holy guillotine." They sacrificed nuns to their machine and cried: "Let us strangle the last King with the entrails of the last Priest!"

Still Marguerite urged her brother to swear allegiance to the new republic. Would taking a wife really be so terrible? Denis would be excommunicated—but that was reversible. Death was forever. Even after the September Massacres, the fool did not have the sense to flee. Denis chose martyrdom instead.

How could Marguerite return to such a country? The France she had known was as dead as her brother. The National Assembly abolished slavery itself, though even this did not appease the negroes on Saint-Domingue. They slaughtered planters and soldiers till they claimed the island for themselves. They renamed it Haïti, as if *they* were the Indians' rightful successors.

Thousands of refugees from France and Saint-Domingue sought asylum in the former British colonies. After all, Frenchmen had helped these United States win their independence. Now, the fledgling country could repay its debt. Many of the Saint-Domingue émigrés brought their slaves with them. Apparently their property was more precious to them than their lives. If crocodiles devour your neighbors, Marguerite thought, you do not leave the swamp and take the crocodiles with you!

The whites from Saint-Domingue made her anxious too. Someone might know Gabriel had no legitimate heirs. The refugees sought her out to commiserate. Marguerite always turned the conversation to France. They consoled her with platitudes like: "We would find the winters there difficult, after so many years in the tropics." They rejoiced in Charleston's similarities to their lost island: "The architecture! The flora!" She would counter: "The hurricanes! The earthquakes! The mosquitos!"

Worst of all were South Carolina's mulattos, so like Saint-Domingue's: the vain descendants of black whores and soft-hearted white fathers, some of them appallingly wealthy. The island's mulatto émigrés joined Charleston's Brown Fellowship Society, where they congratulated each other on the number of slaves they owned and on the complexion of their daughters' fiancés. They shunned anyone who looked more African than themselves.

Some of these mulattos would have rejected René. Marguerite's regimen of milk baths did nothing to lighten her grandson's skin. His nose remained wide in spite of the clothespin she kept on it whenever they were alone. At least it had a bridge. She could do nothing about his lips. Wigs and even powder fell out of fashion before he was old enough to wear them. She hated his obstinate black hair. But Charleston inundated René with English, while Marguerite and Thierry spoke French to him. So her grandson soon lost his Creole, and surely he forgot all about being colored.

Thierry suggested that the boy have a "mammy," but Marguerite would not hear of it. The last thing her grandson needed was another negress encouraging his bad habits. Marguerite kept him away from Thierry's slaves as much as she could. Mightn't they recognize one of their own kind?

No one white read the truth in his features. The word "Spanish" covered a multitude of doubts, as did René's disposition. Far from lazy or violent, the boy was industrious and reserved, if independent. Perhaps that was the Indian strain. His African blood had certainly not dulled his mind: he was brighter than she could have hoped.

Often René reminded her so much of Matthieu, Gabriel, or Étienne, her heart literally ached. In those moments, she knew she had made the right choice. Her grandson belonged here with her, not amongst savages. But after all she had done for him, the boy never warmed to her.

For years, he pestered her with questions about his mother. Questions meant he did not remember, Marguerite assured herself. She would repeat her story about the tragic young Spanish woman, or she would change the subject. If her grandson pressed her for details, Marguerite would begin weeping and berate him for asking her, when the thought of Saint-Domingue was so painful. Finally he stopped asking.

Instead, René grew fond of Thierry and their neighbors, and they of him. One by one, houses began to sprout up in the surrounding fields. On the very next lot lived the Saint-Clairs: good Catholics who had fled the revolution in France. Gérard Saint-Clair merely sold and repaired clocks—he was of no consequence—but he had a boy René's age, Sébastien. If her grandson went missing, Marguerite usually found him with Bastien, and often with Bastien's little sister, Anne.

The girl was certainly pretty, fair as sunlight—such a contrast to René. The way Anne followed him around, the way he doted on her, her family teased that a wedding was inevitable. Then, when Anne was four, scarlet fever took her hearing. She forgot how to speak properly, so René and the Saint-Clairs amused themselves by teaching Anne hand shapes from books.

René also endeared himself to Thierry, and the boy seemed to act from genuine affection. He helped the old man capture and catalog his butterflies. In Thierry's final illness, her grandson proved a tireless nurse. René hardly left the man's side, when the slaves could have done all of it.

"I've already written my will, you know," Thierry wheezed. "You won't persuade me to change it." But the old man was smiling. He'd left René everything—except his books and specimens, which went to the Charleston Library Society.

A boy of fourteen needed an executor. The old man named not Marguerite but Gérard Saint-Clair. In the end, René required little guidance. He wanted to attend medical school. So the year Bonaparte crowned himself Emperor, Marguerite ventured back to her homeland with her grandson.

Despite the revolution, Paris still had the best schools. There was even a place for Anne Saint-Clair. Her family's pantomime was not sufficient to communicate why they were sending her away. When Marguerite and her grandson left Anne at the National Institute for Deaf-Mutes, Marguerite was relieved, the girl was terrified, and René was as miserable as if he'd betrayed her.

In a flurry of panic, Marguerite embarked on the quest that had truly brought her back to France: for the copy of their parish register from Saint-Domingue. The record of her grandson's Baptism would note his mother's color and status. Marguerite saw them in her head, those cold terrible words that would change everything:

mulâtresse

quarteron

esclaves

She must find that page and destroy it. She would tear it into pieces and devour it if she had to.

The fawning little Priest apologized, but the volume covering 1789 was missing entirely. Perhaps it had been misplaced during the revolution, or perhaps the ship carrying it to France had sunk. *Sans doute*, the original in Le Cap had been lost one of the times the city burned.

The missing register meant she had no proof of her grandson's valid Baptism. So René was baptized again conditionally just before his Confirmation, his mother's name now officially recorded as Maria Dolores, deceased. *Libre* was not considered necessary. Of course she had been free.

René had studied his catechism without enthusiasm, though he spent nearly as much time at Anne's school as his own. He learned all the signs and wrote her fretful parents of her progress. Before he began his doctorate, by flapping his hands at her, René asked Anne to marry him.

Her own teachers—the ones who could hear at least—worried she could not understand what he meant. Anne's body might be seventeen, but her mind would always be a child's; to make her a wife, a mother, when she could not truly give her consent... There were reasons the courts usually forbade such unnatural unions.

Marguerite herself was appalled. Why would someone so full of promise chain himself for life to a savage, as the Institute's own director had called his charges? Did her grandson suspect what ran in his veins? Did he think no one else would have him? Or was love simply deaf as well as blind?

When Marguerite demanded an explanation, that was René's answer: "I love her, *grand-mère*."

"You *pity* her," Marguerite insisted.

"No, *grand-mère*." Instead of the lechery of his mother's race, the boy had inherited Matthieu's inexplicable devotion to a woman unworthy of him. Marguerite could not let it destroy them both.

A dozen times she began a letter to Anne's parents, then threw it in the fire. Gérard and Jeanne Saint-Clair prided themselves on being the kindest master and mistress in Christendom; but they would never let their daughter *marry* a negro, Marguerite knew— even if she was an idiot. Marguerite could put an end to this engagement at once. Yet in their fury at her deception, whom else might the Saint-Clairs tell?

A part of Marguerite hoped her grandson would never marry. As much as she wanted great-grandchildren, she also dreaded them. What if René's African blood showed in his offspring even more strongly than in himself? She'd read that could happen. Marguerite could only cling to the theory that mulattos always became sterile by the third generation.

So her grandson obtained the Saint-Clairs' blessing, found an attorney to argue his case, and married Anne. They mixed their blood with indecent alacrity. Their firstborn was premature, frightfully small, and too dark for Marguerite's liking—all signs of degeneracy. But René and Anne would not let Joseph out of their sight; they were determined to keep him. The idiot's one attribute was her color, and she'd failed to impart it. At least Joseph was a *little* lighter than his father and responsive to sound.

His sister Catherine was not much of an improvement. She was born during the Russian occupation of Paris, but named for the fourteenth-century Italian saint, not the Tsar's grandmother. Finally Europe settled into peace and René completed his medical studies. He decided to return to Charleston. France was already overflowing with doctors, he said, and Anne wanted to be near her family.

Marguerite tried to dissuade her grandson, but in the end, she could only follow. In France itself, there were no slaves, and so few coloreds they were more a curiosity than a concern. In South

Carolina, René's position and his children's futures would be far more precarious. So surely his choice of residence proved that her grandson did *not* know of his black blood, and *that* was the important thing. Her own children had never known they were illegitimate, so the truth could not harm them. If René thought himself white, if he acted white, others would take him for white.

At least in Charleston, her grandson would escape the influence of his liberal student friends. But Marguerite feared the damage had already been done—that René would remain unorthodox for life.

As soon as they left France, that missing parish register began to haunt her. What if it were not at the bottom of the ocean? What if it had simply fallen into some dusty corner of the archives? *What if someone found it?* Across the Atlantic, she could do nothing to ensure its destruction.

Across the Atlantic, they would be safer from its secrets.

CHAPTER 6

There is nothing they are bad enough to do, that we are not powerful enough to punish.

— Charleston Intendant [Mayor] James Hamilton, *Negro Plot: An Account of the Late Intended Insurrection* (1822)

René had asked his father-in-law to look after his property. Instead, Gérard had improved it. He'd purchased a new pair of slaves. He'd added a three-story piazza to the house. And he'd set up an office for René in the front room, with a desk and two great cabinets: one for books and one for medicines.

Marguerite's grandson might have become wealthy in Charleston, if he'd chosen the right patients. Instead, he threw away most of his talents on paupers, even masterless negroes. When they offered some paltry payment, René often refused it—even as he added more mouths to their household: another girl, Hélène, and another boy, Christophe.

The boy's hair was as yellow as his mother's, but its texture was alarming. And his *nose*! René and Anne did not seem to notice. Fortunately, Christophe died in his cradle one night. Marguerite's fears of discovery, more potent than they'd been the past thirty years, were put to rest with him.

Anne grieved as if she were the first mother to lose a child. She showed herself for the savage she was, wailing like some sort of banshee and then lapsing into a catalepsy. Finally René coaxed her into mere despondency. He decided to take her back to Paris so that she could visit her school friends, who still lived together like nuns at the Institute—sensible men did not want idiots for wives. Marguerite hoped her grandson would leave Anne there, but she doubted it. The thought of crossing the ocean twice more made Marguerite nauseous—and the truth was, René could afford passage only with Gérard's aid. So, while their parents were abroad, Marguerite promised to look after Joseph, Catherine, and Hélène.

At least, she could look after the boy, who generally stayed in one place with his nose in a book (his mother's nose, thank God). Joseph was ten years old now. He still appeared delicate, but his health was surprisingly robust, and his mind was as quick as his father's. "A very prodigy," Gérard liked to call the boy. Joseph was hardly Mozart, though he played the piano ably and sang soprano remarkably.

His true talent was languages. Marguerite's great-grandson could converse in French and in English with equal facility. He'd also taught himself a great deal of Spanish (believing it was his grandmother's tongue), and he knew as much Latin as a Priest. To Joseph, Denis was a hero, their family's very own saint.

Joseph's sisters were more defiant, and they made Marguerite's heart pain her. She should have been able to call on Anne's parents to discipline the girls, but the Saint-Clairs spoiled them as atrociously as René did. If Catherine or Hélène did not find Marguerite's rules to their liking, all they had to do was run bawling to their grandparents through the gate in their shared garden fence. Marguerite had to settle for an occasional whack with her cane as the girls darted by. Saint-Domingue had literally crippled her; she was lucky to have kept both legs.

. . .

THREE DECADES after she thought she'd escaped it, that damned island pursued her. All over again, the slaves planned to gorge themselves on fire and blood. To ingratiate himself with his master, a mulatto domestic revealed this conspiracy rather than joining it. Charleston's dubious Intendant wanted corroboration before he would act, so another mulatto spied on his fellow slaves and returned with a date: Sunday the 16th of June 1822. This time, Marguerite would be ready.

Even as the City Guard patrolled the streets, carrying firearms for the first time in its history, Gérard would not believe the reports. "Surely it's nothing," he tried to assure Marguerite. "*Our* people have no reason to revolt. South Carolina isn't Saint-Domingue. We don't work our servants to death and replace them. We take care of them, and they know it."

The only difference was that in Charleston, the negroes grinned and bowed as they plotted how to murder you. Unlike Gérard and his equally naïve wife, Marguerite refused to sleep inside that Sunday night or to allow the children to do so. What if the slaves set fire to the houses?

Finally Gérard agreed to obtain a pistol for her, but he also came back with a white tent for the children. This was *not* an adventure! Catherine and Hélène dressed up the canvas like the abode of a sheikh. Then the girls chased fireflies around the joined gardens, giggling, till they collapsed and slept like innocents.

Their neighbors took the threat more seriously. Across Archdale Street, the Protestant churches glowed like twin lanterns and reverberated with hymns as the congregants prayed for deliverance from these black devils. Even with all the outbuildings between them, Marguerite could hear Mrs. Mitchell becoming hysterical every time a patrol passed. Again and again, the woman mistook sounds for attacking negroes. Across the south fence, the Blackwood children were sobbing. Catherine and Hélène murmured in their sleep but did not wake.

In the insufficient, unnerving lantern light, only her great-grandson sat soberly beside her. Marguerite swung the pistol between their own slave quarters and the gate to the Saint-Clairs' yard, her hands shaking with more than age. Her heart felt erratic and too large for her chest. While Marguerite tried to forget what Saint-Domingue had done to her boys, Joseph bowed his head over his rosary, murmuring prayers of protection.

He was as weak as his sisters. When the negroes assaulted them, her great-grandchildren would cower and submit. Joseph, Catherine, and Hélène knew nothing of the fear or hatred they would need to survive. From their parents and grandparents, they received only coddling. Marguerite must find a way to educate the children before it was too late.

She knew she had little time left. Her heart worried her more and more, and it had worried René. If she lived through this night, she would soon be eighty years old. Everyone *thought* she was turning seventy-six—she'd carefully maintained every fiction, even, especially, those begun with Matthieu half a century ago.

When the sun rose Monday morning, Charleston still stood. Catherine and Hélène scampered off to the kitchen, as if Marguerite had never warned them that the cook might have poisoned every bite. Marguerite hobbled after the girls to rap their greedy little hands and insist that the cook sample everything she served.

In the days that followed, as more than one hundred negroes were taken to the Work House to be interrogated, Marguerite devoured every scrap of news. It did not surprise her that the conspiracy's leader had been a slave on Saint-Domingue. His fanciful master, a Captain Vesey, had named the boy Télémaque and foolishly taught him to read. Here in Charleston, these English speakers corrupted the negro's name to Denmark. He won $1500 in a lottery, and Vesey allowed him to purchase his freedom. And still Denmark was not content: he wanted his children and all slaves to be free.

So, like Makandal, he began to plot. Over the course of four years, thousands upon thousands joined his secret army. Among Denmark's recruits were "French negroes" from Saint-Domingue.

Blacksmiths forged swords and daggers and pikes. Gunpowder was stashed away for the attack. The slaves planned to burn Charleston to the ground. Denmark wrote to the mulatto who called himself President of Haïti and asked for asylum. The negroes would leave a few ship captains alive to take them there.

As the trials and whippings continued, the executions began: on the 2nd of July, Denmark Vesey himself; another carpenter; a boy belonging to the Blackwoods; and three of the Governor's slaves. Forty-three negroes were sentenced to be "transported," sold to a slower death in the Antilles. Ten days later, two more were hanged: a conjurer born in Africa, who'd claimed he could make them all invulnerable, and Elias Horry's coachman. Like the Intendant, the Saint-Clairs, and most Charlestonians, Mr. Horry was incredulous that his trusted slave could mean him harm. "Tell me, are you guilty?" Mr. Horry had pleaded. "For I cannot believe unless I hear you say so... What were your intentions?" His beloved negro answered: "To kill you, rip open your belly, and throw your guts in your face."

In spite of all this evidence, when Marguerite suggested they take the children to the hangings, the Saint-Clairs reacted as if she were mad.

"Hélène is five years old!" Jeanne cried.

Marguerite could only hope the girl was old enough to remember.

"If René were here, he'd never permit it," Gérard pointed out. Which was precisely why Marguerite *must* take the children—before they became liberal like their father.

Jeanne concluded with a shake of her head: "You'll give them nightmares!"

None of them knew anything about nightmares.

Marguerite had been right about the cook: she was trouble. She wore mourning for the criminals, in defiance of the special ordinance. Too soft to do it themselves, the Saint-Clairs sent her to the nearby Work House to receive her thirty-nine lashes. Marguerite stood on the upper piazza so she could hear the negress's screams.

Since the one cook served both their households and the other slaves were useless in the kitchen, this left Marguerite and Jeanne to puzzle out meals in the sweltering outbuilding. One morning toward the end of July, young Joseph appeared in a daze.

Marguerite scowled, glancing up from the receipt book. "What's the matter now?"

The boy hovered on the threshold. "I was at Grandpapa's shop. Men came and took Jemmy."

"Took *who?*"

Beside her, Jeanne stopped kneading. "The boy we hired from Mrs. Clement, to help with the cleaning and deliveries." She spoke low, as if to herself. "They must think he knows something."

Marguerite raised her chin, vindicated at last. "Or that *he* was one of the conspirators."

Joseph blinked at her. "He was so polite."

"They do that to *fool* you!" Was Marguerite the only person in this city who understood negroes?

"I'm glad Mama isn't here," Joseph murmured, drifting away like a lost buoy. "This would make her worry."

Fifty-three negroes were actually released. Jemmy Clement was not among them. He would hang alongside twenty-one more slaves. Gérard had lost only Jemmy's rent for the rest of the year and the use of his cook for a few days. Marguerite wished the cut had been deeper. Perhaps Gérard had not learned his lesson; but she would ensure that the children did.

As soon as the Saint-Clairs left for their clock shop that morning, Marguerite hurried Joseph, Catherine, and Hélène into their grandparents' open landau. She wanted to secure a good spot, though it would mean missing the procession of the condemned from the Work House. She smacked the floor of the carriage with her cane. "Drive!" she commanded the coachman, who was, of course, a slave. For insurance, she carried the pistol in her reticule.

As the horses carried them northward, people turned at the sound of the landau, peering at them from sidewalks, piazzas, and windows, expecting the criminals. Then the buildings thinned, the fields began, and finally they reached the crumbling walls called the Lines. These had been erected during the War of 1812 as a fortification to protect Charleston from the British. But even then, the greatest enemy had been within.

Their carriage was not the first to arrive. Without anything yet to watch, already an audience was gathering. The people around them displayed the usual spectrum of skin, from alabaster to pitch and everything in-between. The Saint-Clairs would soon realize their foolishness; they would have no customers today. All of Charleston would be *here*.

With twenty-two negroes to execute in one day, Marguerite had expected the city to hang a few at a time. Instead, Charleston chose spectacle. For gallows, long benches had been constructed just in front of the Lines, with the old wall used to support scaffolding above. From these beams dangled all twenty-two waiting nooses. Their coachman found a place so close, the wall's shadow fell across them—a welcome respite, as the late July sun began to climb.

Marguerite returned her attention to the children, only to discover that they were signing to each other. "Stop that!" She slapped Joseph's hand, since he sat beside her. "You know I don't understand what those mean! What is *this*?" Marguerite mimicked his last gesture, tapping her chin with her crooked index finger.

The boy glowered at his shoes and mumbled: "Nothing."

Marguerite glared at the girls, but they offered no translation either. "I've *told* you not to do that in public—you look like idiots. Speak properly! English is bad enough." She sighed and changed the subject. "You know they're hanging your grandfather's shop boy today?"

The children did not respond. Even their hands were still.

"Will you point him out to me?"

Hélène's chin trembled. "Jemmy wouldn't have hurt *us*, right, Cathy?"

"Of course not," Catherine told her. "We're too little."

"Don't lie to her!" Marguerite ordered. "They've been planning to murder you since you were a baby!"

In spite of the heat, the girls huddled together on the seat across from her.

"Do you know what Denmark Vesey had to say about white children?" Marguerite continued. "He said: 'What is the use of killing the lice and leaving the nits?' You would have been *lucky* if they killed you. I heard they were planning to sell some of *us* as slaves. You don't *want* to know what they would have done to little girls."

After that, the children behaved themselves. Marguerite kept watch with a pair of opera glasses. At last the criminals appeared in carts, sitting atop their coffins. Most looked solemn, but one had clearly lost his few brains. He was waving, chattering to the crowd, and *laughing*. Perhaps he thought this behavior would earn him clemency. Marguerite hoped not.

The City Guard had to force a way through the throng so the condemned could reach their nooses. The wave of people following them crashed into the mass already waiting. Only with difficulty did their own coachman keep their horses from bolting. Nearby, Marguerite heard screaming and caught enough words to surmise that at least one person had been trampled.

"Can't we go now, *bisaïeule*?" Joseph begged beside her.

"It hasn't even started!" Marguerite snapped. At the thought of leaving, palpitations seized her heart again. She had waited thirty years for this.

The negroes descended from their coffins.

"I want to go *home*!" Hélène wailed.

Marguerite yanked on the girl's bonnet ribbon and forced Hélène to look at her. "Act like a lady!"

Joseph muttered, "There are no other ladies here."

Marguerite released Hélène and glanced around them. The crowd was full of snivelling colored women, and a few white women of low character. The rest were all men and boys. Fools. *Everyone* in this city should bear witness, so no one would forget their negroes' intentions. They were *not* "like family."

Awkwardly, with their hands bound behind their backs, the criminals mounted the benches, and the guardsmen looped the ropes around their necks.

"You're going to remember this day," Marguerite told her great-grandchildren in a voice low and fierce. "You're going to remember it for the rest of your lives, every time someone asks why your children don't have a black nurse. And you!" She jabbed a finger at Joseph. "Don't you *ever* trust a negro with your shaving razor! Do you hear me?"

Without ceremony, a guardsman kicked away the first bench, and then the second. The criminals dropped—except, they did not drop far or fast enough. They only *began* to strangle. Some of the men's feet scraped the ground. They dangled, kicking but not dying. They were so close, Marguerite could hear the gagging distinctly. Nearby, one negro tried to keep his legs lifted long enough to choke himself.

Marguerite smirked. What an inept hangman. Or perhaps a wise one. Let them suffer. They had planned to burn children alive. They had mutilated *her* children. They had left her with a fool for a grandson and weaklings for heirs.

Across from Marguerite, both girls were blubbering now. Without a word, Joseph left the seat beside her and tucked himself between them. His sisters buried their faces against his shoulders and clung to him. He cooed at them but glared at Marguerite. She barely noticed.

Wobbling on their toes like children's tops, many of the hanged men could still speak, a chorus of hoarse voices begging for mercy among the gasps and shrieks of the crowd.

With a curse, the captain of the City Guard succumbed. He drew his gun and began shooting the criminals, one by one. The impact spun their bodies anew.

Marguerite remembered the pistol tucked into her reticule and laughed. She withdrew it, cocked it, and aimed at the nearest negro. His head burst like a mushroom. One of the guardsmen wrested the pistol from her, as if she had more than one shot.

They couldn't stop her from admiring what she'd done to her target. It was not an impertinent *mulâtresse*, but it was something.

. . .

THE NEXT MORNING, when Joseph came to give his great-grandmother a letter from his father, he found she had passed away in her sleep. In the July heat, she already smelled horrible, and she was already attracting flies. But before he ran to tell his grandfather, Joseph said a quick prayer for Marguerite's soul. He knew she needed it. He closed his eyes tightly, because there was a very strange smile on her face.

PART II
A PURE BOY, FAITHFULLY PRESENTED

1822-1825

CHARLESTON

Though to visit the sins of the fathers upon the children may be a morality good enough for divinities, it is scorned by average human nature, and it therefore does not mend the matter.

— Thomas Hardy, *Tess of the d'Urbervilles* (1891)

CHAPTER 7

Appearance oft deceives.
— Giovanni Torriano, *A Common Place of Italian Proverbs* (1666)

Joseph would never forget the day of his Confirmation, and not only because of the Sacrament.

Bishop England looked like royalty, his black hair and grey eyes set off against his red and gold episcopal robes. Yet His Lordship did not rule like a monarch—he preferred American government. He'd written a Constitution for their diocese and begun annual conventions in which a House of Lay Delegates and a House of Clergy made decisions together.

Joseph's Mama and his grandparents were always praising Bishop England. Apparently he irritated Archbishop Maréchal, but Joseph didn't understand why. Everything His Lordship did seemed wise. He had written the first English catechism in the United States and translated the Missal too.

Bishop England was a Doctor of Divinity like Papa was a Doctor of Medicine; many people called him "Dr. England." His Lordship made house calls throughout the three states in his diocese: North Carolina, South Carolina, and Georgia. In Rome, they called him "the Steam Bishop" for his energy. His Lordship was born three years before Papa; he was thirty-four when he came to Charleston. That sounded old enough to Joseph, but Grandpapa said it was young for a Bishop.

Joseph's little sister understood and respected none of this. After Mass in the cathedral, Hélène marched up to Bishop England, who was deep in conversation with someone else. Joseph chased after his sister, but he was too late. His Lordship turned to meet Hélène's scowl and her disapproving words: "Mama says you're from *Ireland*."

"That I am." Amusement tugged at Bishop England's mouth and sparkled in his eyes, as if he knew what was coming.

"Then why is your name *England*?"

"Where are *you* from, lass?" His Lordship knew this too. Papa had tended the Bishop during his most recent illness.

Hélène frowned. "I'm from here."

"Your name must be America, then?"

"No! It's Hélène Lazare!"

"Well. Be thankful 'tis not Asparagus."

Hélène made the same face she always made when Mama insisted she eat that dreaded vegetable.

Beside her, Joseph tried not to laugh. He wondered if Bishop England had learned his sister's least favorite thing through divine revelation, or through Papa. Joseph took Hélène's hand. "Come on, Asparagus."

She tried to pull away. "I'm *not*—"

"That can be *your* Confirmation name," Joseph suggested.

"It has to be a saint's name! There wasn't any Saint Asparagus!"

"Your sister is learning her catechism almost as quickly as you did, Joseph." When he glanced back, Joseph saw His Lordship smiling at him the way his parents, grandparents, and teachers so often smiled at him, as if they expected him to part the Red Sea.

Joseph colored. He would disappoint them. He already had.

Yet Joseph could still feel the chrism oil on his forehead; he could still feel grace entering his body, washing him clean from the inside out. He was a new person now: Joseph *Denis* Lazare. He'd chosen the name to honor his great-granduncle Denis, the Priest who had died during the Terror rather than abandon his parish-ioners. With the intercession of such a martyr, strengthened by God's Sacraments, maybe Joseph *could* do great things someday, or at least resist his own sinfulness.

~

THE NEXT MORNING, when Mama began to say grace, Hélène tapped her wrist and signed: 'Don't start without Papa!'

'He had to visit a patient outside the city.' Mama could see Hélène wasn't finished, but she made her wait till after the prayer.

Joseph's little sister frowned at her hominy. 'Papa said he'd take me to Grandpapa's shop today.'

Mama stirred her tea, then answered, 'He can take you tomorrow.'

'But Grandpapa told me he would receive a new shipment of clocks today! Could you take me, Mama, *please*?'

'Sweetheart, you know I can't.'

'Why not?' Hélène pouted. 'You never want to go anywhere except church!'

Joseph knew why Mama never wanted to go out. Even at church, there were often new people. People who didn't understand how Mama communicated. People who stared. And some of the people who'd known them for years *still* stared, even though they spoke without words too. The looks on their faces said: *You don't belong here.*

'Do you think someone will buy all the best clocks before you see them?' Cathy laughed.

'They might!' Hélène argued. 'It isn't far, Mama, and I know the way. I could go by myself.'

'Absolutely not.'

'Then I'll take May—or Henry.'

Mama went pale and glanced over at May, who was adding biscuits to the table. After the hangings that summer, Mama had watched their slaves with fear in her eyes.

Joseph himself didn't know what to think. The Grands seemed

worried now too. They had decided to sell their cook, since she'd mourned Denmark Vesey and his conspirators. If Papa acted any differently toward their negroes, he was even nicer to them. He'd bought Henry's mother Agathe to be their new cook, against the Grands' objections—she'd grown up on Saint-Domingue, though Agathe's old master had brought her to Charleston long before the slave revolt.

To Hélène, Mama said only: 'Henry and May are busy.'

'I could take Hélène,' Joseph offered. He was a Soldier of Christ now. Surely he could protect his little sister through a few Charleston streets. He liked Grandpapa's clocks too. The shop wasn't much farther than the Philosophical and Classical Seminary, and Joseph was allowed to walk to school by himself now. Although Mama still fretted about that.

'Your father and I have indulged you too much since—since we returned from Paris,' Mama decided. 'Hélène will make her first Confession soon. She must learn that we cannot always do what we want to do. We must ask ourselves: "Will it please Our Lord?"'

Hélène frowned. 'Why does God care if I see Grandpapa's clocks?'

'God cares about *everything* we do.'

'But...' Hélène's chin, her lips, even her nose began trembling, and she made a little whimpering sound as if her kitten had run away. She was very good at this, acting as though the world would end if she didn't get what she wanted. Her pouting was particularly effective because she rarely asked for anything unreasonable. Often Hélène begged for something entirely selfless. If Papa were here, he would be pudding. Joseph himself felt his heart breaking. Behind him, he heard May snigger. Cathy just rolled her eyes.

Mama chewed her lip and squeezed one of their hands in each of hers as if she might never see them again. Finally, she gave in. Mama made them promise to go straight to Grandpapa's shop and come straight back.

. . .

AS HE AND HÉLÈNE passed beneath the palmettos and chinaberry trees, as they darted across the sandy streets ahead of approaching horses, Joseph saw two negroes for every white person. Men delivering messages, dressed in livery so everyone knew who owned them. Women in head kerchiefs carrying baskets of brightly-colored fruits or briny-smelling fish and crabs from the market. Even from here, you could see the flags atop the tallest ships in the harbor.

Apart from his sister stepping in manure as they crossed Broad Street, they arrived safely. Hélène left her soiled pattens in the alley, and they entered the shop. They were greeted by the familiar sound of the clocks tick-tick-ticking away all around them like a hundred mechanical hearts.

Many of the cases were wood or porcelain, but these were not Joseph and Hélène's favorites. The truly memorable pieces were *ormolu*, gilded bronze, each design different from the last. The clock-face might be set in the rose window of a miniature cathedral; might be disguised as the wheel of Napoleon's cannon or a maiden's chariot; might overlook an entire scene from an opera or a myth.

Hélène spotted a new clock. She pointed to the gold bas-relief on the base, where a man carried a limp woman in his arms, followed by a monk. "Is this Romeo and Juliet?"

Joseph studied the figures on the top of the piece. A mostly naked man sat painfully beside the clock-face, his hands bound above his head to a palm tree. A golden woman stood over him, her hands on the ropes. The final clue was the dog in the bas-relief. "It must be *Atala*. It's a story by Chateaubriand, set here in America." Joseph pointed to the man, then the woman. "Chactas is an Indian. Atala is half-Spanish like Papa. She does kill herself like Juliet."

"Because she can't be with her beloved?" Hélène sighed, her elbow on the counter and her chin in her hand. She loved romantic stories.

Joseph nodded. He supposed this was not the time to remind his sister that suicide was a mortal sin. "Atala made a vow to her mother and the Blessed Virgin that she would stay chaste."

"She wants her beloved to chase her?"

Joseph laughed. "C-h-a-s-t-e. It means…that you're pure, that you don't get married. Like Priests and nuns." He saw Hélène still didn't understand, but he didn't understand it himself, what exactly husbands and wives did together to make themselves impure.

"*That's* why she can't be with her beloved? A silly *vow?*" His sister's forehead was wrinkled in protest. "Why doesn't she just say she's sorry and then marry him?"

"Vows are sacred, El. You can't break them."

"It's better than killing yourself," Hélène muttered as she wandered to another clock.

Chactas was supposed to be a pure-blooded Indian, yet on this clock, his skin was as black as a negro's. Often Joseph couldn't tell which figures were Indians and which were Africans, since they all had headdresses and skirts made of feathers and the same black patina for skin. Grandpapa said the French artists had probably never seen Africans *or* Indians. But they made all the savages and animals a solid gleaming black on purpose, because of how strikingly it contrasted with the white of the clock-face and the gold of the rest of the piece. These black-and-gold clocks had been popular for decades. They sold better than the time-pieces with figures of Frenchmen, Greeks, or angels, because those were entirely golden.

One jet-black man toted a clock on his back, while another pushed his in a wheelbarrow. Four wooly-headed boys carried a clock on poles. Their lips nearly touching, a black-skinned couple draped over another time-piece in an embrace that always made Joseph avert his eyes. One of the man's hands cupped the woman's bare breast.

Hélène pulled Grandpapa over to a new sculpture. Standing on a golden pedestal and flanked by two cherubs, it was the bust of a black girl with a feathered turban on her head. Below her broad nose, her lips were slightly open in an eternal smile. "They sent you the wrong thing, Grandpapa!" Joseph's sister scowled. "There isn't a clock in this one."

"But there is, *ma petite*," he smiled. "Queen Marie Antoinette herself had a clock like this. Watch closely now." Grandpapa pulled on the left earring of the negress, and her eyes rotated in her head.

Hélène shrieked in delight. She stood on her toes to see better.

The right eye of the negress now contained an X, her left eye a 13. Her turban must be full of clockwork.

Some of the other clocks were simple automatons: as the gears kept time, hidden mechanisms would cause parts to move. The arms of little musicians pulled bows across their instruments. A ship bobbed on the waves.

Beside Joseph, a fat negro nodded his head over and over, his wide red lips dipping toward his long-stemmed pipe. The clock-face sat inside his round belly, surrounded by his golden robes. Joseph half expected his huge eyes to blink, but the negro just kept nodding.

"That's supposed to be Toussaint Louverture," Grandpapa said behind him. "Do you know who he was?"

"The leader of the slave revolt on Saint-Domingue." Joseph imagined the finely dressed, grinning negro drenched in blood and shuddered.

"I put that model away, after…Vesey," Grandpapa told him. "But then someone asked for it. I sold another one last week." He shrugged. "Maybe people find it comforting."

The wide-eyed negro with the clock in his belly did look harmless, his head nodding and nodding as if he would agree to any command. *"They do that to fool you,"* Joseph's Great-Grandmother Marguerite had said.

But she'd been wrong about so much. She'd been wrong to take them to the hanging. Mama, Papa, and the Grands all said so. Hélène had slept in Joseph's bed that night, because Cathy refused to share hers. Joseph couldn't say no when Hélène started sobbing. He'd prayed with her, and she'd fallen asleep clinging to him.

In the morning, Hélène had beamed at him as if he'd performed a miracle. "I didn't dream about them at all, Joseph! God listens to *you*! You're as good as a Priest!"

But Joseph himself had dreamed about the hanging men, that night and many nights after. More than the sight of their kicking bodies, it was their *sounds* that came back to him, their last desperate struggles for breath. Sometimes, Joseph would feel the terror burning his own throat, and only an ejaculatory prayer would allow him to breathe again.

WHEN JOSEPH AND HIS SISTER returned from Grandpapa's shop, they found Mama in her bedchamber, kneeling on her prie-Dieu. Before she could rise, Hélène threw her plump arms around Mama's neck. Mama disentangled her gently but immediately.

'Joseph kept me safe!' his sister signed.

'I am so glad.' Mama rose. 'But you know what I've told you about embraces, sweetheart.'

Hélène frowned. 'But I *love* you, Mama!'

'And I love you.' Again and again, Mama pressed her hands to her heart: 'I love you and your brother'—she smiled at Joseph— 'and your sister and your father… But we must not forget that someone else deserves our love first.' Mama cast her eyes to the portrait on the wall, where Christ held His own shining heart. 'He is the one who truly kept you safe today.'

'I do love Our Lord, Mama—but I can't hug Him!' Hélène pouted. 'Why can't I hug you? Don't you like it?'

Mama grimaced as if she were in pain. She reached toward Hélène, then withdrew her hand and closed her eyes for a moment. 'I like it *too much*. I think you are old enough to understand now. It is very hard, so we must help each other to be good.' Mama looked at Joseph to make sure he was watching her hands too. She made the signs slowly and deliberately, first striking her chest with her fist: 'It is a sin to take pleasure in anything except Our Lord.'

Hélène kept frowning. She did not look like she understood at all.

CHAPTER 8

What matters deafness of the ear, when the mind hears. The one
true deafness, the incurable deafness, is that of the mind.
— Victor Hugo, 1845 letter

Joseph had been sitting on the piazza with his book for only a
few minutes when he heard Henry's voice from the garden:
"What you reading today, Master Joseph?"

Henry was always interested in his books. Joseph knew negroes
weren't allowed to read for a reason. Denmark Vesey had been able
to read, and he'd twisted verses from Scripture to suit him. But the
thought of opening a book and seeing meaningless black marks…
"It's part of a set Mama bought about the lives of the saints. It's by
feast day."

Henry was using a garden syringe to spray tobacco-water on
Mama's roses and kill the insects. "Whose day is today?"

"Saint Calixtus. He was a Pope." Joseph scanned for more
details, and his eyes widened. "But he was born a slave!"

Joseph tried to imagine Henry being elected the next Holy
Father. He would have to become a proper Christian first—like
most of the negroes Joseph knew, Henry was a Methodist. He was

also married to May, at least as married as slaves and Methodists could be. But as far as Joseph could tell, Henry was a kind man, even a wise one.

"I don't suppose Calixtus was an African, though," Henry commented.

Joseph shook his head. "He was a Roman. But there *are* African saints." Maybe he could save Henry yet. Why hadn't he thought of this before?

Beneath the brim of his straw hat, Henry wiped his forehead with his sleeve. "That right?"

Joseph nodded. "I know there's Saint Moses the Black, and Saint Benedict the Moor. Saint Augustine and his mother, Saint Monica, were both from Africa, too." Joseph didn't know what color they had been. Negro blood would explain how wicked and lazy Saint Augustine had been in his youth. But Saint Monica was so virtuous.

There must be other African saints. Joseph would find them. He would ask Bishop England. Maybe Joseph could talk to His Lordship tonight—surely he would be at the party.

Joseph had intended to skim the rest of October for African saints, but he stopped at Saint Teresa of Ávila, who had been Spanish like his grandmother. When she was seven years old, Teresa and her little brother ran away, because they had "resolved to go into the country of the Moors, in hopes of dying for their faith." Their martyrdom was thwarted by their uncle, who brought them home almost immediately.

Papa's voice interrupted Joseph's reading: "Henry, your mother says she needs about ten more okra pods." Papa must have been in the kitchen talking to Agathe again. Because Henry's mother was from Saint-Domingue, she spoke a Creole dialect, and Papa seemed determined to learn it. He spent an odd amount of time talking to their slaves, and not about anything important like their souls.

Papa stepped onto the piazza. "Are you ready, son?"

"Yes, sir." Reluctantly Joseph set aside his book.

"Have your mother and sisters come down yet?"

"No."

"Shall we see how close they are to perfection?"

Upstairs, he and Papa found all the females clustered around Mama's dressing table. Mama was attending to Cathy's hair, while May dressed Hélène's. This might take a while yet. Joseph perched on the trunk at the end of his parents' bed to watch.

There was more hair to arrange than ever before. That morning, his sisters had squealed with delight at the arrival of their strange package: the severed, glossy tresses of peasant women that had come all the way from Italy.

For as long as Joseph could remember, Cathy had been whining about her hair. She couldn't grow it long or shape it properly because it was too frizzly: it only stood out from her head. Looking like a hedgehog might have been the fashion in Great-Grandmother Marguerite's day, but not now! Lots of women added false curls, so why couldn't she? "Maybe when you're older," Papa answered again and again, till at last he surrendered. And Hélène wanted whatever Cathy wanted.

Hélène spotted Papa in the mirror and darted away from May to tug on his sleeve. "Am I pretty now, Papa?"

His smile seemed sad. "You have always been pretty, *ma poulette.*"

Cathy actually stuck her nose in the air while she admired her reflection. From long habit, she signed and spoke at once. "Hers don't match as well as *mine.*" It was true: the added hair was slightly darker than Hélène's own.

Mama scowled at Cathy, in the way only Mama could. 'Vanity is a mortal sin, Catherine. Remember your patron saint. When she wasn't much older than you, her brothers wanted her to marry. But Saint Catherine knew she was a bride of Christ, so what did she do?'

Cathy rolled her eyes but signed: 'Cut off all her hair to make herself ugly. But I don't *want* to marry Christ, Mama! I want to marry a *man!*'

Hélène had run back to the mirror and was tilting her head sideways so she could see the curls better. Her lower lip trembled, and her ragged breaths threatened to become sobs.

"No one will notice, sugar," May soothed. "All we do is add a little decoration." The black woman plucked two ideas from the dressing table. "Feathers, or flowers?"

Hélène weighed a choice in each hand as if her entire future lay in the balance. "Oh, May, I can't decide! Which do *you* like?"

Cathy laughed. "Don't be ridiculous, El. Everybody knows negroes don't have *opinions*; they just do what they're told." Cathy motioned to the blue kerchief wrapped around the black woman's head. "Does May *look* like she knows anything about hair? Negroes only have wool! Don't they, May?"

"Yes, miss," she replied quietly, her eyes lowered.

Meanwhile, Papa was noticing that Mama still wore her frilly white wrapper. 'You haven't chosen a gown yet?' he asked with his hands and a smile.

Mama avoided Papa's gaze. 'You go with the children.'

He frowned. 'You said you wanted to meet the new Priest.'

'I'll meet him later.' What she meant was: *When there aren't so many other people about.* This was an old argument. Mama had never liked parties, and Papa was always trying to get her to go places besides church. There, she would hide behind her mantilla. Mama had even asked their family not to sign to her in public. They didn't always obey.

Joseph hopped off the trunk and caught Mama's attention. 'The Grands will be at the party. You can talk to them.'

'Only with my hands.'

Papa lifted one to his lips and kissed Mama's knuckles. 'Then use your hands.'

'I'll embarrass you.'

'No you won't, Mama,' Hélène assured her.

"May?" Papa asked aloud, turning to her. "Would you find Anne something to wear that doesn't have too many hooks?"

May looked puzzled. "Sir?"

Papa grinned. "Something you can get her into *quickly*."

The black woman chuckled. "I'll try, sir."

. . .

APPARENTLY THERE WERE STILL a great many hooks. By the time they arrived at the house party, it was already dark, and all that remained on the table were nuts and prunes. Hélène pouted.

Father Laroche's health was poor, so he was leaving them. The new Priest was named Father McEncroe. He said he had been ordained three years ago and had known Bishop England in Ireland.

At first, Father McEncroe made the mistake of talking too loudly at Mama, as if this would make a difference. But then the Priest saw their expressions, stopped at once, and apologized. He seemed sincere, and he waited patiently while Papa translated.

The Grands soon found them, and Mama looked relieved. She positioned them carefully in a corner so they could talk without anyone else seeing their hands. Her signs were so contained, so different from Papa's bold ones. When *he* had something to say, he didn't care if the whole room took notice. The Grands' gestures were somewhere in-between, though their eyes were nearly as cautious as Mama's, always alert about who might be watching and what they would think.

Eventually, Joseph began wandering. He found Mr. Künstler, and they discussed Plato. Mr. Künstler was one of the lay teachers at the Philosophical and Classical Seminary. At first, Joseph had been wary of him, because he walked with a cane like Great-Grand-mother Marguerite. Mr. Künstler leaned on his even more heavily, and he could not stand for very long at one time, because he had a club-foot. But Mr. Künstler could not have been more different from Joseph's great-grandmother. He actually listened when Joseph spoke.

Mr. Künstler said he'd seen Bishop England in the garden. On his way there, Joseph passed the drawing room. A haze of cigar smoke drifted through the barely-open doorway. Inside, men's voices rolled and boomed. When he heard the word "deaf-mute," Joseph paused.

"Can you imagine a more perfect wife?" a man practically shouted, his words slurring. "You'd never have to listen to her! I mean: You'd *never* have to *listen* to her!"

"That Lazare is one lucky man," someone else agreed, as if there could be any doubt about who this "perfect wife" was. Joseph felt as if claws had gripped his heart. He wanted to run away, but his legs wouldn't move.

"Think about it, gentlemen: a perpetual child bride." That was the first voice again. "She'd be *totally* dependent on you. She wouldn't think a thing unless *you* put the thought into her head."

"She'd never defy you."

"She wouldn't know *how*."

Someone made a slurping noise.

"You could do anything you liked to her." The first voice had changed now, become darker. "She literally couldn't complain."

There were a few beats of silence, then a new man interjected: "It must be better than keeping a colored girl!"

Everyone laughed.

Somehow Joseph managed to make his legs obey him. By the time he reached the piazza, he was running. Too fast. His tearing eyes were on his feet, not on what lay ahead. Joseph collided with a man standing at the bottom of the steps and crashed sideways onto the ground.

It wasn't a man—it was the Bishop! As he struggled to rise, Joseph wobbled uncertainly: *left* knee to honor His Lordship, *both* for Penance. Joseph grabbed Bishop England's right hand to kiss his ring and sank deeply onto both knees. "Forgive me, my lord!"

"Joseph!" The Bishop's hand caught him gently under his chin, titling up his face, though Joseph did not let himself look up. "Are you all right?" He must have seen Joseph's tears, the ones that had started before his fall.

"Are you hurt?" chorused a female voice at his side, one Joseph recognized: the Bishop's sister, Miss Joanna, who had come with him from Ireland.

Joseph murmured, "I know it's a mortal sin to strike a Priest." He'd almost knocked over a Bishop.

"Only if that was your intention, lad. Did you run into me on purpose?"

"No, my lord!"

"Then you don't need Absolution, son. You didn't injure me." The Bishop laid a hand on his shoulder like a benediction. "Only be more careful in future."

"Yes, sir."

"Will you show me *you* aren't hurt?"

Joseph swiped away his tears and rose slowly. He felt a twinge in his hip where he'd struck the ground. The knees of his trousers were stained, too. He pictured May scrubbing them in the yard and felt even worse.

"Should we find your father?" Miss Joanna suggested.

"No. Thank you." With his eyes lowered, Joseph could see only Bishop England's leather shoes and the hem of his sister's grey gown.

"Sure weren't we speaking of Joseph a few minutes ago, John?"

"Indeed. We were discussing yesterday's Vespers and how blessed we feel every time we hear you sing."

"Like a foretaste of Heaven, Joseph." Miss Joanna touched his arm. "'Tis a gift from God you have: the voice of an angel." Joseph knew he was blushing. Then the Bishop's sister added with a sigh: "'Tis truly a shame your mother cannot hear it."

Joseph nodded haltingly. He'd thought it himself, about so many sounds. Every morning and every evening, Joseph prayed that God would restore Mama's hearing. But even if He granted a miracle tomorrow, Mama would never know what Joseph's little brother had sounded like when he giggled. "My lord...when we *are* in Heaven" —if Joseph ever achieved it—"will Mama be able to hear me then?"

"Yes, son. At the Resurrection of the Dead, we shall all be transformed. We shall have *perfect* bodies."

All? Joseph dared to glance up. "Will there be negroes there, too?"

"Absolutely. The Revelation of John the Apostle is clear: he saw 'all nations and tribes and peoples' standing before God's throne, praising Him."

Side by side? Would the negroes still look like negroes? How then could they be perfect, cleansed of their sin and washed "as white as snow"?

Joseph was unable to voice these questions. He saw someone else standing nearby, waiting to talk to His Lordship. Joseph was reluctant to relinquish him, but he knelt quickly to kiss the Bishop's ring again and left them. Joseph still felt sore and unsettled from his fall, as if it might happen again. And what those men in the drawing room had said about Mama—and Papa...

Joseph retreated deeper into the garden. Their host had set out lanterns. Along the high wall separating the garden from the neighbors' yard, a white bench stood out, set between two crêpe myrtle trees with orange leaves. On the bench, a girl was hunched over with her face in her hands. Joseph heard her sobs almost in the same moment he realized it was his sister.

He hurried to her. "Cathy?"

She glanced up, recognized him, and hid her face again.

Joseph sat beside his sister on the bench. "What's wrong?"

"Theodosia Lockwood!" Cathy choked out. "She said it was about time I got better hair! She said I need it, because my *real* hair looks like a colored girl's!"

"That's ridiculous." Joseph remembered he had a handkerchief and offered it to his sister.

"I know!" Cathy blew her nose loudly.

"Did you tell Theodosia that our grandmother was a Spanish noblewoman—and *that's* where you got your hair?"

"No," she moaned. "The other girls started laughing at me, and I ran away."

"Do you want me to talk to them?"

Cathy drew in a shaky breath and sat up straight. "No; I should do it." She glanced down at the sodden kerchief, then at Joseph. "Do you want this back?"

He chuckled and shook his head.

His sister blew her nose one last time and tucked the handkerchief into a pocket. "Thank you." Cathy stood up and raised her head to its usual angle. "I'm going to tell Theodosia that my hair isn't nearly as ugly as her *teeth*."

Joseph smiled in spite of himself. He knew he should advise his sister to behave like Christ and turn the other cheek. But he also knew Cathy wouldn't listen. He watched her stride back to face her enemies.

Joseph stayed on the bench until Mama appeared. They moved closer to a lantern, but it was still hard to see all her signs clearly. Joseph gathered that the Grands had gone home and Hélène was falling asleep. Papa was also ready to leave because Mrs. Prioleau was after him again. Joseph laughed. The old woman always wanted to describe some new rash.

'Have you seen Catherine?' Mama asked him.

Joseph nodded, but he decided not to tell Mama what Theodosia Lockwood had said. It would only upset her.

He turned when he heard hushed voices behind them. Two boys climbed onto the nearby bench, and then one boy hoisted the other to the top of the garden wall. Even in the half-light, Joseph recognized them: brothers a few years older than himself and also French Creole. More than once, they'd disturbed Mass by making ridiculous noises. Now, the first boy hauled the second atop the wall with him, until they were both wobbling on the ledge.

Scowling upward, Mama clapped her hands to attract their attention. When she succeeded, she made a sharp pointing motion at the ground.

The brothers turned back to each other and sniggered. Joseph caught the words: "That's the dummy!"

Joseph's face grew hot. He was glad Mama couldn't understand. She clapped her hands again, louder.

"Only if you say 'please,' dummy!" one of the boys taunted, speaking as if to a child. His brother found this hilarious.

Then the boys ignored Mama entirely. They stuck out their arms to balance like unsteady tight-rope walkers as they peered into the next property. Each lot was supposed to be its own private domain. It was bad manners to look through your own windows on the side that faced your neighbors. What the boys were doing was disgraceful as well as dangerous. Joseph wondered if *he* should say something, but surely the brothers wouldn't obey him either. Should he run and find Papa?

Then, Mama commanded the boys with words. Her syllables

sounded broken, and they startled even Joseph. He'd never heard her speak before. Even laughing seemed to embarrass Mama. He thought she was trying to say "Get down right now!"

In response, the boys on the wall broke out in unsuppressed guffaws and nearly fell off. First one brother then the other imitated her sounds, distorting them even worse. Though Mama couldn't hear them, she understood that the boys were mocking her. She clamped her mouth shut, drew in a few unsteady breaths, and turned back toward the house.

Before he followed her, Joseph shouted up at the brothers: "She was *trying* to keep you from breaking your worthless necks!" Sometimes he wasn't very good at behaving like Christ either.

JOSEPH AND MAMA found Papa carrying Hélène, her arms around his neck. Hélène waited till Mama wasn't looking, then she squinted an eye open and grinned at Joseph. She wasn't sleepy at all. She'd simply found the perfect excuse for a hug—with Mama right there.

When they reunited with Cathy, Joseph raised his eyebrows in question. His sister nodded and smiled. She didn't need words either.

At home, May met them in the hall with a lamp, and Mama noticed Joseph's stained knees. Papa set down Hélène and followed Joseph into his bedchamber. Joseph disrobed to his long shirt, and Papa confirmed that Joseph's only injury was the bruise already forming on his hip. Papa said he had a salve in his office.

Joseph didn't want him to leave yet. "Papa…can Mama speak?"

"*Did* she?"

Joseph nodded haltingly and explained about the boys on the garden wall.

"That is why she *stopped* speaking," Papa said quietly, "and why she tried so hard. Adult cruelty is usually more subtle, that's all."

"Does she remember how to speak from before she went deaf?"

"Perhaps a little. She tried to learn again at the Institute in Paris." Papa sat heavily in Joseph's chair, and Joseph settled on the edge of his bed. "The Abbé de l'Épée founded the Institute on sign

—he called it the 'natural language' of the deaf. But many of the men who came after him have dismissed sign as primitive and refused to learn it. One of them was a doctor named Itard. He insisted that deaf children should speak." Papa stared out Joseph's window at the dark piazza, but he seemed to be seeing the school all those years ago. "That was what your mother wanted: to appear 'normal.' She and so many other pupils struggled for *years* to form sounds they couldn't hear. Of course their speech was imperfect, and when they tried to read other people's lips, they could understand only fragments. Your mother was in tears almost every day. She could read and write French and sign beautifully, but she thought she was a failure." Papa shook his head. "I wanted to strangle him, that Itard. He was the worst kind of physician."

Joseph frowned. "Because he wouldn't learn to sign?"

Still Papa addressed the window. "Itard also tried to 'fix' the deaf children. He shocked their ears with electricity. He forced probes through their noses. He burned their skin with poultices. He purposefully took a hammer and fractured their skulls! He accomplished nothing but suffering. He *killed* a boy, trying to make him hear again—and your mother was heartbroken because Itard was experimenting only on the male pupils. So she begged *me* to fix her."

Joseph held his breath. What a terrible choice. But if there was a chance she could be cured... "Did you try?"

"No!" Papa cried, staring at him as if Joseph hadn't been listening.

Before Joseph could respond, they heard a timid knock. The door crept open, and Mama peered around it. 'Is he all right?' she signed.

Papa nodded and stood. To Joseph, he said: "I'll find that salve."

CHAPTER 9

In a higher world it is otherwise, but here below to live is to change, and to be perfect is to have changed often.

— John Henry Cardinal Newman, *Essay on the Development of Christian Doctrine* (1845)

Joseph wondered what color he was. He suspected he had passed pink quite some time ago and turned downright crimson. Not only his cheeks but his entire body felt as if it were on fire, and it had nothing to do with the temperature of the air.

"Do you have any questions?" came Papa's voice from the other side of his desk.

Joseph shook his head and kept his eyes on his shoes. He'd thought that painting of the Virgin's breast was the most dangerous thing in Papa's office. He'd been wrong. Spread out between them now were half a dozen proximate occasions of sin: distressingly detailed anatomical diagrams.

"I know I've made you uncomfortable, son, and your modesty does you credit. I considered waiting another year. But your body is starting to change, and you've such a keen, curious mind. I would rather give you the truth early than have you grow up gathering lies the way other boys do. And believe it or not, what I've just told you is a *fraction* of what you'll need to know before your wedding night."

Already Joseph's head was swimming. Mama said taking pleasure in anything except God was a sin. But Papa spoke as if a husband's pleasure was inevitable and his wife's pleasure was his responsibility. How could a man ask a woman to let him do—*that* to her *unless* he made it pleasant?

"Would you like to borrow any of these books?"

Joseph shook his head again. Perhaps too quickly: Papa understood that he really wanted to nod.

He chuckled. "If you can't stop thinking about women's bodies, son—even if blood has gone somewhere besides your cheeks—that isn't a sin. It's perfectly natural. It's necessary!"

If such a thing was possible, *more* blood rushed to Joseph's face. There was none left to go anywhere else.

Joseph heard Papa closing books. "Or, if you can't imagine yourself doing such a thing, that's perfectly natural too. Just come to me when you've changed your mind. Will you do that, Joseph?"

He nodded. At the edge of his vision, he watched Papa stack the last volume. Joseph felt both relief and disappointment.

Papa's hands lingered on the book, but he seemed to have forgotten its contents. "I know I'm gone more than I'm here…"

Jealousy stabbed Joseph in the stomach. When Papa *was* home, Joseph wished he wouldn't spend so much time talking to their slaves. But Joseph understood why Papa often left early and returned late. "Your patients need you. I know that." Joseph looked up. "Your work is important."

"*You* are important too, Joseph." Papa held his eyes till Joseph believed him.

The mantle clock chimed then. Papa raised his eyebrows. "*Tempus fugit*, indeed. If you're sure you don't want to ask anything, I need to pay a call on a botanist friend. I promised your mother I would find out why there are black spots on the leaves of her roses."

"May I come with you?"

Papa seemed to hesitate. "My friend's garden is up on the Neck. It will be a long, hot trip."

"I don't mind." Joseph did have a question to ask.

Papa glanced toward the parlor. He looked worried. "I suppose your mother and sisters are still over at the Grands'."

Right now, the thought of being in the same room with a woman—any woman—was terrifying. But Joseph didn't want Mama to fret. "Should I tell them I'm going with you?"

"No—don't." The response was surprisingly quick and sharp, more like a prohibition. Papa tried to soften it: "Henry can tell them when they come back."

Papa brought his medical satchel—he took it everywhere, whatever his plans—and they retrieved their hats from the hall. Henry had already harnessed their old mare to the chaise.

"Thank you, Henry!" Papa called with a wave as the black man closed the gate behind them.

When they'd turned onto Coming Street, Joseph asked: "Papa, did you ever serve at Mass?"

"No…"

"Yesterday, Father McEncroe spoke to our class—about how we might think we have nothing to give to Our Lord, because we're only boys, but we *do*: we can assist His Priests. Father McEncroe said we should ask our parents first. I haven't talked to Mama yet, but I know she'll say yes."

"Of course she will," Papa answered without taking his eyes from the mare.

"M-May I, Papa?"

"I was hoping you were going to ask me something about *women*," he murmured. "You're already in the choir. Why do you want to be an altar server too?"

Joseph stared at Papa. *Because God made me, and you, and everything—because He DIED for me—and I've done so little to thank Him! Because Holy Communion will help me fight my wickedness!* He was deciding what to say aloud when Papa interrupted his thoughts:

"Oh, Joseph—I'm so sorry."

He followed Papa's eyes. They had passed outside the city and were approaching the Lines. The walls were empty now, but Joseph looked away quickly. He would see those twenty-two hanging men until the day he died.

"I came this way without even thinking..." Papa urged their mare past the ruins.

"It's all right," Joseph murmured, even though lying was a sin.

"Hélène told me how you comforted her that day. I have never been prouder of you, Joseph. Your mind is exceptional—everyone tells you that. We should also tell you how impressive your heart is."

"You were prouder about my comforting Hélène than you were at my Confirmation?"

Papa sighed. "If you want to be a server, you have my blessing. But there are more important things than saints and Sacraments, Joseph."

If lightning struck them right now, would Papa go to Hell?

"You are certainly your mother's son. She wanted to become a nun. Did you know that?"

Joseph shook his head. "Why didn't she?"

"I wish I could say she chose me instead. The truth is, no order would accept her. Can you believe that? Your mother is the most devout woman I know. And who would keep the Great Silence better than a deaf-mute? Those nuns were *blind*: they couldn't see past medieval ideas that deafness is proof of God's displeasure, that it 'prevents faith.' One Mother Superior said your mother could live in their community as an act of charity, but not as a postulant. Those nuns humiliated her. I told your mother: 'You are perfect just as you are. Take your vows with me.' *That* is the Church you are so eager to serve."

"But it was a Priest who started the National Institute for Deaf-Mutes."

"The schools and the hospitals the Church has established—absolutely commendable. I'm not saying it's entirely bad. But neither is the Church all good."

Joseph had planned to argue, but a noise in the woods up ahead distracted him. Faint but distinct, it sounded like a bell—not a church or plantation bell, but the kind put on animals. No human voice accompanied it. Their mare lifted her head and turned an ear toward the bell too. Joseph hoped it wasn't attached to a bull or anything dangerous. "Papa, do you hear that?"

He pulled back on the horse's reins, making her slow to a walk. The jangling continued, sounding faster now, almost frantic, but they couldn't see its source through the trees. "A loose sheep, probably." Papa raised the reins to urge the mare back into a trot—and then the cracking of a branch and a human groan came from the woods.

"Is someone hurt?" Papa called, stopping their horse.

No response from the trees.

"I'm a doctor," Papa explained. When the stranger still didn't answer, he added: "I keep my patients' secrets."

The silence continued till Joseph was certain the groan had been some trick of the wind. Then a deep voice replied, almost too quiet to carry across the distance: "You know how to set bones?"

"I do." Papa handed Joseph the reins and jumped out of the chaise.

The voice inquired, "You alone?"

"My son is with me." Papa led their mare to one of the pines nearby, where he tied her. "He can keep a secret too."

Joseph frowned at his father as he leaned in to retrieve his medical satchel.

"Would you prefer to stay here?" Papa asked.

Joseph shook his head and accepted Papa's hand to help him down from the carriage.

"I ain't close to the road, understand."

"We'll come to you," Papa replied. "If you think something is broken, try not to move."

"It's my arm," the man explained, the slow clang of the bell punctuating his words. "I gots to move a little, so as you can hear me, I reckon."

Papa chuckled. "Just keep talking. We're on our way."

The man did not offer his name. They picked their way through the trees for several long minutes before Joseph saw the bells—two of them, suspended from a pair of arched iron bars that resembled horns. The bells were brass perhaps, round with slits at the bottom and swaying slightly, but Joseph could hear only one ball rattling. His eyes followed the horns downward. They sprouted from the shoulders of a young, bushy-haired, dark-skinned negro, from either side of the iron collar around his neck. He sat on the fallen trunk of a dead tree, cradling his bloody right arm in his lap.

Joseph stopped. He felt a little sick. Much as he admired Papa, Joseph knew he could never be a doctor himself.

The negro glanced up at the bells. "I was tryin' to be careful, but one of 'em caught on somethin', and I fell wrong."

On the dead tree, next to this wild negro, Papa set down his medical satchel as calmly as if they were in a Charleston bedchamber. Joseph kept his distance while Papa peered at his patient's arm and the raw flesh of his palm. "What I need to do will hurt before it helps." He offered the negro a leather strap from his bag. "You might want to bite down on this."

"I don't suppose your regular patients would appreciate that much." The negro accepted the strap but only gripped it in his good fist.

"My 'regular patients' come in all shades," Papa informed him, blotting at the wound with loose cotton and something from a bottle. "Joseph, would you find me a splint, please? If you need tools, my surgery set is in the bottom of the satchel."

Joseph was glad to keep away. As he hunted for a suitable piece of wood, he did not hear the next few questions Papa asked or the negro's answers. But every time he moved, or even breathed, one of the bells above him clanged. The negro was a runaway—he had to be. This must be his second attempt, or his master would never have resorted to such punishment.

"Do you have to sleep in that thing?" Papa asked.

"Haven't slept for weeks now," the negro muttered.

Joseph crouched over an old, fallen trunk that the weather had mostly split for him. He decided he'd still need a tool and began to pick his way back to Papa's satchel.

"My sister, she stuffs the bells at night to keep 'em quiet." With a grimace, the negro watched Papa pushing a needle through his skin. "She stuffed 'em 'fore I left, but it's worked out-a that right one."

Joseph paused to gape at the boldness of his disobedience.

The negro glanced at him; he must have sensed Joseph's reproof. "I'm not running away, not permanent. I'm going to see my wife, is all."

Joseph dug in the medical satchel. "Can't you do that on Sundays?" He hadn't meant to say the words aloud, but he wasn't sorry. No master made his slaves work on Sundays.

"Not anymore. My wife, she near Orangeburg now. Last time, took me two days just to get to her."

Then he should ask for a pass. If he couldn't get one as often as he liked—well, he must learn to be content. Suffering was part of God's plan. It taught you virtues like humility and patience. Joseph selected the largest amputation knife and returned to the promising trunk. "Servants, obey in all things your masters," he murmured, remembering the verse he'd heard many times.

"As you would that men should do to you, do you also to them," Papa called loud enough that Joseph could hear him over the wood splitting. "You're quoting Saint Paul. I'm quoting God."

The negro chuckled, which made his bells wobble.

Joseph returned with the splint and handed it to Papa without meeting his eyes.

"Perfect! Thank you, son."

Joseph turned his back while Papa set the negro's arm. He was nearly through wrapping the splint when a new voice shouted from the direction of the road. "Halloo!"

Joseph heard the negro suck in a breath and hold it, which of course the bell marked.

Someone must have come upon their chaise and horse. "Are you in any trouble there?" the man inquired. Was it a slave patrol? Papa might be imprisoned for helping a runaway!

"No trouble!" Papa called back. "My son's dog took off after a rabbit, is all." It was appalling how easily he broke the Eighth Commandment. Perhaps Papa thought the bell would be more difficult to lie away; he caught it with one hand to keep it silent.

"Do you need help with your search?"

"No, thank you. We've got her in hand now."

There was a moment's pause. At last, the man answered: "All right, then—good day to you!"

"Good day!"

Joseph thought he heard hoof beats on the road. The negro released his breath, and slowly Papa let go of the bell, which rattled in protest.

"I can't reach 'em up there myself." The negro glanced at the bell, then down to the bloody cotton Papa had discarded. "D'you think—you could take some of that and…"

"I have a better idea." Papa finished the splint and turned to his surgery set. He extracted the bone saw. "Do you trust me?"

"You just proved I could." Still the negro looked dubious.

Papa took back the leather strap and walked around behind his patient. He fed the strap between the negro's neck and his collar, where one of the rivets held it closed. Then Papa sawed carefully till iron shavings began falling.

For a while, Joseph watched, frowning. Papa spoke to the negro about how his arm would heal, not about the crime he was committing. He kept sawing for what seemed like ages. Joseph poked an anthill with a long stick, and the tiny creatures swarmed around the disturbance. He retreated a safe distance and sat down to wait.

At last Papa broke through. He folded open the two halves with their horns. The negro helped him, and together they dumped the broken collar on the forest floor. The right bell clanged its warning a few moments more.

The negro stared down at the collar as if he didn't believe it was gone, though it had left behind raw marks all around his neck and shoulders. He looked up at Papa with the same kind of disbelief, as if he were seeing him for the first time. "You some kind of foreigner?"

Papa cased his bone saw and smiled. "Just a doctor."

"Well, I'm much obliged to you, Doctor." The negro stood up from the dead tree, holding his splinted arm against his chest. "You a good and decent man. I hope your son there takes after you inside as well as out."

Joseph watched the dark form disappear into the trees, while

Papa snapped shut his satchel. Joseph knew what he was feeling was another sin, that if he spoke up, he would be breaking the Fourth Commandment. But if your father criticized the Church, couldn't you criticize him? "You had no right to do that."

"No right to treat a wounded man?"

"I mean about—" Joseph glanced down at the slave collar, but found he couldn't name it, so he only pointed. What Papa had done was like theft. How would he feel if someone stole one of their negroes? "He wasn't yours to free."

Papa sighed. "He only wants to see his wife."

"He was probably lying."

Papa made a noise that was more like a snort than a laugh. "Because all negroes lie." He said the words in a way that mocked them. "Does Henry lie? Does May?"

"Jemmy did."

Papa sat on the dead tree and stared down at the iron collar for a long time. When he spoke, his voice had changed somehow. "Pick it up."

Joseph blinked at him, puzzled.

"*Pick it up*," Papa repeated more harshly, glaring at him. When Joseph only looked at the collar, his father barked: "Do as you're told, boy!"

Fear gripped Joseph's throat. This wasn't Papa. Papa didn't speak like this, not even to their slaves.

"NOW!" he bellowed.

Joseph jumped and moved to obey. He didn't have a choice. He stooped over the great iron contraption and gripped it below each bell. The right one rattled as he tried to lift the collar, and it was even heavier than he'd thought. *Too* heavy. He could barely get it off the ground. Surely that was all Papa expected him—

"Don't let go until I tell you to!" commanded the man who had been his father. "Not even if you think your arms are going to break!"

Joseph couldn't breathe, and he certainly couldn't look up. Hot tears pricked beneath his eyelids, and every one of his muscles burned. The collar would drag him into the earth.

His tormenter knelt beside him, his voice suddenly Papa's again. "Can you imagine what it is like, Joseph, to have your body, your entire life, and all the people you love ruled by someone else's whims?" He took the collar away and caught Joseph by the shoulders, or he would have fallen. "Can you understand why the negroes are tired, why they are angry?" Papa cradled Joseph's head in his hands, knocking off his straw hat. "Are you all right?"

Joseph nodded numbly, his eyes averted.

"I'm sorry, Joseph. But do you understand?"

Joseph kept nodding, though he did not think he understood anything, least of all his own father. Papa wrapped his arms around him, but Joseph remained stiff.

"I love you. You know that," Papa breathed against his ear. "But please, Joseph, open your eyes. Don't believe everything people tell you, or what books tell you. Look for yourself. You are so good with your mother and your sisters—even with Henry and May. You *know* what's right." Papa pulled back to gaze earnestly into his face. "You are the wisest, kindest boy I know. Don't hide that light under anyone else's bushel. Trust yourself."

They walked back to the road in silence. Their mare was still waiting with the chaise. It seemed they had left her weeks ago. When Papa helped him into the carriage, Joseph's arms ached.

Eventually, he and Papa reached a great tract of land filled with ordered rows of bushes and trees, many of them in bloom. There were hothouses and sunken beds too. Papa directed their mare to a trough and tied her up. He led Joseph toward the two figures in the nearest field. One was a tall man with grey hair, an aquiline nose, and a kind face. He was walking slowly between rows and pointing out plants to a boy a little younger than Joseph. The man was white, but the boy was mulatto.

They turned as Joseph and Papa approached, and the man's face melted into a smile. "René! It's so good to see you again!" he called in French.

"And you, Philippe." Papa and the man exchanged a quick embrace and half-kissed each other's cheeks. Then Papa addressed the young mulatto: "How are you today, Louis?"

"Fine, sir," the mulatto smiled, looking Papa in the eyes as if they knew each other too. His French was good, and his clothes were fine. Joseph wondered what he was doing here.

"Is this Joseph?" the man asked, delighted. How peculiar, to hear his name from a stranger's lips as if the man knew all about him.

Papa nodded and placed a hand on his shoulder. "Joseph, this is Philippe Noisette. He lived on Saint-Domingue too. But we met in Charleston only a few years ago, while he was director of the Medical Society's garden."

"Noisette, like our roses?" Joseph maintained the French.

"*Exactement!*" the man smiled. "Noisette roses were named after my brother Louis Claude and myself. I sent him one, and he made it famous in France." Monsieur Noisette gestured to the young mulatto. "Allow me to introduce *my* son, Pierre Louis."

Joseph's eyes went wide. He'd thought this day could not become any stranger. Monsieur Noisette looked like a pure-blooded Frenchman. If this boy was his son, that meant he had— With a *negress*!

Joseph saw mulattos every day in the streets. But until this morning, he had not really understood how they happened. And no one he knew had openly admitted to causing them. *This* man felt no shame for what he'd done. Noisette seemed *proud* of his colored son.

The boy had extended his nut-brown hand.

"Joseph!" Papa hissed in English. "Have you forgotten your manners?" He acted as if this situation were perfectly normal, as if conventional etiquette applied. Joseph was beginning to think he did not know his father at all.

Joseph couldn't move. He couldn't even look at them. At the edge of his vision, he watched the mulatto drop his hand.

Noisette cleared his throat and turned back to his flowers. "I was just testing Louis to see how many of these plantings he could name by genus and species. How's your Latin coming, Joseph?"

"*Bene,*" he muttered at the ground.

"Do you know that all plants have Latin names? For example, *Digitalis purpurea* is foxglove—your father is familiar with that one.

The Latin names are important, because they allow botanists in different countries to communicate with each other. Even in the same language, a common name can refer to different plants, or many common names can refer to the same plant. Linnaeus was a doctor too, but he wasn't thinking of medicinal uses when he designed his classification system. Do you know *why* he grouped plants the way he did? What criteria Linnaeus used?"

Joseph shook his head.

Noisette grinned and dropped his voice as if he were telling a secret. "Very meticulously, one by one, he counted the plants' sexual organs."

Joseph gaped at him, afraid to look down. "Plants have…"

Noisette nodded, still smiling. "Usually several!"

Joseph swallowed. Did Mama know this?

Papa chuckled. "I think you've scandalized the poor boy, Philippe."

"If a flower has both male *and* female parts," Noisette continued, "what do we call it, Louis?"

"A 'perfect' flower," the mulatto answered.

"*Très bien!* Let me show you one." Noisette took them over to a cluster of white lilies. "This is called the pistil." He touched the bulbous tip of a stalk that was darker than the petals and jutted out from their center. "Would you say this part is male or female, Joseph?"

He knew he was blushing. Wasn't it obvious?

"It's *female!*" Noisette declared. "These stamina with the pollen, *they're* the male organs."

Joseph averted his eyes. Lilies were obscene. Lilies! In paintings and statues of the Blessed Virgin and Saint Joseph, white lilies often accompanied them. Mama had explained that lilies symbolized the *purity* of Christ's human parents, how they had never corrupted their bodies by lying together. Mama and those artists certainly did not know about *this*.

Papa asked Noisette about their spotted rose leaves. He talked to the mulatto as if he were any other boy. Finally, he led Joseph back to their chaise.

After they'd climbed inside, Papa sat staring at the reins. "That's twice today you've disappointed me, son. But before I lived in Paris, when I was your age, I saw the world the way you do: black and white, so to speak." Papa looked over the field to the distant figures. "In some things you're so mature, I forget how young you really are, and that all you've ever known is one small corner of Charleston. I should have introduced you to the Noisettes years ago." Joseph felt Papa's eyes on him, but he didn't raise his own. "Have you noticed them at Mass?"

Joseph shook his head. He always kept his attention on the Missal or the Priest.

"That's because the Noisettes sit in the gallery. The colored members of our congregation also receive Communion last. In the so-called Catholic Church! At the cathedral, Dr. England's solution is to offer a separate Mass. If you *truly* want to serve God, Joseph, remember: 'never do to another what you would hate to have done to you by another.' I've seen inside white *and* black bodies, son. They aren't any different."

"If you really believe that," Joseph asked quietly, "why haven't you freed our slaves?"

Papa's sigh was almost a groan. "Because South Carolina has made it impossible! Since the Act of 1820, the state legislature has to approve *every* petition, and they've shown time and again they'll free slaves only for 'heroic deeds'—only for exposing revolts like Denmark Vesey's. Why didn't I free Henry and May *before* 1820, when manumission was merely difficult? Why don't I submit a petition now on principle?" Papa's voice became a mutter, as if he were talking to himself. "Because of what your mother and her parents would think. Because I'm a hypocritical coward."

WHEN THEY REACHED HOME, Mama met them in the front hall, and she glared at Papa. Joseph had not meant to stay and watch their hands. But when he reached the first stair landing, he glanced down and saw Mama making his sign name. Joseph couldn't resist the temptation.

'He wanted to go!' Papa answered. 'And I think my son should know my friends.'

'Was that woman there?'

'Philippe's wife has a name.' Smoothly and rapidly, Papa spelled each letter with his fingers: 'C-E-L-E-S-' That was as far as he got before Mama rolled her eyes and turned her head away.

'She is his *slave*.'

Lightly but firmly, Papa tapped her shoulder till she looked back at his hands. 'Even if he managed to free her, Celestine would have to leave South Carolina.'

Mama raised her eyebrows as if to say: *How would that be bad?*

'Philippe and Celestine love each other! They've been together most of their lives! They have four beautiful children, and they love each of them just as—'

'Those children should never have been born.'

'What?'

'They are his slaves! Did your friend think about how *selfish* he was being? The offspring of—couplings like that aren't black, and they aren't white! Where do they belong? They're unnatural! I will not have *our* children associating with—'

'"Unnatural"?' Papa echoed aloud as well, as if he'd misunderstood.

'Blacks and whites are *different*.' Mama lingered on the sign: starting with two fists in front of her and then drawing them apart as far as her arms would reach. 'God made them different for a reason. They do not belong together. Not like that.'

'Many people say you and I don't belong together. That I shouldn't have married a deaf woman. That you shouldn't have married at all.'

'We are nothing like them!'

'Why not?'

'Because you and I *aren't* different! When I was born, I was like you! Our children are normal, not cursed. I praise God for that every day.'

'I don't want normal children! I didn't want a normal wife! But sometimes, Anne, you are entirely too conventional!'

Mama's breath caught, her hands trembled, and she turned away from Papa. She closed her eyes and made a sound that was halfway between a whimper and a sob.

Papa stepped forward quickly and took her by the shoulders till she opened her eyes. "I'm sorry!" he said with words as well as with his fists against his heart.

Tears still descended her cheeks, but she submitted to his embrace.

Papa kept speaking aloud, the way he would sometimes, even though he knew Mama couldn't hear him. "The last thing I want is to hurt you, Anne." Papa stood holding Mama near the pier glass, and he seemed to be examining their reflection. "But you call me 'unnatural'…"

On the stair landing, Joseph scowled. No she hadn't: Mama had called *mulattos* unnatural. Joseph must have misunderstood some of their signs. He wasn't used to reading hands and faces from such a high angle. This was why you shouldn't spy on other people's conversations.

As he turned away, Joseph heard Papa murmur below him: "You see what you want to see…"

CHAPTER 10

It is a melancholy fact that many hundreds of Catholics live for years without ever seeing a Priest and die without receiving the Last Sacraments...

— Father John McEncroe and James McDonald, *Respectful Appeal of the Roman Catholics of the State of South Carolina* (1827)

Before Joseph could serve at the altar, he had so much to learn: how to fill and swing a thurible; how to pour the cruets; how to hold a paten; how to hand the Priest his biretta; how to bow moderately and then profoundly. There were many wrong ways to do these things, and there was a proper way. It was a like a mathematical formula: if they did everything right, the living God would come into their midst, would change the bread and wine into His own Body and Blood.

The other boys behaved as if serving were only a duty to be endured. How could they not see what an honor and blessing it was, to assist every day in a miracle! Father McEncroe was patient with all of them, and he praised Joseph's pronunciation of Latin. "When you speak," the Priest told them, "remember that you represent the entire congregation."

Joseph supposed Father McEncroe meant the coloreds in the gallery too. Sometimes during Mass, when he was only standing or kneeling and waiting, Joseph would allow himself to look up. Noisette was not as easy to pick out as Joseph had thought; the Frenchman's skin was tawny from the sun, so he was darker than a few of the colored people. Glance by glance, Mass by Mass, Joseph found the children who were also his slaves: Louis, his two older brothers, and a little girl with braided hair who often sucked her thumb. A colored woman sat with them—that must be Celestine. She and Noisette would sometimes lean their heads together and whisper.

"Celestine" was Latin for "heavenly." There had been five Popes named Celestine. Joseph was thinking about this when Noisette's Celestine approached the rail to receive Communion at Easter. Joseph realized she was expecting another child, and he nearly dropped the paten.

Mama spent weeks sewing Joseph a soutane and embroidering a surplice. The first time he wore them, she held his face in her hands and started weeping.

'They fit me perfectly, Mama!' Joseph assured her.

'Yes, they do,' she answered. 'I am not crying because I am sad!' Mama raised his hand to her lips and kissed his knuckles. 'I have prayed for this since the day you were born. *This* is why Our Lord did not allow me to become a nun. I doubted Him then, but I understand now.'

Joseph did not think it was a good exchange. A nun's vows were perpetual, and he would serve only a few years.

Sometimes, he was sorry to put on the soutane and surplice. He knew he should not mourn anyone who died in Christ. He should rejoice at such funerals. Still Joseph wished God had allowed Grandpapa to stay with them a little longer.

Grandpapa had been ill for years. The pain was worst when he relieved himself. Papa said it was all because of a stone lodged inside him. Finally Grandpapa allowed one of Papa's doctor friends to cut it out. (Papa was a physician, not a surgeon.) Everything went well, and Grandpapa seemed to be healing. But three days after the surgery, he began shivering and sweating. Neither Papa nor his friend could stop it. Bishop England himself gave Grandpapa Extreme Unction, Absolution, and Viaticum. Grandpapa died without fear.

Joseph's Uncle Bastien was not so blessed. That winter, Joseph returned from school to find Mama trying to comfort Grandmama on their piazza. Mama's own eyes were red from crying.

'Joseph, do you remember your Uncle Bastien?' she asked. 'You would have been six, seven years old when he went to North Carolina.'

Joseph recalled only a few things about his uncle, but he knew Papa, Mama, and Bastien had been inseparable when they were children. Unlike her sister, Mama's brother had eagerly learned how to sign. Even after Uncle Bastien left Charleston, he corresponded faithfully.

'Today we received a letter from his wife—his *widow*. There was an accident at his mill…'

'It's been *months* since Bastien last saw a Priest!' Grandmama snatched up her handkerchief to blot her eyes and her nose.

'You understand what this means, Joseph?' Mama said with shaking hands. 'Your uncle is in Purgatory, and he will be for a very long time unless we help him. Father McEncroe has already agreed to say the first Mass for Bastien tomorrow. You will pray for him too, Joseph?'

It didn't seem fair. Why should a faithful Christian have to suffer for hundreds of years in Purgatory just because there wasn't a Priest to give him the Last Sacraments? And if Uncle Bastien had committed a *mortal* sin with no chance to confess it…

Mr. Künstler joined their family at the first Mass for Uncle Bastien's soul. When it was over, Joseph walked with his teacher to the seminary, letting Mr. Künstler lean on him as well as his cane.

"There are not nearly enough Priests in this diocese." Joseph's teacher shook his head. "And those who do come leave almost as quickly."

"Why don't they stay?"

"There are many reasons," Mr. Künstler sighed. "America is still a missionary country. The congregations are small and usually poor, so they have trouble supporting a Priest. Many of the Priests can't speak English well. Our diocese has an added obstacle: the peculiarity of our climate. 'Stranger's fever' is called that because it is most fatal to new arrivals. Some never recover, and those who do suffer relapses, like Bishop England. To a European Priest, coming to our Southern states is an exile if not a death-sentence."

Joseph hadn't thought of their country that way. It sounded as bad as Africa or China.

"As Dr. England has said many times, what we need is a *native* clergy. That's why he established this seminary." They passed through its door. Once, it had been only a house. "You understand that the school for boys your age, the minor seminary, is meant to support the major seminary? Financially for now, but soon—we *hope* —pupils will continue from the one to the other."

Most of the other boys weren't even Catholic. They came to the school because their parents had few other choices. His Protestant classmates complained about it while they mocked Joseph for wanting to kiss the Pope's feet.

It was early yet, so the classroom he and Mr. Künstler entered was still empty. "A native clergy is essential if we are ever to convert our separated brethren. Protestants view us with suspicion at best. They see that we are mostly immigrants, and they are convinced that we serve the Pope first, that we'll never be truly American." Joseph's teacher sat heavily in the chair he kept at the front of the room. "We need Priests who understand American democracy and language, who have grown up in this climate. But there are so few American vocations. And a Priest born in *this* city of Sybarites— well, he would be a true *rara avis*." Mr. Künstler rubbed his bad leg, but he smiled. "Can you tell me the origin of that expression?"

"Sybarites or *rara avis*?"

"Do you know both?"

Joseph nodded eagerly. He always paid attention during lectures. "Sybaris was a wicked city in ancient Italy, like Sodom and Gomorrah —so a Sybarite is someone who lives only for luxury and pleasure."

Mr. Künstler looked very proud of him, so Joseph continued: "*Rara avis* comes from Juvenal. Literally it means 'rare bird.' He was talking about a black swan. For centuries, people thought they didn't exist."

"Technically, Juvenal was talking about a perfect wife—he said such a woman was as rare as a black swan!"

Joseph knew Mr. Künstler was still a bachelor. Was that why? He'd never found his *rara avis*?

Joseph realized the humor had drained from his teacher's face. "I know you weren't born in America, Joseph, but you're very nearly a native." Mr. Künstler was staring at him in the strange, expectant way adults often stared at him. "Surely God has been calling *you* to the Priesthood? Have you been listening?"

Joseph could hardly breathe. "M-Me?"

A few days ago, as Joseph extinguished the altar candles, Father McEncroe had commented: "*I think you have a vocation, Joseph.*" He'd said it so warmly and casually, Joseph had assumed Father McEncroe simply meant assisting him.

When Mama had wept and kissed his hand to see him in his soutane and surplice, when she told him she'd been praying for this… She'd meant the Priesthood too. He *hadn't* been listening.

Joseph had dreamed about becoming a Priest—of course he had. He dreamed about it every day when he watched Father McEncroe raise the Host, or when he heard Bishop England preach. But he wasn't like them. He was a terrible sinner. Surely they never had impure thoughts. Joseph felt unworthy even washing a Priest's hands. And he was not as brave as his great-granduncle Denis, who had died rather than renounce his faith. But Joseph wanted to be brave like that.

"Yes, Joseph," Mr. Künstler assured him. "I've seen you when you're serving at Mass. You make it look effortless—like you *belong* there. When you say, 'I will go to the altar of God, Who gives joy to my youth,' you mean it, don't you?"

Joseph nodded. His Protestant classmates—and most of the Catholic boys—cared only about new clothes, impressing girls, hunting, and card games. Nothing important. Nothing that would last. Joseph wanted to be useful like Papa. But even Papa's medicine wouldn't last for all eternity.

"Envy is a grave sin," Mr. Künstler mused, "yet I envy you, Joseph—the chance you have. I wanted desperately to be ordained myself." His expression darkened, and he stared down at his club-foot. "But a Priest cannot be damaged. He must be perfect." Mr. Künstler drew in a deep breath and laid his hands on Joseph's shoulders. "*You* are an exceptional young man, Joseph. You would make an exceptional Priest. Promise me you will pray about it, and listen for God's voice?"

Joseph nodded. He still couldn't breathe.

CHAPTER 11

Unless you expect the unexpected, you will never find truth…
— Heraclitus (500 B.C.)

J oseph ran to church before the rest of his family woke. Thank God it was Saturday, so Father McEncroe was expecting Confessions. Joseph waited on his knees, praying and sweating, till at last the Priest entered the confessional.

"Bless me, Father, for I have sinned," Joseph pleaded. "I mean, I think I have sinned. It can't have been pleasing to God. I didn't *like* it; I thought I was dying and—"

"Slow down, son." Father McEncroe stifled a yawn. "Take a deep breath. *Then* tell me what happened."

"I was asleep, but it woke me up. It felt like I had wet the bed. But I'm too old for that; I'm thirteen! When I looked, it was thicker, and whitish…" Joseph lapsed into humiliated silence.

Father McEncroe released a breath that sounded like a chuckle. "You're growing up, son; that's all. You haven't committed a sin."

"But—isn't that what happens when…" Priests did *know* about that, didn't they, even if—

"You said you were asleep?"

"Yes."

"Then you couldn't give your consent. If there's no volition, there's no sin. Do you understand?"

"I think so."

"Nocturnal pollutions are beyond our control. We can guard our waking thoughts, but we can't guard our dreams. Now, did you abuse yourself in any way last night?"

Joseph caught his breath. He knew *that* was a mortal sin. "No, Father."

"When you woke, were you touching yourself then?"

"I—I don't think so." The thought was horrible: his hand wandering on its own, violating him against his will.

"Calm down, son. You have your own rosary?"

"Yes."

"Try wrapping it around your hand before you go to sleep, with the crucifix in your palm. That should help. Do you say your prayers every night?"

"Yes, Father."

"Good. Now you have something else to pray for, that you will be spared this. But I must warn you: it will probably happen again. It's the nature of our flesh. It is weak."

Joseph frowned. "W-What did you call it?"

"A 'nocturnal pollution.' As I said, I don't need to absolve you. But I'll bless you—how's that?"

"Thank you, Father," Joseph murmured. He didn't want to be polluted. He wanted to be pure like his patron saint.

AFTER THAT, Joseph did go to bed with a rosary wrapped around his hand. Hour after hour, he would lie awake in the dark, his weariness battling with his fear. His flesh might rebel as soon as he lost consciousness. He could never be a Priest if he couldn't master his own body. He longed for the distraction of a hair shirt. His cotton night-shirt and drawers were far too comfortable. The more Joseph tried to concentrate on his prayers, the more his thoughts would stray—the more his body would respond. So he would imagine the consequences of surrendering to impurity: the bottomless lake of fire.

This was not difficult to do as summer stalked Charleston. But in Hell, there would be no winter—no end to the heat, the agony, the gnashing of teeth. Hell would go on and on and *on*, forever and *ever* —and he could earn that eternity of torment with a single *moment* of weakness.

ONE HOT NIGHT, as he lay counting his beads, a strange odor drifted into the room. Joseph frowned. It smelled like…smoke. As if his fantasy of Hell were coming to terrifying life. He sat up, eyes wide. It could be another slave uprising. Negroes were setting fire to the city!

Joseph threw aside his mosquito netting, sprang to the floor, and peered out his window. The acrid smell of smoke grew stronger on the breeze. From his bedchamber, he could see only the upper piazza, and beyond it, the dark wall of Grandmama's house. At least she was safe: away in the mountains, taking the waters for her health.

Still carrying his rosary and still barefoot, Joseph tucked himself through his open window. He climbed onto the piazza and hurried to the back end. There, he could peer down into the work yard. It was their kitchen on fire!

"Papa!" He wheeled across the piazza toward his parents' open window. Within, a lamp was already lit. The thin white curtains swayed in the slight wind, shifting for just a moment so that Joseph could see inside.

The rosary dropped from his hand. The cord must have snapped: the beads clattered on the piazza, bounced over his bare feet, and careened in a dozen directions. Thoughts of the fire fled just as quickly. He was mistaken; the mosquito netting had distorted things; he couldn't have seen—

But he *heard*, too: Mama, so careful never to make sounds, was moaning.

The curtains swayed aside once more, and Joseph glimpsed it

again, the hideous tableau. His mother's delicate, expressive hands reduced to bloodless fists, gripping vainly at whatever bound them to the bedposts. Her own stockings? Between her spread arms, her head tilted unnaturally to one side. Her beautiful face was screwed up in such pain that she had to bite down on her lip, and tears trickled from her closed eyes. Her skin was flushed with shame, and every inch of it was bare, her pink nipples rising from the tangle of her golden hair. And Papa—Joseph didn't know what he was doing to her; he didn't want to know—but he saw his father's dark head moving between Mama's white thighs.

Joseph clamped his eyes shut and stopped his ears with his palms. What kind of monster would— To a woman who could not even cry out for help in words anyone would understand! He had *bound her hands*—the only way she could beg him for mercy.

The men in that drawing room had known: *"Can you imagine a more perfect wife?" "You could do anything you liked to her."*

His father had said it himself: he was a hypocrite. When he'd explained with his medical books how men and women joined together, hadn't his father insisted that the *woman's* happiness must be the man's first priority?

When his father had lied without hesitation, practically stolen another man's property, and bellowed at Joseph in the forest, *that* must have been the real René Lazare, not the kind man he pretended to be when everyone was watching. His father hated nuns and flaunted a sacrilegious portrait of the Virgin. How could Joseph have deceived himself for so many years that these were aberrations? The truth had been screaming at him all along.

He'd known it all his life. He'd been born eight months after his parents' wedding. *Eight* months, not nine. How many times had his father told the story? Joseph was born early; they were worried about him because he was so small; they'd kept him close to the hearth for warmth. All that must have been an elaborate lie.

Joseph understood now: he'd been conceived *before* his parents married. They *had* to marry, because his father had raped Mama and forced her to become his wife, when *she* wanted to become a nun. It was Joseph's fault. Mama was trapped with this monster for the rest of her life because she had been expecting Joseph against her will...

A profound, urgent clanging penetrated his thoughts then: the bells of St. Michael's, sounding the alarm. A deeper banging noise erupted somewhere much closer. Gingerly Joseph relaxed his hands till he released their seal over his ears. Between the peals of the fire bell, his father cursed and Mama whimpered. Very slowly, Joseph opened his eyes. Mercifully, the still curtains concealed the inside of his parents' bedchamber.

In the hall, Henry's voice boomed: "Master René, sir? I'm sorry to disturb you, but it's our kitchen on fire."

"The fire's here?" his father answered. "Is it spreading?" Joseph heard him moving around in the bedroom, heard cloth rustling.

"No, sir. I think we nearly got it out now."

"Is anyone hurt?"

"My ma's arm, some. Can you come see her?"

"Of course." His father's voice seemed to come from the hall now. Then Joseph heard quick, heavy steps on the staircase and soon on the lower story of the piazza.

Joseph supposed he must reappear. He must not add to Mama's worries. He hoped his father had had the decency not to leave her bound. Joseph glanced down at the remains of his rosary, then snuck back to his window. He crawled inside his bedchamber so he could come through its door and everyone would think he'd just woken.

In the lantern-lit hall, his sisters were trying to pry details of the catastrophe from May. Mama stood beside them in her frilly white wrapper, her tears dried. When she saw him, she turned. 'Joseph! Everything is all right.'

It was not. He'd nearly convinced himself he'd imagined the hideous tableau. But when Mama signed, her sleeves fell away from her wrists. Pink still wreathed her skin in the pattern of her bonds. She realized he'd seen the marks, blushed again, and yanked down the white frills to cover her wrists. Then her attention returned to his sisters. The fear vanished from her face. Mama did not suspect that Joseph knew *why* her wrists were pink.

As soon as his father returned, Joseph would confront him.

And then? What would that accomplish? His father would only laugh, because he knew Joseph was powerless to stop him. He was nothing but a boy. If only Grandpapa were still alive! He *might* have been able to free Mama, but no one else could. The monster had married his victim: Mama belonged to him almost like a slave. She was his wife, so he could do anything he liked to her. The law did not protect her, and neither would the Church. She was his till one of them died.

This mockery of a marriage must, somehow, be part of God's plan. For enduring such suffering on Earth, Mama would be spared even an hour in Purgatory.

When they all returned to bed, Joseph lay awake for a new reason, dreading what he might hear. He begged the Blessed Virgin and Mama's patroness, Saint Anne, to watch over her.

But his father was insatiable. For the first time in his life, Joseph wished he were as deaf as his mother.

MAMA WAS A LIVING SAINT. On the stairs the next morning, she smiled at her husband and accepted his arm as if she had not cried out beneath him a few hours before.

Though Hélène knew nothing, she was still fretful. Not only was their cook injured, they no longer had a kitchen. "Are we going to starve, Papa?"

"Of course not, *ma poulette*." He crouched down to her level as if he were a caring father. "First thing this morning, I asked Henry to take a message to your Aunt Véronique and Uncle François. They've already responded that we are welcome to join them for breakfast."

"But...what about dinner?"

Their father only laughed.

Uncle François was a banker, and his house showed it. Though Aunt Véronique was Mama's sister, she'd learned only a few basic signs, so Mama could not really participate in the table conversation. At first, Joseph's father tried to translate everything that was said, but it was hard for him to keep up, because Aunt and Uncle did not wait. They behaved as if Mama were not even there. Finally, when his father tapped her, she just shook her head and kept her eyes on her quail.

Joseph's cousin Frederic was nearly eighteen. When he discovered Joseph didn't know how to ride, Frederic promised to teach him. "I bet you don't have the right boots, though." They determined that Joseph did not. Their family's shoemaker didn't even make riding boots. "My man can make you some, then," Frederic offered. "That's all right, isn't it, Father?"

"It's your allowance," Uncle François answered without interest.

Frederic was as good as his word. They set off as soon as they'd finished breakfast. Joseph's cousin walked with a silver-tipped cane he didn't need, because he thought it made him look elegant. Frederic extolled the virtues of his boot-maker, and they were only half watching where they were going. They nearly collided with another pair on the sidewalk: an elderly colored man and woman who were finely dressed. Their eyes lowered immediately.

Gripping the head of his cane, Frederic glared at them. "Well?" he prompted.

Slowly the colored man guided the woman to the edge of the sidewalk so that Joseph and his cousin could pass.

"And they didn't even apologize!" Frederic muttered as they continued. "These free coloreds get so full of themselves!"

Joseph liked the way the boot-maker's shop smelled: sharp and rich from all the leather hanging about them. The boot-maker was a free mulatto who owned slaves. One of them took Joseph's measurements, and his cousin helped him choose a style.

On the way back, Frederic paused at the corner between St. Philip's and the Huguenot Church, staring down Queen Street toward the docks. "Father said I could have a new valet for my birthday—the one I have is getting too old. You don't mind if I take a look at the stock while we're here, do you?"

Joseph could only shake his head and follow his cousin. He'd never entered this part of the city, but he knew what it contained.

He'd only glimpsed slave auctions from a distance while his parents or grandparents hurried him and his sisters along.

Frederic turned onto State Street. "We're looking for a trader called Hart. Let me know if you see his sign."

Some of the buildings here resembled warehouses or stables, but most looked like houses, except for the high white-washed walls surrounding their yards. Negroes stood in lines along the sidewalks, sometimes on little wooden footstools to elevate them above the milling crowd. They were all clean and neat: the men in suits and many in top hats, the women in calico dresses and tidy head kerchiefs. Joseph tried not to stare at them—he imagined enough people did that.

Most of the negroes kept their eyes on their shoes, but one woman seemed to be gazing vacantly across the street. Joseph tried to follow her eyes. He saw nothing unusual, only a sign on the façade of one of the buildings that said:

PRICE, ARMSTRONG, & CO.
DEALERS IN SLAVES

"Here we are!" Frederic cried, almost in the same moment a white man stepped in front of them. He had bushy whiskers on his cheeks, and the band of his hat declared in bold letters:

CASH FOR NEGROES!

The man smiled coolly. "Out for a stroll this morning, gentlemen?" He seemed to be assessing them.

"Not at all—I am quite in earnest." Frederic produced a card from his pocketbook. "My father is *François* Traver. He's purchased from Mr. Hart's firm before."

Uncle François's name seemed to satisfy the man, who gave a sharp bow. In fact, Joseph saw another dealer turn his head and frown in disappointment. "Are you looking to sell or to buy, Mr. Traver?" asked the man in the *CASH FOR NEGROES* hat.

"Both. I need a new body servant."

"Of course." The man led them to the red door of a three-story building that looked like a house. "If you'll step into our showroom, I am sure we have just what you need."

The *CASH FOR NEGROES* man directed them down a sparse hallway to a room that resembled a large parlor without much decoration. It did contain several chairs and a sideboard topped by crystal decanters. Beside it waited a dark-skinned boy of about fifteen in livery. Other negroes stood with their backs to the long wall while white men contemplated and questioned them. At the far end of the room, an elderly man sat in a fine chair and puffed on a cigar while he eyed two mulatto girls.

A well-dressed man shook hands with one of the other buyers in parting, then greeted Joseph and Frederic with the tip of his hat. "Simon Hart, at your service."

Frederic introduced himself.

"And the young master?"

"This is my cousin, Joseph Lazare."

"Will Mr. Lazare be doing business with us as well?" Hart queried in a voice like a chuckle.

"How are your negroes treating you, Joseph?" Frederic grinned.

At least, his cousin sounded like he was grinning. Joseph had returned his eyes to his shoes. "Fine," he mumbled. Joseph didn't think such a suggestion was at all amusing. Henry and May had served his family for as long as he could remember. Even thinking about trading them made him feel disloyal. He didn't like Agathe's food as much as he had their old cook's—she used strange spices— but Agathe was Henry's mother.

"Would either of you gentlemen care for a drink?" Hart asked now. "Perhaps a lemonade for Mr. Lazare?"

Joseph nodded weakly. His throat was certainly dry. He accepted a lemonade from the young slave. It was very sweet.

Hart continued: "Do you prefer dark-skinned domestics, or mulattos?"

"I'm not sure." Frederic swirled his brandy. "I've a dark valet now, and he's very faithful." He took a sip and considered the young black boy, who was as still as a statue again. "Aren't mulattos more trouble? My father says they inherit only the worst of white traits. He says they become sick more often than pure-blooded negroes, and because they have a *little* intelligence, they're more likely to run away."

Hart grasped his lapels and puffed out his chest as if he had been insulted. "Not *our* mulattos, sir. We offer a guarantee."

"Do you offer them on trial as well? My mother is very partic- ular about faces."

"Absolutely, sir."

"I need someone young, but already trained."

"Of course, sir," Hart nodded. "What else are you looking for?"

"My family does not tolerate impudence," Frederic emphasized his words with his glass, and the liquor sloshed in the wide bowl. "I want someone who knows his place."

"If you'll wait here, I have just the man." Hart hurried from the room.

Joseph made himself drink a little more of the lemonade.

Frederic peered down at him. "You've never visited a slave pen before?"

Joseph shook his head. His father had purchased Agathe directly from her old master. Henry and May had been presents from Grandpapa, already installed at the house when Joseph's parents moved back from Paris. Had Grandpapa bought Henry and May in a place like this?

Frederic stepped to the window behind the black boy and pulled aside the white curtain. Through its panes, Joseph saw the high white-washed wall surrounding the yard. It matched the wall around the jail on Magazine Street, where Denmark Vesey and his conspirators had been kept before they were hanged. Joseph remembered that slave pens were also called "nigger jails." What had the slaves here done to deserve such imprisonment? "Where do they come from, the negroes who are sold here?"

"Hart sends agents out to the countryside—even to other states. They buy up negroes from masters who have too many or who need money, and the agents bring them here." Frederic sipped his brandy as he stared into the yard. "Last year, one of Hart's men took my father and me on a tour of the establishment. They have a tailor's shop, a kitchen, and an infirmary. Everything is very clean and organized."

Joseph stepped closer to the window. Now he saw the tall iron fence dividing the yard down the middle. Men and boys waited on one side, and women and girls waited on the other. Some of the negroes were alone, others in groups, a few even playing cards; but all their shoulders drooped. They kept to the shade of the buildings and the high outer walls, except for five negroes who clustered in the full sun: a woman and two girls who clung to the fence separating them from a man and a boy. Even from this distance, Joseph could tell they were a family.

One of the little girls started to climb the fence. A white man appeared and pried her off. The negress took the girl, who was crying now, and the man ordered them all away from the fence. He did not carry a whip, but some sort of paddle.

Joseph lowered his eyes again. "Why do they separate the women from the men?"

His cousin chuckled into his brandy. "You know how these negroes are: animals constantly in heat."

Hart returned with a tall mulatto who looked about twenty-five years old. "I think we can meet all your needs, Mr. Traver." The dealer appeared pleased with himself and his merchandise. "And the tall ones are always impressive in livery."

"They're also more expensive," Frederic grumbled, then addressed the mulatto directly. "What's your name, boy?"

"Fred, sir."

"Well, that wouldn't do," Frederic smirked. "We'd have to call you something else. My current valet is named Peter—that would be easy to remember."

What would happen to the old Peter? Joseph wondered.

"You don't have any family you'll be begging me to buy as well, do you, Peter?"

"No, sir," the mulatto murmured. "Master wouldn't sell them."

"Would you like me to be your new master? Would you like to live in one of the finest houses in Charleston?"

The mulatto glanced up for only a moment. "Yes, sir." His voice lacked enthusiasm.

"You have experience as a valet, Peter?"

"More than ten years, sir."

Frederic made the mulatto open his mouth and then touch his toes. "Any problems I should know about? Are you sound?"

"Of course he is!" answered Hart in a bluster.

Frederic shot the trader a look. "I asked *Peter.*"

Hart cleared his throat and remained silent.

"Let's have you prove it." With his cane, Joseph's cousin motioned to the hall. "Could we have him run up your stairs?"

"Naturally."

Hart, Frederic, and Joseph walked out to stand beneath the staircase, where they watched the mulatto run up to the third floor and down again.

Finally Joseph's cousin allowed the mulatto to stop, satisfied that the man's breathing was normal. Then Frederic inspected his hands. "Remember, Joseph: whether he's to work in the fields or in the house, *always* examine a slave's hands. They are the most important parts of him—dexterity is essential."

Frederic released the mulatto's hands and addressed Hart again: "You have somewhere I can see, uh, all of him?"

"Of course, sir." The trader offered them a small room across the hall.

Wordlessly the mulatto removed his fine clothing, neatly folding each article onto a little table. Joseph kept his eyes on the carpet. He felt his cheeks growing hot with shame, as if *he* were being forced to expose himself.

"You *are* an innocent, aren't you?" Frederic chuckled. "A man has to see what he's buying."

Joseph glanced toward the mulatto, who had nothing left to reveal. Checking the slave's back for scars made sense, but what did the man's genitals have to do with his being a good valet? His skin there was darker than the rest of him, just like Joseph's. "Why do you have to see his…?"

"I am *not* a Molly, if that's what you're implying!"

Joseph had no idea what that was, but he'd never heard Frederic so angry.

"These bucks and wenches have to be kept in two separate yards because outside this pen, they're at each other night and day! Do you know how many diseases that causes? I don't want one who's spotted and runny! He'd be ill constantly, and then who would dress me?" His cousin took a few breaths and calmed. He gestured to the naked, motionless mulatto. "It doesn't embarrass *them.*"

He might as well be made of stone, Joseph thought, till he realized the man was trembling.

"Africans run around naked in Africa," Frederic assured him. "They'd prefer to stay that way all the time. They're like animals, Joseph. You don't turn red when you see a horse penis, do you?"

Actually, those did make Joseph uncomfortable. And how did they know being naked didn't embarrass the negroes? The problem was, you couldn't tell when they were blushing.

CHAPTER 12

This little girl struck her fancy, and [Madame Talvande] offered to educate her, making one stipulation... Monkey (whose real name was Charlotte) could only visit her Mother occasionally...
— Mary Chesnut, *Two Years* (1877)

Uncle François invited Joseph's family to stay in his new cottage on Sullivan's Island. Joseph had received his boots, and Frederic said the beach would be the perfect place to learn to ride. But his cousin's friends were also visiting, and Frederic was occupied with them.

So the first day, Joseph walked along the shore with his parents and sisters. They had taken the ferry to Sullivan's Island many times before. Joseph and his father would swim in their under-clothes. Hélène would wade out with them in her own bulky bathing attire and dunk herself, screaming with delight. Mama permitted it because Hélène was still young. Mama and Cathy entered the ocean only with the aid of bathing machines. They did not seem to enjoy themselves but endured the process like a purgative. Usually Mama and Cathy simply strolled or sat. They rarely even took off their boots.

They were still looking for a place to settle when they came upon a woman with a group of girls, accompanied by their maids.

Cathy gasped. "That's Madame Talvande!"

Joseph recognized the name of the founder and headmistress of the French School for Young Ladies, because his sister talked about it incessantly. Madame Talvande's establishment was the most exclusive girls' school in Charleston.

First, Cathy fretted about not having a mirror or her false curls, though her hair was mostly hidden under her bonnet. Finally, she ran up to the woman and curtseyed. "*Bonjour*, Madame Talvande," she began in a stream of easy French. "I am so pleased to meet you. My name is Catherine Lazare, and I hope to attend your school very soon."

"But your French is already perfect!" the headmistress replied in her native language. "Are your parents French?"

Cathy nodded, then frowned: "Well, my grandparents are French. My parents are Creole. Papa was born on Saint-Domingue."

"Ah. My husband and I are also from that unfortunate island. I prefer this one."

"Here's Papa," Cathy announced. "He's a doctor. His name is René Lazare. Have you heard of him?"

Their father chuckled and kissed Madame Talvande's offered hand.

"I believe Bishop England has mentioned you, Dr. Lazare," the headmistress smiled.

He turned to introduce Mama, who was hanging back as usual. But they were interrupted. "*Monkey!*" shrieked one of Madame Talvande's pupils in exasperation, as a plump little girl darted toward Joseph's sisters. "Monkey" was younger than the other girls. Her hat hung from two ribbons down her back, revealing a mass of coiled black hair. Her dark eyes wide, Monkey stared at Cathy and Hélène as if she wanted to say something, but then she dropped her gaze to the sand. Cathy glared at her.

Madame Talvande *tsk*-ed. "What have I told you about your hat, Monkey?"

Without looking up, the girl tied it back on her head.

Hélène curtseyed. "Pleased to meet you...Monkey. My name is Hélène Lazare."

"Monkey isn't her Christian name, of course," the headmistress explained as she straightened the girl's hat. "If it weren't for this hair, you'd hardly know, but she's *colored*." Madame Talvande stepped back to assess her work. "Monkey is my little experiment—a true test of my powers. I said to myself: 'If I separated her from her parents, could I make a proper lady of her?' She sleeps at the foot of my own bed. She's become quite the pet of the other pupils." The headmistress looked up to see Joseph's father frowning. "She doesn't *eat* with the other girls, of course."

"Is it true Bishop England dines with you every week?" Cathy put in.

"We do have that honor."

Cathy kept worshipping Madame Talvande. Monkey peered hopefully at Hélène again, who produced a shell from her pinafore to show the girl.

Joseph realized that one of the maids was staring at his father. The negress stood a little apart from the schoolgirls. Perhaps sixty years old, she wore a yellow head kerchief and large gold hoops in her ears. Her skin was ebony, yet Joseph could see a pattern of raised scars across her cheeks. They must have been done long ago in Africa.

Perhaps she felt his gaze: the negress turned her attention to Joseph. He scowled, but she approached him anyway. "Pardon, sir, but you are the son of René Lazare?" It took Joseph a few moments to understand her, to translate in his head. Joseph had studied Creole out of curiosity. He was not fluent, but knowing French helped.

"*Oui*," he answered cautiously. Who did this negress think she was, addressing him so boldly?

"Your father was born in the parish of Acul on Saint-Domingue? About two years before the Revolution there?"

"I was," Joseph's father answered for him. He'd stepped closer.

The negress grinned. "I thought you must be him. Lazare, it is not a common name. I am called Ninon. You would not remember me, but I helped bring you into this world." Then she glanced at Madame Talvande, who was still occupied with Cathy. The negress looked anxious. She moved farther away from the others and closer to the water, still carrying her basket.

Joseph's father trailed after her, as if it were something they'd agreed to do. He looked worried too, but eager at the same time. Joseph had to follow. His father glanced over his shoulder and frowned at him, but he didn't tell Joseph to leave. Perhaps he thought Joseph wouldn't understand the woman's patois, or that he wouldn't be able to hear anything over the roar and hiss of the waves.

When his father and the negress stopped, they stood with their backs to him, staring out at the ocean instead of each other. Joseph pretended to be fascinated by the holes in the sand and the bubbles they emitted each time a wave retreated.

His father asked the negress: "You knew my mother?"

"Only a little."

"What was she…like?"

The woman turned to him. "She did not leave Saint-Domingue with you?"

Joseph's father shook his head. "I came to Charleston when I was two years old with only my grandmother, Marguerite Lazare. She told me my father, her son, died during the first uprising. My grandmother said my mother died when I was born—and that she was Spanish."

"Spanish!" The negress laughed as if this were a joke. "That was clever. But your mother didn't die when you were born. I came back to that plantation maybe a year later, to catch another baby, and your mother was still with you then. It was good to see her happy. You were just learning to walk. She was so proud of you."

"You mean she didn't…" His father's voice faltered. He was staring down at his feet. "She had every reason to hate me."

"Oh, no. She was stronger than that. Your birth, it *was* very difficult—that was why they called me. Your mother was only a child herself. I don't think, *that* night, she knew how she felt about you yet.

She was in so much pain, and she was angry at your— But when I came back, and I saw her with you, I could not doubt it: your mother adored you. You were her whole world. She *must* have died before you left Saint-Domingue, or she would never have let you go." Her head was turned so that Joseph could see half her smile. "Even if you do look more like your father."

"Ninon!" Madame Talvande shouted behind them, startling Joseph. "Mademoiselle Foster wants her luncheon." The head-mistress stood beside a pouting blonde girl and pointed at the maid's basket.

"*J'arrive*, Madame," the negress called back.

Before she left him, Joseph's father caught her arm. "What was her name?"

"She didn't tell me what *her* mother called her. But her slave name was Ève." Without waiting for him to reply, the negress hurried to the schoolgirls.

Joseph's father took a step toward the ocean. And then, he sank onto his knees in the sand.

Joseph kept scowling. His grandmother's name had been Maria Dolores. What did the negress mean by her "slave name"? None of this made any sense. Joseph must have misunderstood again. Hadn't he learned his lesson about eavesdropping?

Why was the thought of his grandmother being Spanish amusing? Why had his father assumed his mother hated him? Why was he acting as though all of this was very important?

The negress couldn't have meant— She couldn't—

Joseph didn't want to know. He didn't want to understand. He wanted to be far away from it. He turned and fled from his father.

The wind snatched Joseph's hat from his head, and the sun stung his eyes immediately. He did not stop, though the sand beneath his feet seemed determined to swallow him. Behind him, over the pounding of his heart in his ears, Joseph heard his father calling his name.

No sooner had Joseph arrived at the cottage and caught his breath than Frederic appeared on the back porch with his friends.

His new valet accompanied them, a dark-skinned boy who could not be more than twenty.

"Joseph!" Frederic greeted him. "We were just going swimming. Would you care to join us?"

Joseph nodded fiercely. He trailed behind Frederic and his friends but kept ahead of the slave. His side ached from the effort. As they hurried along the beach, Joseph wondered why they had to go swimming at such a distance from the cottages.

At last they halted. Frederic and his friends began peeling off their clothing, tossing pieces at the negro, who caught most of them. Joseph shrugged his braces from his shoulders and unbuttoned his trousers. But the other boys did not stop undressing when they got to their shirts. They did not even stop when they got to their drawers. Joseph averted his eyes at once.

Frederic noticed his hesitation. "You *can* swim, can't you?"

Joseph nodded without looking up. He was quite fond of it, the freedom he felt as he floated in the water. But he *never* swam naked.

"Come on, then!" Frederic encouraged as he threw his drawers at his slave.

"What's the matter, kid?" one of his cousin's friends laughed. "Afraid a fish might emasculate you?"

"I bet he's still hairless as a baby!" teased the other boy.

Joseph made the mistake of raising his eyes. Whooping like wild Indians, the naked trio dashed into the breaking waves—but not before Joseph caught a glimpse of their own hairy genitals. What startled him was not the hair but the color of their skin there. Very like the color of his mother's nipples, or the Blessed Virgin's.

Joseph felt as if there were sand in his throat. It was true—what the negress and his father had said, what they had implied. Even if he had wanted to, Joseph could not disrobe like Frederic and his friends. They would see him and *know*. Where the sun should never reach, in the most private part of themselves, the other boys were pink. Joseph was brown.

He was colored. Just like his monstrous father, and his grandmother the slave. Just like those hanging negroes who had plotted to burn the city, the naked mulatto in the pen on State Street, and that nodding clock in Grandpapa's shop.

You couldn't be *part* African. You were either pure white or incurably colored. Joseph had wanted to be Charleston's first native Priest. He had wanted to be a black swan. Instead, he was just black.

When Mama had called mulattos "unnatural," this was why his father had defended them—why he was friends with Noisette and their own slaves. This was why his father abused his mother, and why Joseph struggled so often with his own lusts. Negroes couldn't control themselves—everyone knew that.

Their black blood explained everything. *Il porte le vice dans le sang,* the French would say. Great-Grandmother Marguerite had used that expression when a bastard became debauched like his father. Of course he had: *He carries vice in his blood.* But *vice* meant other things in French, too: *defect, flaw, blemish, viciousness.*

Joseph tried to tell himself that the water in his eyes was because of the sun. He sat half-dressed on the sand while his cousin's slave folded the three sets of clothing and finally settled beside him, at a respectful distance. Eventually Joseph realized that the longer he stayed there under the sun without his hat, the more he would resemble the negro.

Unsteadily, he rose, re-dressed himself, and followed his foot-prints back toward his family. Four white boys and one black had left these tracks, he thought. Three white boys and two blacks would retrace them.

"There you are, Joseph!" Cathy cried, startling him. He was only halfway back to the cottage. "Mama didn't want to start our picnic without you, so Papa made me come looking for you. We found your hat."

He pulled it back on, hard.

Cathy turned on her heel to walk beside Joseph. She kicked at a piece of driftwood and muttered, "I hate Papa."

"Why?" Joseph asked cautiously.

"He says I can't attend Madame Talvande's, that it's too expensive! That's because she teaches girls how to be ladies! If I don't go to Madame Talvande's," Cathy wailed, "I'll never attract a good husband!"

His sister was eleven; he did not think she should be despairing about her prospects just yet. At least, not because she lacked feminine accomplishments. Cathy lacked *breeding*. Should he tell her about their grandmother? If their places were reversed, wouldn't he want her to warn him? Joseph began walking more slowly. "I think…it might be dangerous for you to attend Madame Talvande's, Cathy."

"What?"

"Aren't most of her teachers from Saint-Domingue?"

"Yes! They're French! The best in the city!"

"But one of them might have known Father there."

"How could *that* be dangerous?"

"I overheard him talking to one of Madame Talvande's slaves—a midwife. She witnessed his birth."

"And?"

Joseph realized they'd nearly reached Uncle's cottage. He could see their father, Mama, and Hélène seated at the table on the back porch. From here, you couldn't tell anything was wrong. Joseph stopped. "His mother wasn't Spanish, Cathy. She was a slave."

"A-An Indian?"

Joseph shook his head.

His sister's eyes widened, then slitted in indignation. "That's impossible. The midwife was lying."

"She had no reason to. Great-Grandmother Marguerite did." The woman made a little more sense to him now. "The slaves killed her husband and all their children. Our father was the only family she had left."

Cathy gaped at him.

"The way Father talked to the midwife—he already knew."

"But—" Cathy turned her attention to their father. Her hand went to her hair. "You mean—when Theodosia said I looked like a… She was *right*?"

Joseph nodded.

"What are you two doing?" Hélène ran out to them and yanked on their arms to pull them after her. "*I'm* starving!"

At the table on the porch, Mama chided them for their long faces and the fact that they weren't eating. 'I know Cathy is upset about Madame Talvande's,' Mama prompted. 'Is Frederic neglecting you, Joseph? Is that what's bothering you?'

Joseph could only nod. He certainly couldn't meet his father's eyes. Instead, Joseph studied him when his father's attention was elsewhere. He saw the truth written in every line of his father's face —in the broadness of his nose, the thickness of his lips, and the dense coils of his hair. *Why have I never noticed this before?* This man was born a slave. He should still be a slave.

He had no right to a woman like Mama. When he bound her wrists to his bed, did his father laugh? Did he congratulate himself because he had made a white woman his slave? Joseph stared at his father's hand against Mama's on the tabletop: at the difference in their skin, at his fingers trapping hers any time she was not signing. Joseph shivered in spite of the heat.

AFTER LUNCHEON, Joseph wanted to escape again, but he got no farther than the porch steps. He felt as if he'd never leave this island, or at least that a different boy would leave it. Before Sullivan's Island became a summer resort, he remembered, it had served a different purpose: as a quarantine site for Africans.

His father found him on the steps. Joseph sprang up immediately and strode toward the ocean. "Joseph!" his father called behind him. "Come back, please!"

Joseph ignored him. He did not slow down till he felt wet sand beneath his bare feet. He did not stop till the tide washed up and splashed against his thighs. He was still in his trousers, but he didn't care.

His father followed him, relentless, wading out to him through the next crest. "You understood my conversation with Ninon, didn't you?"

Above the snap of the wind and the churning of the waves, Joseph was practically shouting. "How long have you known?"

"I didn't, till today," his father yelled in return.

Joseph glared at him over his shoulder.

He heard his father's sigh of acknowledgement only because the man was so close. "I have *suspected* for a long time. Since I was a child."

"Then how could you do this to us?" Again and again the ocean smashed into them, but Joseph refused to retreat. If only that foam could wash him white.

At the corner of his vision, he saw his father narrow his eyes. "What exactly have I done?"

You "suspected" what you were, and you violated Mama anyway! Even now, Joseph could not say it aloud. "You took advantage of the Grands! They didn't know, did they?" Every wave sucked at the sand around his feet, burying him deeper. "If I hadn't overheard, would you ever have told me?"

His father hesitated before he replied. "No."

"Why not?!"

"Because of the way you're acting right now!" Joseph's father spread his hands as if the answer were obvious. "For Heaven's sake, son, I haven't given you syphilis! Everyone acts as though African blood is some kind of curse."

It *was*. It even had a name: the Curse of Ham. Ham had seen his father Noah naked and mocked him, so Noah cursed Ham and his descendants with black skin. The curse followed all of them, no matter how distant the connection: Joseph had heard that black skin could show up in children whose parents looked white.

"It's a lie, but it is *so* deep…" his father continued with all the passion of his race. "I think some of the slaves believe it—that they are worthless, that they are *less*."

If everyone treated you like you were less, then you were. Joseph stared down at the buried stumps where his feet had been. He wished the sand would cover him completely, or that the waves would carry him out to sea.

"I know what you're feeling, Joseph, because I've felt it too. I wanted to spare you that. I know what that feeling has done to your mother. She *despises* herself. She thinks it's a sin to be special. She wants to disappear into God like a nun. It doesn't have to be like that. I hope someday you'll meet the deaf men I knew in Paris. They're *proud* of who they are. Their deafness—something the rest of the world sees as a burden—it makes them stronger. It makes their lives richer than you or I can imagine."

When his father gripped his shoulder, Joseph flinched but did not pull away. The sand held him fast.

"You must never, ever think there is anything wrong with you, Joseph. *I'm* the mistake. *You* were desired, anticipated, welcomed…"

Joseph closed his eyes against his father's lies. If only he could close his ears too.

"Don't ever be ashamed of who you are."

In his mind's eye, Joseph saw only Mama bound to her bedposts —all the proof he needed that there *was* something very, very wrong with his father, with him.

Over the churning of the waves, it took both of them a minute to realize that a new voice was crying out behind them: "Papa? Papa!"

Joseph opened his eyes and turned his head to see Cathy standing above the reach of the water. Even from this distance, tears glistened on her cheeks.

"I'm coming, *ma minette!*" Their father climbed the beach toward her.

Joseph dragged himself from the sand and followed.

Cathy didn't move. "Joseph told me."

Their father stopped just shy of her. "I wish he'd let me do that."

I wish you weren't our father, Joseph thought.

"Then it's true?" Cathy peered up desperately at their father. "You're really a… And I'm—a quadroon? An octoon?"

"You are the same beautiful girl you were this morning."

"But I might have looked like…" She was trembling. "If I have babies, *they* might look like…"

"I don't think that's possible, unless you marry a colored man."

"I don't *want* to marry a colored man!"

"You can marry whomever you like, *ma minette*."

"No I can't! I'd have to tell him!"

"He hasn't told Mama," Joseph cut in.

Cathy gaped at their father. "Mama doesn't know?"

He put his hands on her shoulders. "No, and you mustn't tell her. Promise me."

"How could you not tell her?"

"Your mother—" He couldn't meet Cathy's eyes. "Your mother has enough to worry her."

"How could you ask her to marry you and not—"

Their father dropped his hands from Cathy's shoulders. He looked past her toward the cottage as if Mama might be standing there, but the porch was empty. "When you fall in love yourself, *ma minette*, you'll understand: how fragile it is—how terrifying." His voice grew quieter with every word. "I'd hoped one day... But it's too late now."

Cathy glared at him. "Are you going to tell Hélène?"

"Do you think I should? Joseph? We should decide this together."

"She needs to know," Cathy murmured.

Joseph nodded.

When they entered the cottage, Mama asked why Joseph and his father had gone swimming in their trousers. She was distracted by Cathy, who'd started crying again. She buried her face in Mama's puffy sleeve like she hadn't done in years. Mama thought it was still about Madame Talvande's school.

Their father found Hélène reading in her bedchamber. Joseph hovered at the threshold to listen while their father told Hélène that everything she knew about her grandmother was a lie. "A fairy tale," their father called it.

Hélène did not cry or run away from him, but she looked very serious. They should have waited to tell her. Eight was too young to understand. Her first question was: "Do you remember your real mama?"

"I don't." Their father shook his head. "I've tried." He stroked Hélène's hair. She had always been his favorite. "I have dreams sometimes...but they're only dreams."

"I bet she was nicer than Great-Grandmama."

He smiled back. "I bet she was."

"May is nice. So are Henry and Agathe. Am I related to them now?"

He kissed the top of her head as if she'd said everything right. "We are *all* related, *ma poulette*. God created every one of us. Remember that."

CHAPTER 13

Among our Catholic negroes we sometimes find exemplary instances of that to them most difficult virtue,—purity. … negroes are, as a race, very prone to excesses, and unless restrained, plunge madly into the lowest depths of licentiousness.

— Patrick Lynch, Third Bishop of Charleston, *Letter of a Missionary on Domestic Slavery in the Confederate States of America* (1864)

Now more than ever before, Joseph knew he must become a Priest—if Holy Orders were even possible for a colored man. Was such hot blood capable of celibacy?

His sisters' friends had started to peer at him and giggle, to look away shyly but invitingly. They seemed especially interested when Joseph was wearing his soutane and surplice. Little did they know what his vestments truly concealed.

In his encyclopedia on Saint-Domingue, Moreau de Saint-Méry had written: *"The mulatto's only master is pleasure."* Some scholars argued that the Curse of Ham resulted not only from Ham disrespecting his father but also from Ham violating God's command that everyone on the Ark remain continent. Ham was the only one who disobeyed and lay with his wife, so his skin turned black to bear eternal testimony to his wickedness, and Ham's descendants were cursed with servitude.

But weren't Priests servants too? Wasn't total devotion called "holy slavery"?

Joseph longed for a voice telling him what to do, for God to speak to him as He had to Noah and so many saints. Because Joseph heard nothing, did that mean he didn't have a vocation? But he *felt* something when he served at Mass, or even kneeling alone before the altar of the cathedral as he was doing now.

Their Saint Finbar's wasn't a proper cathedral, the Grands had told him many times. They had worshipped inside proper cathedrals in France. Those were made of stone. Bishop England's was of wood, small, squat, and shingled. Its altar was simple, but it held what mattered: a Tabernacle—and inside it, the Real Presence of the living God. That was what Joseph felt, rippling the still air: power and peace, something—*Someone*—that started outside him but filled him, exciting him into action. Surely that meant God *was* calling him.

But Joseph wanted *words*. He wanted God to cry out: "Whom shall I send?" so that Joseph could shout back: "Here am I, send me!"

Perhaps he was not showing sufficient humility. In the aisle of the cathedral, Joseph lay prostrate. He rested his forehead on his hands and begged for a sign.

"Take, Lord, all my liberty…" He had been following the Spiritual Exercises of Ignatius of Loyola. Joseph had recited this prayer so many times, he knew it by heart:

> "Accept my memory, my understanding, my entire will. Whatsoever I possess Thou hast bestowed; to Thee, I surrender it wholly. Grant me only Thy love and Thy grace—with these I am rich enough and desire nothing more."

He waited and waited. No answer came. Though he struggled against them, tears fought their way up behind his eyelids. "Accept me, *please*…"

Then Joseph did hear voices—and they seemed to be coming from the altar. He raised his head. He realized with disappointment that the voices were attached to bodies: Bishop England and Miss Joanna were standing outside the sacristy door.

She was carrying fresh altar cloths. His Lordship was reading his sister something from a newspaper, and he sounded angry. Framed by her mantilla, her face was a portrait of worry. Then Miss Joanna noticed Joseph and smiled.

"My lord!" Joseph pulled his legs beneath him in order to rise and honor his Bishop. But he hesitated. He should not cross the altar rail unless he was serving.

"Please, son—stay where you are."

Joseph *wished* he were this man's son, though he knew that was impossible.

"We didn't intend to interrupt your devotions." Bishop England folded his paper.

"You didn't. I wanted…" Joseph remained kneeling, his eyes downcast. He wasn't sure how to explain, so he greeted Miss Joanna instead.

She answered with her usual kindness. She set the clean altar linens on the priests' bench and genuflected to Christ in the Tabernacle. Then Miss Joanna went about her work, gathering the used altar cloths. She handled the linens with utmost care because they might hold the remains of Christ's Body.

His Lordship also genuflected before he passed through the altar rail. He sat in a pew and set his paper aside. "Can I help you at all?"

Joseph must begin somewhere. "My lord…I read about Pope Saint Calixtus, how he was born a slave. I know *he* wasn't an African, but it made me wonder: Can a colored man become a Priest?"

"Of course. The Church has had a presence in Africa since the time of the Apostles. We have ordained many men there."

His gaze on his knees, Joseph swallowed his disappointment and nodded. "A black Priest couldn't serve here."

Bishop England sighed. "Unfortunately, in this country, people would see only the color of his skin. They wouldn't respect him."

Joseph couldn't ask about becoming a Priest himself, not today, or His Lordship might—

"If, on the other hand, his parishioners don't *know* of his African heritage; if they believe his grandmother was *Spanish*, for example…"

Joseph sucked in a breath and his eyes snapped up.

His Lordship was smiling. Still he glanced across the altar rail at his sister (still busy with her task) before he whispered: "Your father told me, Joseph."

Joseph's first reaction was anger at his father, though relief soon replaced it. He no longer had to worry about concealing their secret, and he knew they could trust Bishop England. "A-A man's blood doesn't matter to the Church, then?"

His Lordship shook his head. "The Church welcomes *everyone*, whatever their origins. That's why it's called Catholic—universal, for *all* men. You mentioned the Pope who was born a slave. Pope Sixtus V, who finished the dome of St. Peter's in Rome, was once a swineherd." Bishop England's eyes rested on the paper beside him now, his dark brows pulled together. "And do you understand, Joseph, that many people despise the Irish as much as they do blacks? I have heard my countrymen called 'white negroes,' even— if you'll pardon me—'niggers turned inside out.' Many Englishmen and Americans view the Irish as a race of savages: filthy, indolent, ignorant, drunken, and helpless."

Joseph scowled. He'd heard negroes called all those same things.

"Perhaps you've seen some of the newspaper drawings. The artists make us look like apes. Even the Irishwomen." Bishop England's attention returned to Miss Joanna, who was folding the last soiled altar cloth. She looked like an angel, or at least a saint. "But God doesn't see us the way men see us. He sees an island of saints. He sees white souls beneath black skins. He sees Popes in slaves and swineherds."

"But there are men who *can't* be Priests, aren't there? No matter how badly they want it? Men like Mr. Künstler?"

His Lordship opened his mouth, hesitated, and then tapped the seat beside him. Joseph obeyed gratefully; his legs were falling asleep from kneeling so long on the bare floor.

"I know Mr. Künstler's story must *seem* like a tragedy. But he's found another way to serve."

He was only a teacher. He wasn't God's representative on Earth.

"You must understand, Joseph: training a Priest takes at least a decade. It requires an enormous investment of time and resources. The Church must ensure that as many seminarians as possible will be able to serve for a lifetime. The duties of a Priest are exhausting even for someone in perfect health. An army cannot accept every soldier who wishes to join its ranks. Sometimes, unfortunately, 'the spirit is willing, but the flesh is weak.'"

There were many kinds of fleshly weakness. Joseph glanced nervously toward Miss Joanna, who was laying out the new altar linens. Joseph lowered his voice. "Someone could be too wicked to be a Priest, couldn't he?"

"He could, if he refuses to turn away from his wickedness."

"*How* wicked is too wicked?"

"Are we talking about *you*, Joseph?" Bishop England's words carried a lilt of amusement.

Joseph wished he understood why. He couldn't meet His Lordship's eyes. Here there was no confessional grille to separate this holy man from his own shame. At last Joseph whispered: "I have impure thoughts *every day*."

"At your age, son, unfortunately that is normal."

Joseph didn't want to be normal.

"Time, self-discipline, and most of all *grace* will make those thoughts subside. Chastity isn't something we accomplish on our own—it's a divine gift. You understand that with every Sacrament, God grants us a measure of His grace? When a man becomes a Priest, God gives him the strength he needs to keep his vows. *Volition* is what matters. Do you *want* to set aside the things of the world and choose the things of God?"

Joseph nodded fiercely. He was afraid the tears might return. "I do." When he raised his eyes, Bishop England was beaming.

"I have longed for this day!" He touched Joseph's head the way his father used to do. From His Lordship, it felt like a blessing. "I *knew* Our Lord was calling you, Joseph. My sister and I have quarrelled over you more than once."

Joseph too looked across the altar rail to where Miss Joanna stood grinning at him with her hand pressed over her heart.

"She insisted that I must let *you* come to *me*."

"Wait till you hear what he has planned for you, Joseph!" With that, Miss Joanna gathered up the old linens and scurried back to the sacristy.

"My first question is this, son: Do you know any Italian?"

Was that a requirement for the Priesthood? Joseph shook his head.

"But your Latin is flawless, and I understand you've taught yourself some Spanish as well?"

"Yes."

"Those will give you a good foundation. I am certain you will master Italian quickly. Your lectures and examinations will be in Latin, of course. But you will want to explore the city."

"What city?"

Bishop England kept grinning, his grey eyes shining like silver. "Joseph, how would you feel about attending seminary in Rome?"

"Rome?" Joseph gasped. To kneel at the tomb of Saint Peter! To receive a blessing from the Holy Father himself! "I thought I would stay here."

"The truth is, son, my little seminary cannot give you the education you deserve. As I said, I've been anticipating this, and I've made enquiries already. You are familiar with the Sacra Congregatio de Propaganda Fide?"

"The Sacred Congregation for the Propagation of the Faith." Joseph nodded. "The Cardinals responsible for missionary work."

"A young man of your intelligence, the first candidate from a new diocese—I'm certain the College of the Propaganda will accept you and pay your expenses." Bishop England studied Joseph. "It will mean leaving your family. That is the first sacrifice a Priest must make. If we hurry with your application, you could start in November. Do you think you are ready?"

Joseph swallowed. He didn't want to leave Mama. He would miss Grandmama and Hélène—and Cathy, too. But going to Rome also meant he would not have to live under the same roof as his father. At last Joseph nodded. "The sooner I begin…"

"…the sooner you will be a Priest." Bishop England squeezed his shoulder as if to confirm he was real. "Will you promise me something, Joseph?"

"Anything, my lord."

"Promise me you won't *remain* in Rome? I know it will be tempting, but we need you here—desperately. Even ten years from now, I don't think that will change."

Joseph nodded. "I will complete my studies as quickly as I can."

His Lordship smiled again, then averted his grey eyes. "I suppose Saint-Sulpice would feel more like home. You could apply there as well."

The Parisian seminary was famous. But Joseph remembered Bishop England's struggles with Archbishop Maréchal. Joseph asked cautiously: "You're not very fond of Frenchmen, are you, my lord?"

Bishop England sat back and raised his hands to protest his innocence. "I have no objection to them whatsoever—apart from their insufferable arrogance and their refusal to learn English!" His Lordship laughed his warm Irish laugh. "You, dear boy, are guilty of neither fault. You know you have *my* recommendation. We will also need a letter from a physician—someone besides your father."

"A physician?"

"'Tis nothing to worry over, son—simply a confirmation of your good health." Bishop England stood. "I will ask Dr. Moretti. Perhaps he can even teach you a little Italian! Now, have you discussed your vocation with your family?"

"I will." Joseph knew most of them would be pleased. He suspected his father would be furious.

AFTER JOSEPH CROSSED QUEEN STREET, he paused at the sight of the two steeples ahead: the Unitarian Church and St. John's Lutheran. He thought of the congregations who assembled there every Sunday and the graves in those churchyards: so many lost souls… Once he was a Priest, Joseph could baptize them and grant them Absolution; he could save all those people—the living ones, at least. All he had to do was convince his father.

Resolutely, Joseph continued down Archdale Street toward home. He found a tall, grey-haired man standing outside their gate. The man turned at his approach, and Joseph slowed. It was Philippe Noisette, holding a cutting in a pot. "Ah, Joseph! What fortunate timing. I am in need of an ambassador." Noisette lowered his voice. "I *know* your mother saw me, but she is pretending she didn't."

Joseph was tall enough now to peer through the slats at the top of their gate, and he followed the Frenchman's gaze into their yard. Mama strolled the garden beds alongside the piazza, selecting blooms to take inside. Careful to keep her back to the gate, she glanced surreptitiously over her shoulder and scowled at Noisette. Deafness had few advantages, but the freedom to ignore someone you didn't like was one of them.

"The sign says your father is out, but I promised him this cutting." Noisette extended the flower-pot, so Joseph had to look back at him. "Would you take it? It's rooted, but best to leave it in the pot another week."

Reluctantly Joseph accepted the cutting. For a minute, he only stood there on the sidewalk and stared at the small severed branch. Joseph wanted nothing to do with this man or his plants. Noisette lived in sin with one of his slaves; he could legally sell his own children—and yet…that also meant he *understood* the Curse of Ham in a way Bishop England never could. Perhaps African blood did not matter to God, but it mattered to everyone else. "You know about my father, don't you?"

Noisette's caution gave Joseph his answer. The Frenchman glanced again toward Mama. She glared back and hurried into the house, slamming the door behind her. Finally Noisette replied: "I know he is a skilled physician, a loyal friend, a devoted husband, and a doting father."

Joseph clenched his teeth. "I *mean* about…" He was not going to say it aloud. They were completely exposed, but he wasn't about to invite Noisette in. Joseph glanced behind him. Two men approached on the other side of Archdale Street, deep in their own conversation. Strangers, Joseph told himself, who would not draw conclusions from a few guarded French words.

Noisette leaned closer and dropped his voice to an urgent whisper. "What I know beyond a shadow of a doubt is this, Joseph: the prevailing theories that mulattos inherit the worst of each race, that they're weak, even sterile—it's absolute rubbish." He pointed to the cutting in Joseph's hands. "Noisette roses have been so successful because they possess the qualities of both *Rosa moschata* and *Rosa chinensis*. They don't *lose* anything. Botany *thrives* on hybrids: taking two good things and combining them to make something *great*."

People weren't plants.

"Other men of science—*and* men of color—will argue that mulattos are superior to negroes because of their white blood. That is equally ridiculous. I know my children's virtues didn't come from me alone. Your father's intelligence, his humor, his compassion, his courage—do you really think *all* of that derives from his French blood? Do you really believe that you have inherited nothing good from him and his mother?"

Perhaps Joseph's father was intelligent, but so was Satan. His father's humor was usually ribald. As for his *compassion*… Where was the compassion—or the courage—in raping a deaf woman? Noisette saw only what he wanted to see.

CHAPTER 14

His situation is peculiarly unfortunate and disturbing…
— "The Humble Petition of Philippe Stanislaus Noisette" to
emancipate Celestine and their children, denied 1820s

Grandmama took her meals with them now, so Joseph could
tell everyone about his vocation at once. He was so anxious
he could hardly eat, yet the words wouldn't leave his tongue. When
Cathy asked to be excused, finally he managed: "Wait—I have…"
Haltingly his hands followed his speech so that Mama would understand too. "I talked to Bishop England today, about attending the
College of the Propaganda in Rome."

"Are you going to be a Priest?" Hélène gasped in delight.

"I want to be," Joseph answered, careful to avoid his father's
stare.

"Rome!" Grandmama hurried down the table to kiss the top of
his head. "Your grandfather would be *so proud*!"

Mama broke her rule about embraces. In fact, Joseph wondered
if she'd ever let him go.

'The Propaganda hasn't accepted me yet,' he reminded her.

'They will,' she assured him with a smile on her lips but tears coursing down her cheeks. 'I *know* they will!'

"They're fools if they don't," Cathy agreed.

Finally Joseph had no choice but to meet his father's eyes.

He stood scowling at the end of the table. "May I speak to you in my office, Joseph?"

He knew it wasn't really a question. So he left the approval of his sisters, his Mama, and his Grandmama to obey.

His father told Joseph to close the door behind him. At first, he couldn't even look at Joseph. He only stared at his painting of Saint Denis, one hand braced against the wall and the other hanging limply at his side. The decapitated forms of Denis's fellow martyrs lay bleeding at the edges of the frame. At the center, Denis's headless body groped for what it lacked. In the dim light that penetrated the white curtains, his father's skin resembled the martyrs': he was the color of a corpse. "I have dreaded this day," Joseph's father murmured without turning. How different his reaction was from Bishop England's. "Must God have *both* my sons?"

At first, Joseph bristled at such an equation. His brother Christophe was *dead*. Then Joseph remembered that becoming a Priest was a kind of death. Wasn't that what he wanted, to die and be born again, better than before? He would enter seminary as a sinful colored boy but emerge as pure and white as new snow. He would cease to belong to his family, because he would belong to God and *all* families. He would wear black to remind himself and everyone else that he was dead to the world.

"It would be one thing if you were staying here." His father dropped his eyes to the floor. "You could come home every day. We could talk. I could keep you from becoming someone I don't recognize."

"You want me to become like you."

"No, Joseph." His father turned sharply. "But neither do I want you to become like your mother: terrified and ashamed of your own —" He stopped and began again. "I want you to have the chance to become *yourself*, Joseph." His father pushed off the wall, but he still looked unsteady. "You're barely thirteen years old!"

"Many boys start studying for the Priesthood when they're—"

"Even younger! I know! That doesn't make it right! You can't possibly understand what you're sacrificing—and that's precisely why they take you so early. I know what happens in those seminaries. The Church locks boys away from the world and tries to prevent them from ever becoming men. They'll tell you: 'virginity is as superior to marriage as Heaven is to Earth.'"

It *was*.

"The Canon that mandates celibacy, do you know the reason it gives? 'Since Priests ought to be temples of God, vessels of the Lord, and sanctuaries of the Holy Ghost, it is unbecoming that they give themselves up to marriage and impurity.' As if the two were interchangeable! Even between husbands and wives, the Church will not permit pleasure. It is obsessed with purity—an *impossible* standard."

Impossible for him, perhaps.

"All celibacy does is make Priests miserable. It is unnatural and unhealthy and ridiculous. God is not enough—human beings need each other."

That was heresy. God was *everything*. And Priests were no longer human. They were something more, something greater. Ordination changed them, made them *super*natural. *Of course* that came at a cost.

Joseph winced and stepped back as his father threw open the curtains to let in the afternoon sunlight. He scowled. He must *try* to make his father understand. "'It is good for a man not to touch a woman.'"

"'It is not good for man to be alone.'" His father laughed, but there was no mirth in the sound. "You're quoting Saint Paul. I'm quoting God. *He* does not demand celibacy—the Church does. *Men*."

Divinely inspired men.

His father pulled open the glass doors of his bookcase and began hunting for something. "Priests are taught to hate half their parishioners! The things Fathers and Doctors of the Church have said about women! '*You* are the Devil's gateway,' Tertullian tells them. Women are blamed for all sin." His father pulled a worn volume from a bottom shelf and leafed through it. "Blessed Albertus Magnus—Albert the supposedly Great, teacher of Thomas Aquinas, Bishop—he went even further." Joseph's father found the passage he wanted. "*This* is what Albert taught: 'A woman is nothing but a devil fashioned into human appearance. ... One must be as mistrustful of every woman as of a venomous serpent.'" He slammed the book shut. "I *won't* have you thinking of your mother or sisters that way. Milton had it right: woman is 'Heaven's last, best gift'."

You cherished a gift. You didn't abuse it. Again his father proved himself a hypocrite. "The Church doesn't hate women. It *honors* them. You're forgetting Our Lady."

"Mary is honored only because she is 'alone of all her sex'—conceived without sin, sinless, and above all 'ever virgin.' Heaven forbid she and her husband should actually touch each other!" His father motioned with his book to that dangerous portrait of the Holy Family, where the Blessed Virgin nursed the Christ Child and the white-haired Saint Joseph stood aloof.

Joseph's eyes strayed once more to the Virgin's breast. He forced them back to Saint Denis.

His father continued: "Mary is the Mother of God, yet the Church doesn't permit her to give birth! They claim she bore Christ as if He were light and she were a window!" Joseph's father threw the book on his desk. "Human mothers must conceive and bear children vaginally, so they have to be 'churched' afterwards in order to 'purify' them."

That had been a Jewish custom first; he couldn't blame—

"Motherhood is not a sin! And neither is sexual pleasure between a husband and wife! Don't you ever tell your parishioners that!" His father stopped, but Joseph thought it was only because he was out of breath.

"You're not *forbidding* me to go to Rome, then?"

His father threw up his hands. "How can I? You would despise me."

I already despise you, Joseph thought.

"I know what it's like to have a vocation..." His father sank onto the chair behind his desk. "But *is* that why you want this? Don't become a Priest for the wrong reasons, Joseph."

He hesitated, but he knew he must ask. "What are the wrong reasons?"

"Are you doing this because of my mother?" His father leaned forward earnestly. "Because you see the Priesthood as an escape? Because you're seeking sanctuary?"

"N-No." He wasn't really lying. That wasn't the *only* reason.

"Is this some kind of Penance?"

Joseph shook his head again. "I—I want to do what you do. I mean: I want to be useful."

"And that is laudable, son. But there are other ways."

"No way that is equal to the Priesthood."

"I am begging you, Joseph: question everything they tell you. If you don't…mark my words: you will regret this. Maybe not tomorrow—but ten, fifteen years from now. I can only hope those scales fall from your eyes before it's too late."

DR. MORETTI also had an office in his home. Joseph's father said he knew the man only by reputation, that they had never met face to face. He offered to walk Joseph to the doctor's house for the examination, but Joseph refused. He could not risk Dr. Moretti seeing his father and realizing they were colored.

The Church might not care that Joseph had African blood, and Bishop England might not care, but what if Dr. Moretti did? He might believe that mulattos were weak, that Joseph's mind could not survive the rigors of seminary and his body could not survive the rigors of celibacy. The doctor might fail Joseph before he ever had the chance to prove himself.

On the walls of his office, Dr. Moretti had no paintings of dismembered or half-naked saints, only a diagram of the nervous system and a chart for testing vision. The doctor sat behind his large desk with a portfolio open in front of him. He had not looked up since Joseph entered the room. Dr. Moretti wore spectacles, and he had lost much of his hair. "In addition to the examination, Dr. England has asked me to complete another portion of the application with you. He feels it is appropriate to have an impartial amanuensis. So I have several questions for you, Mr. Lazare, and you must answer truthfully. Do you understand?"

"Yes, sir."

"Have you ever struck a Priest?"

"No, sir!"

"These are possible impediments. We must be thorough. An oversight now will only cause disappointment later." The morning sunlight reflected off the doctor's spectacles and obscured his eyes. "Dr. England has copies of your Confirmation and Baptismal records already...we'll also need one for your parents' Marriage. They were married when you were born?"

Joseph swallowed hard. Dr. Moretti hadn't asked if they were married when he was *conceived*, so Joseph could answer: "Yes, sir."

"I understand your mother is deaf?"

"Y-Yes."

"Was she born deaf?"

"She could hear until she was four years old. It was scarlet fever."

"Have you noticed any problems with your own hearing?"

"No, sir."

"Good." Dr. Moretti asked many other questions about the illnesses Joseph had had. Finally he said: "Now, I'll need you to undress."

"Yes, sir." Joseph tried not to sound reluctant. This sudden flutter in his stomach was ridiculous. He was perfectly healthy, and surely the doctor did not need to examine anything below his waist.

Joseph shrugged off his coat and draped it over the nearby chair. He unbuttoned his waistcoat and laid it on top. He pulled his braces from his shoulders, gripped his shirt just above his trousers, and stopped. His nipples were brown too. Would Dr. Moretti be able to tell from those that Joseph was not pure-blooded? Maybe he didn't need to take off his shirt at all. He looked up.

The doctor stood waiting with his stethoscope. "Your shirt too," he confirmed.

Slowly Joseph freed the bottom of the shirt from his trousers. He worked the fabric up his back and turned it inside-outwards over his head, so that he could clutch it against his chest like a shield.

"Is there something wrong with your spine, Mr. Lazare?" Dr. Moretti asked as he approached.

"No, sir."

"Then stand up straight."

Joseph obeyed. The doctor made him set down his shirt. He pressed the end of his stethoscope against Joseph's back and asked him to breathe in and out. He listened to Joseph's heartbeat, studied his pulse, and poked his armpits. He peered at Joseph's teeth and throat with an amplified candle. Dr. Moretti tested Joseph's eyes and then his ears.

The doctor concentrated on Joseph's hands, asking Joseph to spread his fingers and then make fists. Joseph remembered what his cousin had said at the slave pen. A Priest's hands must be even more important than a slave's; they would perform Sacraments.

Dr. Moretti made Joseph touch his toes, but he did not ask him to run up any stairs. He returned to the other side of his desk and dipped his pen in the inkwell again.

With relief, Joseph reached for his shirt.

"Now the rest," said the doctor.

Joseph froze. "Pardon?"

"I need to see *all* of you, Mr. Lazare."

Surely he didn't mean... Joseph's eyes slid in horror to the front of his trousers.

At the edge of his vision, Dr. Moretti motioned to the windows. "No one can see through the blinds. I need to confirm that you're whole."

"W-Whole?"

Dr. Moretti frowned the way Joseph's father did when something interested him and looked up from his papers. "Are you a Jew?"

"No..." Being a Jew was better than being colored, but not by much.

The doctor returned to his notes. "Your hair; it made me wonder."

He was starting to suspect! "My grandmother was Spanish," Joseph blurted, then closed his eyes for a moment in repentance. He'd promised to tell the truth.

"You might still have Jewish blood. I am a descendant of converts myself. In any case, by 'whole,' I didn't mean 'uncircumcised.' That doesn't matter."

"I'm not—"

"Whatever you look like, whatever you're worried about, Mr. Lazare, I do not care—unless you are a castrate."

"*What?*" Just because his voice hadn't changed much yet, that didn't mean—

"If you *are* a castrate, that is an impediment."

Joseph didn't know why the suggestion felt like an insult, when those parts would be utterly useless to him. "N-Nothing is *missing!*"

"Unfortunately, I cannot take your word for that, Mr. Lazare. I must see for myself." Dr. Moretti set down his pen.

Joseph didn't move. He couldn't. He was becoming a Priest so that he could be *free* of this body! Even now, it had found a way to betray him.

If the doctor had asked to cut open his chest instead, Joseph would have agreed instantly. That would have felt like less of a violation, less of a risk.

Dr. Moretti would see the dark skin of Joseph's genitals. He would see the black wool sprouting there. He would also see the pale splotch on Joseph's left thigh. Until this summer, Joseph had found the birthmark interesting, like a permanent, vertical puddle of milk. Now, he knew it drew unmistakable attention to the fact that the rest of his skin was not so white. And was a birthmark an impediment?

Dr. Moretti was still waiting. "You begin a new life today, Mr. Lazare—provided, of course, that you pass these tests. I think it is only fitting that you begin your new life as you did your old one. 'Naked I came from my mother's womb, and naked I will depart...'"

"*The Lord gave, and the Lord hath taken away,*" Joseph continued in his head, *"blessed be the name of the Lord."* The words were from Job, but they recalled that prayer of Saint Ignatius: *"Take, Lord, all my liberty…"*

If Joseph revealed himself to this man, the liberty of his entire family might be taken away. Surely his father could not be re-enslaved now, but they could very well lose their freedom to live as whites. Joseph's father would lose most of his paying patients; his sisters would have to marry colored men; Mama and Grand-mama… How would they survive the shame? If Dr. Moretti learned the truth, he might tell anyone. He might mention it casually to some colleague, not even meaning any harm…

On the other side of the desk, the doctor sighed. "Do you or do you not want to be a Priest, Mr. Lazare?"

Joseph nodded haltingly. "I do." But it was selfish and impossi-ble, this dream of his; he must surrender it, for his sisters' sakes, for Mama's.

No, he argued with himself, it was *selfless*: he was doing this to save souls. How many thousands of people would spend eternity in Hell if he didn't rescue them? His family's souls weren't in danger, only their lives.

Perhaps his lie about being part Spanish would explain his color-ing. Joseph had never seen a real Spaniard, let alone seen one naked. Perhaps Dr. Moretti hadn't either. If God wanted Joseph to be His Priest, He would save him. God would blind the doctor to this one truth.

If God *didn't* want Joseph to be His Priest…

His breaths were coming faster and faster, yet none of the oxygen was reaching his brain. Joseph feared he might faint. Then Dr. Moretti would never declare him fit. Joseph stumbled over to the edge of the chair and sat heavily, tugging off his shoes and getting his head more on a level with his heart.

Somehow he stood again and his fumbling fingers unbuttoned his trousers. Drawers next—all that shielded him from disaster. He wouldn't look; if he didn't look, he could imagine he was normal and that Dr. Moretti would see only a normal, colorless boy.

At last Joseph let his drawers and his trousers drop down his legs together. Eyes determinedly closed, he stepped out of them into nothingness. It was June; how could he be so cold?

This is the first and last time anyone will ever see me naked, he chanted in his head like a prayer. *This is the first and last time anyone will ever see me...*

For the rest of his life, this most intimate skin would be safely veiled behind not only drawers and trousers but also soutane, surplice, alb, dalmatic, and chasuble, layer after layer of linen, broadcloth, and silk always protecting his secrets.

"Thank you, Mr. Lazare. That is sufficient."

Before the last word had left Dr. Moretti's mouth, Joseph wheeled back to the chair in relief. He snatched up his shirt and yanked it over his head. It fell to his knees and allowed him to breathe again. He heard the doctor's pen scratching against a page. "Did—Did I..."

"I see no impediment to your becoming a Priest."

Joseph didn't even care that his shirt was inside-out.

PART III
THE MAN THAT WAS A THING

1825-1835

Rome,
Paris,
and Charleston

So free we seem, so fettered fast we are!

— Robert Browning,
"Andrea del Sarto" (1855)

CHAPTER 15

However pure and sparkling the rills at which others may drink, he puts his lips to the very rock, which a divine wand has struck, and he sucks in its waters as they gush forth living.

— Nicholas Cardinal Wiseman, on being a seminarian in Rome, *Recollections of the Last Four Popes and of Rome in their Times* (1858)

In Rome, Joseph lived in a palace—the seventeenth-century Palazzo di Propaganda Fide. His own chamber resembled a monk's cell, though it was for sleeping only, locked during the day. His desk was in a study room monitored by a proctor, who would pace the rows murmuring over his breviary until he noticed something amiss. Joseph had brought a few favorite books with him. Two were confiscated. He should have known better than to bring Donne.

The Palazzo housed a hundred seminarians who spoke twenty-five languages. After Ordination, they would return to their own dioceses and celebrate Mass in one tongue all across the Earth—truly "one holy, catholic, and apostolic Church." There was even an African student, a boy of fourteen with skin as dark as jet. He came from the colony of Saint-Louis in Senegal, so he knew French. His Latin was minimal—his Italian, nonexistent. The African sought out Joseph their very first week, since the prefect told him Joseph spoke French.

Joseph tried to be civil. But he saw how the other seminarians stared at the black boy, how they stared at *him* when they were together. Joseph had been stared at all his life because of his mother. This was supposed to be a fresh start for him, an opportunity to become someone new, to escape his African blood and "vanish into Christ." If the other students realized that Joseph shared more with the black boy than language...

Their lives were ruled by the bells, and there were few times during the day when the students were permitted to speak, so Joseph could prepare. When the African approached him between classes, Joseph would have an excuse ready, or he would simply pretend he hadn't heard.

He was keeping his distance for the African's sake as well as his own, Joseph told himself. Hadn't their professors warned them that they must not form friendships? They must surrender their love for their families and never again become attached to another human being. They must remain aloof from this imperfect world. All their attention must be focused on God.

Joseph first noticed the African's absence in their music class. The boy's voice had already deepened to a rich bass, and their polyphony was markedly poorer for its loss. Their choir-master told them the African had returned to Senegal and said no more about it.

Sacred music was Joseph's favorite subject, but he could no longer concentrate. When they filed into the chapel, he stared at the painting behind the altar with new eyes. King Balthazar's white turban and black skin stood out distinctly against the blue sky—he was the only one of the Magi not yet kneeling before Virgin and Child.

Had he done this, Joseph wondered? Had the African left because of *him*? What would happen to all the souls in Senegal that the boy would have saved? Hadn't Joseph doubted his own decision to come here? Those first terrible nights, hadn't he lain awake in the cold dark, fighting back tears and feeling as though the loneliness would drown him?

He might have been kind to another lonely soul. Instead, he'd been selfish.

Joseph had known seminarians lived liked monks, but he hadn't understood what that meant. At the College of the Propaganda, they ate in silence while the older seminarians practiced homilies. Some were interesting. Others seemed interminable. During the silences, the Priests and students communicated through simple hand signs. Joseph longed to teach his classmates how to truly talk with their hands. Then he reminded himself that such desires—to circumvent the rules, to form a bond with the other boys—only showed his weakness.

With his teachers and classmates, Joseph explored every permitted corner of St. Peter's and the Vatican Palaces, and he admired a thousand other marvels of stone, paint, and mosaic. But his favorite place in Rome was a small convent church not far from the seminary, unassuming outside but so ornate within: Santa Maria della Vittoria, consecrated to Our Lady of Victory.

In the vault over the nave, the Queen of Heaven vanquished Heresy. *Holy Mary, give me victory over doubt,* Joseph begged her on his knees. *Blessed Virgin, give me victory over temptation.* Somehow she made him feel closer to his own mother, who remained in his prayers every day. No matter how hard Joseph tried, he could not conquer his affection for his mother.

In addition to the high altar, Santa Maria della Vittoria possessed eight side-chapels. For the altar-piece of the Cornaro Chapel, Bernini had depicted the Transverberation of Saint Teresa of Ávila. Large as life, at once fluid and frozen, this magnificent sculpture was the reason Joseph returned to Santa Maria della Vittoria. Only Bernini could make marble shudder and float.

Joseph wished he could witness this miracle every day. Instead, he had to wait several months between visits, which made every moment more precious. Seminarians weren't permitted to leave the college alone, and Joseph's walking companions didn't share his fondness for Saint Teresa. One student dared to criticize Bernini: "That nun is far too young and beautiful. When she experienced this vision, Saint Teresa was nearly fifty. The angel's instrument of Divine Love should be a spear, not an arrow; and both should be 'afire.'"

"But the other nuns who witnessed Teresa's death reported that it was equally miraculous," Joseph argued. "They said she became young again. I think Bernini is combining that moment with her Transverberation." The sculptor had captured Teresa's *soul*, her "mystical union" with Christ. Teresa had died not of infirmity but of love—she had perished in ecstasy.

Sometimes, Joseph's meditations at the chapel were interrupted by visitors with even less respect for Bernini's genius. Two separate men had peered into the altar niche and *sniggered* at Saint Teresa and her angel. Once, a grey-haired woman had glanced at the statue with disapproval, at Joseph with censure, and then scurried from the church.

He didn't understand why. Was it because Bernini had sculpted a nipple on the young angel, where his robe fluttered low? He did look somewhat pagan; that smiling face surrounded by curls seemed more appropriate for a faun. The visitors could not find anything indecent about Saint Teresa herself. The nun was so swaddled in her habit that only her feet, hands, and face were uncovered. In-between, she hardly seemed to possess a body at all, or at least it had become weightless, her head back and mouth open in rapture.

Saint Teresa inspired him. Her own patron had been Saint Joseph, and Teresa even had tainted blood. In her time and place, sixteenth-century Spain, that meant she was the granddaughter of a *converso*, a Jew who had converted to escape the Inquisition. Teresa too had been tempted in her youth—again and again in her writings, she called herself a "broken vessel" and a "wretched worm."

Yet no saint he knew had given herself so completely to God. Teresa wished she were all tongues, so that every part of her could praise the Lord. How He rewarded her, what visions He granted her: of Hell, yes, but also of Heaven. What must it be like to experience such ecstasy, to be freed from your body and find union with

Someone greater? Saint Teresa had made herself so empty, so open to God's love, she had actually levitated.

In Bernini's sculpture, Saint Teresa seemed like a bridge between Heaven and Earth, just as a Priest was supposed to be. She hovered behind the rail and above the altar of the chapel. Joseph longed to reach out to her—to touch that exquisitely shaped bare foot. What might such contact transmit, what glimpse of the divine like a lightning bolt through his soul?

In the streets of Rome, Joseph's thoughts were rarely directed toward Heaven. His explorations of the city became gauntlets to run, tests he always failed. The College of the Propaganda bordered the Piazza di Spagna, and his walking companions frequently wanted to climb the Spanish Steps. Joseph dissuaded them whenever he could. Perhaps the other seminarians could pass that way without sinning, but Joseph could not. On that wide sweep of steps lurked pairs of lovers and beautiful models hoping to catch the eyes of artists.

Joseph met thousands of pilgrims come to this center of Christendom. He would direct the visitors to St. Peter's Square, St. John Lateran, or St. Paul Outside-the-Walls. The husbands and fathers would pretend they hadn't needed any help, while the daughters and mothers would smile with relief and bless Joseph. The mother would pat Joseph's hand and tell him he would make a fine Priest. But he would know the truth: he hadn't offered to walk with them because their destination was close or because he was going that way already—he had lingered because the daughter was pretty.

More than once, a girl had leaned close and confided, "We would have been *lost* without you!" His pride—and another part of him—would swell at such feminine attention. Before Joseph could stop himself, he would imagine how that flushed cheek might feel beneath his fingertips, even what a few opened buttons might reveal. He could not control these thoughts any more than he could keep his voice from becoming baritone, like his father's.

Whenever he could, Joseph visited the Scala Sancta to do Penance. The antithesis of the Spanish Steps, the Holy Stairs had been brought from Jerusalem by Saint Helena. His head bowed in shame while he climbed the twenty-eight marble stairs on his knees, Joseph would remember *his* Hélène. He must imagine that each of those lovely pilgrims was his sister.

Joseph would meditate on Christ's Passion, how He had ascended these very steps on the way to His terrible death for Joseph's sins. Christ had been a man once too; he had had a—

He had also been tempted, but He remained pure. When Joseph's knees started aching, he would remind himself what he purchased with this pain: nine years' indulgence for every step he climbed.

He spent only a few minutes in the company of those pilgrims. He would have many more occasions to sin against female parishioners. He'd been an arrogant fool to believe he could achieve purity. Not with this black blood coursing through his veins, the very color of sin. In one of Saint Teresa's visions, when a demon appeared to her, he resembled "a horrible little negro."

At seminary, they received the Sacrament of Penance face to face; he could not hide in the anonymity of a booth. Now Joseph's confessional was often a garden. During the summers, to escape the heat in Rome, the students stayed at the Propaganda's villa. His confessor, an elderly Tuscan named Father Verchese, had managed the grounds there for almost forty years. But with every passing day, the Priest's arthritis made it more difficult for him to do the manual labor.

So Joseph became the old man's hands, as he would soon become God's. His confessor warned him to take utmost care and wear proper gloves. "To lose the use of my hands after a lifetime of service, that is one thing," Father Verchese explained. "But if *you* were to damage your hands, my son, you could never be ordained. Those hands will perform Sacraments. They must be without blemish."

Joseph promised he would remember. But sometimes, when he was alone, he willfully disobeyed. He could not resist the temptation to remove the hot, restricting gloves and trace his fingertips up some tender shoot, across the satin petals of a blossom, or even through the richness of the earth.

At home, Henry had done the hard work in both their kitchen and ornamental gardens. Now, Joseph found he enjoyed teasing life from the soil. Even the way the labor drained him was a blessing. In time, perhaps he could work out his salvation and exhaust his lust by hauling water and carting manure. He could be a gardener in a monastery too—where he would be safe from women altogether, and they from him.

As he watched Joseph turning the soil, his confessor reminded him: "You attend the College of the Propaganda—for the Propagation of the Faith. Four years ago, when you accepted a place here, you agreed to become a missionary, not a monk."

Joseph frowned at the disturbed earth. "Sometimes they grant dispensations, don't they?" In a monastery, he could even change his name.

"My son, you must ask yourself: 'Why do I want to join an order?' A monastery may be a fine hiding place, but cowardice is a sin. A desire to disappear into Christ is laudable. A desire simply to disappear is not."

Joseph remained on his knees, listening to the trickle of the fountain behind them. "I can do a great deal of good in a cloister, with my prayers."

"You can do *more* good in the mission field, and you know it." Father Verchese tapped his shoulder.

Though it was difficult with his gloves, Joseph accepted the mustard seeds from his confessor's gnarled hand. He accepted the truth more slowly, as he sprinkled the seeds. One of his other professors concluded every class with the cry: *"Souls are waiting!"* Souls who would *truly* be lost without him.

"Didn't you promise your Bishop you would return?"

Immediately Joseph felt the stab of guilt, and he nodded. He was here only because of His Lordship. Joseph could not betray him. But Bishop England did not have to battle black blood. Joseph stood, grasped his hoe, and hacked too hard at the soil to cover the seeds. "I'm not strong enough to live in the world, Father. I don't *want* these impure thoughts. I beg God to take them away, but—"

"Do you doubt Our Lord?"

"O-Of course not." Joseph stopped hoeing.

"He is refining you, my son. We all endure that refinement, and it *makes* us strong. When you are ready, at your Ordination, He will reward you with His grace—like a suit of armor. Remember what Saint Paul wrote to the Corinthians: 'God will not suffer you to be tempted above that which you are able; but will make also with temptation a way to escape.'"

"How do I escape from my own mind, my own body?"

"You must stop thinking of them as *your* mind and *your* body. They are God's; you are returning them to Him. You must make yourself empty so that He can fill you."

Like Saint Teresa. *And remember that prayer of Saint Ignatius*, Joseph berated himself as he watered the mustard seeds. *Surrender yourself wholly*. Not "mostly." He was *trying*…

"Purity is a habit, my son. You must practice it."

"But how do I begin? Everything I've tried has failed."

"You are an intelligent young man, Joseph. Perhaps at this stage, a little reason will help." Father Verchese picked up a pair of shears from the nearby bench. His hands shook, but he used one of the blades like a saw to remove a bloom from a climbing rose. His confessor laid the blossom in Joseph's gloved palm: freshly opened, damp with dew, and an exquisite shade of pink. "Beautiful, yes?"

Joseph nodded. He couldn't take his eyes away. His filthy glove seemed an unjust resting place for such a treasure.

"Today, it is beautiful. But tomorrow, its beauty *will* fade. Admire it—chastely—on the vine, but remind yourself that such beauty does not last." Father Verchese chuckled. "And remember the thorns! Myself, I do not envy husbands."

Joseph smiled back, but without conviction. Because in this moment, the rose *was* beautiful.

"Celibacy is a sacrifice; but *every* man makes sacrifices, whether he chooses the Priesthood or an earthly family. The question is not: 'What do we give up?' but: 'What do we gain?' There is more freedom and *joy* in the Priesthood than laymen can comprehend. To be able to perform God's work *wholeheartedly*, without distractions or divisions in our affections; to step within the Holy of Holies and experience the divine as only a handful of His creation can; to transform ordinary bread and wine into the Body and Blood of the God Who existed before time…"

Joseph remembered the longing he felt when he assisted at Mass, and he nodded. But he had not let go of the rose.

His confessor settled on the bench. "When I was in seminary, I had a friend who struggled until his final year."

Joseph sat beside him.

"Let us call my friend Lot. As we progressed in our studies, as our Ordination to the Subdiaconate approached, Lot grew increasingly restless, increasingly curious: what was it really like to *know* a woman? Finally he…stumbled, shall we say. And afterwards, Lot confided to me not only his profound regret but also his disappointment. The forbidden fruit proved far less delicious than he had imagined."

Joseph frowned. That possibility had never occurred to him.

Father Verchese wagged his finger at Joseph. "Woman fell short of his expectations. But God will always surpass them."

"Your friend still became a Priest?"

His confessor nodded. "Lot confessed and did Penance. Now, he is a fine pastor."

Joseph stared down at the rose in his palm. He wondered what had happened to the woman who'd shared Lot's sin. "What about… would you recommend mortification of the flesh?"

Father Verchese considered. "It has proven effective for numerous saints. When they were tempted, both Saint Benedict and Saint Francis stripped to the skin and threw themselves into thorn bushes."

Joseph grimaced.

"One of the Desert Fathers found that even while fasting in the wilderness, he was haunted by obscene visions of one particular woman. Eventually word reached him that the woman had died, but even this did not quell his lust; he still dreamt of her. Finally, the Father travelled to the place where she had been buried months before. He unearthed her coffin, opened it, and dragged his robe through the putrescence that had been the woman's body. After that, whenever he lusted after her, he could bring the robe to his face, inhale the stench, and remember what had become of the flesh he'd so desired."

Joseph closed his eyes against the image, but he should have pinched his nostrils: somehow the stench of that robe reached him even here. Or it might have been the manure he'd spread that morning. When Father Verchese patted his knee, Joseph started as if his confessor were a corpse—or a woman.

"Perhaps the mere thought of their fortitude will strengthen yours, my son," Father Verchese chuckled as he stood.

Joseph swallowed and nodded. He admired the rose one last time. Already it was wilting. He leaned down to lay the bloom on the earth beside his bench. *"Remember, man, that thou art dust, and unto dust thou shalt return."*

CHAPTER 16

It seems that 60 men deprived of hearing and speech should have constituted a painful and grievous sight; but no, not in the least. The human spirit so animates their faces, most of which are truly beautiful, it so shines forth from their lively eyes, it blazes its way so rapidly to the tips of their fingers, that instead of pitying them, one is tempted to envy them.

— Société Centrale des Sourds-Muets de Paris, *Banquets des sourds-muets* (1842)

At the Propaganda's villa, the seminary routines of silence and prayer changed little. Even if their families had been close enough to visit, such a prolonged return to the world would have offered dangerous temptations. Joseph found that swimming, clothed and alone, helped to ease the restlessness still humming in his rebellious body.

Though there were no lectures to attend during the summer, he and the other seminarians continued their studies through guided reading. Not a moment must be lost, or souls would be lost. While Canon Law stated that a Priest could not be ordained before the age of twenty-five, the Holy Office frequently granted dispensations,

especially for missionaries. Bishop England had entered the Priesthood at the age of twenty-two.

The seminarians were permitted letters from their families,
although the seals were broken. Most of Joseph's correspondence
was with his mother, his grandmother, and Hélène—nothing the
censor judged harmful to his vocation. Joseph suspected that many
of his father's letters were destroyed, but it hardly mattered; he only
glanced at the ones he did receive. When Bishop England sent a
missive, Joseph cherished every word.

In 1830, Joseph received a rare letter from Cathy. Its contents
made him realize just how long he'd been away. Five years. Long
enough for his sister to become a young woman of sixteen. A young
woman whose hot blood had dictated her future.

> Joseph, I am married. His full name is Peregrine McAllister,
> though I call him Perry. He is your age and a Scot. He's also a
> good Catholic, but Papa likes him anyway. Papa has been wonder-
> ful. He never said "No"; he only said "Wait." Mama and Grand-
> mama are the ones who turned up their noses. "He's beneath
> you," they said.
>
> We gave them no choice.

Here some of the letter was cut away, but Joseph surmised that
Cathy had allowed her lover to compromise her.

> Now that Perry has married me, Mama and Grandmama are
> usually civil, though they still think I deserve someone finer. But
> we know better, don't we, brother?
>
> I told him, Joseph, and Perry says it doesn't matter. He doesn't
> understand that it would matter to anyone of quality. But I don't
> want to be someone's mistress. I want to be a wife—even if that
> means being a mother too. Perry says he loves me, and he makes
> me feel beautiful, at least for a little while. I'm not like you, Joseph.
> I'm weak.
>
> For now, we'll share Grandmama's house. Don't tell anyone
> else yet, but in a few years, when he's saved enough money, Perry

and I plan to leave Charleston. He wants to own land even if that means going westward. I want to go where we'll be safe, where no one knows Papa.

There was a postscript in Hélène's hand that made Joseph smile.

Don't worry, dear brother: I shan't get married until <u>you</u> can marry me!

THE NEXT SUMMER, Cathy wrote again to tell Joseph he was an uncle.

We had him baptized David Joseph, since you'll never have a son, and so you'll remember him when you offer Mass. Mama and Papa say he looks just like you when you were a baby, only fatter. I am simply grateful he does not resemble Papa's mother.

Sweating and alone beneath an olive tree, Joseph closed his eyes against the words: *"since you'll never have a son..."* He thought he understood some small shard of what Christ felt in the Garden of Gethsemane. A part of Joseph envied Cathy and her husband. A part of him wanted to beg his Heavenly Father to take this bitter chalice from him.

What was his sacrifice next to their Savior's? Joseph made himself pray as Christ had: "Not my will, but Yours be done."

THE MONTH AFTER JOSEPH'S TWENTY-FIRST BIRTHDAY, Bishop England came on his visit *ad limina*, to kneel before the tombs of Saint Peter and Saint Paul and report the state of his diocese to the Holy Father. Joseph had not seen his Bishop for eight years, and at first he hardly recognized him. But the smile that reached all the way to Bishop England's eyes was unmistakable.

Once, he had seemed like a giant. Now, Joseph found himself looking down on this great man, at least literally. His Lordship was no longer as vital as Joseph remembered him, heavier in body, his dark hair gone grey. He must be forty-seven, but he looked even older, as if he were carrying the weight of the world on his shoulders—or at least, the weight of three American states.

They turned onto the Ponte Sant'Angelo, lined with Bernini's angelic statues. Each bore an Instrument of Christ's Passion. "Have you already met with the Holy Father, my lord?" Joseph asked.

Bishop England nodded, keeping his eyes downcast. "Yesterday. I wanted to draw the attention of His Holiness toward the American souls we have been neglecting: the souls of the negroes and Indians. His first step in addressing the problem is one I had not anticipated." His Lordship stopped beneath the statue of the angel with the scourge. "The Holy Father has appointed me Apostolic Delegate to Haiti."

"Haiti?" Joseph felt as though he'd uttered a curse. "Does His Holiness not understand that you are Bishop to three states full of slaveholders?" The mere word "Haiti" inspired terror and hatred in Southerners. In their eyes, the island contained only fiends, fallen too far to ever be redeemed. Its name might as well have been Hades.

His Lordship looked ahead to the angel with the great Crown of Thorns. "My current flock will distrust me because I go to serve former slaves who freed themselves through violence—and those former slaves will distrust me because I have not condemned the slavery in my diocese. If the Haitians were to discover that I myself own a man…" Bishop England met Joseph's eyes and added in explanation: "His name is Castalio. His former master left him to me in his will. And this is how it happens, you see? The heirs of slaveholders are born into a trap—a burden carried from generation to generation." His Lordship started forward again. "Slavery is 'the greatest moral evil that can desolate the civilized world'—I wrote that for a pamphlet published in Ireland last year. But in the United States, we Catholics walk a razor's edge of resentment already. If I were to condemn slavery from a Charleston pulpit, I would be hanged in effigy if not in fact, and all the gains I have made for our Church these thirteen years would come to nothing."

"Can you decline this mission to Haiti?"

Bishop England shook his head. "The question is one of nearly a million souls and of the generations to succeed them."

"But surely someone else could go."

As they passed, Bishop England glanced to the other side of the bridge, where an angel held the Cross against the sky. "What if Christ had given such an answer when God the Father asked Him to sacrifice His life for us?"

Ashamed, Joseph fell silent.

"I would be comforted if I could take with me an assistant I trust, an assistant who is fluent in French...and perhaps conversant in Creole?" Bishop England peered hopefully at Joseph.

Now *he* interrupted their progress; Joseph could only stand gaping. To go willingly toward that scene of slaughter, which Great-Grandmother Marguerite had invoked so many times in his childhood...

"I know—you must complete your studies. But I imagine this mission will continue for a number of years. If you feel called to minister to Haiti, son, I would welcome you at my side."

They'd nearly reached the end of the bridge. Joseph stared at the angel above them now, the one who held the sponge of vinegar. "I-Is it safe?"

His Lordship leaned against the marble balustrade. "The President has invited us—an *homme de couleur* named Jean-Pierre Boyer."

"President, or dictator?"

"President for life." Bishop England looked up to the statue of the avenging Saint Michael atop the Castel Sant'Angelo. "At least he's brought unification and peace. But the *cost!*"

"More bloodshed?"

"No. Did you realize, Joseph, that in order for France to recognize Haiti's independence, in order to finally secure peace, Boyer had to agree to pay reparations to the slaveholders for their lost property? The indemnity is 150 million francs!"

For a moment, Joseph stared down at the muddy Tiber. He had

heard about this: as the heirs of a Saint-Domingue planter, Joseph's father, his sisters, and Joseph himself were eligible to receive part of the indemnity. But his father had refused to apply for it. Joseph had been relieved—surely such a claim would risk exposing his father's illegitimacy and their true color. "By 'lost property,' the French don't mean only the land," Joseph murmured.

Bishop England shook his head. "France has forced the people of Haiti to purchase themselves."

∼

JOSEPH AND HIS BISHOP AGREED that he would depart from the College of the Propaganda the following year, so that His Lordship could confer on him all three of the major orders. Joseph would spend his months as a Subdeacon and Deacon in Charleston and complete his studies at the seminary there.

Before he left Rome, Joseph visited Santa Maria della Vittoria one last time. He found with alarm that the church had been invaded by scaffolds, tarps, and workmen. A fire had ravaged the apse and licked at the crossing. The high altar had been reduced to ashes, but Saint Teresa and her angel remained untouched, luminous in the gloom. Joseph knelt before the altar-piece that now seemed more miraculous than ever. *Help me to be like you, Saint Teresa,* he prayed.

A saint would have recognized the money his father had sent him as an occasion of sin and put most of it in the offering box. Instead, Joseph left the Papal States and did something that certainly was a sin for the pleasure he took in it: he attended an opera, Donizetti's *L'elisir d'amore.* As soon as he reached Paris, Joseph sinned again, twice. A Mozart aria was almost worth eternal damnation.

He'd come to visit the National Institute for Deaf-Mutes. Joseph learned that its board of directors was discarding the deaf teachers and suppressing the language of signs. The Abbé de l'Épée, who had founded the Institute, would not have approved. He'd celebrated Masses in the manual language of his pupils.

In response to the school's hostile new board, the deaf community decided to commemorate the Abbé's birthday. That year of 1834, sixty men gathered for their first annual banquet: printers, engravers, painters, cabinetmakers, farmers, teachers—their only commonality was their deafness, but this made them immediate allies.

The deaf men invited Joseph and two other outsiders, but this night was to celebrate sign, so they agreed not to use their voices.

'Do you ever dream that you can hear and speak?' Joseph asked one of the deaf men with his hands.

'No,' the man answered with a wistful smile. 'I dream that everyone in the world can sign.'

In this, Joseph's father had been right: these deaf men amazed him. Their difference gave them a place to belong, yet they did not let it limit them. Every day they fought tirelessly to prove themselves proud and intelligent Frenchmen, who deserved nothing less than the rest of their countrymen.

JOSEPH RETURNED TO CHARLESTON through the port at Nantes, in order to make a pilgrimage to the place of his Great-Granduncle Denis's martyrdom during the Terror. Only forty years ago, in the country of Joseph's own birth, to be a true Priest had meant treason, and treason meant death. Before his capture and execution, Denis had been forced to live and minister in hiding, sleeping in caves and celebrating Mass in stables. With one simple oath to the Republic, he could have saved his life by damning his soul.

Joseph could not help but wonder what he would have done in Denis's place. Would he have been a martyr, or a coward? What price was *he* willing to pay for his faith? *Help me to be like you, Father Denis,* Joseph prayed. *Help me to be worthy of carrying your name. Help me to be worthy of the Priesthood.*

CHAPTER 17

Do you really think…that it is weakness that yields to temptation?
I tell you that there are terrible temptations that it requires
strength, strength and courage, to yield to.
— Oscar Wilde, *An Ideal Husband* (1895)

From his childhood in Charleston, Joseph knew he must remove his soutane when he left Catholic Europe. For the first time in nearly a decade, he wore only a black woolen coat, waistcoat, and trousers over his shirt and drawers. He felt lighter but practically naked, like a knight deprived of his armor. Until Joseph's hair grew out, his hat would cover his tonsure—that too was abandoned in hostile countries. The true badge of a Priest was his conduct, not his dress.

Joseph soon learned the new pitch of American persecution toward the true Church. In Charlestown, Massachusetts, Protestant citizens believed nuns were being held against their will, or at least the mob used this fiction as their excuse. Fifty men dressed like Indians rampaged through the Ursuline Convent and school, setting it alight. The nuns and their pupils fled in terror. Firemen were called, but some joined the mob, and the others simply watched the convent burn. Thirteen rioters were arrested, but all were acquitted or pardoned to applause in the courtroom.

Four Ursulines had just arrived in Joseph's Charleston to set up a girls' school. The Sisters of Our Lady of Mercy had established themselves five years before. Perhaps Bishop England had invited these holy women in order to ease the loss of his own sister Joanna to stranger's fever. His Lordship had retained Castalio, a quiet negro about thirty years of age, who served as his valet and also as coachman when the Bishop toured his diocese. Father McEncroe had returned to Ireland to recover his health.

Their church on Hasell Street had taken the name St. Mary's. But His Lordship had given Joseph's family permission to attend Mass at St. Finbar's Cathedral now, since Joseph would be serving there. He suspected this decision had been painful for his mother and grandmother. Even if it was the cathedral, St. Finbar's lacked the pedigree of St. Mary's. Most of its congregation was lower-class Irish instead of upper-class French.

The changes Joseph noticed most keenly were those in his own family. His black-haired nephew, David, was already learning to read. Cathy and her husband had also welcomed a daughter named Sophie. Peregrine McAllister had grown up in the Scottish Highlands and spoke with a brogue, but his love for his wife and children came through clearly.

Joseph decided to forgive Perry for compromising his sister, though the Scotsman had little to offer her. For now, he worked as a carpenter. Cathy was learning how to cook and clean from Agathe and May. When the McAllisters moved out to Missouri, they would begin a very different life. Cathy understood that wives must submit to their husbands. But she did not always obey with Christian fortitude. Sometimes she snapped like a cornered animal.

When Joseph found an opportunity to speak to his sister alone, it was wash day. Cathy was in the yard, her sleeves rolled up and her hands submerged in a tub.

"Perry is good to you, isn't he, Cathy?" Joseph asked.

"Of course," she answered without looking up. She seemed to

be scrubbing one of Sophie's diapers. "Most women would count themselves lucky to have such a husband."

"You don't?"

Cathy dropped the diaper. Soap splashed on her pinafore. "Do you think *this* is what I dreamt about when I was a girl?" She thrust her fists toward him, glaring at Joseph over her inflamed hands. "Do you think I *want* to be a drudge on some farm?"

Joseph hesitated. "I think Perry would remain in Charleston if you asked him to."

"He would *hate* it." Cathy snatched up the diaper again. "Soon enough, he would hate *me*. He longs for the wilds, my Peregrine. He longs to see what's over the next hill. His parents named him well. I knew that when I married him."

Then why *had* she—

"I dreamt of marrying a prince once, or at least a gentleman." Cathy threw the diaper into another laundry tub. "But a gentleman wants a *lady* at his side, not a woman like me. *My* choices were a man of Perry's class or life as a spinster."

She might have become a nun.

"Did I understand the implications of my choice when I was sixteen?" Cathy continued, half to herself. "Of course I didn't. But I've made my bed, and now I must lie in it." With a wooden paddle, she fetched a chemise from a third laundry tub. "Or should I say: Papa's father made my bed for me, when he went after his *mulâtresse*. I am the granddaughter of a slave, so I must work like one."

HÉLÈNE ALSO REJECTED A RELIGIOUS LIFE. She often aided the Sisters of Mercy in their labors with orphans and invalids, so their mother urged her to take vows. But Hélène doted on her niece and nephew. She wanted her own children and husband. She was eighteen now and pretty, though she had not lost the plumpness of her girlhood.

Upon their reunion, his family had exclaimed about how Joseph's voice had changed and how tall he'd grown. He had never seen his mother's smile last so long. She remained beautiful, but strands of silver had invaded her golden hair. She was, after all, a grandmother in her forty-fourth year of life. His father was two years her senior. Surely by now his lust had cooled.

Still Joseph wondered, worried, and prayed for his mother. He was grateful when Bishop England suggested Joseph share his own modest residence next to the seminary and cathedral. Joseph was a new man now, or nearly, and it would be inappropriate for him to remain in his childhood bed as if nothing had changed. He was no longer a son or a brother, and he could never truly be an uncle. He was a seminarian, and before the end of the year, he would be a Priest. How much better to share a roof with his spiritual father, the man he wished to resemble.

HENRY TOO HAD AGED ALMOST A DECADE, so he welcomed Joseph's help in the garden. Even in early January, there was a great deal to do on a mild day. While Henry spread hay over the daffodil bulbs, Joseph harvested spinach from the cold frame, since the black man's knees bothered him. Apparently Joseph's garden gloves, like the rest of his few possessions, were still making their way across the Atlantic. Henry's gloves did not fit Joseph, but slicing through spinach stalks was a simple enough task.

His father emerged from the house and watched Joseph for a time. Finally his father asked: "Do you like gardening because it keeps you perpetually on your knees?"

Joseph leaned back down into the frame so he wouldn't glare at his father and decided not to dignify that with a direct response. "There's a long and proud tradition of botanist Priests and Friars. Men of the cloth have whole genera named after them: *Camellia* for the Jesuit missionary Georg Joseph Kamel and *Plumeria* for the Franciscan Charles Plumier." Joseph set another handful of leaves in his basket, then stood to take the spinach to Agathe. "Did you know 'seminary' is Latin for 'seed plot'?"

"Yes. It comes from the same root as 'semen.' Will you really be satisfied if the only things you ever plant are flowers and vegetables?"

Agathe disappeared into the kitchen. Joseph was glad she didn't speak much English. "There is no need to be vulgar."

"*Life* is vulgar, Joseph—and sublime."

That gardenia bush was becoming unwieldy, Joseph decided; it needed pruning. He could make a start, at least, with his knife. Much as he wanted to, Joseph shouldn't walk away to find the shears while his father was still arguing. But Joseph didn't have to look at him.

"God gave us bodies as well as souls, Joseph. To reject one of them is to *insult* Him, not—"

"God gave us bodies, but our sin corrupted them; it divided our natures. Before the Fall—" Joseph looked quickly from the gardenia to Henry, who was rubbing linseed oil into tool handles. Then he remembered that the black man was also a husband, and that nothing he could say would shock Henry. Joseph returned his attention to pruning. "Before the Fall, our souls had mastery over our bodies. Now 'the law of our members fights with the law of our mind'; they 'rise up against the soul's decision in disorderly and ugly movement… Beware, lest that bestial movement—'"

"I don't want to hear another word from Saint Augustine! The man was a hypocrite and an idiot!" His father loomed over him. "Your body is not 'ugly' or 'bestial,' Joseph! You—and your member —are a miracle and a masterpiece!" Joseph's father finally paused in order to glance over at the black man. "You'll have to pardon us, Henry—I do not mean to imply that you are any less miraculous. But *you* are not willfully throwing your life away!" Joseph felt his father's eyes again. "At twenty-two years old!"

If his father had been a loving husband, Joseph might have countered: *You also made a life-long commitment at twenty-two.*

"This order of Subdeacon that happens next month—that's your Rubicon, isn't it? That's when you make some sort of irreversible promise?"

Joseph nodded, kneeling to remove the lower branches of the gardenia. "I will be 'perpetually bound to the service of God'."

"And to celibacy."

"'Henceforth you must be chaste,' yes."

His father sighed heavily and turned away for a minute while Joseph worked. Unfortunately, he soon turned back. "There is another doctor my own age who lives a street away. His name is Latour—a fine man and a fine physician. But when the families in this neighborhood need a doctor, they call on me first. Do you know why? Because Dr. Latour is a bachelor. He doesn't know what it's like to watch his own wife and children suffering. My patients trust my judgments because they know I am also a husband and father."

Remember what he did to Mama in order to become a father. Joseph would never allow *his* hands to torment a woman.

"I know all my patients' names and I care about what happens to *them*, not their diseases. I don't just spout words I've memorized from a book."

HE is the hypocrite. He is a beast; you are a beast; and your only hope—

Joseph saw the bright well of blood before he even felt the pain, before he realized what he'd done. He'd been distracted; the knife had slipped past the wood of the gardenia and sliced into the heel of his hand. He dropped the blade, and panic clamped down on his chest. He struggled to stand, as if he could escape from his own flesh, but the world was going bright and black at once—he only collapsed to his knees again.

"Henry! Get my bag!" his father yelled somewhere far away. "Quick as you can!"

Joseph could not take his eyes from the hot blood spilling down his wrist and soaking into his sleeve. He felt as if he was watching his vocation drain away, drop by drop—every hour of his life this last decade utterly gone, utterly wasted because of his carelessness. Tears began welling too.

"Joseph." His father was kneeling with him, his hands on Joseph's shoulders. "Look at me, son. You're going to be fine."

Still Joseph stared at the gash in his hand. Breath wouldn't come, no matter how hard he fought for it. Why was he even fighting? He was nothing now. He could never be a Priest. He might as well have slit his wrist.

"It isn't as serious as it looks. You're not going to lose your hand."

He couldn't promise that!

"Signing will be awkward for a while, that is all—and you may have some trouble buttoning your trousers." His father was actually *chuckling*! He took his medical satchel from Henry. "Do you want laudanum for the pain?"

"You don't understand! A Priest can't have damaged hands!"

His father paused in his rummaging. How could he be so damned calm? As if they had all the time in the world, his eyes locked with Joseph's. "Are you telling me that if I do a poor job on these sutures, I can prevent you from becoming a Priest?"

Now Joseph's heart stopped. *Dear God...* If there'd been even a chance this could heal—

His father sighed, then bent over Joseph's hand. "I wouldn't do that to you, son. This is your decision, not mine. I can't be a bad doctor any more than you could be a bad Priest."

Joseph closed his eyes in relief and thanksgiving. He felt his father probing the wound, and he tried not to flinch. Before he opened his eyes again, he murmured, "You think I'll be a good Priest?"

His father did not look up from his work. "You will be an *excellent* Priest, as soon as life teaches you a few things." He pierced Joseph's flesh with a needle. "You would also have been an excellent botanist —and an excellent husband and father..."

Joseph averted his eyes. "Cathy has already given you grandchildren. They just don't carry your name."

"I don't care if you give me grandchildren, Joseph. I do care about your happiness."

"I *am* happy—I will be."

"Are you absolutely certain, son?"

He hesitated for only a moment. "Yes."

"I shouldn't have insulted you. I'm sorry, Joseph." After another few minutes, his father sat back to admire his work. "I doubt you'll even have a scar."

Joseph stared down at his hand, wrapped in its clean white bandage. "Thank you," he whispered.

"*Alea iacta est*," his father muttered.

JOSEPH PROTECTED HIS SUTURED HAND as if it were made of porcelain. He could scarcely sleep for fear he would roll on it. He visited his father's office each morning so that he could change the bandage and inspect the wound. The cut continued to heal with no signs of inflammation, but every day Joseph peered at his palm with trepidation. The new flesh was smooth and shockingly pink. Had he thought the skin would grow back dark like his Haitian grand-mother's?

On one of these visits, his father picked up the new bandage only to set it down again. He sat on the edge of his desk, facing Joseph. "This little omen hasn't changed your mind?"

"Of course not." Joseph kept his eyes on his wound. "I intend to resume gardening as soon as possible."

His father gave a dry chuckle. "In a flower bed or in the 'vine-yard of the Lord'?"

"Both."

He was sober again. "Then while I have your attention, son, there is something I must say."

Something *else*, he meant. Joseph contemplated finding another doctor.

"I imagine part of your seminary training involved your respon-sibilities as a confessor and counselor?"

"Yes." He would say as little as possible, Joseph decided, so that this lecture might end sooner.

"I implore you, son: do not judge your parishioners either rashly or harshly."

"I won't."

"It comes to this: your teachers have all been Priests. Assuming they have kept their vows, such men have a, shall we say, *limited* knowledge of women and of sexual congress. I, on the other hand, possess more than two decades' experience, not only as a husband but also as a doctor. I have friends who are husbands and doctors as well. We often seek each other's advice. You are young, Joseph, and you have been very sheltered—like a hothouse flower. Sooner or later, a penitent will confess to you some act or desire that will shock you. You will find yourself at a loss how to respond. When that happens, I will gladly place my knowledge and experience at your disposal. I will give you no names, and you will give me none. We will *both* be bound by the Seal of Confession."

That will not be necessary, Joseph thought. *If I need advice, I will go to another Priest, just as you go to fellow doctors. You cannot diagnose sin. You don't even wish to cure your own.*

~

ON THE DAY he became a Subdeacon, Joseph's palm retained little evidence of the wound. Bishop England assured him the damage was not sufficient to constitute an impediment, but he advised Joseph to be more careful in future. His Lordship added with a grin that Joseph was blessed to have such a fine physician.

Perhaps Joseph's hand remained unsteady. His very first act as an Ordinand, when Bishop England called his name, was to respond "I am present" and step forward. But somehow, carrying the weight of the unaccustomed vestments and the expectations of an entire diocese, Joseph dropped his candle instead.

Miraculously, even as it rolled away from him, the candle remained lit. When he stooped to snatch it up, the tasselled ends of his cincture swung dangerously close to the flame and nearly caught fire. Everyone in the cathedral seemed to gasp and then release his breath at once.

Probably Joseph's father thought this was another omen. After all, a clergyman's cincture symbolized his chastity. As Joseph tied the white cord around his waist in the sacristy, he had prayed: *"Gird me, O Lord, with the cincture of purity, and extinguish in my heart the fire of lust."*

Afraid he'd somehow invalidated the rite, Joseph raised his eyes nervously to his Bishop. His Lordship granted him a reassuring smile before continuing the Mass. Joseph's heart calmed as again and again, Bishop England addressed him as "dearly beloved son." Each time felt like an embrace.

"Consider that this day of your own free will, you desire a

burden," His Lordship proclaimed in booming Latin. "For after you have received this Order, you will no longer be free...you will be obliged to observe chastity and to work always in the ministry of the Church."

Joseph lay prostrate, rose, and answered "Amen" at each proper place. Bishop England conferred on him all the vestments and duties of a Subdeacon. And it was done. He was safe. Joseph belonged now to God, and no woman would ever belong to him.

CHAPTER 18

No thief hugging his ill-gotten gains; no murderer, fleeing from
city to city, like a deer chased by the hounds, passing night after
night in but fitful slumbers, ever was haunted more by fear of
discovery, or lived in greater suspense.
— Ralph W. Tyler, "1,000 Passing in Washington," *New York
Age*, September 16, 1909

Shortly before Easter, Joseph agreed to accompany his father to
the funeral Mass for Philippe Noisette. Afterwards, they stood
in St. Mary's churchyard in the drizzle, watching Celestine, five of
her children, and three grandchildren pay their last tearful respects
to the Frenchman. Joseph asked his father in a low voice: "What will
become of them now?"

"Philippe did all he could for them. He sent Louis to apprentice with his brother in France, so at least he is safe. Philippe has
two other siblings—hopefully they won't contest his will. He recognized all his children and made arrangements to support them and
Celestine through the sale of his estate, which is considerable. But
the only way to guarantee their freedom is for the Noisettes to
leave the South—and they want to stay. Philippe's eldest son,

Alexandre, wants to continue his father's business at the garden. Philippe named Joel Poinsett and Francis Duquereron his executors—good men and powerful ones. If they become, at least nominally, the Noisettes' masters, Philippe's family can remain in Charleston."

His father walked Joseph back to the seminary, still clearly troubled. "I don't intend to die anytime soon, but neither will I live forever; I need to make my own provisions. Agathe and your grandmother's maid will probably predecease me, but I've been thinking a great deal about Henry and May. They have family here—brothers, sisters, nieces, nephews—owned by other masters. But if Henry and May stay in South Carolina, they will always be slaves. I can't free them in my will."

"As long as Mama is alive, she'll need someone in the household who understands sign."

"Henry and May have agreed to help teach their successors—who will be free men or women, I'm determined on that. I have agreed to reduce Henry and May's tasks as they age. Then, they deserve a few years of rest—and they will need a protector who is free. Cathy and Perry are leaving next year, and all the other men I trust are my own age or older. But Dr. England tells me he wants to keep you in Charleston."

"You would be safer if I sent you to the far missions," His Lordship had admitted to Joseph. *"No one in North Carolina knows your family—and even if the people there did discover your heritage, fewer would care. But I cannot conscience such a waste of your education, Joseph. My seminary needs teachers, and you are qualified in every subject."*

Now, his father stopped on the sidewalk and looked Joseph in the eyes beneath his black umbrella. "I know being a Priest doesn't prevent you from owning slaves, and this would be in name only. Can I will Henry and May to you, son?"

Joseph hesitated. If they wanted security for Henry and May, shouldn't his father will them to someone white?

"Will you give me your word that you'll let them have their time? You would allow Henry and May to live where they chose. You would assist them whenever their status legally prevented them from accomplishing something. And you would never, ever sell them."

"Of course—I mean, of course not." What a burden his father was offering him—what a privilege, to someday serve the people who had served his family for so many years.

"Will you do this for me, Joseph? Will you do it for them?"

"I will." South Carolina law couldn't be any more complicated than Canon law.

In *The Southern Patriot*, Noisette's obituary observed that "His death was much lamented by all his friends and acquaintances." It did not mention Celestine or their children, yet it concluded: "The writer of these lines has often heard Mr. Noisette repeat this sentiment of Pope: 'An honest man is the noblest work of God.'"

BEFORE HIS NEXT MISSION TO HAITI, Bishop England turned his attention to the negroes of Charleston. Slaves were forbidden to read; but it was not against the law to teach free blacks. The Protestants already had colored schools in the city, and the true Church was losing souls. So His Lordship opened a school of his own for blacks. To teach the girls, he appointed two nuns. To teach the boys, he asked two seminarians. One of them was Joseph.

He was a Deacon now (mercifully, the ceremony had passed without incident, candle and all). He would not make the solemn promise to obey his Bishop until he was ordained a Priest, yet Joseph felt he could not refuse such a request. And how could he deny anyone the chance to read?

To his surprise, Joseph enjoyed teaching—opening the children's eyes to the world. Or at least, the corner of the world their color allowed them to occupy. It did trouble Joseph, the way some of the boys would peer at him. Especially the mulattos. Joseph wondered if they recognized his African blood. Did he make them proud or simply envious, hiding like this in plain sight?

Soon His Lordship's new school had more than eighty pupils. But in the middle of the night that July of 1835, Joseph and his

Bishop were startled awake by shouting from the street below. Joseph yanked his trousers over his night-shirt. He was still pulling his braces over his shoulders when he stumbled from his bedchamber to find His Lordship already in the hall. Together they hurried down the stairs to admit their agitated visitors through the back gate. Joseph couldn't remember the men's names, but he knew they were Irish.

"Have you heard about the tracts, my lord?" the taller man was asking. "The ones the Anti-Slavery Society sent?"

"Nobody asked them to," muttered his companion. "Meddling abolitionists."

"Bags and bags of tracts! To people they don't even know, because—"

Rubbing his temple, Bishop England interrupted: "Gentlemen, what exactly is the emergency?"

"There was a mob, broke into the post office a couple hours ago, took the bags of tracts to the Arsenal square and made a bonfire."

"They also burned effigies of the abolitionists. We were curious, my lord—we saw the light of the fire and went to investigate. They didn't know we were Catholic."

"Thing was, Your Lordship, we overheard the mob planning where they'd go next. 'We should do here what they done in Charles*town*,' the men said."

"They were talking about burning the convents, the seminary, the cathedral, and your house!"

"They said your name, Your Lordship! They said: 'Did we not free ourselves from *England* fifty years ago?' and 'That Papist Bishop deserves Lynch's law! Ain't he been bowing to those bloodthirsty Haitians and teaching our niggers to put on airs?'"

Joseph was now fully awake.

What the shorter man said next arrested his heart: "We even heard the crowd saying one of your teachers is a mulatto!" He looked directly at Joseph. "Is that true?"

Joseph couldn't breathe, let alone answer. Had one of his students betrayed him?

The taller man put a hand on his companion's shoulder. "They said it was one of the nuns who teaches the *white* girls, Pat. I bet Deacon Lazare doesn't even know her."

"You mustn't believe every rumor you hear," Bishop England put in.

"We called up the Irish militia corps already, to protect Your Lordship, the nuns, and everything else," the shorter man assured them. "They be here, 'fore you know it."

"I appreciate your initiative, Mr. Cleary," Bishop England replied. Castalio had appeared from the garret. His Lordship directed his slave to wake the seminarians and their housekeeper. "Joseph, would you follow me to the cathedral and help me vest?"

"Of course."

"We must pray for God's protection and guidance. God willing, these are threats only."

WHEN THE MOB RETURNED to the post office the next day for more tracts, Postmaster Huger scared them off with a shotgun. For two nights, armed sentinels stood anxious guard around the Bishop's residence, the seminary, the convents, St. Finbar's Cathedral, and St. Mary's Church. Thanks be to God, the vigils proved without incident.

Finally, in the light of day, a committee came to demand that Bishop England close his colored school. His Lordship pointed out that the Protestants also had schools for free blacks. Why had his been singled out? The city then decided to close *all* the colored schools.

A few days later, while they dined together, Joseph gathered the courage to ask Bishop England: "Is it true, about one of the nuns being colored?"

His Lordship stared at his fish stew. "I spoke to her superior. At first, Madame Héry denied everything. Then, she admitted that the young woman's papers were forged."

"What will you do?"

"I can't let her stay." Slowly Bishop England looked up. His grey eyes added: *You must understand, Joseph.* "She's in danger—and it's against the law."

Had His Lordship forgotten that Joseph directed the choirboys, that in the autumn, he would be teaching seminarians? In four months, Joseph would be a Priest. His colored hands would place the Body of Christ onto the tongues of slaveholders. At each and every Baptism, Joseph's very breath and saliva would usher their children into the Kingdom of God.

Even if Bishop England believed the chrism of Priesthood would wash the color from Joseph's body, did he really think Charlestonians would agree? *What if someone starts a rumor about me?* But Joseph's mouth refused to ask any more questions with answers he did not want to hear.

Perhaps this explained why His Lordship had not assigned Joseph to St. Mary's Church. On the surface, it would have been a better fit. Its parishioners were cultured; they would appreciate a Priest trained in Rome. Most of them were French Creoles; they would welcome a confessor who spoke their language. But most of them were also slaveholders, who knew intimately the signs of African blood.

The congregation at St. Finbar's Cathedral was very different. It consisted mostly of lower-class Irish immigrants who could not afford to own negroes—and a small percentage of the communicants were slaves themselves. Perhaps Bishop England had reasoned: *My negro Priest will be safer there.*

CHAPTER 19

Adam was but human—this explains it all. He did not want the apple for the apple's sake, he wanted it only because it was forbidden.

— Mark Twain, *The Tragedy of Pudd'nhead Wilson* (1893)

E very week that separated him from Ordination seemed to stretch out like a month. He should have had more than enough to keep him occupied. In addition to teaching at the seminary and directing the cathedral's choir, Joseph had many other duties as a Deacon. Bishop England also allowed him to dine with his family once a week. Yet in the midst of it all, there were hours when Joseph felt restless.

He suggested creating a Biblical garden on the lot between the cathedral, the seminary, and the episcopal residence. His Lordship was so delighted by the idea, he offered some of his own limited funds. Joseph's grandmother also contributed.

Autumn was the perfect time to begin. Joseph planned out the beds, and Henry and Castalio helped him prepare the soil. Around a statue of Saint Rose with her crown of blossoms, they began to plant herbs, bushes, and trees mentioned in the Scriptures that might grow in South Carolina as well.

One fair Tuesday in early November, Joseph was transporting a pomegranate sapling in a wheelbarrow when he heard something so beautiful, so ethereal, he thought he must be imagining it. Or, on the eve of his Ordination, was God granting him a Heavenly visitation, an experience like Saint Teresa's?

As he pushed the wheelbarrow deeper into the garden, the lilting sounds grew more distinct: a woman's clear, pure soprano, singing words Joseph did not understand, though he suspected the language was Irish. Then, between the statue of Saint Rose and his pear sapling, he saw a burst of blue: the bodice and skirt of a graceful figure seated on one of the stone benches. He stopped, afraid to frighten her, as if she were a songbird instead of a woman.

The morning sunlight caught the gold in her resplendent brown hair. She wore it in braids that encircled her head like a halo, adorned with a pink camellia. A few wisps dangled beside a face he could not quite see as she rocked a red-haired little boy in her arms. Madonna and child. She was singing a lullaby, Joseph realized. He felt a ridiculous stab of envy that his own mother had never soothed him so sweetly.

The young woman must have felt his eyes on her; she looked up. Her singing broke off, and her lips opened in a gasp instead. Her face was as beautiful as Bernini's Saint Teresa; it possessed a perfection of shape and proportion only an artist could explain. Her eyes were the same remarkable shade as her hair: a complex brown as glorious as metal, but infinitely softer. She was twenty at most, her child perhaps two. Her day dress, worn but clean, was the breathtaking blue of woad. "I'm so sorry—should I not be here?"

It took Joseph a moment to find his voice. He kept it low, so he would not wake the little boy. "Of course you should. I created this garden for you. I mean: for visitors." Joseph knew he was staring. He set down his burden and dropped his eyes to the pockets of his leather gardening apron. "So that people can see what hyssop and spikenard look like—all the plants from the Bible I can make thrive." Since he didn't actually need anything from his pockets, he could not resist glancing up again.

"What a brilliant idea!" The young mother looked around herself at the half-bare beds. Her lips turned up in a smile that lit her whole countenance. Her accent was not as heavy as some of the other Irish he knew, but it possessed that musical rhythm. "I shall have to tell my brother Daniel—he is a gardener. So there will be olives and grapes and lilies? I love the scent of lilies!"

He loved her enthusiasm. "All of those, eventually." Joseph pulled out his garden plan and pretended to examine it. "Plus a few other appropriate plants—Passion-flower, perhaps."

Now she frowned. "Passion-flower? How is that holy?"

Joseph realized her mistake and grinned. "It was named after *Christ's* Passion."

The young mother blushed, covered her face with her hand, and tucked her head over her child's, exposing the camellia in her hair again. "One of my brother's books said Passion-flowers grow in hot countries, so I assumed..." Her voice was hurried and hushed, as if she were admonishing herself more than speaking to him. "You must think me so ignorant—perhaps even wicked."

"Not at all," Joseph chuckled as he put away his plan. This pomegranate needed transplanting, he reminded himself. He picked up his wheelbarrow again.

"I *am* a Catholic in good standing with the Church."

"I am glad to hear it." He set down the sapling beside the bed he'd chosen earlier.

"*Silentium est aurem*—I should leave you to your work."

Now Joseph had to stare. "You know Latin?"

"Only a little." She shifted the weight of her slumbering child. "Mostly proverbs. My father is a schoolmaster."

Silence was not golden when one's companion had a voice and a mind like hers. What else did she know? "*Quid plura?*"

The young mother considered. She decided on: "*Vita sine libris mors est.* 'Life without books is death.' 'Tis one of my father's favorites, and mine as well."

Joseph withdrew his shovel and watering-pot from the wheelbar-row. *"Optimus magister bonus liber."*

"'The best teacher is a good book,'" the young mother trans-lated slowly, and beamed at her success.

He could not help smiling back. She knew more than she thought.

"But—with respect, sir—I'm not sure I agree. Much as I adore them, books cannot answer questions. May I ask how Passion-flowers earned their name?"

Joseph tried to concentrate on his digging. "Jesuit missionaries thought parts of the plant resembled the Instruments of Christ's Passion: the scourge, the Crown of Thorns, the nails."

"I look forward to seeing such a plant. I imagine I shall have to wait till next spring?"

"For Passion-flowers, we'll have to wait till July. But I'm trying to plant something for every season."

"I'm amazed there are still things in bloom here—so different from County Clare in November." The young mother touched the camellia in her hair. "This had already fallen, I promise."

"I never thought otherwise," Joseph assured her. The roseate bloom could have no better setting, though her beauty needed no embellishment. Joseph swallowed and lowered his eyes again. *Admire her—chastely—on the vine*, he reminded himself. Even if he were free, she was not—there was the child, living proof of her union with another. "Your lullaby—it was Irish?"

"'Twas."

"It was beautiful." In a few days, he would be granted the grace of the Priesthood, and he would no longer struggle like this.

The young mother was blushing anew as she caressed the red hair of her sleeping son. She was particularly lovely when she blushed. "I had to do something to calm him. Thomas and I had quite a fright earlier; we saw a snake. We don't have them in Ireland, thanks to Saint Patrick."

If Joseph could not look without lust, he must not look at all. "Was the snake dark with yellow stripes?"

"Yes! You've seen it here before?"

With his eyes on the earth, he could still hear her mellifluous voice. From her lips, the simplest of phrases were like caresses. *She is not pleasing you purposefully.* "It's a garter-snake. They're harmless."

"Thomas will be relieved."

She is a mother. She is your sister in Christ.

"And who is this watching over us?" At the corner of his vision, the young mother nodded toward the statue at the center of the garden.

"Saint Rose of Lima. She was the first American saint *and* a gardener, so I thought her appropriate."

"Lima in Peru?"

"You know your geography."

"Remember, I'm a schoolmaster's daughter. I helped my father with the younger children. But I never knew there was a Saint Rose. Can you tell me anything else about her?"

Perfect. Recalling the saint's mortifications would help chastise his own flesh. "Rose was a mystic and ascetic. That crown of roses on her head—underneath, it's full of metal spikes." Joseph kept digging. "Rose fasted constantly, surviving only on gall, bitter herbs, and the Blessed Sacrament. Sometimes she slept on a bed of thorns and broken glass. God rewarded her with ecstasies that lasted for hours. Rose also made a vow of chastity, but she was as beautiful as her name, so men still pursued her. Finally she offered her beauty to God by cutting off her hair and burning her face with lye."

"To be that strong…"

When Joseph glanced up, the young mother's eyes were closed, her brow troubled, as if she also felt the saint's pain. He wanted to comfort her.

The child was safe to look at. He was still sleeping.

"Are there any saints from the United States?"

"None have been canonized yet. They may be living among us." Joseph measured the hole he'd dug.

"What are you planting now?"

"A pomegranate."

"I remember a pomegranate in the myth of Persephone. They're in the Bible as well?"

Joseph nodded before he lifted the sapling from the wheelbar-row. "They're mentioned in the Canticles—but more importantly, many scholars believe *this* was the Tree of Knowledge." He lowered the pomegranate into its new home. "Apples don't grow very well in Mesopotamia, where the Garden of Eden must have been."

"The forbidden fruit was really a pomegranate?" Her voice skipped with delight, the way his heart did every time something marvelous took him by surprise. The way his heart was skipping right now.

"Quite probably, yes." *Fill the hole. Whatever you do, do not look at her.* "When you see one, you'll understand—pomegranates are even more appealing than apples."

"I cannot wait to tell my father *and* my brother. If it weren't for you, we'd never have known."

"Pomegranates are also messier than apples—the juice leaves permanent stains." Joseph forced himself to layer water and soil around the little tree.

"Beside me, is this a pear?"

He glanced up again automatically. At the moment, the pear sapling bore neither flowers nor fruit, and few leaves remained. "You have a good eye." Was she a gardener, too?

"We do have pears in Ireland. Where are they in the Bible?"

"I'm stretching the rules again—pears are from Saint Augustine's *Confessions*. He uses them to meditate on human nature." Around the pomegranate, Joseph pressed down on the soil with his boot. "In his boyhood, Augustine stole pears from a neighbor's tree—even though he had pears in his own yard. 'I pilfered something which I already had in sufficient measure,' Augustine wrote later." *God's love is more than sufficient. You do not need this woman. You only WANT her, because she belongs to someone else and you are perverse.* "'To do this pleased me all the more because it was forbidden. … It was foul, and I loved it. I loved my own undoing.' The theft of those pears haunted Augustine for the rest of his life."

"Is there anything, sir, you do not know?" Over the head of her son, the young mother beamed. "A gardener who is a Latinist, a hagiologist, a Biblical scholar, and can quote from Saint Augustine —I can understand why Bishop England engaged you."

Joseph smiled back. "Horticulture is merely my hobby." He gave the pomegranate one last drink of water. "I learned it and everything else I know at seminary."

Her smile disappeared, and the color drained from her face. For a moment, the young mother only stared at him, her lips slightly open. At last she whispered: "You're a divine."

Joseph nodded. "A Deacon, at the moment. Come this Saturday, a Priest." Had she never seen a clergyman out of his soutane before? He did not look very holy at the moment, it was true; he was dirty and sweaty. Joseph set down the watering-pot and took up the shovel again to spread mulch.

The young mother began glancing around as if she'd forgotten something. "I should have…" Did she think she'd behaved inappropriately? That *he* had?

He must fix this. But he had so little experience with women. "You and your husband are welcome to celebrate with us at the cathedral."

"I don't have a—" She dropped her eyes to the boy in her arms and went scarlet. "Thomas isn't mine."

She is free. His damned heart actually leapt in his chest, as if the news made any difference to him.

"His mother and I were on the ship together. I watch him sometimes."

Remember what you are, wholly apart from your vocation. If this young woman knew what you carry in your veins, she would not flush—she would flee. Leave her to a better man. He must find something normal to say. "Did you emigrate recently?"

"A month ago." She fiddled with her little drawstring bag. "We've attended at the cathedral, but I—I haven't seen you."

"I've been assisting His Lordship at the early Mass." The one for the colored parishioners. "You came to Charleston with your father and your brother?"

"Only with my youngest brother, Liam—William Conley. I am Teresa Conley." She must be named for Teresa of Ávila! Joseph would have told her about Bernini's sculpture, but she seemed so uncomfortable now.

"My name is Joseph Lazare." He smiled in an attempt to put her at ease again. Perhaps they *were* breeching etiquette—but circumventing formal introductions was one of the prerogatives of a clergyman. "I would kiss your hand properly, Miss Conley, but…" He grimaced as he pulled off a filthy gardening glove. Beneath, his hands were perspiring. "Will you come? On Saturday?"

"Of course." Still Miss Conley looked as though she wanted to flee, perched on the edge of the bench. In her arms, little Thomas stirred and whined. He did not want her to move any more than Joseph did.

"I know you won't recognize *all* the Latin, but Bishop England translated the Rite of Ordination a few years ago. We still have copies of the pamphlet, if you'd like to read it beforehand. I can get one for you—it would take half a minute."

"Yes, thank you."

Joseph dashed to the Bishop's residence, scraping off his boots as quickly as possible. He blessed himself using the holy water stoup at the door, and this put things in perspective. For fifteen minutes in that garden, Joseph had let himself lose sight of what was important. He was not a lover and he never would be. He was above all that. Miss Conley was a parishioner, nothing more. He grabbed the Ordination pamphlet from the library and raced back to the garden.

She hovered near the gate, looking more ill at ease than ever. Miss Conley was taller than he'd expected—almost as tall as Cathy. Thomas stood beside her, sucking his thumb and gripping the skirts that concealed her long legs.

Parishioners did not have legs.

"Here it is." Joseph held the pamphlet by a corner, so there would be no chance of their fingers brushing.

Miss Conley took it just as gingerly. "You must be overjoyed. You've been preparing for this for…"

"Ten years. Truly, all my life."

Miss Conley nodded shakily. She would not meet his eyes. She looked as if she were about to cry. A few minutes before, she had seemed so comfortable with him.

Had she realized his attraction to her? "Miss Conley...have I offended you in some way?"

She shook her head vigorously. "I cannot imagine better company." She tucked the Ordination pamphlet in her bag. Her hands were trembling.

"You could stay and read it here. If the snake returns, I promise to keep him away from you."

"Thank you, but…" She picked up little Thomas.

"Whatever is troubling you, Miss Conley, you can tell me. In fact, I could use the practice as a confessor."

She turned away from him, so he saw the camellia again, so he hardly heard her words: "It will be difficult, I imagine, to know the true foulness of your companions."

"Sin is only the beginning. When I become a Priest, I can offer penitents Absolution. I can make their souls clean again and show them the way forward. Our God is a God of justice, yes; but He is also a God of love and forgiveness."

Over her shoulder, he saw Miss Conley's profile for only a moment before she left him. "You will be a wonderful Priest, Mr. Lazare."

People had been telling him that half his life. For the first time, Joseph thought he believed it. Hadn't he just passed his final test?

HIS MIND KNEW WHAT WAS IMPORTANT, but his body did not. Before the next dawn, Joseph awoke to the proof—to the pollution that had not plagued him since his Ordination to Subdeacon. Now it was infinitely fouler. The holiest man in America slept across the hall, a man who believed Joseph worthy of the Priesthood. And always before, when Joseph remembered his dream, his partner in impurity had been a faceless abstraction. He curled up in shame, as if he could will the stuff back into his body. He'd thought he'd outgrown this. He'd been wrong.

Before he crawled from his soiled bed, he whispered the prayer for purity to his patron. He'd never meant the words more than he did now:

> "Guardian of virgins, holy father Joseph, to whose custody Christ Jesus, Innocence itself, and Mary, Virgin of virgins, were committed, look mercifully upon my infirmity. I beseech thee, that I may be preserved from all defilement…"

He took the ferry to Sullivan's Island, ran till he was alone, and swam till he was exhausted. The chilly ocean numbed his stubborn flesh, and he felt almost clean again. When his side started cramping, he dragged himself up the beach and retched onto the sand.

Why these sudden, paralyzing misgivings? People said grooms became uneasy on the eve of their weddings, no matter how much they loved their brides. That was all this was. It would pass.

CHAPTER 20

At the altar each day we behold them,
And the hands of a king on his throne
Are not equal to them in their greatness;
Their dignity stands all alone;
And when we are tempted and wander,
To pathways of shame and of sin,
It's the hand of a priest that absolves us—
Not once, but again and again…
— "The Beautiful Hands of a Priest,"
from a Catholic prayer card

On the day of his Ordination, Joseph was particularly careful about how he tied his cincture and how he held his candle. Bishop England had timed the ceremony to coincide with the Twelfth South Carolina Convention of clergy and laymen, so as many people as possible could witness Joseph's transformation. As he progressed through the incense up the aisle of the cathedral, he caught the eyes of his family and of Miss Conley. She had come. She offered him a small smile, and he could see she was holding the Ordination pamphlet.

His Lordship's homily concerned the wonder of the Priesthood, but also its difficulty. At the end, he prayed for Joseph: "May the Immaculate Virgin Mary, the mother of Priests, and Saint Joseph, her most chaste spouse, intercede for you always."

For the first time of many, Joseph knelt before his Bishop, who stood in his full vestments and mitre. "As far as I can perceive, the conduct of this Deacon is pleasing to God... If any person has anything to allege against him, let him come forward and speak." His Lordship paused to allow an objection.

Joseph bowed his head lower, held his breath, and waited. Would someone expose him as colored? Would Miss Conley reveal the lust she had seen in his eyes?

There was only silence in the cathedral. Joseph reminded himself that most of the audience did not know Latin. Even if they were trying to follow along in the translation, they might not have understood the placement of this pause.

Satisfied, Bishop England resumed the rite. "Imitate that which you handle," he admonished Joseph, "so that in celebrating the Mystery of the Lord's death, you are careful to mortify your members concerning all vices and lusts. Let your doctrine be a spiritual medicine for the people of God. Let the fragrance of your life be the delight of the Church..."

Joseph lowered himself to the floor of the cathedral until he was prostrate, his forehead resting on his folded arms. He lay in the very spot where, a decade before, he'd begged God to accept him, and Bishop England had assured him He would. They chanted the long litany of the saints, which included Saint Joseph but not Saint Teresa.

At last Joseph rose to his knees again. First Bishop England and then each of the other Priests laid their hands upon Joseph's bowed head. He was sure he could feel the power tingling through them into him: this unbroken apostolic succession, transmitted across eighteen centuries all the way from Saint Peter—from Christ Himself. "We beseech Thee, O God, infuse the blessing of the Holy Ghost and the virtue of Priestly grace upon this Thy servant..."

His Lordship positioned the stole across Joseph's breast. "May he preserve pure and undefiled his ministry…may he arise in inviolable charity a perfect man…"

Bishop England removed his gloves. Trembling—for he knew what was coming—Joseph held out his hands. His Lordship dipped his thumb in holy oil and anointed Joseph's palms. "O Lord, consecrate these hands by this unction and"—he made the Sign of the Cross—"our benediction."

Though his throat was tight, Joseph replied, "Amen."

His Lordship placed Joseph's palms together, and Father Baker bound them with a spotless white cloth. Bishop England brought a Host and a chalice, and Joseph touched them. "Take this power to offer sacrifice to God, and to celebrate Masses, both for the living and the dead."

The cloth was removed from Joseph's hands. The prayers of the Mass continued, in which Joseph now took part. He kissed the altar and the episcopal ring. He received from Bishop England the Body and Blood, the soul and divinity of Christ under the appearance of bread and wine.

In time, Joseph joined his hands again, and His Lordship placed his around them. "Do you promise to me and my successors obedience and reverence?"

"I promise," Joseph answered, and Bishop England offered him the Kiss of Peace. Their cheeks were both damp with tears.

I am a Priest, Joseph thought, stricken with awe, relief, and joy. *I am a Priest, forever.* No one could take this away from him. At long last, his life could begin.

When the Mass concluded and the congregation spilled into his Biblical garden, Joseph's family descended on him. Perched on her father's hip, even little Sophie was wide-eyed and speechless. "Bless me first!" demanded his five-year-old nephew, yanking on Joseph's chasuble.

"Soon, David," Joseph told him. "A new Priest blesses his *parents* first."

Joseph's mother was so overcome, she forgot she never signed in public. 'Now we have *two* doctors in the family: a physician of the body and a Physician of the Soul!' Though she kept dabbing at her eyes, she was beaming. 'Isn't it wonderful, René?'

He managed only a wan smile. 'Just don't expect me to call my son "Father."'

When Joseph held his hands over his mother's head to begin the First Blessing, his father knelt beside her. But afterward, he rose without kissing Joseph's anointed palms, when his father needed the indulgences far more than his mother.

Nearby, Miss Conley was weeping. She stood next to a young man with her coloring—that must be her brother Liam. Eschewing etiquette, Hélène began chatting with them while Joseph blessed his grandmother, Cathy, Perry, and their children in turn. Then Miss Conley approached. Her eyes downcast beneath her mantilla, the young woman knelt before him, her white skirts billowing around her on the ground. *She looks like an upside-down flower,* Joseph thought as he gave her the blessing. *Like a fallen camellia.*

When he offered his palms, Miss Conley took them in her own hands. Perhaps she could not afford gloves; her slender fingers were bare and warm in the chill November morning. The intimacy took him by surprise, and every muscle in Joseph's body tensed. This was the first time they had touched. It was the first time any woman had ever touched him skin to skin—any woman unrelated to him, and that made all the difference.

Miss Conley took possession of his hands in a grasp that was gentle but impossible to resist. The wound he'd incurred while pruning the gardenia had left the barest imperfection in his flesh, invisible to anyone who did not know where to look. Yet somehow, when Miss Conley raised Joseph's palm to her lips, she kissed him exactly there.

His reaction was weak but nonetheless electric, like one last convulsion in the tail of a dying fish. Clearly the chrism had yet to reach his loins.

When Miss Conley kissed his other palm, Joseph tried to keep his arm limp; but at the last moment, his tendons contracted as if controlled by some invisible puppeteer. As she let go, his fingertips brushed her silken throat.

"Will you pray for me, Father?" Miss Conley pleaded in a hoarse whisper. His hand was still so close to her mouth that Joseph could feel the trembling caress of her breath. Her eyes flickered, as if she were not sure where to look. When she closed them, more tears seeped between her long lashes.

"O-Of course." He wanted to fall to his knees and take Miss Conley's face in his hands. He wanted to dry those tears with his stole and beg her to tell him what was wrong so that he could make it right.

But how would that look? He would soil his vestments—it had rained last night.

Hélène saved him from doing anything foolish. Without waiting for his blessing, she promptly followed Miss Conley's example— except when his sister grabbed Joseph's hands, she was sniggering.

Joseph took control, patting Hélène's cheeks in admonishment as though she were a child, since she was acting like one. "It has to be done *devoutly*, El. It doesn't count if you're giggling." Still he couldn't help smiling himself.

Hélène huffed in mock effrontery and sprang up to embrace him instead. "I love you, Joseph! I don't care if that earns me indulgences or not!" His little sister then lost no time in introducing everyone to the Conleys. She invited them to dinner.

At the prospect of guests, Joseph's mother fretted as if her deafness were contagious. His grandmother gave Hélène her wide-eyed jaw-clench of disapproval, which was already too late.

'*Look* at them, Grandmama!' Joseph's sister argued in sign. 'They're so thin! And we always have plenty of food!'

Mr. Conley watched Hélène's hands with interest. "What's she saying?" he asked Perry, who must have seemed less intimidating than the rest of them.

Perry had learned a great many signs, but he chose his own translation: "She is saying that a new Priest must become acquainted with his parishioners."

～

THE CONLEYS JOINED THEM for dinner the day after Joseph's first Mass. Being served by Henry and May clearly made them uncomfortable, but brother and sister did their best to hide their reaction. For most of the meal, Miss Conley was gracious but withdrawn—so different from the vivacious woman he'd met in the garden.

Of course their guests wanted to hear about Rome. Joseph imagined he would be recounting his years in the Eternal City for the rest of his life, but he did not mind. Then Perry and Mr. Conley commiserated about the cruelty of landlords. Perry's family had been victims of the Highland Clearances. Mr. Conley's ire was fresher and seemed even deeper. During this conversation, his sister became as white as death. The young Irishman quickly changed the subject, but Joseph longed to know their whole story.

Hélène asked Mr. Conley a surprising number of questions. Joseph had not realized she was so interested in Irish politics. Their guest was eager to discuss Catholic Emancipation, how life in Ireland had changed since the Relief Act of '29—and how it had *not* changed. The "Tithe War" still raged.

"Catholic farmers who can barely feed their children are forced to pay for *Protestant* clergymen!" Mr. Conley exclaimed. Clashes between tithe agents and Catholics had taken hundreds of lives.

"Please do not take my brother for a revolutionary," Miss Conley interjected quietly. "My family holds with the Great Emancipator, O'Connell: we do not believe in *violent* protest."

"No matter how much we are provoked," Mr. Conley muttered.

Joseph gathered that Mr. Conley's father had sent his youngest son to America for much the same reason the Church had sent Bishop England here: they had both been agitating their countrymen with their pens. What an Irishman called justice, the British Crown called treason.

Joseph's mother had tried to disappear before their guests ever arrived, but his father had refused to allow it. The Conleys were very patient as they waited for translations. They even wanted to learn a few signs. Mr. Conley was genuinely interested in the legal barriers faced by the deaf in France and in America. The young

Irishman had found work as a copyist for a lawyer on Broad Street, and someday he hoped to practice law himself.

"I'd heard that the deaf could communicate with their hands," Mr. Conley observed over dessert. "But it isn't just your hands—you use your entire countenance!"

"We do," Joseph's father smiled.

"A year ago in Paris, I attended a banquet for the deaf," Joseph added, signing as he spoke. "There were speeches without speech. Some of the men even recited poetry." He waited for the Conleys' gasps of astonishment. "Poetry composed in sign doesn't rhyme, of course—it finds its rhythm in the shapes of the signs themselves: how they reflect one another and grow out of one another. It's quite beautiful."

Miss Conley ventured: "Do you remember any of the poems, Father?"

"Not well enough to do them justice. I'm sorry."

"Have you composed any poems in sign yourself?"

Joseph chuckled. "I'm afraid not. Homilies are difficult enough."

"The one you gave yesterday was excellent."

"I am relieved to hear it."

"I think the best parts of Joseph's Mass were his chants," Hélène declared. "Your voice is truly divine, brother. Which is why you *must* sing for our guests!"

"What, now?"

"Dinner is finished—why not?" His sister stood, kissed their mother's forehead, and said only in sign: 'I apologize, Mama.'

'It's all right, sweetheart,' she answered. 'I'll see if David and Sophie have finished *their* dinner.'

Hélène flew to the piano. "I finally received the sheet music I've been waiting for, a ballad everybody else already has! It's supposed to be a man singing, so it doesn't sound right when *I* do it."

Joseph frowned at the sheet music. "This looks like a love ballad."

"It *is*." Hélène was already teasing the tune from the keys. "It's about a man who renounces his love, so it's perfect for you."

"Whom have I renounced?"

"Everybody! Must I really explain celibacy to a Priest? Now *sing*!"

Joseph sighed and capitulated:

> "I'd offer thee this hand of mine,
> If I could love thee less;
> But hearts as warm and pure as thine,
> Should never know distress.
> My fortune is too hard for thee,
> 'Twould chill thy dearest joy:
> I'd rather weep to see thee free,
> Than win thee to destroy…"

When the ballad was finished, everyone offered their praise. Joseph heard only Miss Conley's.

"Surely one of our guests will favor us with a song as well?" Hélène urged.

Miss Conley lowered her eyes. "Oh, no, we couldn't—especially after—"

"Don't be so modest, Tessa," her brother encouraged. "Everyone always said you had the sweetest voice in our parish."

The sweetest voice in all of Ireland, Joseph would wager.

At last, Miss Conley conceded. She needed no accompaniment. She sang a lament in her own language, wild and ancient and absolutely breathtaking. She kept them at a distance, then drew them in and left them intimate strangers.

Joseph let the others shower Miss Conley with acclaim. His only compliment was wordless, an exchange of smiles from one singer to another. He was afraid that a true admission of how Miss Conley's voice affected him would reveal how much of the man remained in him, how his transformation into Priesthood was not as instantaneous as he'd hoped.

PART IV
A PRIEST FOREVER

1835-1837

Charleston

The Lord has sworn, and He will not repent:
You are a Priest forever…

— Psalm 109:4

CHAPTER 21

In a short time the persons begin to act towards each other not like angels…but like beings clothed with flesh. The looks are not immodest, but they are frequent and reciprocal; their words appear to be spiritual, but are too affectionate. Each begins frequently to desire the company of the other. And thus…a spiritual devotion is converted into a carnal one.

— Saint Alphonsus Liguori, *Dignity and Duties of the Priest* (1760)

At a glance, Joseph continued to resemble other men. Outside the cathedral and seminary, he wore a simple black suit. To stroll down the streets of Charleston in his soutane would have been akin to carrying a pillory. To most Protestants, he remained incognito; his neck-cloth only appeared out of date or too formal for day wear.

But Catholics could identify him as a Priest by this "choker," a white silk neckerchief. It contained a great deal more cloth than a stock or a cravat, so it took a bit of practice to make it tidy. Castalio had to help him the first time. Joseph learned to wrap the folded neckerchief around his shirt collar thrice, then tie the ends at his throat. Finally, he pushed the knot up out of sight, like a second

Adam's apple, and tucked the tails into his waistcoat. In the winter this thick neck-cloth was a boon, though Joseph suspected he would feel differently come summer.

Unfortunately, some of the Protestant boys also grew to recognize him. Their favorite projectiles were *Melia azedarach* fruits. In Charleston, these trees were called chinaberries. In Europe, they were called bead trees, since religious orders often dried the berries to make rosaries. *I am being pelted with prayer beads*, Joseph would think. They stung nonetheless.

The boys had an endless supply: the berries lingered on the branches well into winter, looking like shrivelled yellow marbles. As if they were playing Indians, his tormentors shot them out of improvised blow-pipes. Even when the berries hit his clothes and caused little pain, Joseph always started, and the boys always laughed.

Give thanks to God for the chance to share in His sufferings, Joseph reminded himself.

He ran this gauntlet daily. His duties as a curate were neverending. His immediate superior, Father Richard Baker, was not only pastor of the cathedral but also president of the seminary, chaplain of the Ursuline Convent, superior to the Sisters of Mercy, and editor of the diocesan newspaper. The dedicated Irishman was strong in spirit, but malaria had rendered him weak in body. Years after his first attack, he remained vulnerable not only to recurrences but also to other diseases. So parish calls fell mostly to Joseph, and Father Baker authorized him to perform Sacraments and create sacramentals.

Everyone sought a blessing from the new Priest for themselves, their children, their homes, shops, scapulars, rosaries, carts, carthorses… Joseph told himself these visits would become less exhausting once he knew all his parishioners. But he soon realized this was impossible. New faces appeared every day. In addition to the babies he baptized, Charleston was a port city.

Many Catholics came from the German states, but the majority of the immigrants were Irish. Some became established, even wealthy, in Charleston. Most were terribly poor. They lived in the worst part of the city, tightly packed into ramshackle tenements near the Cooper River wharves.

Sweet olives and gardenias perfumed gardens only a few streets away, but these alleys stank of excrement, fish, and the decay peculiar to the Low Country. By day, sharp-eyed vultures perched on the rooftops, watching for offal; by night, rats and cockroaches scurried amongst their leavings.

The filthy, ragged state of the children here pained Joseph to the quick. He could do very little to improve these people's earthly lives. Instead, he directed their thoughts toward Heaven. He reminded his parishioners that this squalor would not last forever. If they remained faithful, God would reward them.

Every morning during Mass, Joseph struck his breast and cried thrice: "Lord, I am not worthy that Thou shouldst enter under my roof." Who was Joseph to ask the living God to change a wafer into His own Body? Who was he to consume that divine flesh?

Yet what humbled Joseph most were the times he administered the Last Rites. To hear a stranger's deepest regrets and assure her she was forgiven; to hold her hand as she died and watch the stranger *smile*...this was the reason Joseph had been ordained, to embody the unseen for those who had almost lost hope.

THE FIRST SUNDAY OF ADVENT, Joseph decided to knock at one more door before dusk. "It's Father Lazare, the new Priest," he announced.

"Father! Come in!"

Joseph opened the door to reveal a familiar figure standing by the window, hastily tucking stray hairs behind her ears. Not *so* familiar—only unforgettable: Miss Conley.

Joseph took in the room at a glance. There was little to see. A cracked hearth with books on the mantle shelf. Two worn trunks that doubled as tables. A frayed blanket strung up in one corner. Beyond it, he glimpsed a washstand with a battered basin, pitcher, and dressing mirror. The only adornment was a crucifix, hung between the two beds. Unless the mold on the walls counted as decoration.

Of course Miss Conley lived like this. She was poor. But the sight of her beauty in this ugly little room seemed so incongruous. To call her a pearl among swine would be uncharitable to her neighbors. Most of the Irish were good, pious people—and no one should live like this, unless they chose it as a Penance. But certainly Miss Conley was a rare flower in need of a better bed.

Better SOIL, Joseph corrected. *You must see her as Christ would. He would care only for Miss Conley's spiritual beauty.*

She assisted at Mass every day. As a parishioner, Joseph had not understood the truth of that phrase, how the faithful in the pews could "assist" the Priest in his sacrifice. But as the celebrant, when Joseph knelt before the altar, when he elevated the Host, he felt their prayers joining his, strengthening them, strengthening *him*. Especially Miss Conley's prayers.

She knelt before him now, and as he blessed her, a ridiculous wish occurred to him: that this invocation could transform her drab dress into a ball gown, as if she were Cinderella.

When he'd finished the blessing, Miss Conley took his hand and kissed him just above his knuckles for what seemed like an eternity, but must have been a moment. His reaction to her touch had hardly dulled. Few of Joseph's other parishioners greeted him in such an intimate manner, though the practice had been common in Italy— he had often kissed Priests' hands himself.

He must say something to discourage Miss Conley without her suspecting his true reasons. He had asked Father Baker, and there were no indulgences for kissing a Priest's hand after his Ordination and first Mass. "Miss Conley," Joseph stammered, "I do not know the practice in Ireland, but in this country, it is customary to kiss a Bishop's hand only, not a mere Priest's."

She had not let go. "But your hands are also holy. Every day they hold the precious Body of Our Lord."

Joseph sighed. He could hardly explain: *When you kiss me like that, my thoughts are anything but holy. I imagine not Our Lord's body but—*

Slowly Joseph realized that Miss Conley's expression had

changed. Still on her knees, she was squinting up at him quizzically. When Joseph frowned, Miss Conley quickly lowered her eyes and let go of his hand. "I'm sorry, Father."

"What is it?"

She bit her lip and pointed gingerly toward his head. "There's a...small yellow ball in your hair."

Joseph chuckled, stroked his fingertips below his hat brim, and withdrew a chinaberry. This explained why Mrs. O'Flaherty had been staring at him out of the corner of her eyes when she thought he wasn't looking, and why Frankie Doyle had been gaping outright. "Thank you."

Suppressing a giggle, Miss Conley rose from her knees. "Could I make you some tea, Father?"

Parishioners were always offering him food and drink—people who could ill afford to spare it. "No, thank you; I'm quite all right." Joseph stepped before the hearth and tossed the berry into the fire.

"Perhaps a seat, then? I imagine you've been on your feet for hours."

She was right. "Yes; thank you."

Miss Conley offered him the room's larger chair, which must belong to her brother. As if she'd read Joseph's mind again, she added: "Liam is still at the office." She frowned. "That lawyer keeps him so late—and pays him so little."

As Joseph sat by the fire, he noticed the pincushion, spool of thread, and pair of ladies' gloves on the table by the window. The gloves were rose silk, finer than anything Miss Conley herself would wear. "Please don't stop your own work on my account."

"The sunlight is going, anyway. I should move to the fire." Even candles must be beyond the Conleys' means. She transferred her chair to the hearth across from Joseph, then gathered her sewing. "I help Liam all I can, but my skills are limited. And I didn't realize I'd be competing with—" She broke off and fell silent, lowering her eyes to her task.

"With negroes?" Joseph prompted.

Miss Conley nodded. "We knew there were slaves in South Carolina, of course, but somehow we'd thought they were all on plantations, that I'd be able to find work easily in a city… I know that must sound naïve."

"I'm sure I harbor just as many misconceptions about Ireland."

"Perhaps," she smiled, glancing up at him. "But most of your ideas are probably accurate. Many Irish do believe in fairy folk. My own father—who is very God-fearing—calls me his *aisling*."

Joseph held his hands to the warmth of the fire. "I'm sorry, I don't recognize the word."

"You must understand, Father, I am my parents' seventh child, but their first daughter." Miss Conley concentrated on her stitching as she spoke. "While my mother was carrying me, both my parents prayed for a girl. My father claims he had a dream in which a beautiful woman assured him I was coming. *Aisling* means 'vision'—she appears to dreamers and foretells change. My father swears the *aisling* he saw nineteen years ago looked like I do now."

Even in the gathering gloom, Joseph saw a flush in her cheeks— pleasure at her father's compliment but embarrassment that she'd just called herself beautiful. It was nothing less than the truth.

How different her hair looked by firelight. In full sun, the strands shone like the brass of his thurible. Now, their color was darker and deeper, like the fragrant myrrh he burned within. Her halo of braids was looser as well, her long tresses barely contained, so he could better estimate their full glory. Unbound, they might cascade to the floor.

He must look somewhere else. Joseph's gaze landed on the books lined up along the mantle. Some were law tomes, but many of the volumes must belong to her. "I know you share your father's love of books. You said you have some teaching experience as well?"

"Oh, yes!" She stopped stitching. "Do you know of a position?"

"I'm afraid we can't pay you very much, but we do need another catechist. I was thinking: once you become acquainted with the parish's children and their parents, it might lead to other things— perhaps a position as a governess."

"It might. Thank you, Father."

He would do anything to inspire such a smile. "When the weather's mild, if you can bring your sewing work with you, you're welcome to sit in the Biblical garden afterward. The light must be better."

"You wouldn't mind?"

"On the contrary."

Joseph was both disappointed and grateful when Miss Conley returned her eyes to her sewing. "I had a letter from my mother this morning. My eldest sister-in-law has been safely delivered of her tenth child. They named her after Our Lady."

"I imagine your parents chose your Christian name to honor Saint Teresa of Ávila?"

Miss Conley nodded. "I was born on her feast day."

"Have you read any of her writings?"

"I have. For my Confirmation, I asked for an English translation of her *Life*. It took my father almost a year to procure it, but finally he did." She looked up to the last book on the mantle and smiled.

Joseph read the spine with its antiquated spelling: *The Flaming Hart, or, The Life of the Gloriovs S. Teresa.*

"That copy is nearly two hundred years old! I cannot understand why, but Saint Teresa seems to have fallen out of favor."

"You've not read her other works, then? I think my set is from the seventeenth century as well."

"You own the set?" Miss Conley gasped, abandoning her work on her lap. "Might I see the other volumes?"

"You may borrow them, for as long as you like."

"Oh, thank you, Father!"

Joseph was becoming very warm by the fire. He stood and moved to the window.

Though she remained seated, Miss Conley turned in her chair. "Isn't Teresa extraordinary?"

"She certainly is." Joseph tried to stare into the alley; he tried to keep himself detached. He was not successful.

"I realize I'm prejudiced, but I think she is truly unique. She's so honest, so human, even humorous—but also so utterly holy that she leaves me in awe. Her yearning for union with God is palpable, there on the page. The way she writes about Christ, as if He is her dearest friend…" At last Miss Conley lowered her eyes. "Yet she never forgets His divinity or her unworthiness."

"We are all of us unworthy. But I think she must be precious to Him, too." Joseph decided that if he stayed at the window, it was safe to admire her. "There's a chapel devoted to Saint Teresa in Rome. In the vault above it is an inscription from one of her visions, one I don't think she mentions in her *Life*. Christ said to her: *Nisi coelum creassem ob te solam crearem.*" Joseph waited to see if Miss Conley understood.

She wrestled visibly with the Latin, furrowing her brow and catching her lower lip between her teeth. Finally she shook her head. "Something about creating Heaven…"

"'If I had not already created Heaven, I would create it for you alone.' Teresa insisted Christ meant that for all of mankind…but He said it to her."

She held his eyes for one long moment in the firelight, before her brother entered the room.

CHAPTER 22

When I returned to Charleston from Hayti, the dogs that were set to guard against negroes began to bark at me, though previously they had allowed me to pass.

— Bishop John England, 1834 letter

As Christmas approached, Joseph imagined the Conleys trying to celebrate in their shabby little room, separated forever from their parents, siblings, nieces, nephews, and homeland. How he wished he could invite the brother and sister to spend the holiday with his family. But Joseph could not justify such an offer, especially since he himself no longer resided with his parents.

Hélène saved him. During her visits with the Sisters of Mercy, she discovered where the Conleys lived. Since her home was much closer to the cathedral than their lodging, Hélène offered them a place to rest between the vigil Mass Christmas Eve and the three Masses on Christmas Day: Joseph's old chamber, with a trundle-bed for Mr. Conley. Joseph was relieved and delighted to know the brother and sister experienced those hours of comfort and happiness.

The Conleys were two among many. Why their fate should

matter so much to him, Joseph did not understand. Brother and sister were devout and warm-hearted, but most of their countrymen were the same.

They were a schoolmaster's children; they were bright; they were readers. Poor as they were, they cared about the world beyond their own quotidian concerns. Perhaps this was what elevated them above the rest of the immigrants in Charleston. And simply because you could not help everyone, it did not mean you should help no one.

Before, between, and after his duties at the cathedral, Joseph joined his family and the Conleys to play parlor games, dine, and exchange French and Irish carols. Young David heard Miss Conley sing for the first time, and he looked almost as mesmerized as Joseph. Mr. Conley had a fine voice as well, although Joseph thought Hélène's praise of it rather effusive.

Miss Conley proved herself one of the few people who could keep little Sophie entertained. *She is going to be a wonderful mother*, Joseph thought. But what kind of life could she give her children? What bleak future awaited them—awaited her? Surely Miss Conley would marry another Irish immigrant, and they would always be poor.

It was useless to dream about another life in which he was white, in which he was some respected botanist, in which *he* could rescue her.

Shortly before they parted, while Joseph's mother taught Miss Conley a new stitch, the young Irishman explained why his parents' precious, only daughter had joined him in exile. Joseph was learning that these sorts of confidences were the privilege and burden of his Priesthood.

"Our brother Daniel works as a gardener at our landlord's manor," Mr. Conley told Joseph in a low voice. "Even as a child, Tessa shared Daniel's way with plants, so sometimes she would assist him. It was a chance for Tessa to be around beautiful things, flowers we could not afford to grow ourselves. Our landlord wasn't even there to admire his gardens most of the year—he spent months on end in England. Neither he nor his agent cared if Daniel had an assistant; they didn't pay her.

"But one day our landlord...*noticed* Tessa. Daniel did not need to forbid her to visit him after that; she understood what the old man's leer meant, and she was terrified. When Tessa did not return to the manor, our landlord sought her out. We tried to keep her hidden from him, but he would demand to see her.

"Our landlord would make foul jokes, like: If we ever came up short on rent, he would gladly accept Tessa as payment. My sister would stand there trembling, and he'd be molesting her with his eyes and his suggestions, dragging the tip of his riding crop down her body. My father, my five brothers, and myself—we were utterly powerless against one old lecher. If he raised our rent, if he evicted us, we had no recourse, Father—nowhere to go."

Joseph nearly snapped the handle from his teacup. He'd heard Irish tenants compared to slaves.

"Even Daniel couldn't secure work elsewhere without a reference. At the manor, he'd heard terrible stories—that our landlord had forced himself on maids. And of course those women were powerless to prosecute him. What if the old man took the next step? What if he ordered Tessa to the manor? If she refused, how would he retaliate?" Mr. Conley stared down into his brandy. "Worst of all, Father, we feared she might accept."

"Pardon?" Joseph was sure he'd misunderstood.

"We feared Tessa might sacrifice herself for the rest of us. The only way we could save her was to help her escape. Every Conley— and many of our friends—saved for months to pay for our passage."

"*Did* your landlord retaliate, when he learned you and your sister had fled?"

"We knew he might," Mr. Conley acknowledged. Then, he chuckled. "But apparently the old man was so angry, he died of an apoplexy. Divine justice at last."

"You could return to Ireland," Joseph observed.

"I suppose Tessa could," Mr. Conley mused. "I prefer America. Here, even a poor man without a college education can become a lawyer. Here, I can speak my mind without fear. Until Ireland is free of landlords like *that*—until she is free of their sons and their grand-sons—I cannot remain silent."

Miss Conley could hardly travel such a distance alone. Besides, how would she pay for another passage across the Atlantic? Once again, she was trapped.

This knowledge of Miss Conley's sufferings accomplished in Joseph what the admonitions of his confessor had not. It shamed him into celibacy at last. He imagined Miss Conley's terror at that old lecher's approach, and admitted that his own attraction to her was every bit as vile. Joseph was not of her race; he was not even of her species—he was a Priest now, not a man. Miss Conley must understand that he cared for her; he'd hardly concealed it. But she could not suspect there was anything carnal in his affection, or she would not have been so receptive.

Miss Conley remained unsuccessful in finding a position as a governess. Charleston's parents wanted teachers with a formal education and letters of recommendation. But Miss Conley's lack of credentials did not prevent her catechism students from adoring her.

The catechetical school shared the seminary's building, so Joseph was able to see her more often than glimpses during Mass. When the weather was fair, Miss Conley brought her sewing to the garden. Sometimes as she worked, she would hum. Even this was exquisite, but if Joseph was very lucky, she would sing quietly to herself. He would listen as he tended the plants. He could read the prayers in his breviary only after she departed.

As spring approached and the Biblical garden began to show signs of life, other parishioners visited more and more. There were only three benches, so Joseph learned to leave his tools on Miss Conley's favorite one till she appeared.

One morning when the garden was nearly empty, Joseph brought over his class of students from the minor seminary to explain about pomegranates being the forbidden fruit. The boys spotted Miss Conley sitting alone on her bench.

One of them pointed. "It's Eve!"

"No it isn't," another boy argued. "Were you even listening to Father Lazare? Eve was *naked*!"

Which set off an outbreak of sniggers that infected even Miss Conley and Joseph, before he composed himself and scolded his students.

~

A MONTH-LONG ILLNESS had prevented Bishop England from embarking on the second Haitian mission. Instead, he sent his coadjutor, Bishop Clancy, who made little progress on the island. That spring of 1836, Bishop England would return to Haiti himself.

The second week of Lent, Joseph was hardly through his parents' gate when his mother accosted him. 'Joseph! You must make your father see sense!'

Joseph glanced to his father on the piazza. 'About what?'

'When Bishop England returns to Haiti, your father says he's going with him!'

Joseph's father stepped forward and drew her attention. 'I *am* seeing sense, Anne. Dr. England needs me. I speak French as well as Creole. And if he falls ill again'—Joseph's father grinned—'don't you want him to be in good hands?'

'What if *you* fall ill? What if you die of fever thousands of miles from—'

'Nothing is going to happen to me, Anne.'

'You cannot promise that! How can you do this to me? I'm already losing Cathy *and* our grandchildren in a month!'

'They're not dying, Anne—they're moving to Missouri.'

'Halfway across the continent, surrounded by Indians! And now *you* want to go sailing off to a godforsaken island full of murderers!' She turned away and covered her face with her hand for a moment. Tears filled her eyes, but she managed a few more signs. 'I don't know what I'd do without you, René.' She rushed to their Mary Garden and knelt to beg the Virgin's intercession.

Joseph and his father followed but kept their distance. Joseph felt a surge of hope: his mother seemed genuinely grieved at the thought of losing his father. Surely this proved the man had stopped tormenting her. Joseph still didn't understand him. He asked in a low voice, as if his mother could hear: "How can you wish to visit a place where—where your father was beheaded?"

"He probably deserved it. And my going to Haiti has nothing to do with him. I am going to visit my mother."

Joseph frowned. "You...know where she's buried?"

"She isn't buried anywhere. She's still alive."

Joseph gaped at him.

His father glanced over the gardenia bushes to ensure that his wife was still at her prayers. "After we met Ninon on Sullivan's Island and she told me the truth about my mother, I started wondering: If she didn't die when I was born, what if she wasn't dead at all? What if she didn't *want* to give me up? You know what my grandmother Marguerite was like." He sat on the bench nearby, and Joseph joined him. "I met with Ninon again. She told me everything she could remember about the plantation where I was born. I wrote it all down, and added a few details I learned from other Saint-Domingue émigrés. Two years ago, before Dr. England left on his first mission to Haiti, I asked him to take my information to President Boyer, to see if enquiries could be made. You know how easily Dr. England wins people over, so Boyer agreed to help. Having a dictator on your side has its advantages. Last year, when Dr. Clancy returned from Haiti, he brought word that my mother had finally been found, very much alive."

Bishop Clancy knew they were colored now, too? Even if the news had been sealed in a letter, no good could come of this. Joseph's father was putting all of them at risk. If their secret became known in Charleston... Joseph could transfer to another parish, and Cathy was already planning her flight with Perry. But for Hélène, their mother, and their grandmother, starting over would not be so easy.

Movement drew Joseph's attention to his mother, who rose from her prayers. She threw Joseph a hopeful glance and returned to the house.

His father murmured in her wake: "I don't think you can understand, Joseph. You've had a mother all your life. This is my only chance to meet mine."

Joseph also knew that state law would not permit *her* to visit South Carolina instead.

"You could come to Haiti with me, son."

"I'm a Priest now."

"You know very well that Dr. England could use a second pair of consecrated hands there even more than here."

"I have classes to teach at the seminary. Besides, Mama would never let us both go."

His father sighed. "Would you write your grandmother a letter, then?"

"Can she read?"

"I'll read it to her."

"What would I say?"

"Anything. Tell her about yourself. She'll be as proud as I am."

"I doubt she's even Catholic."

"Anyone would be proud of you, Joseph."

"Because I'm the first colored Priest in America?"

His father stood and scowled down at him. "Because you're a wise and compassionate young man. *Most* of the time."

A FORTNIGHT after Joseph's father sailed for Haiti with Bishop England, Cathy, Perry, David, and Sophie left for Missouri. To distract their mother from her grief, Joseph and Hélène coaxed her into visiting the orphanage run by the Sisters of Mercy. Several children had lost their hearing to fevers. Joseph and Hélène had taught them basic signs, but few people had the time or patience to converse with the children, let alone teach them to read.

Soon, Joseph's mother and grandmother were visiting the orphans together. They'd always made little gifts for the children. Now they presented these in person. The Sisters of Mercy reported that what the orphans cherished most were their laps and their arms.

His mother and grandmother must have been visiting the orphanage on the day Joseph stopped at his parents' house to retrieve a book. Even Henry and May were out, because no one greeted him. Everything was quiet till Joseph entered the hall and heard the murmurs in the parlor. He recognized Hélène's voice, and the other sounded like…

Then Joseph saw them: his little sister and Mr. Conley seated together on the sofa, bare hands clasped, knees practically touching, a flush of pleasure suffusing her cheeks as he whispered something that sounded like poetry.

When she realized they were not alone, Hélène sprang up instantly in front of her lover, as if to shield him from Joseph's wrath. "This isn't what it looks like! You needn't challenge Liam to a duel!"

Who'd ever heard of a Priest fighting a duel?

To his credit, Mr. Conley was also blushing, and trying vainly to move in front of Hélène. She wouldn't let him, and neither needed protecting; Joseph was frozen in place on the threshold.

"Well, it *is* what it looks like, but nothing *happened*!" Hélène continued at the speed of a locomotive. "And nothing happened at Christmas, either! I promised Papa I wouldn't follow in Cathy's foot-steps. Papa already knows about Liam and me—and he gave us his blessing!" She dropped her eyes to the rug and pouted. "Except he's making us wait…"

"…until I have established myself as a lawyer," Mr. Conley completed. "Until I can support your sister properly. Not in the manner she's accustomed to, and not in the manner she deserves— I'll never be wealthy—but…"

"Liam *will* make a name for himself; I know he will," Hélène gushed. "He's going to represent people like Mama, and immigrants and colored people!"

How many of his clients would be able to pay him?

His sister darted forward to squeeze Joseph's hands. "I told Liam the real reason Papa is visiting Haiti."

"Hélène!"

"Your family's secret is safe with me, Father. On my life, I shall tell no one."

"Surely we can trust Tessa," Joseph's sister cut in.

Emotion climbed Joseph's throat—and not all of it was dread. If she already knew... "You've told Miss Conley too?"

"Not yet, but—"

Joseph shook his head. "You can't, El. She teaches children. She might not *mean* to reveal anything, but—" One of her students might speak cruelly of negroes, and before she thought of the consequences, Miss Conley might scold him by declaring that her dearest friend was a colored woman... "This is how rumors start." Joseph turned to the Irishman. "Have you been reading the laws of your new state, Mr. Conley? Do you realize what we're facing if the wrong people find out?"

The Irishman averted his eyes. "Your father could never return to South Carolina—none of you could leave and ever come back. If you remained in Charleston, you'd be forced to find white guardians, pay a capitation tax, and obey the same curfew slaves do. You'd be barred from restaurants and theatres and constantly reminded of your 'inferior position.'"

And their treatment in the Northern states wouldn't be much better.

Mr. Conley met Joseph's gaze with defiance. "But such injustice will not change unless we fight it, Father."

"You'll be risking exposure *by* fighting."

"I'm not afraid," Hélène insisted.

Mr. Conley smiled at her. "Your sister is afraid of nothing. She has a heart the size of a cathedral. After all, she loves *me*. For the rest of my life, I shall strive to be worthy of her."

"Will you give us your blessing, Joseph? Will you say our wedding Mass? Even if it doesn't happen till"—Hélène bit her lip and threw a mournful glance at her suitor—"ten years from now, when Liam can support me?"

Joseph sighed. "Mama and Grandmama won't approve of this

match, El." No doubt they were still hoping Hélène would marry a Middleton or a Pinckney.

"That's why we haven't told them yet." Her brow furrowed. "Do *you* approve, Joseph?"

"Of course. I'm happy for you." First he offered Liam his hand as a brother. The Irishman gripped it with obvious relief. Then Joseph blessed their betrothal as a Priest.

Technically, Hélène and Liam were condemning their children to two decades of indentured servitude and themselves to seven years. Because of Cathy and Perry, Joseph had asked his father if there was a law against amalgamation in South Carolina. There wasn't—but there was a colonial statute calling intimate relations between whites and blacks "unnatural and inordinate copulation" and making the perpetrators and children of such offenses into virtual slaves.

Joseph thought Miss Conley close to perfection. He could hardly object to her brother marrying his sister. This union would make Miss Conley a permanent part of Joseph's life. He would have a legitimate reason to worry about her and enjoy her company, because they would be family. In the eyes of the Church and the law, Joseph and Miss Conley would become brother and sister. Intimate yet entirely safe.

IN JUNE, Joseph's father and Bishop England returned from Haiti, sunburned but otherwise intact. Now there were two colored Priests in the Americas: during the mission, His Lordship had ordained a Mr. Paddington, who had been born in Haiti and educated in Ireland and Rome.

Bishop England related this over dinner in the presbytery. Joseph's father didn't wait for his weekly visit; he found Joseph in the Biblical garden the next morning, eager to speak and heedless of anyone who might overhear.

Joseph hurried him into the garden shed and closed the door. Until they lived in a kinder world, such revelations belonged in the shadows. While Joseph tidied his tools, his father recounted his journey to meet his mother. Joseph could hear it in his father's voice: part of him had wanted to stay in Haiti.

In Great-Grandmother Marguerite's day, Charleston's free blacks had had to purchase numbered copper badges to wear on their breasts at all times or they'd risk the Work House. Even now, the law demanded that slaves hired out by their masters wear such badges—much like the city's dogs. Yet the way Joseph's father spoke about their African relatives, it was as if he wore an invisible badge over his heart—and he was proud of that badge, no matter its cost.

"I have six brothers and sisters and nineteen nieces and nephews. My mother and her husband have a little land but not much money." Joseph's father stared through the wall of the garden shed all the way to Haiti and raised his shoulders in a shrug. "Yet they are content. They have each other, and they are free. I wish you could have met them, Joseph. My mother has a scar on the side of her head, and she's missing the top of her right ear—because my grandmother *shot* her in order to steal me. My mother was sixteen years old when it happened—fourteen when she gave birth to me. We cried for *hours* and talked for two days straight. Her mother's people, my people, your people—they're called the Yoruba. My mother's true name is Ìfé."

Joseph could only guess at how that might be spelled, but the pronunciation wasn't far from her French name, Ève.

"Before I was baptized René, my mother named me Ekúndayò."

How easily his father might have been someone else. How easily Joseph and his sisters might never have been born.

"Ekúndayò," his father repeated. He scratched at the peeling skin of his sunburned wrist, but he was smiling. "It means: 'sorrow becomes happiness.'"

CHAPTER 23

The majority of women (happily for them) are not very much troubled with sexual feeling of any kind.

— Dr. William Acton, *Functions and Disorders of the Reproductive Organs* (1857)

After more than a year in Charleston, the Conleys' fortunes had not altered. Liam remained a copyist, Miss Conley a catechist and seamstress. At least Joseph's mother and grandmother seemed to be warming to the Irish brother and sister. Bereft of Cathy and Perry, the Lazare women welcomed the Conleys for another Christmas holiday. Hélène and Miss Conley had become as close as sisters—in truth, closer than Hélène and Cathy had been. They called each other "Ellie" and "Tessa" and cherished their shared secret: someday, they would be sisters-in-law.

While Hélène and Miss Conley taught each other French and Irish carols at the piano, Liam watched them with a broad smile. He exchanged knowing looks with Joseph and his father. *Do you see?* the Irishman's expression said. *We're already a family.* Miss Conley was even wearing one of Hélène's altered gowns. Liam's coat must be the finest he owned; but its elbows showed clearly his sister's repairs.

SHORTLY AFTER THE FEAST OF SAINT VALENTINE, Joseph sat in the confessional, leaning into the winter light that entered through the barred door so he could read his breviary while he waited for penitents. He'd had few today, all seminarians. Most people confessed and received the Eucharist only at Christmas and Easter.

A few members of his congregation were more scrupulous, like Miss Conley. Every Sunday, she knelt at the rail to receive the Body of Christ from him. But she had never confessed to him. Sometimes Joseph worried that he'd done something to make her distrust him. Her countenance brightened whenever she saw him; she seemed to enjoy their conversations as much as he did. But some kind of unease remained hidden behind her eyes. Might Miss Conley suspect how he struggled to admire only her soul?

Then Joseph reminded himself that no one in his family had chosen him for a confessor. He recalled how much easier it had been for him to make a good confession in Paris, where all the Priests had been strangers.

Finally Joseph heard the rustle of skirts that announced a female penitent. He closed his breviary and sat upright. Even with the grille, he was careful to shield his eyes with a cupped hand.

"Bless me, Father," the young woman whispered beside him. "I confess that I am sinfully happy!"

Joseph sighed, dropped his hand, and abandoned the rules. "Good afternoon, Hélène."

For a moment, his sister grinned at him through the grille, but it quickly turned into a pout. "Don't you want to know *why* I am sinfully happy?"

"Only if you're going to make a *proper* Confession. You don't sound at all contrite."

"I'm not!" At least she seemed a little sorry about *that*. "But I knew you'd be here, and I couldn't wait to tell you!"

"This is a *Sacrament*, Ellie."

"No one else is waiting!"

"A real penitent could arrive at any moment."

"Then I shall tell you my news *outside*." Hélène flung aside her curtain. Then she yanked open the door of the confessional booth, exposing Joseph to the light.

He squinted and scowled up at her. "Hélène! This is entirely inappropriate!"

His sister stood with her hands on her hips as if *he* were being unreasonable. She was going to spend millennia in Purgatory. "I'm hardly causing a scandal! No one is watching—and even if they were, they know I'm your sister! You *do* want to hear my news?"

"*Yes*." Joseph removed his violet stole and folded it atop his breviary on the seat. He allowed Hélène to pull him from the confessional.

"Liam has an apprenticeship!" his sister shouted to the entire empty cathedral. "We'll be married before we're thirty!"

Joseph frowned. "He said it would take him *years* to afford an apprenticeship."

"Liam doesn't have to pay for it anymore—the lawyer who's training him will soon be his brother-in-law!"

How could Liam have a future brother-in-law other than Joseph? Unless—

"Tessa is engaged now too! And you'll never believe who proposed to her!"

Joseph gripped the back of a pew. "Who?"

"Edward *Stratford*! His father owns a plantation on the Ashley!" Hélène exulted at her usual speed, her hands excited fists under her chin. "Edward is the youngest of three sons—but still: a Stratford! It's like the prince and Cinderella! Now Mama and Grandmama cannot possibly object to Liam and me! Can you believe we'll be related to the Stratfords?"

In truth, Joseph had barely heard of them. "This Edward Stratford will not interfere with Miss Conley's religion? He'll allow their children to be Catholic?"

"Not only that, Joseph—Mr. Stratford agreed to convert! Tessa said he'll call on you."

Hélène soon flitted homewards. Joseph retreated into the confessional and shut the door. He was glad of the bench and the concealment. His legs felt as if he'd just raced up the Spanish Steps; they'd threatened to buckle beneath him. His heart felt... This was envy. He was in the wrong seat.

JOSEPH SHOULD BE REJOICING. Miss Conley had turned a lost soul toward the true Church. If they could win *one* Stratford, might not others follow? At the very least, there would be Catholic Stratfords in the next generation. Soon Miss Conley would sing lullabies to her own children. She would bear them in comfort, and they would want for nothing.

Joseph should be falling on his knees in thanksgiving. Most men of Mr. Stratford's class would not hesitate to ruin a young woman like Miss Conley for their own momentary pleasure. He could have seduced her with a promise of marriage and abandoned her. But to his credit, Mr. Stratford recognized Miss Conley for the jewel she was, and he wanted her on his arm for a lifetime.

The young man was certainly besotted. When he spoke about his intended, Mr. Stratford's countenance matched Liam's when he spoke of Hélène: it was breathless and reverent. Mr. Stratford was earnest, humble, and open-hearted. Not only had he secured Liam an apprenticeship with his eldest brother, he had saved the Conleys from their appalling lodgings. He rented them a suite of rooms, modest but completely respectable, which Liam could purchase from him over time, where Hélène could live one day. Miss Conley had been able to give up her sewing. Now, other women labored over her trousseau.

Yet for all his qualities, all his wealth, Joseph thought Mr. Stratford utterly unworthy of Miss Conley. He was simply...dull. It was like yoking a unicorn to an ass. An ass could not help being an ass, but it was still an ass. What did they talk about? Mr. Stratford was eager to discuss crop yields, but his interest did not extend to ornamentals. He had no appreciation for poetry or even music, though he happily took Miss Conley to plays and concerts.

What man COULD be worthy of such a woman? Joseph chastised himself. He was being unfair. He knew nothing about love, and he rarely saw the couple together. Even then, Miss Conley practiced modesty and hid her affections in public.

Mostly Joseph met with Mr. Stratford alone in order to prepare him for his Confirmation. The Stratfords were Episcopalian, at least officially. Like the rest of his family, Mr. Stratford viewed religion as something to do on Sundays and ignore the rest of the week.

When Joseph inquired why he wished to convert, the young man answered: "Because it will please my Tessie." Mr. Stratford was only two years Joseph's junior, but sometimes he seemed like a little boy —or perhaps a puppy wagging its tail, begging for attention.

"It isn't as if much will change, right?" he asked Joseph with ignorant cheerfulness. "I mean, Episcopal services, Catholic services —they have more commonalities than they do differences."

"Transubstantiation is not a small matter," Joseph informed him as calmly as he could.

"Well, yes, but there's really only that and the Latin—which I think sounds much grander than English; I can understand why you kept it. And of course the celibacy of Catholic Priests, which I also approve. I mean, I wouldn't want to do it myself! But that's the point, isn't it? What I'm saying is: I admire you, Father. That kind of sacrifice sets you apart, doesn't it? It makes you special."

MR. STRATFORD INSISTED on making his first general Confession to Joseph. The young man admitted to self-abuse and impure thoughts, especially about Miss Conley. But Mr. Stratford confessed no visits to prostitutes or harassment of slaves. He understood the wages of sin. Joseph was confident that he would be a faithful husband.

After Joseph granted Mr. Stratford Absolution, they walked out to the Biblical garden, where they found Miss Conley reading. For a moment, Joseph imagined that her gaze leapt to him first, and that her smile wavered when she looked to Mr. Stratford. Ridiculous. Joseph lowered his eyes and noticed a weed threatening his *Passiflora*. He knelt to remove it.

Mr. Stratford did not yet cross the garden to his intended.

Instead, he confided to Joseph in a low voice: "Sometimes I envy her. I know Tessie doesn't struggle the way I do." He sighed. "*I try to read or to concentrate my attention on anything else, and all I can think about is our wedding night.* Virtue is so much easier for women. They're born pure and that's how they remain—at least if they're ladies."

No one was born pure; they were all sinners, male and female alike. Joseph's experience as a confessor had taught him that even ladies felt lust. But there in the presence of Miss Conley, Joseph did not correct her intended. The young man would learn soon enough.

ANOTHER DAY, Mr. Stratford asked: "Have you heard of this book by Maria Monk? *Awful Disclosures?*"

"Unfortunately." It was the latest anti-Catholic invective, the most ludicrous—and most popular—so far. It was a gothic novel masquerading as the autobiography of a pregnant nun who had escaped a convent to save her child's life.

Mr. Stratford squinted at him. "Is any of that true, Father?"

"Are you seriously asking me if I force myself on nuns? If I strangle our newborn children and then throw them into a pit?"

"Well, I figured *that* part was fictional. But what about the rest of it? The kneeling on dried peas for Penance and sticking a pin through your—"

"If you want to know the secrets of the Catholic Church, Mr. Stratford, read the catechism, the Missal, the Ordination rites. Bishop England translated them years ago, not only for the benefit of the faithful but to prove to the rest of the world that we have nothing to hide."

The young man looked disappointed.

"My life isn't the stuff of novels, Mr. Stratford."

CHAPTER 24

O fairest of creation, last and best
Of all God's works…
How art thou lost, how on a sudden lost,
Defaced, deflowered, and now to death
    devote?
—John Milton, *Paradise Lost* (1674)

Young Edward would not be the first Stratford to marry a
Catholic, Joseph discovered. His middle brother, Laurence,
had settled in Louisiana several years before, on land recently taken
from Indians. There, Laurence had married a Catholic heiress who
had already given him sons. This probably explained why Edward's
father had not objected to Miss Conley—that, and the old widower's reputation as an eccentric who indulged his own whims. He
bred racehorses and hosted the only Mardi Gras ball in South
Carolina.

The Stratfords' connection to Louisiana also explained the
appearance of their plantation house on the Ashley River. Joseph
visited it after ministering to nearby Summerville. Mr. Stratford had
said Joseph could not miss the house, and he was right: there was

nothing else like it, at least not in this state. As fond as South Carolinians were of their piazzas and porticos, they stopped at one or two per dwelling. Mr. Stratford's father had completely surrounded his home with two-story, twelve-foot-wide verandas supported by twenty-four Tuscan columns.

"It's a common design in Louisiana," the old planter explained. "Keeps the sun off *all* the windows, and looks damned impressive from every angle!"

"He's as proud of those verandas as if he had sawn every board and laid every brick with his own hands," Miss Conley observed.

She knew who had truly remodelled the house, who harvested the Stratfords' rice fields, and it troubled her. As the youngest son, Edward would not inherit his father's columned masterpiece or his plantation. But the old man had given Edward and his intended a house in Charleston that they would occupy upon their marriage— and four domestics to care for it. The house needed repairs and decorations; the garden needed pruning and restocking; already Miss Conley must act the mistress.

"Our own Emancipator, O'Connell, called slaves 'the saddest people the sun sees.' In Parliament, he was instrumental in passing the act that abolished slavery in the British West Indies," Miss Conley explained to Joseph in a low voice as they watched a negro repainting the piazza. "I never, ever thought I would own another human being. 'Tis a sin, isn't it?"

This was not the first time Joseph had been faced with the question. "The sin is in how you treat your slaves," he answered, echoing Bishop England and the other Priests he'd consulted. "If you are a good, Christian mistress, you can improve their earthly lives and even save their souls."

For the first time he could remember, Miss Conley peered at him doubtfully, before she looked away and nodded.

∼

JOSEPH WAS HONORED that Miss Conley and Mr. Stratford had asked him to celebrate their wedding Mass. Still, he wished they'd not chosen *late* morning. Usually the Eucharistic fast seemed a small discomfort. Today, he'd suffered keenly each empty hour since midnight, for sleep had eluded him. The insects outside his window had irritated him inexplicably. Never before had they sounded like an alarm.

He resented each layer of vestments, when the summer air already hung thick and heavy around him. In such heat, without the aid even of water, he feared he was approaching delirium. These past eighteen months of his Priesthood, he'd performed this sacrifice hundreds of times, yet he felt suddenly unsteady, as if he were trying to stand upright in an earthquake.

Joseph looked to the bride, to remind himself how important it was that he not falter: this was a day she would always remember. But he found no encouraging smile; Miss Conley's veil obscured her face.

Joseph forced himself to concentrate on Saint Paul's letter to the Ephesians: "Let women be subject to their husbands, as to the Lord…"

Miss Conley knelt before him with her bridegroom. Joseph instructed them to join their right hands. The vows were not part of his Missal; Joseph must recall them from the notes he had scribbled in the margins, notes that had smeared. "Now, repeat after me, please: 'I, Joseph Lazare, take thee, Teresa Conley—'"

Only when a tide of sniggers rippled through the witnesses did Joseph realize what he'd said. He sucked in a mortified breath and dropped his eyes to the floor, where the pooled satin of Miss Conley's gown nearly reached his feet. No couple would ever ask him to say their wedding Mass again.

When Joseph managed to speak, his dry throat half-strangled the words: "You say your own name, of course, Mr. Stratford."

"I, Edward Stratford," the bridegroom obliged with a grin.

"Take thee, Teresa Conley, for my lawful wife…" Joseph prompted.

"Take thee, Teresa Conley, for my lawful wife…"

After the exchange of vows, Joseph made the Sign of the Cross over the wedding ring and sprinkled it with holy water. He returned to Latin: "O Lord, bless this ring…that she who is to wear it may render to her husband unbroken fidelity…"

Mr. Stratford slipped the ring onto his bride's left hand.

Joseph prayed: "O God, Thou hast consecrated the Marriage union, making it a Sacrament so sublime that the nuptial bond has become an image of the mystical union of Christ with the Church." Joseph turned to the bride and smiled, hoping *she* could see *him* through her veil. "O God, mayest Thou regard Thy handmaid with bounteous kindness. … May she be fruitful in offspring… Plighted to one husband, may she fly from forbidden intimacies, fortifying by stern discipline the weakness of her sex…"

"Amen," the bride and the others responded.

In spite of his exhaustion, Joseph did not sleep that night either.

CHAPTER 25

"Oh! come, then, best beloved of my heart; come, Lamb of God, adorable flesh...nourish, cleanse, and purify my soul...all unworthy as I am to receive thee..." Ardent love swelled her throbbing bosom...for her amiable spouse...

— John D. Bryant, describing his heroine's reaction to the Eucharist, *Pauline Seward* (1847)

Several days later, after making sick calls, Joseph was returning the pyx to the cathedral when he noticed the new bride sitting alone in the pews. At first, he hardly recognized her. She wore such fine gowns now (this one of violet silk) and her long hair was hidden beneath a large, frilly bonnet. But more than that, her posture had altered. Her shoulders, neck, and head—everything above her corset—drooped like a bruised flower. She stared down at her hands, sheathed in black lace mitts. They lay limp on her lap beneath a crumpled handkerchief.

He could not pass her by. "Are you all right, Miss Conley? Pardon me: Mrs. Stratford?"

She released a harsh puff of breath. "I wish—" She broke off suddenly and closed her eyes. Her jaw clenched, and the tendons in her slender neck tensed above her lace collar. "Please, Father: I wish you'd call me Tessa." She turned her reddened eyes to him and attempted a smile—the barest quiver at the edges of her lips, as if they'd forgotten the shape. "We shall be family soon, after all."

"Then you must call me Joseph."

"I-I couldn't, Father." She dropped her eyes to her lap again. "It wouldn't be right." She raised the handkerchief and blotted her nose. Before Joseph could formulate a question, she looked up to the altar. "'Tis such a comfort, knowing He is always here, whenever I need Him." Her strained voice belied her words, as if she sought comfort but had not found it. "In County Clare, most of the churches must also serve as schoolhouses or threshing-floors. So God resides in the Tabernacle only when the Priest is celebrating Mass." Her fingers worried the handkerchief in her lap. "I only wish I could receive Him every day. When I take Him into my body, I can feel His strength suffusing me. I can feel Him inside me—not an invasion but a completion."

"Daily communion isn't only for Priests. You are welcome to receive every day."

She squeezed her eyes shut. "How am I to approach Someone so holy when I feel so unclean?"

"You haven't been reading any Jansenists, have you?"

She kept her eyes closed. "If I've—lain with my husband... " It was only a whisper.

Suddenly her distress and her exhaustion made sense. She was passionate about their Lord, horticulture, and music; of course she would bring that passionate nature to her marriage bed. Perhaps she'd startled her husband (hadn't he thought ladies incapable of desire?) and they'd quarrelled. Now, she was struggling to reconcile the yearnings of her body with the yearnings of her soul.

Nervously Joseph glanced behind him to confirm that no one else had entered the cathedral. He should speak of sexual matters only inside the confessional. But how could he ask her to uproot herself when she looked too weak to stand? Slowly Joseph sat, an arm's length away from her, and lowered his voice. "Provided you do nothing to preclude conception, finding pleasure in the marital act is only a venial sin, and you need not confess venial sins before you receive Our Lord. He recognizes your contrition."

"But if I refuse my husband, that is a mortal sin?"

They should definitely be inside the confessional. "Has he asked something unnatural of you?" *Please, please don't ask me to define—*

She shook her head.

"Then, yes: if your husband desires intercourse and you refuse him, you commit a mortal sin."

Her eyes opened slowly, though she only stared at the back of the bench before them. "What if I *want* to refuse him? Is that also a mortal sin? I feel *nothing* but dread and repulsion and…"

Joseph had been wrong.

"I knew it would be painful the first time, but not— I think there is something wrong with me." She shielded her face with her hands, muffling her words. "I'm so sorry, Father; I shouldn't be telling you this."

"Have you discussed it with your husband?"

"How can I?" She opened her hands. "It would humiliate him!"

"He must know something is wrong."

She shook her head fiercely. "*He* is quite content."

The man was even more obtuse than Joseph had feared. Had her husband really mistaken discomfort for purity? "But—the act remains painful for you?"

She nodded miserably.

This was so far beyond his ken… What would a physician of the body ask? She'd been married only a week; perhaps this despair was premature. "How many times…?"

She gripped the back of the other pew for support. "Every night."

Joseph swallowed. "Surely his ardor will fade in…" A month? A year? If she were *his* wife…

She nodded again, pulled herself to her feet—merciful God, did Joseph only imagine it, or did she wince at the movement?—and turned away from him. "I will bear it. I *must*." She hurried into the aisle. "He is my husband. 'Tis all he asks of me, and all I have to give him."

Joseph followed. "Tessa, wait."

She was muttering as if to herself. "I want children; if this is the cost, I must—"

"Tessa!" Joseph loped ahead of her. As gently as he could, he grasped her arms just below her shoulders. Finally she stopped her flight, though still she trembled. Joseph stooped so he could look up into her distraught face instead of down at her. She must not feel threatened; she had already suffered enough at men's hands. "First and above all: Never think that your body is all you have to give. It is not even the most remarkable part of you."

Her eyes flickered to his—only a moment, but her breaths seemed to be calming.

"Second: Would you allow me to consult with my father?"

Was her new gasp relief, or trepidation?

"He will not know I am asking on *your* behalf," Joseph promised.

At last she nodded. "If I were braver, I would ask him myself. He has been nothing but kind. But *this*; 'tis so difficult to speak of."

"I am glad you spoke to me. You can, Tessa, always—no matter the problem. I will find you a remedy."

JOSEPH WENT IMMEDIATELY TO HIS PARENTS' HOUSE. The sign declared his father at home. Through the open window, Joseph saw him at his desk. Yet Joseph lingered on the sidewalk as if he were mired in quicksand. How exactly did one begin such a conversation with one's father, with the rapist of one's mother? But who else could he possibly ask? Joseph wished Hélène and Liam were already married. Sometimes his father *seemed* so compassionate…

Joseph hesitated so long that his father looked up from his medical journal and peered through the window. "Is that you, Joseph?"

He made sure no one on the street was close enough to hear. "Your offer of a medical-sacerdotal consultation…"

"It remains open." His father stood, pulled the door wide, and smiled. "My door is *always* open to you, son."

Joseph was careful to shut it behind him. He closed the windows and the door to the hall. Keeping his eyes on the rug, he crossed to face the desk where his father waited. He felt he should not sit, and he could not look at his father. "The marital act…it should not be consistently painful for the wife?"

"It should not."

"If it *is* painful, might there be a medical reason?"

"There might. I don't suppose this woman described the *nature* of her pain to you?"

"No." Joseph gulped the word.

"Could you not persuade her to see me?"

"I promised her anonymity. She is understandably reluctant to speak of such matters."

"Then I must find my way blindfolded. But in my experience, it is most likely that her husband is simply a fool."

I think that is very likely.

"This couple, how long have they been married?"

Joseph could not be specific without betraying Tessa's confidence. "Not long."

"Did both of them enter the marriage as virgins?"

"Yes."

"I stand by my diagnosis: their problem is ignorance, and it is easily remedied. If I cannot see them… Are they literate?"

"They are."

"Then I shall write a letter. I shall offer as much information as I can and extend my own invitation. Will that suit?"

"Yes; thank you."

"Thank you for coming to me. I should address this letter to the wife?"

Again Joseph nodded.

His father began hunting among his books. "I will need a few hours to prepare my prescription."

WHAT HIS FATHER PRODUCED wasn't a letter or a prescription. It was a treatise—so many pages crammed into an envelope that it bulged.

At Joseph's incredulous expression, his father shrugged. "I have seen the cost of ignorance too many times. I would write a book, but your mother would probably die of mortification upon its publication. And I might be arrested for indecency. So, I must disseminate my gospel one couple at a time. I left it unsealed purposefully, Joseph, so you can read it yourself. This woman will not be the first wife who will come to you anguished and confused. You are wise to reach out, and you would be wise to educate yourself for the future." Now his father seemed reluctant to release the letter. "Whether you read it or not, promise me you will deliver it tomorrow."

"I promise." Joseph took the envelope.

His father must have heard the hesitation in his voice. "Make no mistake: This woman is in pain—unjust, utterly unnecessary pain. Pain that is not only physical but spiritual. She doubts her love for her husband, his love for her, her decision to marry at all—she doubts even God, that He should require such a thing of her. If that doubt is not lifted, it will drive a chasm between this woman and her husband, between her and God. You hold her salvation, there in your hands."

PASSING THE LIBRARY, Joseph bid good-night to Bishop England and Father Baker. The bulging envelope felt like a heated brick in his coat pocket. Joseph retired to his chamber and set the letter on his desk. He resolved not to read it.

He finished reciting the prayers for the day. He reviewed his notes for his homily tomorrow. He undressed for bed and washed his face and hands. He leaned over to blow out his lamp.

But the envelope beckoned to him from his desk. Much like the Serpent in the Garden, promising forbidden knowledge. Things other men already knew.

It was the mention of God and the Psalms in the first lines that lured him in.

Dearest daughter—for I shall speak to you as I have my own daughters—God has given you a remarkable gift. "I praise Thee for my wondrous fashioning," the Psalmist cries, "marvelous are Thy works." None of God's works is more marvelous than <u>your body</u>, my daughter. You know already its capacity to nurture and bear life. God has also fashioned your body for limitless pleasure.

A woman's body <u>is</u> as capable of experiencing pleasure and pleasure's climax as a man's. In fact, your pleasure will be more complex and of longer duration than your husband's—if you continue to read this letter.

A woman's climaxes do require more skill and patience than a man's. For this reason, they are more rare. Women cannot climax through penetration alone—but this is all husbands think they must do. When his climax is complete, the man believes the act successful. He is only half right. He is entirely wrong to leave you incomplete.

"But his seed in my womb is all that is necessary for conception," you say. "That is the purpose of sexual intercourse. To do more simply for the pleasure of it is sin." I may not be a catechist, but I know the female body. And I return to your "wondrous fashioning." God has given you a unique organ called a clitoris. He created it for one purpose only: to transmit pleasure from the crown of your head to the tips of your toes. But you must give yourself permission to experience this pleasure.

You do not yet believe that God wishes you to do so? Open a Bible. Find the Canticle of Canticles. Do not tell me it is only an allegory of Christ's love for the Church. Would an allegory make us blush? Would it stir our blood and make us desire our mates?

The Canticles do use poetic symbolism. The woman's body is a garden. The man's genitals are fruit. Her arousal is honey and wine. Pay particular attention to the first verse of the fifth chapter. The couple has consummated their love—and God definitely approves: "Eat, O friends, and drink, and be inebriated!" These lovers do far more than penile-vaginal intercourse. Experiment! Discover one another fully! "Everything created by God is good, and nothing is to be rejected if it is received with thanksgiving" (Saint Paul to Saint Timothy).

Do you think me too Protestant, to quote only from Scripture?

Then I shall add the wisdom of Blessed Alphonsus Liguori. Rome has decreed his writings "free from error." Liguori concludes that the female climax has a purpose because "nature does nothing in vain." If their husbands are unable or unwilling to do so, wives "may excite themselves before copulation" or stimulate themselves afterwards in order to achieve climax—without sinning. Spouses may engage in sexual acts not only to conceive children but also "for reason of health" and "to foster mutual love."

His father went on like this, page after page. He described in shameless detail how to locate the clitoris and stimulate it—not only with the penis but also with fingers and mouth! How to caress the breasts. The signs by which a husband might recognize his wife's excitement and when she "came." How she might heighten his excitement. *"A true lover will find his greatest joy not in pursuing his own pleasure but in pleasing his beloved."*

How could this be the same man who had raped a deaf girl, who had forced her to marry him and abused her for years afterward? Joseph had realized long ago what his father must have been doing with his head between his mother's thighs—but the fact remained that he had been doing it against her will. Her bonds and her tears proved she had not consented. The man himself admitted here: *"Not all women enjoy all kinds of stimulation."*

His father also explained that when a woman was excited, her "glands of Bartholin" should produce a mucus (hardly honey and wine!) to facilitate penetration. If this mucus was insufficient, intercourse would be painful, so he recommended...!

Olive oil was the matter of Sacraments. It had anointed Joseph's forehead at Confirmation and his hands at Ordination. Joseph himself used it to cleanse the five senses of sin when he administered Extreme Unction. But the application his father suggested... The olive oil could hardly be called virgin after *that*.

If their father had told Cathy half of what was in this letter, no wonder she had thrown herself beneath the first man to flatter her. The Devil could certainly quote Scripture—out of context—to serve his own ends. Joseph's father blithely ignored *most* of Liguori, such as his condemnation of "imperfect acts" that served no purpose, like kissing.

This letter was a prescription for sin. A manual of lust. A carnal catechism. Joseph should burn it immediately. He stood up abruptly, gripping the vile pages. The indecent state of his own body was proof these obscene words must be destroyed.

Then his father's plea returned to him: *"Promise me you will deliver it tomorrow... This woman is in pain—unjust, utterly unnecessary pain."* But pain was part of God's plan. It taught you humility and—

Tessa was in pain. Even now, at this very moment...

Ashamed at last, his arousal subsided, and Joseph sank back into his chair.

How could he face Tessa again empty-handed? How could he see the desperation and hope in her eyes and crush her with a platitude? She was a pious woman as well as an intelligent one. She would take what she needed from this letter and discard the rest.

His lamp was sputtering. Instead of extinguishing it, Joseph replenished the oil and read his father's manual a second time before he sealed the envelope.

WHEN HE SLIPPED TESSA THE LETTER after Mass, she clutched it to her breast and thanked him as if it were the pardon from a death sentence.

Two weeks later, Joseph called on her at home. Her husband was at his law office. Tessa showed Joseph around the garden they had planned together, and he recommended a few more plants to fill the gaps.

Before he left her, Joseph managed to ask: "Was my father's letter a help to you?"

Tessa blushed and averted her eyes. At last she nodded and whispered: "'Tis not so painful now." The words were grim, not joyous, as if she meant: *"'Tis still painful, but less so."*

Joseph frowned. As Tessa walked beside him, he allowed himself to read in her posture and her countenance what he'd been trying to deny. Very little had changed since the day he'd found Tessa slumped in the pews beneath the weight of her marriage.

"You must give yourself permission to experience this pleasure," his father had written. Joseph had feared Tessa would embrace too much of his father's advice. Now he feared she had embraced too little.

CHAPTER 26

From time immemorial, women have regarded the barren womb as a great calamity. All their hopes of happiness are centered around the hope of giving birth to children.

— William B. Mills, *Inaugural Dissertation on the Signs of Pregnancy*, University of Nashville (1857)

On the Feast of Saint John Chrysostom, when the worst of the summer heat had passed, Joseph and his sister called on Tessa together. Now that she herself was provided for, the young Irishwoman eagerly joined Hélène in her charity work, and Joseph often combined his visits with theirs. Today they would bring baskets of food to the tenements near the wharves. Tessa had not forgotten her former neighbors.

As they approached the Stratfords' house on Friend Street, Hélène squeezed his arm. "Joseph, look!"

The door leading onto the piazza was open; and within its frame, Mr. Stratford was kissing his wife good-bye. Far more importantly, Tessa smiled after her husband. Whistling, he sauntered down the street.

Hélène grinned up at Joseph. She too had been worried about

Tessa. But clearly, something had changed. Perhaps the new wife had employed some of their father's advice after all.

Joseph and Hélène set down their baskets on the piazza. Tessa said her cook was still finishing her contributions. While they waited, Tessa offered them tea in her garden.

Though it would not enter its full glory till spring, Joseph thought it was coming along very well, this joint project of theirs. They sat in the shade of the magnolia tree, its red seeds beginning to burst from the pods on their tiny cords. But Tessa herself was the brightest thing in her garden. Joseph had not seen her so ebullient since the day they'd met.

Hélène was equally happy. "Have you seen Liam in his new uniform? Doesn't he look *handsome?*" Like many other Irishmen, Liam had joined the Phoenix Fire Brigade (partially, he admitted to Joseph, to impress his future mother- and grandmother-in-law, who remained ignorant of the betrothal). Every few months brought an opportunity for heroism when a blaze threatened some part of the city. Hélène leaned toward her friend and confided in a loud whisper: "Liam let me feel his arms through his shirt. They're hard as coconuts!" As a matter of pride, and to distinguish themselves from the slave companies, volunteer firemen eschewed mules and pulled the engines themselves.

Tessa's cook brought out her baskets. "Would you mind very much if I carried only the bread?" Tessa inquired.

"Are you still feeling unwell?" Hélène worried.

Tessa smiled into her teacup. "Afternoons are easier."

His sister selected another little cake from the table. "Joseph can carry the heavy things. He may not be as strong as Liam, but he's stronger than he looks."

"Thank you," Joseph responded. "I think."

"He swims a lot. That must be it."

Tessa sat back in her chair and drew their attention again with a sigh at once resigned and contented. "I expect I shall be ill again tomorrow morning."

Hélène frowned and said around the cake, "You should really talk to Papa."

"I did." Tessa lowered her eyes to the front of her pink bodice, where she placed a spread hand. When she looked up at Joseph, a blush suffused her cheeks, so that they nearly matched the silk. "Father, is there a special blessing for…a woman 'in a delicate condition'?"

Joseph's cup clattered in the saucer, when he'd only meant to set it down. *Of course.*

"You're going to have a baby?!" Hélène squealed.

Tessa nodded and grinned. "Your father confirmed it yesterday."

Hélène sprang up to embrace her friend, then abruptly drew back. "Did I hurt the baby? Did I hurt you?"

"Not in the slightest," Tessa laughed. It was so good to hear her laugh again.

"Can Liam and I be the godparents?"

"Of course you can be the godparents!"

"And Joseph can perform the Baptism!"

"Certainly," he managed, finding it difficult to look at Tessa. How strange, to think that two souls now inhabited one body. Joseph thought he'd accepted his own solitude the day he left for seminary, yet the truth struck him as if by surprise: he would never be part of such blessed news. He would always be a Father, but never a father. He could only watch the progression of others' lives.

"Can you still come with us today?" Hélène fretted.

"You'll have to remember that I tire more easily now, but yes," Tessa assured her. "Irishwomen usually remain on their feet and working till the moment their pains start. We're a hardy race. I certainly won't be pulling any fire engines, but your father says *moderate* exercise is good for me *and* the baby."

"We have to think of names!" Joseph's sister realized. "There are so many lovely Irish names!"

Tessa's smile faded. "Edward says it can't be anything *too* Irish."

"What?"

"You know…like Bridget or Patrick. I don't think he'd want anything Gaelic, either."

Hélène pouted, then squeezed her friend's hand. "We'll find something, Tessa."

"It doesn't matter what we name her. I love her so much already." As she gazed down at the place where new life knit together inside her, Tessa soon recovered her happiness. "Your father said she's only the size of a kidney bean at the moment—so that's what I've started calling her: Bean!"

"That small!" Hélène gasped in wonder.

Tessa nodded. "She's about eight weeks."

"How do you know she's a girl?"

"I *don't*, not for certain. But I…dreamt about her last night. And *b-e-a-n* is the Irish word for 'woman.'"

Hélène stooped over to speak to Tessa's abdomen. "You'd better hurry up, little Bean! We cannot wait to meet you! I'm going to love you *almost* as much as your mama!"

"I talk to her too," Tessa laughed. "I told Bean I'm going to plant a tree the day she's born, so she can watch it grow along with her."

Hélène stood up straight again. "When you've just given birth! I don't care how hardy the Irish are—you will not be planting anything! Joseph will do it for you! Won't you, Joseph?"

"Of course." He tugged at his choker. September was still quite warm.

His sister squinted thoughtfully at the garden beds. "What kind of tree should we plant?"

"Do you have any suggestions?"

"It can't be anything too big: you'll want a tree for every one of your children, or the others will envy Bean."

"Every one of my children?" Tessa echoed with a laugh.

"We must plan ahead!" Hélène turned to him. "What kind of tree would you recommend, Joseph?"

He said the first genus that came to him. "Dogwoods?"

"I think I like those." Tessa stood to assess the space herself.

"They prefer partial shade, so we could plant them against the wall."

"Dogwoods are the showy white trees I've seen in the spring?"

"They can be pink, too," his sister pointed out. "Pink for the girls and white for the boys! It's perfect!" She grasped both her friend's hands, gazing out at the garden. "I can see them, Tessa! Little Bean and all her brothers and sisters tending their trees, comparing their heights…"

"And *your* children will come and play with them."

"Yes!" Hélène's skirts bounced in her impatient joy.

"Oh, Ellie." Tessa embraced her friend. Over Hélène's shoulder, she caught Joseph's gaze for only a moment before averting her eyes. "Everything will be all right now," Tessa predicted softly. "I know it will."

PART V
IN LIMBO

1837-1842

It has pleased Divine Providence to permit us to be sorely afflicted.
Our holy and our beautiful house…is burnt up with fire
and all our pleasant things are laid to waste.

— C. E. Gadsden, Rector of Saint Philip's Episcopal Church,
after the 1835 Charleston fire

CHAPTER 27

Original sin [is] the sin we inherit from our first parents; and in which we were conceived and born *children of wrath...*
— Bishop John England, *Catechism of the Roman Catholic Faith* (1826)

On the second anniversary of his Ordination, Joseph rose before dawn as he did every day. He prayed the morning Office, dressed, and unlocked the cathedral. Anthony, his young server, assisted him with his vestments in the sacristy, then preceded him to the altar, and they began the Mass.

While Joseph was offering Communion, he could not help but notice the negro who entered the back of the sanctuary. The man stood turning his hat in his hands, looking anxious but uncertain. He met Joseph's eyes across the pews in a moment of silent entreaty, then dropped his gaze. The negro was well-dressed, but he'd missed one of his waistcoat buttons. Joseph thought he recognized the man, though he couldn't recall the context.

He tried to concentrate on his solemn task: placing the Body of Christ onto the tongues of communicants. But a drama was playing out at the back of the sanctuary. The negro was whispering to one of the parishioners, who glared at him but answered. Another man rose unhappily to close the door, which the negro had left ajar. Finally he hurried up the stairs into the gallery. Even there, the negro perched on his pew; he was clearly preparing to spring up again.

The last communicant left the rail. Joseph returned the ciborium to the Tabernacle. Anthony helped him to rinse his fingers and the chalice. Joseph gave the final blessing and offered the final prayers. He kissed the altar. Never before had these concluding rituals seemed to take so long.

At last he genuflected a final time and carried the chalice to the sacristy. In the corner of his vision, Joseph watched the negro approach. He came back without unvesting.

"I'm sorry, sir," the negro began. "I didn't mean to disturb your service."

"It's a matter of urgency?"

"Yes, sir."

"Then no apology is necessary. But did no one tell you Father Baker was at the seminary?"

"The mistress asked for you specifically, sir." The negro saw that Joseph hadn't yet recognized him. "My name is Elijah. I belong to Master Edward. He and Miss Teresa, they're visiting the master's father this week, at the plantation. But Miss Teresa, she started... bleeding. Our midwife thinks she's losing her baby."

In spite of his vestments, suddenly Joseph felt cold.

"Your father's already gone to her," Elijah assured him. "I've got to tell Mr. Conley next. Should I come back for you?"

"No, I-I remember the way. But I don't think my father has ever—"

"Your sister is with him. And Miss Teresa is in good hands already, sir, with our midwife." Elijah bowed and hurried away.

Weakly, Joseph turned back to the sacristy. How many hours had elapsed, since Tessa had woken in pain? Even now, she might be— In danger of death, why had she asked for him? He wasn't her confessor.

"Father?" inquired his young server.

"Would you fetch my breviary please, Anthony?"

The boy frowned. "Where is it?"

"My chamber. In the Bishop's residence. On my desk. Don't let the notes fall out."

"Yes, Father."

In the boy's absence, Joseph struggled out of his vestments. He stuffed his surplice, soutane, and a stole into his portmanteau, along with his Ritual. Fortunately, he checked the sick call kit—the bottle of holy water was nearly empty. He was at the font when Anthony returned. Joseph stashed his breviary in the portmanteau, strapped it as quickly as he could, and raced to the seminary. He begged Father Baker to either lead or cancel the classes Joseph usually taught.

Then Joseph had to wait for the liveryman to select, saddle, and bridle a horse. Every lost minute haunted him. Thirteen long miles away, two souls were in peril, and Joseph was powerless to do anything but murmur prayers for them.

Finally he and his hired sorrel were cantering out of the city past carriages and farm wagons. On the open road, Joseph urged the gelding to gallop. Instead, the animal slowed to an awkward trot. Frustrated, then dismayed, Joseph realized something was wrong. He had no choice but to dismount. He discovered that one of the sorrel's shoes was coming loose.

At least the hoof did not look damaged; but if he continued to ride, it might well become so. Joseph stared forlornly down the empty road in the direction of the Stratford plantation and tried to calculate the number of miles that still separated him from Tessa.

He looked back toward Charleston. The sun was already so far above the horizon... Should he return to the livery stable for a fresh horse? How long would it take to *walk* that distance? The thought of literally turning his back on Tessa, even intending to return... It made him physically ill.

He decided to put his faith in a Good Samaritan. He prayed that at one of the houses or inns ahead, he would find someone willing to lend him a mount, though he carried no money. He led the limping sorrel at a walk.

Perhaps the hemorrhage had been a false alarm, Joseph told himself. And surely his father would reach Tessa soon. The road was in decent repair; he was grateful for that. Even more important, their destination was *this* side of the Ashley River; they would not have to wait for a ferry.

Joseph saw a wagon approaching. He waved it down. Then he made the mistake of telling the driver he was a Priest. The man spit tobacco juice on Joseph's boots and slapped his reins against the backs of his mules as if Catholicism were contagious.

His eyes on his filthy boots, Joseph started forward again. He anticipated his upcoming conversation with the next man. He couldn't lie. But if he mentioned that it was a matter of life and death and the man *assumed* he was a doctor...

As if in reproach, a light morning rain began to pelt him. Joseph hoped this was not an omen. At least the rain washed away the tobacco spit, though mud soon replaced it. His stomach complained loudly about the extension of his fast.

Between his desperate prayers for Tessa, Joseph remembered the saints who'd been granted the power of bilocation, like Martin de Porres. While Martin's body remained in Peru, he appeared at the sickbed of a friend in Mexico City to comfort and heal him.

Joseph had done nothing to deserve such a miracle. He kept recalling the afternoon he'd blessed Tessa and her child. In the midst of the invocation, selfish thoughts had intruded: *This could have been my child. This should have been my child.* He'd paused for only a moment. Surely that had not made the blessing invalid. Surely God would not punish Tessa for his own unholy longing.

Over the patter of the rain, Joseph did not hear the rider till he called out: "Father?"

Joseph turned and squinted through the drops to see Tessa's brother reining his horse just behind him. "Liam!"

The Irishman insisted that they switch mounts: "Tessa needs you more than she needs me."

Joseph transferred his portmanteau and pulled himself onto the new horse. Promising to send someone from the plantation to meet Liam, Joseph kicked the mare into a canter.

. . .

AN ETERNITY LATER, Joseph recognized Stratford land passing alongside him. At last he and the borrowed horse turned through the gate and followed the avenue of live oaks to the grand house.

As Joseph dismounted, the elder Mr. Stratford strode out the front door. "Look, Eddy," he called over his shoulder with a chuckle. "It's another Lazare. We're being invaded!" The old widower might be eccentric, but he had not struck Joseph as mad. Surely Mr. Stratford's flippancy meant all was well?

Edward barely glanced at Joseph before he slumped into a chair on the veranda. "You're too late, Father. It's over."

Shivering in the rain and aching from the long ride, his hands on his portmanteau, Joseph waited in vain for Edward to explain. "Mrs. Stratford is out of danger, then?"

"She's alive," her husband muttered.

"And the child?"

"Quite dead." Edward seemed more annoyed than grieved. He might have been reacting to the loss of a horse race. Not the loss of his firstborn. Not the loss of a priceless human soul.

Joseph closed his eyes and crossed himself.

When a negro came to lead away the borrowed mare, Joseph told him about Liam. A second slave carried his portmanteau out of the rain; a third took his wet coat on the veranda; and a fourth brought him towels.

While he blotted the rainwater as best he could, Joseph could not help but overhear the elder Mr. Stratford's monologue to the taciturn Edward: "This is not a reflection on your virility, son. You did your part! These failures are always because of the woman. The first time I saw that one, I thought you were onto something—new blood and all that. Isn't my best broodmare an Irish thorough-bred? Let us hope this little episode is only an aberration. You won't know till you try again!"

Before he was reasonably dry, Joseph seized up his portmanteau and asked one of the slaves to take him to Tessa. Still the old planter's voice followed him: "At least it wasn't a son!"

Joseph and his guide used the staircase at the back of the veranda. He had not climbed to the second floor on his previous visit—this was private space. But here too, the floor-length, triple-hung windows opened onto the veranda like doors. Joseph did not have to ask where Tessa lay: her maid, Hannah, exited one of the bedchambers, her arms full of bloody bedclothes.

Joseph felt his strength draining and stopped. All those years at seminary, he'd not fully realized how often his duties as a Priest would resemble those of a doctor—how often sick calls, Last Rites, and even Baptisms would bring him into contact with the distressing failings of the body.

"Father Lazare." Even with her terrible burden, Hannah bobbed a curtsy. "Miss Teresa will be glad you're here; but we need a few minutes yet."

Joseph nodded mutely and watched her carry the bedclothes down the staircase.

"Don't suppose you want me to announce you, then," observed his young guide.

"No, thank you."

The boy disappeared after Hannah, and Joseph stood alone on the veranda. Curtains concealed the bedchamber's interior, but through the open triple-hung window, he heard the familiar voices of his father and sister. The rustling of cloth, the splashing of water, and the low voices of black women. From these sounds, Joseph understood Hannah's comment: the bed and Tessa's own garments were being changed.

On a bench outside the chamber, Joseph set down his portmanteau. He opened it and withdrew his soutane, as much for warmth as formality. As he fastened the long line of buttons, Joseph tried to remember when Tessa had expected this child. She'd carried it less than four months, by his estimation—closer to three.

Another maid emerged from the bedchamber, carrying a bloody basin. Joseph fished in his portmanteau for his breviary, hoping it would steady him. He should find his notes, the verses Father Baker had recommended for miscarriages. But the renewed conversation inside the bedchamber drew his attention.

At first, the sound of Tessa's voice gave him solace: it was irrefutable proof she had survived. Then the words dispelled peace with pain: "Am—Am I deformed in some way?"

Joseph sank onto the bench. For a moment, he was thirteen years old again, exposing himself to Dr. Moretti, waiting for approval. He had purchased his Priesthood by surrendering his modesty. These past few hours, how many people had seen Tessa even more vulnerable, even more ashamed? That was the cost of her motherhood. But she was not a mother.

A mature black woman, probably the midwife, responded to Tessa first, her voice heavy with compassion. "No, honey."

"You are perfectly formed," Joseph's father assured her.

"Then why couldn't I hold onto Bean?"

"I wish I could give you an answer," Joseph's father sighed. "The truth is: most of the time, we cannot explain why a pregnancy fails."

"I must have done something wrong," Tessa argued weakly. "I should never have left the city; I shouldn't have—"

Joseph's father interrupted: "You did not cause this by riding in a carriage or walking up stairs or anything else."

Hélène spoke up next. "If you want to blame someone, blame me."

"You?" Tessa asked. "Ellie, how could this possibly be *your* fault?"

"I told Bean to hurry up, didn't I?" Her voice broke. "I told her we couldn't wait to meet her."

"Sometimes, the good Lord just gathers these little ones to Himself right away," the midwife soothed. "Sometimes, it's a mercy, I think. In Heaven, your Bean is never going to feel hungry or sick —she is safe and happy and waiting for you, Miss Teresa."

For several long moments, Joseph heard only muffled sobs.

"What I do know is this," his father continued. "My own wife suffered such a loss, and so has Cathy. A miscarriage does not mean you cannot have healthy children."

"But I want Bean," Tessa whimpered. "May I hold her again? Please? Just a few minutes longer?"

Joseph heard water splashing again, then Tessa's breath hitched anew.

"You take as long as you need, honey," the midwife said.

"Oh Ellie, she must have been terrified!" Tessa cried. "I am *so sorry*, Bean!"

Joseph closed his eyes. This was not the first miscarriage he'd attended. A few months ago, he'd arrived in time to speak the cold, conditional words: *"If thou art a human being, I baptize thee…"* What else *would* it be? Its mother still loved it desperately, no matter its appearance, no matter that it clung to life only long enough to receive the Sacrament. He'd been glad for the Latin; he'd hoped the mother had not understood.

Joseph made himself stand, clutching his breviary against the chest of his soutane, begging God to give him the right words.

His father strode through the triple-hung window, blocking his path. Above the waist, his father was stripped to his shirt and smeared with blood, yet he frowned at *Joseph's* attire. "If you are going to increase that young woman's misery, turn around right now."

Joseph did turn around, but only because someone was approaching. Hannah. He returned his attention to his father. "Do you think I am heartless?" Joseph hissed.

"No, but your Church often is."

"It's not—" *It's not MY Church, it's THE Church*, he would have said.

But his father had already moved past him to ask Hannah where he and Hélène might change their clothes.

Cautiously, Joseph entered the bedchamber. Hélène moved from her friend's side to ask: "Joseph, Edward and his father think that because Tessa hadn't felt Bean moving yet, she didn't have a soul yet. Is that true?"

This explained their behavior, though it did not excuse it. Joseph shook his head. "Bean has a soul—as immortal as yours or mine."

Tessa raised her bloodshot eyes to him, but only for a moment.

Hélène promised to return soon, and the midwife left them too.

Propped on pillows, Tessa was swaddled in a baggy blue dressing gown with her knees drawn up beneath the bedclothes. On this support, she cradled in both hands something so small Joseph could not see it even as he came to stand beside her. She sheltered it as one might a baby bird fallen from its nest. As if its stillness were temporary. As if sheer will might infuse it with life again.

"Edward wouldn't even look at her," Tessa whispered.

Joseph gathered the courage to share her pain. The sight was more terrible than he had imagined—not because the little body did not resemble a child, but because it did. What Joseph saw first was an impossibly tiny hand, balanced on Tessa's thumb—utterly perfect yet fragile as glass. Ears, nose, and mouth, already formed. Bean's skin was translucent, revealing the delicate tracery of arteries. Her eyes were veiled promises beneath the surface, just like a baby bird's. Tucked into a folded handkerchief, she filled Tessa's palm, but nothing more. Three inches? Four?

"I baptized her as quickly as I could," Tessa said. "I know the mother isn't supposed to do it, but no one else knew how."

For a moment the image seared through him: Tessa alone but for the slaves and the tiny being in her trembling hand, ignoring her own agony in order to save her child. Of course she was a mother, no matter how brief her daughter's life. "Bean was born alive, then?"

Tessa closed her eyes and shook her head. "The Baptism wasn't valid, was it?"

Joseph stared at his breviary. "No. I'm sorry." Did his father expect him to lie? Tessa had been a catechist; she knew this truth as well as Joseph did. It was right there in the Gospel of John and in Bishop England's catechism: "*Is Baptism necessary to salvation? Yes; without it, we cannot enter the Kingdom of God.*"

"My daughter is damned?"

Yes. But he must soften this. "Are you familiar with Limbo?"

"Isn't that *part* of Hell?"

That was how Albertus Magnus had conceived it; Limbo meant "border." Saint Augustine believed unbaptized children suffered the pains of Hell, only to a lesser degree than wicked adults. Scripture simply did not address the fate of unbaptized children, and the Church had never explicitly confirmed or denied the existence of

Limbo. In the absence of a clear revelation, theologians could only speculate about where and how such souls would spend eternity. But in Joseph's experience, people were even more reluctant to accept *"I don't know"* from a Priest than they were from a doctor. "We do not believe unbaptized children suffer the pain of fire."

"Is their banishment temporary, like Purgatory?"

"No."

"Bean cannot *ever* enter Heaven?"

"Although she committed no fault of her own, because she wasn't baptized, the stain of original sin has not been—cannot now be—washed from her soul. So she can never enter the presence of God."

"Because of my sin?"

"Because of Eve's sin, and Adam's." *Transmitted to her through you.*

Tessa stroked her daughter's tiny head. "Bean won't have to spend eternity like this, will she? She'll have a better body than I could give her? Her eyes will open, and she'll be able to run?"

Joseph clung to Politi's theory: "Yes. At the Resurrection of the Dead, even unbaptized children will be given perfect bodies. She will be a young woman."

"Can I see her, then? Can I—"

"No."

Tessa's grief leaked unceasingly, from her eyes and her nose. "I tried! I *tried*, Bean!"

THE STRATFORDS OFFERED JOSEPH BREAKFAST. He ate without tasting anything. He searched for a gentle way to tell Tessa that Bean could not be laid to rest in consecrated ground. But she already knew. They decided to bury the little girl there on the plantation, at the edge of the Stratford family plot. Hélène helped Tessa fashion a casket from a jewelry box. Inside, they also placed a single kidney bean from the kitchen.

Liam carried his sister to the cemetery as if he were rescuing her from a collapsing house. One of the negroes brought a chair for her. Another slave bore a shovel, but Joseph's father took it from him and dug the little grave himself. Hélène carried the tiny casket. The elder Mr. Stratford did not join them, and Edward looked as if he would rather be anywhere else.

Joseph was forbidden to perform funeral rites, but he offered a prayer: "Lord, as we commit the body of this child to the earth, we commit her soul to Your judgment. Though You have not revealed to us the full fate of these little ones, we trust in Your infinite mercy."

He read from the Psalms: "Show me Thy truth... Have mercy upon me, for I am desolate..."

Joseph closed his breviary. Tessa sat motionless, staring down at the fresh grave. Liam and Hélène stood on either side of her. Tessa gripped their hands so tightly that her knuckles were white, as though she might fall into the earth if she let go.

After several minutes of silence, Liam inquired gently: "Tessa, are you ready—"

Instead of answering, she murmured: "Will it be like she never left my womb?" Tessa glanced to her brother. "Do you remember the Irish name for Limbo?"

He nodded. "*Dorchadas gan Phian*. Darkness without Pain."

"Is that right, Father?" Tessa asked.

Joseph hesitated. Most of the theologians who argued against the pain of fire argued for the pain of loss. Other writers, like Saint Thomas Aquinas, concluded that unbaptized children must remain ignorant of their exile from Heaven. "Bean isn't suffering," Joseph answered. "She doesn't know what she's lost."

But Tessa knew.

CHAPTER 28

Evening crowned the city with peace and plenty…midnight saw its habitations enveloped in devouring flames… One woe is past, and behold another woe followeth hard after.

— Reverend Thomas Smyth, *Two discourses on the occasion of the great fire in Charleston* (1838)

W hen Tessa returned to her house in town, she told Joseph: "Edward doesn't want me to be churched."

Joseph frowned. "Did you tell him that churching isn't only about your attending Mass again? That you cannot resume your… conjugal relations until the rite is completed?"

She nodded and looked away. "But I think he intends to—" She broke off and drew in a ragged breath. Whether she shuddered at the thought of violating the Church's prescription—which he knew the Irish took particularly seriously—or simply at the thought of intercourse with her husband, Joseph wasn't sure. "Edward says everyone will see me there, kneeling outside the cathedral with my unlit candle, and they'll know…"

"We could do it early in the morning, when the cathedral is empty."

"I suggested that. Edward said *someone* is still sure to see."

Joseph hesitated, then decided: "I can give you the blessing here, in private."

She looked up at him with such longing. "Truly?"

He nodded. The abbreviated, private rite was intended for women too ill to rise from their beds months after childbirth. But surely he could make an exception for Tessa.

In January, Tessa conceived again. She confided to Joseph: "With Bean, I felt wonder, excitement, thanksgiving... Now, all I feel is fear."

The Blessing of an Expectant Mother was intended for her confinement. Joseph did not wait. "O God, accept the fervent prayer of Thy handmaid Tessa, as she humbly pleads for the life of her child... Let Thy gentle hand bring her infant safely into the light of day, to be reborn in holy Baptism..."

Every day when he celebrated Mass, Joseph named Tessa in his prayers. Liam, Hélène, and Joseph's mother and grandmother joined in a novena. Reluctantly, Edward agreed to abstain from his marital rights until Tessa was safely delivered and then churched. The stakes were higher now. Fate had turned their unborn child into a prince.

The Stratfords owned a fishing sloop and trained slaves to handle it. Early that spring, Edward's eldest brother Miles was out hunting marlin when a squall caught him in open water. His body washed up the next morning. Miles had had an understanding with a neighboring planter, but he'd been waiting for his betrothed to come of age; he'd left no children.

Edward found another lawyer to complete Liam's apprenticeship. Edward himself had always been more interested in agriculture. Even knowing he would not inherit it, he'd helped manage his family's rice plantation, Stratford-on-Ashley. Now, Edward's father altered his will: the property would be Edward's—*if* he and Tessa could produce an heir. If they failed, Stratford-on-Ashley would go to Edward's nephew, his brother Laurence's second son, who had never even set foot in South Carolina.

To Tessa, this inheritance was closer to a nightmare than a dream come true. Stratford-on-Ashley was nothing without its slaves —nearly one hundred of them. That was not the legacy she wanted to leave the child she carried. Headaches plagued her, and sleep eluded her.

Edward's father sent his own physician to examine her. There was nothing to worry about, he proclaimed. Tessa was a foreigner still acclimating to the Low Country.

Joseph's father wasn't so sure: "There is *so much* we do not yet understand—especially about women's bodies."

Tessa rested as much as she could. To fill the long anxious hours, she learned to paint. She claimed her work was nothing remarkable. Hélène and Liam disagreed, urging Joseph to see for himself.

During Holy Week, he was able to do so. Tessa was capturing the finest blooms in her garden. She was no Renaissance master, it was true; but there was life and beauty on the canvas—Joseph's pleasure and praise were no lie.

He was so entranced, admiring the anemones taking shape on her easel, he did not realize Tessa had turned away from him. She walked straight through her flower-bed to clutch the balustrade of the piazza.

"Tessa?" When he saw her face, Joseph rushed to her side, not caring what he trampled. She was as white as death.

Tessa closed her eyes tightly. "No, no, no, *no...*" She wavered and lost her grip on the balustrade.

Joseph caught her before she could fall. "Hannah!" he shouted into the house. Through the cloud of skirts, he found the bend of Tessa's knees and gathered her into his arms. She clung to his neck, and he felt her hot tears against his cheek. Joseph muttered a prayer as he carried Tessa up the steps of the piazza.

Hannah met them in the entry hall.

Joseph stammered: "I—I think..." *It's happening again.* He couldn't say it aloud, as if this alone would make it true.

· · ·

S HE BLED FOR DAYS. On this slow, inexorable tide came the tiny body in its sac. A little boy this time, but still no sign of life. No hope of Heaven or reunion.

Tessa buried her son beside his sister at Stratford-on-Ashley. Shortly after Easter, she walked with Joseph from the plantation house to the two small graves. Her dress was lavender.

"Edward still won't let me wear mourning," Tessa explained. "'Must everyone know our business?' he says. I pleaded with him: 'I could say someone in Ireland had died.'" Tessa stopped for a moment and murmured: "'Tis a sin to lie, Father, I know."

"I imagine that wasn't the reason your husband refused?"

She shook her head and resumed their path. "He told me: 'Black makes *you* look like a corpse. It's our first social season.'"

Joseph gritted his teeth. Edward wanted to show off his beautiful wife. He cared only that she present a pleasing exterior, not about the misery beneath her masquerade.

"He isn't a cruel man; you mustn't think that," Tessa added quickly. "But 'tis as if…he cannot see through anyone's eyes but his own. Our children aren't *real* to him like they are to me. He didn't carry them; he didn't hold them. I suppose 'tis easier for him, to believe they don't have souls. To Edward, our children are only broken promises, something he would rather forget." They reached the two small markers. "I had to beg him for these." Tessa knelt at the stones. "But Edward said I could name our children whatever I wanted."

Joseph knelt beside her and read the inscriptions:

BRIDGET STRATFORD
NOVEMBER 12, 1837
BELOVED DAUGHTER

CONLAED STRATFORD
APRIL 14, 1838
BELOVED SON

Joseph smiled at Bridget, the name her husband would have rejected for a living child. "Conlaed is also an Irish saint?"

Tessa nodded. "He was the first Bishop of Kildare. And Conlaed was my family name, before the English changed it to Conley."

She should have been Miss Conlaed. "Do you know what it means?"

"'Chaste fire.'" She smiled a little too, and then her face clouded again. "When I lost Conlaed, I told myself: 'At least Bridget isn't alone anymore; at least they have each other.' But how can they— You said that children in Limbo don't know what they've lost."

"If they did know, the spiritual torment would be greater than any fire. So they *must* be ignorant of Heaven."

"But they cannot be ignorant only of Heaven, only of their separation from God!" Tessa cried. "If Bridget and Conlaed knew how much *I* love them, that I think about them and miss them every day, they would grieve as much as I do; they would be suffering! That means—" She could scarcely breathe through her tears. "Do they even know they are sister and brother?"

He had meant to comfort her. Joseph clasped her gloved hand, and she stilled, waiting desperately for his response. "Just as truth is hidden from them, it is hidden from us as well, while we are on Earth. We know only in part; 'we see through a glass, darkly.' Our mortal minds cannot fathom the miracles of God. I am certain that in some way we cannot yet understand, Bridget and Conlaed know they belong together, and they know how much you love them, without yearning for more."

❧

LESS THAN A FORTNIGHT after Tessa's second miscarriage, Hell came to Charleston. The clanging of fire bells interrupted Joseph's evening prayers. Soon the streets of their beautiful city teemed with chaos: the shrieking of families in flight; the bellowing of fire masters through their speaking-trumpets; the creak and crash of collapsing buildings; the boom of explosions as the firemen prostrated structures purposefully to create fire-breaks; the crackle and roar of the ravenous flames.

Joseph was called to the very edge of the disaster, to hear the last Confession of a horribly mangled fireman. The stench of scorched flesh clung to Joseph's clothes. In the unnaturally lit darkness, as more companies of slaves and volunteers tramped past him with their gleaming engines, Joseph imagined Liam amongst them, straining to save his adopted city.

Before dawn, the firemen had not only exhausted their gunpowder but also drained the wells and cisterns dry. A fierce wind carried great black clouds over their heads and threw down ember after ember, setting new houses and shops ablaze. The fires raged down King Street, Meeting, Anson, Wentworth, and Market. They devoured St. Mary's, the Synagogue, and two Protestant churches. They laid waste to more than a thousand buildings, almost a third of Charleston.

While Joseph's father aided the injured, his sister, mother, and grandmother watched in terror as the conflagration swallowed their neighbors' houses. Liam, his fellow firemen, and God's mercy prevented the flames from crossing Archdale Street. But before the fires burned themselves out, Liam's own dwelling became a smoking ruin.

Joseph witnessed the Irishman's reunion with Hélène, who wept with relief and kissed her intended repeatedly in spite of the soot on his face. "Oh Liam, I was so worried! We can tell Mama and Grandmama about us now, don't you think? You saved our house!"

Liam smiled. "After last night, I can face anything—even your mother and grandmother."

While they were not enthusiastic, Joseph detected relief that Hélène finally had a sweetheart.

'You'll have grandchildren who aren't a thousand miles away, Mama!' his sister pointed out.

The older women were impressed by how many signs Liam had learned, and they were placated by the knowledge that the marriage would be deferred at least until he completed his law apprenticeship.

· · ·

MOST OF CHARLESTON HAD NOTHING TO CELEBRATE. Throughout those long days following the fire, Joseph offered blessings and prayers for the thousands rendered homeless. The seminary became a temporary shelter and hospital. In the room where most of the desks were stacked, he found Tessa scraping lint for wound dressings.

Before she looked up, she asked: "Were you able to see him?"

"Pardon?"

"Oh, good evening, Father," Tessa smiled. "I thought you were Hannah." She explained: "Whenever I go out, Edward insists I take Hannah with me, so I let her see her son—if *his* master allows it."

Joseph had thought he'd sensed a loyalty in the negress that went beyond mere duty. Though Hannah was a staunch Baptist, she seemed to have no other faults.

"Were you looking for Hélène, Father?"

"I've just come from her. She said there was a basket of cloths that could be torn into bandages?"

Tessa nodded and motioned under one of the desks.

Joseph retrieved the basket and sat down across from her, glad to be off his feet. "How is Liam settling in?"

"'Tis good to have him under the same roof again. I have missed his company. But—" Tessa broke off.

"But…?" Joseph prompted.

"I know Edward resents the arrangement. The fact that I didn't ask his permission first. The time I spend with my brother when both of them are home." Her voice was a murmur, a reluctant admission. "Whenever Liam and I converse, Edward will sit nearby and pretend to read, but I know he's listening."

Joseph frowned. For a minute, he only tore bandages without speaking. Then he rose to turn up the lamp wick. At last, he voiced a suspicion that had haunted him for months: "Tessa, has Edward ever…struck you?"

"Of course not." But even as Joseph resumed his seat, she kept her gaze averted and added in a whisper: "He has other ways." Before Joseph could ask for more, she continued: "Have you heard they're planning a benefit concert for victims of the fire? They need people for the program, and Liam and Ellie thought I should sing."

Joseph smiled. "You will be the favorite of the evening."

"Edward has forbidden it," Tessa muttered. "He says only fallen women sing in public or for profit. But *I* wouldn't be profiting!" She gestured to the half-open door.

Beyond this little room, family after family huddled with nothing but the clothes on their backs, exhausted by the ordeal that had only just begun.

Tessa bent her head again, pulling away more lint. Her words came slowly at first, then more forcefully, like a flood finally breaking through a dam. "He's never said those words to me before: 'I *forbid* it.' But I always know when he's displeased; he never conceals it. Edward will scowl and say things like: 'I'd rather you didn't, Tessie.' If I do the thing anyway, he'll sulk for days, until I beg his forgiveness. I know very well what I'll face tonight. When he returns home, he expects me to greet him. But I cannot sit around painting flowers while my fellow creatures are suffering! He'd keep me from Mass if he could. He thinks I overtax myself merely by leaving the house, that 'tis my carelessness which..." Her eyes dropped to her flat bodice, and her hands stilled.

"Tessa, you know what my father said: that there was nothing you could have done to save them."

"I am so cautious now. I have been since I lost Bridget. I've stopped visiting the orphanage and my old neighbors, because I might contract some fever... If I thought for one *moment* that being here or reading to old Mrs. Callaghan would harm my babies..." Tessa looked up at him with such pleading in her eyes, as if he were a judge. "*Edward* is the one who insisted I attend Race Week. I told him I was tired!"

There was so much Joseph wanted to say, so many ways he wanted to comfort, encourage, and defend her. But a husband's authority was absolute; there were times when a doctor or even a Priest could not challenge it.

"Edward's father is even worse. *He* thinks I read too much. He says reading is unhealthy for women, that I'm diverting all my blood toward my brain and away from my 'generative organs'!"

Joseph scowled. "That's ridiculous."

"Edward also thinks I should be lacing tighter. But I won't! I can't! And not only for the babies' sakes. What I wore growing up in Ireland was nothing like the corsets that fashionable women are wearing now—I'm simply not shaped correctly!"

She was *perfectly* shaped. How could anyone think otherwise?

Tessa resumed her work and bent her head even more deeply, as if in shame. "I'm so sorry, Father. I'm doing it again: I'm telling you things I shouldn't."

"If you didn't feel you could confide in me, I would be doing a poor job as a Priest."

She smiled weakly. "Somehow, I don't think Father Baker would listen so patiently while I complain about my undergarments."

"He might be more receptive than you think. I suspect the two of you could commiserate."

Tessa frowned. "What do you mean?"

"Corsets aren't only for women, you know."

Tessa's mouth fell open. Her eyes darted toward the doorway, as if someone else might be listening to this slander. For a long minute, she considered the possibility. "Father Baker *does* have remarkable posture... No; it cannot be true! Who would lace it for him?"

"Our housekeeper, Mrs. O'Brien," Joseph suggested.

"She is sixty years old if she's a day!"

"But strong as an ox. I've seen her forearms. They're the size of oak trees."

Pursed lips quivering, Tessa resisted the mental image only a moment longer. At last, she threw back her head and laughed so hard tears sprang from her eyes. Eventually, she recovered enough to say: "Thank you, Father."

"For what?"

"You made me laugh. No matter how dark the day has been."

CHAPTER 29

Is there—*is* there balm in Gilead?—tell me—tell me, I implore!
  — Edgar Allan Poe, "The Raven" (1845)

By the second week of May, Edward had secured Liam new lodgings. By the end of July, Tessa knew she was carrying another child—though Joseph's father had advised Edward to give his wife more time to regain her strength. It was her third pregnancy in the space of twelve months.

Since her first loss, Joseph's father had consulted his doctor friends. After her second, he consulted midwives. He read every book, pamphlet, and article he could find that addressed "spontaneous abortion," as doctors called it. He ordered a treatise from Italy, and Joseph promised to translate it. His father compiled lists of foods Tessa should eat and foods she should avoid.

Edward's father was not satisfied. He sent a phalanx of new doctors to poke and prod Tessa. Most prescribed copious amounts of laudanum, calomel, or venesection. All these interrogations, examinations, and experiments were only making her worse, Tessa pleaded. She trusted Joseph's father. Finally, the Stratford men agreed to return her to his care.

They had no choice. That summer and autumn, every doctor in the Low Country was worked to exhaustion. For the first time since the Conleys' arrival, stranger's fever awoke from its dormancy. Its terrible chills, pains, and vomiting prostrated thousands of Charlestonians. Before the first frost, stranger's fever carried off nearly four hundred souls. By the grace of God, Tessa escaped even a mild case. She was only frustrated that she could not help Hélène and the Sisters of Mercy tend to the dying.

And then, in spite of all their precautions, she began bleeding again.

Joseph's father confided: "One miscarriage is normal. Even after two, there is hope. But *three…*" In his father's eyes, Joseph saw the truth. "Start praying for a miracle."

None was granted.

WHEN THE BUTLER SHOWED JOSEPH IN, Edward was donning his hat. "You're not leaving?" Joseph asked.

"Plantations do not work themselves! At least I can be of use *there*. What can I possibly say to her?"

"Tell her this doesn't change how you feel about her," Joseph suggested, trying very hard to restrain himself. "Tell her this wasn't her fault!"

"How can you *still* believe that?" Edward pointed an accusing finger at Joseph. "Your father is only placating her." He pitched his voice into mockery. "Isn't it a *sin* to lie, Father?"

Said the man who hadn't been to Confession in a year and a half.

When Joseph entered her chamber, Tessa was curled up on the far side of the bed, turned away from him. What he saw first was her hair: unbound, coursing across the counterpane and dripping all the way to the floor like a cascade of grief. He thought of myrrh weeping from its African trees: golden "tears" of sap that turned translucent brown before they were gathered to perfume the incense he burned in the cathedral. Since the day he'd met Tessa, a selfish, sensuous part of him had yearned to see these tresses displayed in their full glory. But not like this.

Hannah stood up from the chair at the bedside and came to him. "She said Irishwomen leave their hair down till they've been churched," the black woman told him. "Said she should have done it before. She won't let me touch her. Said it's bad luck—*she's* bad luck."

When Joseph crossed around the bed, Tessa kept staring sightlessly out the window; she didn't acknowledge him. "Tessa? It's Joseph—Father Lazare."

She did not move. One hand was fisted against her chest. The other lay limp on the pillow beside her.

Slowly, instinctively, Joseph slipped his fingers between hers. Tessa closed her eyes and grasped his hand. He no longer knew what to say, so he said nothing; he only sat with her till Hélène came to take his place.

AUTUMN BECAME WINTER. Stranger's fever released its grip on the Low Country, and Charleston rose from the ashes. Father O'Neill celebrated the first Mass at Saint Patrick's, the new church in Radcliffeborough on the Charleston Neck.

Every day, Tessa drank a tea prepared by the midwife at Stratford-on-Ashley. Around Christmas, she conceived again. She followed every Irish superstition. If she experienced the slightest knock, Tessa would touch her hip so the damage would not transfer to her child. She ceased wearing corsets altogether. She left her chamber only to attend Mass, when she wore a great cloak.

None of it made a difference. In March, the terrible, familiar pains seized her womb again.

"THE TROUBLES OF MY HEART ARE MULTIPLIED," Joseph read over the grave of the little boy she called Patrick. "Deliver me from my distress."

Tessa did not rise from her knees. She clung to Hélène, shivering with grief as spring bloomed all about them. Here in the cemetery, Tessa had planted dogwoods for her children after all. They were beautiful. But she did not see them. "We have a proverb in Ireland," she told Joseph and his sister. "'Three who will never see the light of Heaven: the Angel of Pride, an unbaptized child, and a Priest's concubine.'"

Hélène frowned. "The Angel of Pride is Satan?"

"Yes! Satan, a whore, and a baby—on the same list!"

Doctrinally, the list was perfect. Yet Joseph knew he must give Tessa what comfort he could. He'd asked his old seminary professors to send him every theory they could find about Limbo. "The New Earth that Saint Peter talks about, after the Resurrection of the Dead—there are scholars who think that unbaptized children will inhabit that Earth in their new bodies, forever."

"They will be happy there?" Tessa pleaded. "It will be beautiful?"

"Like your garden in springtime," Joseph promised.

"Without any mosquitoes," his sister added.

Tessa smiled through her tears. "Or like County Clare, without any Englishmen?"

BEFORE THE END OF SUMMER, Tessa miscarried for the fifth time.

Once again, Edward abandoned his wife. Once again, he and Joseph passed in the hall. This time, the man actually scowled at him before departing.

Joseph felt a twist of guilt in his gut. Was he visiting Tessa too often, too long? Did Edward suspect how Joseph felt about his wife?

Of course not, he assured himself. *She is my parishioner. This is a sick call. I have done nothing to be ashamed of.*

But he had *thought* a great deal to be ashamed of.

The butler directed Joseph to the upper piazza. Tessa reclined on a green méridienne, staring at her honeysuckle vine, a little book open on her lap. Again her stunning hair was unbound, so long it pooled on the floor of the piazza. It reminded Joseph of Mary Magdalene. But what sins did this young woman have to repent?

Her thoughts seemed to follow his. Without looking at him, she said, "God is punishing me, isn't He?"

"Of course not."

She thrust the little book at him: Bishop England's catechism, Joseph realized. He read the section she'd underlined fiercely:

Q. What is the reason so many marriages prove unhappy?

A. Because many enter into that holy state from unworthy motives, and with guilty consciences; therefore the marriages are not blessed by God.

Cautiously Joseph raised his eyes to her.

"I never, never should have married Edward. I knew that!"

Joseph sat heavily in a chair at her side.

"But there were so many reasons to say 'Yes,' and only one to say 'No.' I thought, in time, gratitude would *become* love. I thought: *Edward will give me children, and I will love him for that if nothing else!*" Her body convulsed in a bitter laugh. "He was *so* persistent! And I was flattered. He took me to balls and concerts and plays."

What had Hélène said? *"It's like the prince and Cinderella!"* Who could say no to a prince?

"Have you ever been hungry, Father? I don't mean fasting—has there ever been a time when every fiber of your body *begged* for nourishment, and you had nothing to give it but seaweed?"

Joseph shook his head.

"It happens nearly every year in Ireland, between the potato crops—and sometimes they *fail*. Do you know what it's like to watch your nieces and nephews starving?" Fresh tears marred her cheeks. "I didn't want my children to suffer like that. Do you know what it's like not to choose poverty as a vow, but to have it *ground* into you, day after day after day? You think: *There is a reason for this. God is displeased with me. I deserve this.*" Tessa lowered her eyes from his face. "And still you long for what you cannot have, because 'tis right there in front of you. Finally you tell yourself: *Even if I never find happiness myself, I can give it to my brother and my dearest friend with a single word!*"

"Edward promised Liam the apprenticeship if you married him," Joseph realized.

"He— He never said that."

"But you knew if you refused Edward, he would have no reason to help your brother."

She nodded miserably.

Tessa had sold herself. No—that was too vulgar. She had sacrificed herself for the people she loved, just as her family had feared she might in Ireland. She had fled one oppression only to find another.

"God is not punishing you, Tessa—He is *testing* you."

"Then I have *failed*." She stared at him so intently now that it terrified him. "You don't know, Father. You don't know the things I've done—the things I've *thought*."

"Have you confessed these sins?"

"It doesn't matter! I *keep* committing them!" Her voice descended so far into sobs he could hardly understand her. "I'm committing them *right now*!"

"I can hear your Confession, if—"

She shook her head violently, her long hair trembling all about her. "Please, go away."

"Do you want me to send Father Baker?"

"*Leave me alone!*" Tessa screamed. "Why won't you leave me alone?!"

Joseph obeyed.

THREE DAYS LATER, he was in the library at the Bishop's residence when Mrs. O'Brien announced a caller.

Tessa swept past the housekeeper and knelt at his feet. "Forgive me, Father."

"Of course." When she did not rise, Joseph knelt himself and peered beneath her bonnet. A deep flush stained Tessa's face, and rivulets of sweat descended her temples. It was August, after all— and she was corseted again. Joseph glanced to Mrs. O'Brien. "Could you fetch us some water, please?"

He led Tessa to a chair and helped her untie the stubborn ribbons at her throat. When she pulled the bonnet away from her hair, Joseph started as if she were a stranger. Those glorious bronze tresses had been severed at the nape of her neck. He fell into the chair across from her. Joseph remembered a story Father Verchese had told him in Rome: when a wife proved barren, her merciless husband had shorn off her long hair, yelling: *You might as well be a boy!* "Tessa? What happened to your hair?"

She did not meet his eyes. "I cut it. As a sacrifice. So God will let me keep the next child. To show Him that nothing else matters to me." She accepted the glass of water from Mrs. O'Brien and hid in it.

The housekeeper gaped at Tessa's cropped hair till Joseph's glare drove her off.

"Edward is furious," Tessa confided, staring into the glass. "He sent my hair to a shop so they can fashion a chignon, so that when we go out, it will look like nothing has changed. He said if I do anything like this again, he'll send me to a madhouse. But I cannot fast; I cannot do anything that would harm the baby too…" Tessa looked to Joseph at last. "What else is there, Father? Should I wear sackcloth? Smear myself with ashes?"

"Why do you feel you need to do Penance, Tessa?"

She avoided his eyes again. "I cannot tell you that."

"Have you told Father Baker?"

She nodded haltingly.

"What did he advise?"

Tessa's beautiful throat convulsed as if she were swallowing poison. "He told me I must avoid my proximate occasion of sin."

"Will you?"

"I would have to leave Charleston! How could— How could I explain it to Edward?"

"Would you like me to speak to him?"

She shook her head vehemently. "Please don't."

"I want to help you, Tessa."

"I know. But you cannot." She replaced her bonnet.

· · ·

TESSA TOLD NO ONE ABOUT THE SIXTH CHILD until it slipped away from her. "As if I could keep a secret from God Himself," she whispered to Joseph.

In February, when they stood alone before the six little headstones, Joseph read from Lamentations:

> "He hath led me, and brought me into darkness, and not into light. ... He hath broken me in pieces... He hath fed me with ashes. ... The Lord is my portion, said my soul... It is good to wait in silence for the salvation of God."

When Joseph had finished, Tessa responded: "In County Clare, a graveyard for unbaptized children is called a *ceallúnach*. Suicides are buried there also. The *ceallúnach* near my village, 'tis beside an ancient stone circle. As if unbaptized children and suicides are destined for some pagan after-life entirely apart from Heaven or Hell..."

"Tessa, you know there *isn't* a pagan after-life."

"At least I could be with my children then, if I..."

Joseph drew in a sharp breath of cold air. Was Tessa saying she had contemplated—

"I know I would be damned." She wrapped her arms around her empty womb. "I know God created this body, that I have no right to despise or destroy it. But all my body has ever done is betray me—again and again and again."

The most beautiful woman he had ever met despised her own body. "Suicide is not the solution, Tessa. Even this despair is a mortal sin. It means you do not trust our Lord, that you have not resigned yourself to His will. God wishes to purify you. Suffering is an invitation to holiness."

He wasn't sure Tessa was listening. "The Irish believe a *ceallúnach* is a dangerous place—that anyone who steps upon the grave of an unbaptized child will be surrounded by darkness and become lost."

"Surely there is a way to counteract the curse?" He was grasping now. "A second superstition to combat the first?"

"You must turn your coat inside-outwards. What if you're not wearing a coat?"

She was wearing a fine brown cloak. Ridiculously, Joseph stepped toward her and undid the clasps. She stood like a statue; she did not protest or resist. He slipped the cloak from her shoulders, reversed it to expose the white silk lining, and draped it around her again. Anything to pull her out of this despair.

She drew it closed and offered him a wan smile.

At long last, he had more than superstition to offer her. "Tessa, are you familiar with the doctrine of Baptism by desire?"

"How can a child who hasn't even been born desire Baptism?"

He could hear her sliding back into that abyss. "Three centuries ago, a Cardinal named Cajetan postulated that a child still in the womb might be baptized through the desire of its *mother*."

Her eyes snapped up to his. "Truly?"

The Council of Trent had debated whether to condemn Cajetan's theory. The Bishops were split in half. Finally they decided that the Council had more important matters to address. "Even if Cajetan was wrong, I've been rereading Ambrose Politi, who believed that those admitted to Heaven would be able to associate with the inhabitants of the New Earth."

"You mean...I could visit my children? I could hold them?" In an instant, Tessa was holding *him*: she flung her arms around Joseph and clutched him in a thoughtless, exuberant gesture. "Bless you, Father!" She nearly knocked off her cloak.

It took all of Joseph's strength (and ten years of seminary) not to return her embrace. That would have been selfish and sinful. He'd already given her what she needed. After Tessa let go—too soon and far too late—Joseph reminded her: "But you will be able to see your children only if you yourself reach Heaven. You understand?"

Tessa nodded and secured her cloak, which was still inside-out.

CHAPTER 30

A canter is the cure for every evil.
— Benjamin Disraeli, *The Young Duke* (1830)

Joseph still dined with his family every week. He did so on his twenty-eighth birthday. While May cleared away the plates, Hélène asked eagerly: "Could you come out to the stable for a minute, Joseph?"

He smiled. "Have you braided Rocinante's mane again?" He was their father's carriage horse, whose name was *mostly* in jest.

"Yes—that's it." Yet she'd hesitated.

"I have sick calls to make."

"On your birthday?"

"Just like last year and the years before that."

"Surely your parishioners can spare you a little while longer." Hélène looped her arm inside Joseph's, not giving him much of a choice.

Their father followed them to the back of the lot. There, a young negro sat rubbing some kind of oil into a saddle. But Joseph's father never rode; he always drove.

Hélène interrupted his thoughts: "Do you remember Nathan, Henry's nephew?"

Joseph did. "How old are you now?"

"Fifteen, sir." At a nod from Joseph's father, the young man went toward the stall that had always been used for storage.

"Papa bartered with Nathan's master," Hélène explained, "so he can come every day to visit his aunt, uncle, and grandmother and help tend the horses."

As she spoke, Nathan led a new horse from the stable: a stunning dapple grey with dark points, perhaps sixteen hands. His conformation looked flawless. Even across the short distance, the animal seemed to prance, his silky grey tail carried high.

"Watch this." Nathan stopped suddenly and backed up a few steps. He kept the lead rope slack, yet the grey not only halted on cue but also backed without being asked.

Nathan praised him. The horse lifted his head proudly and stretched his long legs behind him. He radiated ease and alertness at once. Hélène cooed at him and scratched his withers. The grey did not shy but leaned into her, closing his eyes in pleasure.

"Are you boarding him?" Joseph asked. "Was that the barter?"

His father grinned. "Yes, and no. What do you think of him?"

Joseph frowned. "He's quite handsome. What did you mean: 'Yes and no'?"

"The barter was my medical services for Nathan's grooming services."

"Then…you're replacing Rocinante?"

At Joseph's confusion, his sister was inexplicably giggling.

"No," his father prevaricated. "The Solomons made us a very good offer on your grandmother's house." The Solomons had been renting it for years now, since Cathy and Perry moved to Missouri and Joseph's grandmother moved across the garden fence to his mother and father's house. "We accepted. So I can finally do something I've been meaning to ever since you were stranded in the rain with that livery nag."

The day Tessa lost Bean.

"What I meant was: I'm boarding him for *you*, son." His father stroked the elegant, muscled neck of the grey horse. "Henry and Nathan will ensure that he's properly shod and exercised and ready when you need him."

Joseph could only gape. A Priest shouldn't own an animal fit for nobility—certainly a curate shouldn't. He was supposed to live in holy poverty. Bishop England didn't even have his own horse. Joseph could only imagine what such an animal had cost. "I cannot accept—"

"He wasn't *quite* as expensive as he looks," his father interrupted.

Hélène shielded her mouth with her hand, as if she were protecting the horse's pride. "His bloodlines aren't pure." She grinned. "But his name is Prince."

Of course it was.

"His former owner was eager to be rid of him—through no fault of his own. Prince just didn't want to work for someone who abused him."

Then their father could sell the grey to someone kinder.

"The moment I saw him, I knew he was the one," Joseph's sister declared. "Papa wanted to buy you this ugly red roan, but I convinced him otherwise."

"I find it difficult to deny your sister anything," their father confided. "Especially since—" He broke off and looked away.

Before Joseph could question him, Hélène continued: "You see, Joseph, you *can't* refuse: you'd be insulting not only Papa, but me as well. Furthermore, you'd deny Nathan the chance to spend time with his family."

"Prince may look like royalty," put in the young man, "but if you're gentle with him, he's willing as a dog."

His sister strode to their father's horse, who hung his head over his stall door. "You must consider Rocinante too. He's been awfully lonely—haven't you, boy?" Hélène offered the older horse a lump of sugar from her pocket.

"How can he be lonely, the way you spoil him?" Joseph pointed out.

"I won't always be—" She stopped suddenly just as their father had.

There was some secret they were withholding; Joseph was certain now. Were Hélène and Liam planning to elope? Joseph would have to remind them that the Church did not condone such behavior.

His sister hurried on. "Prince can keep Rocinante company, when their masters aren't out on their missions of mercy."

"You make house calls just as much as I do, Joseph," his father reasoned. "You *need* a good horse, one you can rely on."

Nathan added: "Prince has the smoothest action you've ever felt —like riding on a cloud."

Joseph moved no closer. His duties required him to leave the city perhaps once a week. Having his own mount was an extravagance. Certainly a mount like this was. He wondered if the ugly red roan was still available. "This horse isn't at all appropriate for—"

"Don't judge him by his appearance," Hélène interjected. "Yes, he's gorgeous—but more importantly, he has a good heart." While she spoke, Prince nosed about her pockets.

"Apparently he has a sweet tooth as well," Joseph observed.

His sister produced a second sugar lump but managed to keep it out of the horse's reach, placing it in Joseph's palm instead. Prince reached toward him with questing lips. Joseph extended his hand, and Prince snatched the sugar.

"No more objections, Joseph," his father said with finality. "Prince is perfect for you. He's young, strong, intelligent, and calm in a crisis. He's even a gelding, so the two of you can commiserate."

"*Papa!*" Hélène slapped their father's arm in reproof, but she giggled.

Joseph only sighed.

Father Baker seemed amenable. Then, he saw Prince. His curate needed a reliable mount; but for Joseph to ride such an animal smacked of vanity. They would wait to hear what Bishop England had to say. After he returned from his latest tour of the diocese and before he departed for the Provincial Council in Baltimore, His Lordship considered the grey horse. Finally Bishop England smiled and asked if he might borrow Prince on occasion. Joseph agreed, and the matter was settled.

Joseph himself warmed quickly to the animal. That abusive owner had been a fool. Prince was certainly spirited, yet he remained docile and responded readily to affection. His action was fluid and steady; he was the most comfortable horse Joseph had ever ridden, just as Nathan had promised. Most of all, Prince offered Joseph a taste of freedom, the freedom other young men must enjoy. To counterbalance the work that filled nearly every waking hour, now and again Prince helped him snatch moments of rest, even pleasure.

Every fortnight that summer, Joseph took Prince with him on the ferry to Sullivan's Island. The island did not have a church, but it had a growing Catholic congregation: Irishmen repairing the breakwaters that protected Fort Moultrie. After Joseph said Mass in the open air or in someone's parlor, he usually had an hour or two before the last ferry left.

He and Prince ran till they were far from the fort, the cottages, and the other bathers, so that no one would be scandalized by the sight of a Priest in his under-clothes. Equally unencumbered, Prince rolled in the sand or snuffled amongst the beach grasses (only once attracting the ire of a crab) while Joseph swam or simply lazed.

When visits to the mission at Summerville took them inland, Joseph often allowed himself to tour the Stratfords' gardens. Edward's father had noted Joseph's admiration of their design and variety, and he'd said Joseph was welcome any time. He always learned something when he chatted with the plantation's gardener, a slave who was a master at his craft.

Sometimes, Tessa happened to be visiting her father-in-law's island cottage or his plantation garden and her husband happened to be fishing or hunting. Then, Joseph lingered.

CHAPTER 31

The poor breast was no where discoloured, & not much larger than its healthy neighbour. Yet I felt the evil to be deep, so deep…
— Fanny Burney, 1811 letter

When Joseph came to dinner at his father's house that autumn, he found Tessa and her brother there. Throughout the meal, Joseph's family was strangely somber. Conversations stumbled and died. His father didn't make his customary jests or try to rile Joseph in any way. His sister, who usually took a second serving, barely touched her food.

Before they were quite finished, Joseph's grandmother begged to be excused. His mother rose too. Joseph's grandmother could no longer walk without assistance. Her daughter's strength also wavered; May had to help them from the room.

Joseph's father stopped poking his apple tart and set down his fork. He looked at Joseph, Tessa, and Liam. "We told them this morning what we're about to tell you." Finally, his gaze rested on Hélène.

She lowered her eyes to her bodice. "It was hardly the size of a pea," she began in a weak voice. "At first I wondered: 'Has that always been there?' I have plenty of flesh in which it could hide—and I am not in the *habit* of fondling myself." Joseph thought his sister was attempting a smile, though it looked like a grimace. "But it's larger than it was before."

What in Heaven's name was she talking about?

"There is a tumor inside my right breast," Hélène clarified.

The clock ticked loudly on the mantle.

All these months, while Joseph had been gallivanting about on his new horse, his little sister had been—

"I *knew* something was wrong!" Liam threw his napkin on the table as if it were a dueling glove, as if he had been betrayed.

Hélène was twenty-four years old. There must be a reason for this, a lesson—

Only Tessa leaned closer to squeeze her friend's hand. "Are you in pain, Ellie?"

"Not— Not yet."

"Why didn't you tell us sooner?"

"We didn't want to distress you unnecessarily," Joseph's father answered. "I needed to monitor the growth, to find case histories and consult with my colleagues. This may be a cyst—it may be benign. That could still mean surgery…"

Joseph shuddered and looked away, as if he felt the knife penetrating his own chest. Sometimes, surgery patients actually died of the pain—shock, it was called. And Joseph would never forget what had happened to his grandfather. An operation lasting barely a minute, an operation meant to extend his life, had instead hastened his death. A fatal fever might follow any surgery, no matter how simple or successful.

"The truth is, we still don't know what we're facing," his father admitted. "There are *many* different types of tumors. But we have decided not to risk a trocar. It would give us a sample of the growth and help us determine its nature; but if the tumor is cancerous, such a puncture would speed metastasis. We would have to operate—amputate—immediately."

Tessa drew in a sharp breath and covered her mouth with the hand that did not hold her friend's.

"The tumor remains small and movable. It is not growing *rapidly*, and it is not affecting Hélène's lymphatic system. We must simply watch and wait."

"I didn't want to add to your troubles, Tessa." Hélène's face begged forgiveness as she looked to each of them. "Joseph, you have a whole parish to worry about. And Liam, I—I know I should have told you. But I was so afraid you'd want to end our betrothal."

The Irishman stood abruptly, his right hand a fist. "That is precisely what I am going to do."

Joseph saw the tears spring into his sister's eyes. She dropped her head. "I understand."

"Liam!" Tessa cried in admonishment and disbelief.

"I meant—" He held up a finger. "*Wait*." Liam turned his back on Hélène, not to flee but to ask Joseph: "Father, how many weeks do you have to announce the banns?"

"Three…"

"Dr. Lazare, sir, I know I've not been admitted to the bar yet, that I cannot offer your daughter the home she deserves—but I should like very much to marry Hélène in three weeks' time." Liam turned back to her. "That is, if *you* still want to, Ellie."

"Of course I do!" She gripped his offered hand as if he were pulling her from a whirlpool. Hélène was weeping in earnest now, but she had never looked happier.

"Liam," Joseph's father warned, "if this is cancer, my colleagues and I will do everything in our power to extirpate it, or at least slow it, but you understand…" His voice failed him.

"I've seen the drawings in Papa's books," Hélène whispered. "It might become—I might become—very ugly…"

Liam nodded solemnly, staring down at their joined hands. "I understand. But the way I see it, we haven't a moment to waste."

Joseph's father rose and grasped Liam's shoulder. "You may marry my daughter in three weeks' time on one condition."

"Anything, sir."

"You will not take her away from us. You will come to live here. You can make the third floor into an apartment."

Liam hesitated and avoided his future father-in-law's eyes, but he answered: "Yes, sir." Hélène too nodded reluctantly.

"The quarters will be somewhat close," Joseph's father acknowledged. "You are afraid Hélène's grandmother, mother, and I will hinder your new-wed bliss?"

Liam went red as a pomegranate.

"Hopefully not as much as you think. I am frequently out visiting patients of an evening. Hélène's grandmother retires early and sleeps soundly." His mouth began to quirk. "And as you know, her mother is deaf."

Everyone smiled—his sister actually giggled—except for Joseph.

Then even his father sobered. "You will have to think carefully about whether you wish to try for children," he added in such a low voice that Joseph barely heard him.

Hélène and Liam obviously intended to consummate their marriage. Was Joseph's father advising them to *prevent* children? They knew that was a mortal sin! Joseph knew he must speak. He could not allow them to pervert the Sacrament of Matrimony. "Wouldn't it be better if you remain as you are?"

His father scowled. "Better for whom?"

Joseph tried to imagine how he would advise strangers in such a case. "Better for Hélène and Liam—for the health of their souls." He turned to them. "I know it is difficult, but you must resign yourselves to God's will, not impose your own. He is allowing you to suffer for a reason. He is trying to teach you to rely on Him, not each other." At the edge of his vision, Joseph saw Tessa lower her eyes and nod. "If you endure this trial patiently and reverently, God will reward you, either in this life or the next."

For a moment, no one said anything. Then his sister responded quietly: "Doesn't Christ say there are no marriages in Heaven?"

"Exactly! *That* is the perfect union: with God. Not with a fellow sinner. If you rush into Matrimony now, merely out of lust—"

"It's called *love*, Joseph," his father interrupted.

Standing beside Liam, still grasping his hand, Hélène raised her chin in determination. "I want this, Joseph. I need this, for what is to come. Please say you'll still marry us."

Joseph sighed. He looked between his sister and her intended. He knew they'd already made up their minds. At last he nodded. He was glad he was not their confessor.

HOW DIFFERENT HÉLÈNE AND LIAM'S WEDDING WAS from Tessa and Edward's. The bride's dress was not satin but wool. For the decorations, Joseph and Tessa did their best, but it was October; they could not compete with a plantation full of summer flowers. The bride and groom grinned at one another throughout the Mass, as if they could hardly wait to say "I will." In the kiss, they lingered unabashedly. Clearly, neither was thinking of God's pleasure.

They spent a week at White Sulphur Springs in the Virginia mountains. When Joseph dined in their company again, Hélène and Liam were still delirious with each other. It was impossible to believe anything threatened his sister's future; she radiated well-being.

Fortunately, their mother had already left the room when their father observed: "I think Matrimony agrees with you, *ma poulette*."

"It does, Papa," she answered dreamily, never taking her gaze from Liam. "More every night."

When their father guffawed, Hélène realized what she'd said. Her eyes widened and darted to Joseph, who was choking on his claret. "Day! I meant: 'More every *day*'!"

CHAPTER 32

At that time when a man moved out West, as soon as he was fairly settled he wanted to move again…

— John Bidwell, "First Emigrant Train to California," *Century Illustrated Monthly Magazine* (1890)

At Christmas that year, Cathy acknowledged receipt of their grave news and imparted her own:

We each have our cross to bear, sister. My husband has only half the sense of yours. Perry has pledged himself a member of the Westward Emigration Society. This means that he has promised to pack us all into a wagon and drive us across the prairies and the mountains until we reach California, or die in the attempt. If your mouths have fallen open, you know how I myself greeted Perry's announcement. But I am his wife, and it is my duty to obey.

Perry thinks Missouri is too crowded. We are struggling, it is true. It is hard to compete with the farmers who have slaves. Perry says everything will be different in California. He says its soil is fertile year-round. David and Sophie will grow up healthy and strong, because malaria and stranger's fever are unknown there.

Perry is not the one who has to sew the wagon cover, tent, and extra clothing. Nor does he have to calculate how much flour, coffee, and soap we'll need. He does not have to decide which belongings he can bear to part with. Perry has his tools and his rifle and he is ready to leave, though we will have to wait until spring.

"But California is a different country!" Joseph's grandmother protested, amongst many other exclamations.

At least, Joseph reflected, the Mexicans were Catholics.

A FORTNIGHT AFTER THEIR DEPARTURE, Cathy passed a letter to a band of trappers returning to St. Louis:

You would hardly recognize me. When one is out in the open, hour after hour without respite, a bonnet can do only so much—already I resemble a squaw. Much of the color is not even from sun; it is dust, dust, dust. It stings our eyes and invades our noses and mouths. And the mosquitoes! They fling themselves even into my dough!

Earlier today, there was a break from both harassments, but only because we had a thunderstorm instead: hail the size of goose eggs and a tornado we were certain would carry us away. Now we are battered and filthy. As soon as we pry our wheels, shoes, and animals out of one mud hole, we become mired in another. Yesterday we were nearly scalped by marauding Indians. Perhaps California is Paradise, but it seems we must traverse Purgatory to reach it.

I have not yet told you my greatest burden: I am expecting another child. I will bear this little one somewhere in the wilderness. There are no true doctors or midwives in our party, but there are four other mothers. At least we can commiserate about the folly of our husbands.

I know Perry is worried about the baby too, though he shows it in his own way. He fashioned me a cart that would make me a laughing-stock in Charleston—an ugly, rough thing pulled by mules. But the other women are envious. No one can ride in the wagons for long—they jar your bones something fierce and turn your stomach worse than biscuits black with mosquitoes.

Perry drives our oxen by walking alongside them. The pace of the wagons is so slow that Sophie can pick flowers—when she has collected enough "buffalo chips." There is so little wood here, I am forced to cook our food with dried dung!

David kept running up to listen to the trappers spinning their yarns about grizzly bears—until I forbade it. These men dress like savages, and I am sure they taught him appalling new language. Now that he is nearly ten, my son is too proud to ride with me, so David walks beside us and sulks with his nose in a book. I worry that we have not brought enough shoes.

God's will be done, I tell myself. He has already blessed this mad venture. Just as the men in our own party were admitting their ignorance of the route, we met a band of missionaries also heading west. These holy men were far better prepared for the journey than we. They are six Jesuits who go to minister to a tribe of heathens in the mountains. Would you believe, these savages actually sent messengers to St. Louis and asked for "Black Robes," because they have heard of the "great medicine" of the white man.

'Jesuits are *not* a comfort!' Joseph's mother argued. 'They *embrace* martyrdom amongst the savages!'

CHAPTER 33

God wishes to punish me for having loved myself too well… What I suffer will no doubt help my salvation…

    — Anne of Austria, on breast cancer, *Mémoires, par Madame de Motteville* (1723)

T he pecan trees in Charleston were beginning to give up their bounty. Joseph could already taste the pralines. He'd promised to help Henry harvest his family's tree. But as Joseph approached his parents' house, he saw his sister wrench open their gate and flee inside as though someone were pursuing her. Puzzled, he peered down the sidewalk, but he saw only Tessa.

She was running herself. When she stopped, she caught the gate for support. It was ajar, yet Tessa stared forlornly through the slats, as if she would be refused admittance. Unshed tears shimmered in her eyes. "Oh Ellie…" She glanced to Joseph. "If I'd known…"

"What happened?"

"We were visiting invalids this morning. I chose the last call: a widow named Mrs. Gordon. I knew she was dying, but…" Tessa shuddered. "Mrs. Gordon has cancer of the breast. Her nurse was changing her dressings." Tessa closed her eyes. "I don't blame

Hélène for fleeing. I could hardly breathe myself." She looked back over her shoulder. "But *I* must return. I must make our apologies."

"Permit me to walk you—"

"Thank you, Father, but 'tis only on the corner of Queen Street. Then I will meet Hannah and return home."

Reluctantly, Joseph watched Tessa disappear. He closed the gate and found Hélène at the back of the garden. She knelt before their statue of the Blessed Virgin, in the shadow of their pecan tree.

Henry's basket lay forgotten beneath the branches. "Are you *sure* you don't want me to find your father?" he asked Hélène.

She nodded fiercely, though her cheeks were stained with tears. She did not raise her eyes from her clasped hands.

Henry saw Joseph and left them alone.

Joseph knelt beside his sister. He knew how difficult this past year had been for her. Their father and his friend Dr. Mortimer had experimented with both internal remedies and external applications, but the tumor in her breast continued to grow: from the size of a pea to the size of a sparrow's egg. The growth did not pain her—though uncertainty caused a distress all its own. "Tessa told me about Mrs. Gordon."

His sister's breaths became even more ragged. "The *smell*, Joseph! Like she was already—like she was rotting *alive*! Her chest is this oozing black *mass… That's* going to happen to me."

"You know Father won't let it progress that far. The moment he believes surgery to be the wisest course—"

Hélène looked up at him miserably. "I begged Dr. Mortimer to tell me the truth. He admitted that even if they take my breast and scrape away all the cancer they can see, it almost always grows back —worse than before, like some kind of Hydra."

"But we don't know it *is* cancer, Ellie."

"I *do* know. I can feel it. You can't understand what it's like, Joseph, to have a part of your own body betray you."

Actually, he had a very good idea how that felt. "Has there been a change?"

She nodded and lowered her gaze again. "There are *two* now—a second tumor growing beside the first."

Joseph caught his breath. "Does Father know?"

"He said we should still watch and wait, that it isn't proof of malignancy...but I could see how worried he was." Desperately Hélène met his eyes. "Will you pray for me, Joseph? Right now?"

"Of course." He pleaded for her in words he had spoken so many times, over his sister, Tessa, and other parishioners, that he no longer needed his Ritual. "*Réspice, Dómine, fáulum tuam in infirmitáte...*"

"Amen," Hélène echoed. "Will you tell me what it means?"

The prayer sounded strange in English. "I said:

Consider, O Lord, Thy faithful one, suffering from bodily affliction, and refresh the life which Thou hast created; that being bettered by chastisement, she may ever be conscious of Thy healing which saved her."

"'Being bettered by chastisement...'" his sister echoed. She averted her eyes again. "I remember what you said when I first told you: that God gave me this cancer for a reason. Mama told me the same thing. 'You must examine your behavior,' she said, 'and determine what you have done to displease God. Perhaps, if you repent, He will spare you.' At first, I didn't want to believe either of you. But the more I think about it...and seeing Mrs. Gordon today... Have you heard the rumors about her?"

He had.

"If it's true for her..." Hélène wiped fresh tears from her eyes. "Do you know how rare it is for a *young* woman to suffer from cancer of the breast?"

Joseph nodded. Privately, he had wondered if their mixed ancestry might be responsible.

"Mrs. Gordon, the case histories in Papa's books, the other patients Dr. Mortimer has treated—they are *twice* my age! There was only one other woman less than forty years old—and she was a prostitute!"

"Ellie. Your sins are hardly equivalent—"

She shook her head to silence him. "I never told you *how* I discovered the first tumor." Hélène covered her face with her hands.

"Waiting to be with Liam was driving me mad…lying in bed at night, I would imagine he was there with me, and sometimes I would— Papa says it is better that I caught it early; but I keep wondering: 'Was the tumor there *because* I touched myself?' I am *trying* to correct my sins, to be less wanton and less gluttonous."

Joseph had noticed she'd lost weight. He'd thought it was because of the regimen Dr. Mortimer had recommended.

Hélène dropped her hands. "But it is too late to correct my greatest sin—the sin I committed against Tessa."

Joseph frowned.

"I claim to be her friend, but when it mattered most, I betrayed her. When Tessa told me Edward had proposed, I encouraged her to accept him! I was envious! I was dazzled by Edward's wealth and his station—I knew what that connection would mean for Liam. I was so blinded by my own love—lust—that I couldn't see Tessa felt nothing for Edward. If I questioned it at all, I told myself: 'Everybody loves differently. I may be shameless, but Tessa is shy.' If I had been a true friend to her, Tessa would never have married Edward. She would never have lost her children."

"But—"

"If Tessa had married a man she loved, a man who truly loved her—*their* children would have lived. My selfishness is the cause of all that suffering." Hélène fisted a hand against her diseased breast. "You and Mama are right. I deserve this."

"Did Father or Dr. Mortimer also tell you that cancer of the breast is more common in religious women? That some people actually call it 'the nun's disease'?"

"Dr. Mortimer said it's more common in women who don't have children," his sister acknowledged. "But I *want* children! We *are* trying, Liam and I!"

Joseph reached out to cradle Hélène's face in his hands. "I cannot imagine that Our Lord should need to punish so many holy women who have already dedicated their lives to Him. We all must search our decisions for how best to please God; and if this disease has made you follow Him more faithfully, then I am glad of it. But I do not think He scourges us so neatly. Here on Earth, the wickedest people rarely suffer the most. God has *blessed* you by sending you these tumors, Ellie. He is allowing you to endure your Purgatory not after death, when you would cry out alone, but here in life, while you are surrounded by people who love you." Joseph did his best to smile. "Perhaps that is what God intends for Tessa, too."

Still he wondered what transgressions Tessa could have committed to require such suffering. *Her* sins were not carnal; at least he knew that.

CHAPTER 34

If Winter comes, can Spring be far behind?
— Percy Bysshe Shelley, "Ode to the West Wind" (1819)

When Joseph saw his father at Vespers, he knew something was wrong. The man seized on any excuse not to attend Mass. Hélène sat beside him, and she did not look any worse than the last time Joseph had seen her. It must be their grandmother. Had another palsy struck her?

Joseph was forced to speculate until after Benediction, when his father and sister motioned him into the Biblical garden. "We've had another letter," his father began.

Joseph sank onto a bench. Each time he thought the last blow had landed, his father added another. In July, the McAllisters' wagon had capsized in the Platte River. Perry had not survived. Cathy made it only as far as a landmark called Independence Rock, where she gave birth to a son and decided to turn back. One of the trappers remained with her and the children while the other wagons disappeared into the mountains. Then childbed fever took the lives of Cathy and her newborn. At least he'd been baptized.

Before the trapper could lead Cathy's surviving children back to Fort Laramie, his horse spooked and threw him. Ten-year-old David and seven-year-old Sophie had been left utterly alone in the wilderness, two hundred miles from help. They began retracing their steps toward the fort; but if they'd not crossed paths with an Indian Good Samaritan, the children would surely have perished as well.

Hélène blotted her eyes with her handkerchief. "Can you imagine?"

"It's a miracle David and Sophie survived," Joseph murmured. "Literally, a miracle." Yet he struggled to praise God for this imperfect mercy.

"They're staying with former neighbors in Missouri now," his father explained. "I've a few things to arrange first—patients I need to refer to colleagues—then I'll fetch David and Sophie."

"You'll be able to take them in to live with you?" Joseph asked.

His father nodded. "We'll make space for them on the third floor, across from Hélène and Liam."

"I don't mind giving up my dressing chamber—truly I don't," Joseph's sister asserted. "It will force me to be less vain. But a boy who's already proven himself a man should not have to share a bedchamber with his little sister. And after what those children have already suffered…it seems so cruel, to bring them into a house where two of us are dying."

Their father the doctor did not contradict her. He only averted his eyes.

Hélène twisted up her handkerchief. "David and Sophie need a refuge, not a cramped mausoleum."

Their father patted her hand. "It cannot be helped."

How Joseph wished *he* had a home to offer his niece and nephew.

~

A FEW DAYS LATER, Joseph celebrated Mass on Sullivan's Island for the Irish workers. He would have welcomed the solitude on the other side of the island, the chance to listen for God's voice and find sense in Cathy and Perry's deaths. But Joseph had made a promise to his living sister.

So he rode Prince only as far as the Stratfords' cottage, where Hélène was staying. He found Tessa reading on the back porch, with Hannah seated beside her doing mending. At Joseph and Prince's approach, Tessa set down her book and came to the railing.

Though her wide straw hat obscured her eyes, her lips were smiling. "You are like something from a fairy story. While you are out of my sight, I tell myself I must have imagined you. Then, you reappear, as handsome as before."

Joseph's mouth fell open.

Tessa added in a rush: "Hélène has been resting. I'll see if she's awake." And she darted into the cottage.

Joseph glanced nervously at Hannah. She too was in shadow, but he thought he saw her smile. The question threatened to tumble from his tongue: *"Mrs. Stratford was speaking to Prince, right?"*

The alternative was ludicrous. To direct such flattery at a Priest would be entirely inappropriate, even sacrilegious. To question Tessa's intentions would be not only the height of arrogance but also calumny to Tessa. He must say nothing at all.

Joseph tied Prince to the railing and climbed the porch steps. He cleared his throat and asked only: "Were Edward or Liam able to come?"

Hannah shook her head. "They're both busy in town." Liam had been admitted to practice in the equity courts only a week ago.

Tessa returned carrying an apple. "Hélène is rousing herself, but she still needs to dress."

Joseph thought Hannah glanced at him before she announced: "I'll help her, Miss Tessa." The black woman disappeared inside.

Tessa offered Joseph the apple. "Have you broken your fast, Father?"

"With the workers." He shook his head to refuse the fruit. "Thank you."

"You have made Prince very happy." Tessa held out the apple to his mount, who devoured it noisily. Tessa kept her eyes on Prince, her expression grave now. "Hélène told me about Cathy and Perry and your little nephew. I'm so sorry, Father."

Joseph stared at his boots. "Wherever their bodies may rest, I am certain their souls are Heaven-bound."

"Hélène also shared her worries about what it will be like for David and Sophie, to watch at such close quarters while their great-grandmother and their aunt…" Tessa trailed off.

"Unfortunately, we have no alternative. My cousin Frederic still hasn't surrendered his bachelorhood. David and Sophie need a mother. My Aunt Véronique and her husband have the space and the pecuniary resources to raise another family, but they say they want to travel." Joseph leaned against the railing and sighed. "In truth, we were relieved. Véronique is a cold woman. She's not what any of us want for the children. They need a true mother."

Still Tessa did not raise her eyes. "Father…I know *I* am not family, but—"

"Of course you are! We are practically sister and brother, you and I."

Tessa smiled, but it did not last long. Hélène appeared, and Tessa addressed her too. "Since I learned about David and Sophie, I've been pondering and praying… It has been more than a year since— I must accept that Our Lord does not wish me to bear my own children."

Hélène came to squeeze her friend's hand.

Tessa looked up to her and then Joseph, hope and supplication in her brown eyes. "But I should very much like to be a mother to your nephew and niece—if your family would agree to it."

Cautiously, Hélène voiced the question before Joseph could: "Would *Edward* agree to it?"

"There was a time when he would have refused," Tessa acknowledged, "when he would have been jealous. But now, Edward is married to the plantation more than to me. We are like strangers sharing the same roof. We each inhabit our own little country, and I think I can welcome David and Sophie into mine without disturbing Edward's very much." Tessa lowered her eyes. "I will find a way to convince him. I cannot promise he will be a good father to the children." She looked back to Joseph. "But they will have you, Father, and their grandfather. I would never wish to separate David and Sophie from their true family. They would be only two streets away; they could visit you often, and you could visit them."

To Joseph's shame, the thought foremost in his mind was: *I could visit Tessa often.*

"It's a marvelous idea, Tessa." Hélène embraced her friend. "We will ask Papa before he leaves. But I am certain he will agree. He's as fond of you as we are."

Over his sister's shoulder, Tessa's eyes searched Joseph's. "Do I have your blessing, Father?"

"Of course. I could not choose a better mother."

When they'd broken their embrace, Tessa stared down at Hélène. "Are you really wearing them?"

Hélène grinned. She pulled up her skirt and a single petticoat to reveal the black trousers underneath.

Joseph smiled too. "They're Liam's?"

His sister nodded. Then guilt darkened her face. "I know we've been planning this for weeks; but we're in mourning now. I feel disloyal, enjoying myself so soon after Cathy…"

"It was your father's—your physician's—idea," Tessa reminded her. "And it's our last week on the island." It was already October. Very soon, the Stratfords' slaves would close up the cottage. They would not return to the island till spring. And only their Lord knew how profoundly Hélène's condition would change in six months' time.

"Cathy would understand," Joseph assured Hélène. He suspected Cathy would *not* have understood; but she should have.

Hélène was persuaded. Joseph led Prince, walking beside his sister and Tessa till they were out of sight of the other bathers and strollers. Then Joseph helped Hélène onto the horse's back. Tessa arranged her friend's skirts, and Joseph adjusted the stirrups. They had no side-saddle, so his sister had settled on trousers to allow her to ride astride. *"Besides, I would confuse Prince,"* she'd said, *"hanging off one side of him like that!"*

As it was, the grey proved himself quite amenable to his new rider. With Tessa watching and laughing, Joseph dashed along the sand, leading Prince. Hélène leaned back into the sunlight, her face awash with peace, and lifted her arms as if she were flying.

CHAPTER 35

Show me your garden…and I will tell you what you are like.
— Alfred Austin, *The Garden that I Love* (1905)

Joseph's father agreed to entrust David and Sophie to Tessa. Edward and his father consented upon several conditions. The children would be wards. Edward would provide David with an education and Sophie with a dowry, but he would deed them no property. Nor would they take the Stratford name.

Instead, the Stratfords stipulated that the children use their mother's name. Thanks to Joseph and his father, Lazare was known and respected in Charleston, whereas the name of an obscure dead Scotsman meant nothing to anyone. Except his children. Joseph's father bristled at this qualification, but finally he signed.

"Did the Stratfords think I would neglect my grandchildren if they carried a different name than me?" he blustered afterwards. "Maybe that's how their set behaves, but *not mine*!"

Joseph knew it also rankled his father that near-strangers could provide for his grandchildren better than he could, at least financially. He'd already spent most of his nest-egg: on a gift to start

Cathy in California (which David had used to return to Missouri), on Hélène and Liam's wedding holiday, and on Prince.

Since the cathedral had no cemetery and St. Mary's churchyard had no corner unfilled, Joseph's father used the remainder of his funds to purchase a plot at St. Patrick's in Radcliffeborough. There, two of his patients, free colored artisans, built a brick mausoleum. The men carved LAZARE on the sandstone arch above the door and three names on a limestone panel inside: Cathy's, Perry's, and the name of their newborn son, Ian. But of course the crypt behind the panel held no remains.

Joseph reflected on the words he would say in remembrance of his sister, his brother-in-law, and the nephew he would never meet. He decided it was fitting that the name Lazare should appear on an empty tomb. It was, after all, the French form of Lazarus. One day, Cathy, Perry, and Ian would arise too.

AS IF TO EMPHASIZE THE DEPTH of his own pockets, Edward purchased a new house on Church Street, in one of the oldest parts of Charleston. This house was twice as large as Joseph's father's, with a total of twelve rooms (not counting the piazzas or the cellar). Edward wished to avoid his wards, it seemed.

Tessa admitted her relief at leaving Friend Street and its memories behind. Tessa still visited her children's graves; she still prayed for them; but she would no longer be forced to live in the house where she had lost them. Her wedding night had taken place in the Friend Street house, too. In the new house on Church Street, Tessa and her husband would occupy separate bedchambers.

She was particularly delighted by her new garden. Edward had considered a house on the Battery with a smaller lot, but Tessa had persuaded him to take this one. "The moment I saw the garden, I felt as if I *belonged* here," she told Joseph. The previous owner, a widower who would take up permanent residence at his summer home in Rhode Island, seemed relieved to have found a successor who appreciated his roses. These thrived against the brick wall that bordered Longitude Lane. At the back of the large lot, fruit trees and vegetables beds supplied the kitchen. Many of the ornamentals had become overgrown, however, while others suffered unnecessarily. "All the better to make a new start," Tessa said.

Charlestonians favored parterres: geometric beds bounded by low hedges and wide paths. To please Edward, Tessa would keep a parterre in the area between the house and the front wrought iron fence. And she would not dream of uprooting the roses. But in the rest of the space, she would make the garden her own.

She took her cue from Capability Brown. With suggestions from Joseph and assistance from her slaves, Tessa began to create an informal garden: a small oasis of shrubs and trees joined by grass that might be mistaken for a natural woodland glade. "As little brick and oyster-shell as possible," Tessa declared. "I want it to be *soft*—so it can be a play-ground for the children. I want them to feel at home here too." She could hardly wait until spring.

In the house itself, Hélène helped Tessa decorate David and Sophie's chambers in preparation for their arrival. Joseph visited one evening for the sheer pleasure of watching Tessa smile—not for a few moments but for hours. His sister's humor rebounded easily; he did not fear so much for her. Tessa's despair was more stubborn, her joy more timid. Finally, she seemed to have found her way again. Joseph had not seen Tessa aglow like this since she was carrying Bean.

Perhaps this was why God had denied Tessa her own children, Joseph thought: so that her heart and her home would be open for David and Sophie.

That wicked part of him protested: *Do you really think she could not have been mother to them all?*

Perhaps her suffering had served merely to persuade Edward to pity her.

In fact, Joseph's grandmother did not live to see David and Sophie again. Abiding by her wishes, Joseph laid her to rest not in the Lazare mausoleum but atop her husband at St. Mary's. Joseph, his mother, and his sister assured Tessa that their agreement would not change; she would not lose the children. Even now, on their long journey back to Charleston, Joseph's father would be telling them about Tessa.

When Sophie saw the *chevaux-de-frise* atop the Stratfords' wrought iron fence, she gasped: "It's like Sleeping Beauty's castle!" These brambles certainly might be the work of a deranged fairy: iron spikes longer than a man's hand that canted in half a dozen directions. Tessa wanted to remove the *chevaux-de-frise*, but Edward refused. In the wake of Denmark Vesey's slave plot, many Charlestonians had installed these iron spikes, like porcupines bristling their quills.

When Tessa first showed the children her garden, Joseph accompanied his niece and nephew. David hung back, as if he didn't belong with them, but everything intrigued Sophie. Her favorite part was the old brick wall with the climbing Noisettes. Joseph had seen the roses at a distance, but he'd not indulged himself by lingering or asking questions.

"Allow me to introduce you," Tessa smiled, tipping a white rose to face them. The blossom was so densely petalled, it turned downward under its own weight. "This is Lamarque."

"It looks like your petticoats!" Sophie exclaimed.

Tessa laughed. She *did* wear fuller skirts than Joseph's mother or sister—that was the fashion, so that was what Edward required.

Sophie had her nose in one of the Lamarques. "And it smells like lemonade!"

"I think so too," Tessa agreed. "But this rose down here—I can't decide what it smells like. Will you help me?"

Sophie nodded and skipped ahead of them, toward another climbing Noisette. Against the light green of its foliage and the faded red of the brick, this rose was even more stunning—not the color of crisp linen but soft flesh.

Tessa tried to engage David: "Lamarque and this other rose that's still in bloom—they're siblings, just like you and Sophie. Their parents are Blush Noisette and—"

"There's a *secret door!*" Sophie cried, and dashed to it. The canes, leaves, and blossoms of the flesh-colored rose half-concealed a narrow gate set into the brick garden wall. Sophie stretched up onto her toes and craned her neck, but she still couldn't reach the wrought iron window at the top of the gate. "Where does this go?"

"Only onto Longitude Lane," Tessa told her. "This house's previous owner was a merchant, so he used the gate as a shortcut to the wharves."

Joseph's niece rattled the doorknob. "Do you have the key?"

"Of course. We can use it in the spring, if you like, when we take the ferry to Sullivan's Island."

Sophie nodded in anticipation but still stared longingly toward the window. "Give me a boost, Uncle Joseph?"

"A *what?*" he asked, though he understood. As he obliged, Tessa laughed too, clearly unconcerned that her new ward did not speak like a Charleston lady. Through the round grille of the window, Joseph and his niece saw the neighbors' live oak reaching across the cobbles and flagstones of Longitude Lane. "French gardeners have a term for this kind of openwork," Joseph told them, nodding at the wrought iron window. "They would call it a *claire-voie.*"

Sophie puzzled it out. "A light-way?"

"*Très bien!*" Joseph praised as he set her down. "You know your French."

Her face darkened. "Mama taught us."

"Did *she* have roses, at your home in Missouri?" Tessa asked.

The girl nodded.

"If you remember what they looked like, we could plant them here, too."

"Mama's roses weren't as pretty as these." Sophie touched the nearest bloom.

Joseph could see now that the roses weren't truly flesh-colored. He examined them in awe. The blossoms were golden at their centers, then peach till they flushed pink at the tips of their petals.

"Can you imagine anything more beautiful?" Tessa asked.

He couldn't—at least, not in a rose.

"They're called Jaune Desprez. They were the first Noisettes to show any yellow. They've been quite the sensation—and not only for their appearance. What do *you* think these roses smell like, Sophie?"

The girl sniffed, then hesitated. "Peaches?"

"There isn't a wrong answer," Tessa assured her. "But they make me think of Passion fruit. Did you have Passion vines in Missouri?"

Sophie stuck out her lower lip in thought.

"We called them maypops," David interjected quietly.

His sister gasped and nodded.

"Your Uncle Joseph has a Passion vine in his garden at the cathedral," Tessa told the children. "If you ask him, I'm sure he'll bring you a few fruits next summer."

He promised to do so.

"Now you try it, Uncle Joseph!" Sophie commanded, pointing at the nearest rose.

He closed his eyes and obeyed. The scent of the Jaune Desprez proved even more complex than its color, luscious yet elusive. Beneath the sweetness of fruit came a hint of musk, perhaps jasmine... "It reminds me of pineapple," he decided. He'd tasted pineapple only once. *This must be the ambrosia of the gods,* he'd thought, in a moment of pagan fancy.

Sophie didn't understand. "What kind of apple?"

Joseph smiled. "Pineapples grow in places even warmer than Charleston, and they're *much* better than apples."

"Sometimes ships bring us pineapples," Tessa told Sophie. "I'll ask our cook to watch for them at the market, so you and your brother can try one."

Joseph's mouth watered at the mere thought.

Tessa looked to David. "Would you like that?"

The boy nodded wordlessly, then mumbled: "May I go back inside now?"

"A-All right." Joseph could hear the disappointment in Tessa's voice. David slunk away.

Sophie turned back to the Jaune Desprez and inhaled again. "I wish we could eat *these!*"

Tessa smiled. "We can, if you'll help me candy some of the petals."

Sophie's eyes widened, and she nodded eagerly.

"Perhaps your uncle will help us pick the blossoms at the top of the wall, so we can still enjoy the lower ones?"

He bowed. "I am at your service, ladies."

CHAPTER 36

In the devil's mirror the loveliest landscapes looked like boiled spinach, and the handsomest persons appeared hideous... The mirror fell to the Earth, where it shattered... When a fragment flew into a person's eye, it stuck there unknown to him, and from that moment, he saw everything the wrong way...
— Hans Christian Andersen, "The Snow Queen" (1844)

While Sophie blossomed under Tessa's nurturing—"She isn't like the stepmothers in stories at all!"—David remained somber and withdrawn. Tessa confided to Joseph: "I know he has nightmares. But when I try to comfort him, he denies it."

Another day, Tessa said: "You know I'm a reader myself—normally I would applaud it. But reading is all David does! He actually asks Father Magrath for more schoolwork. I haven't seen David playing even once. I tried to choose toys a ten-year-old boy would enjoy. I asked the children if they'd like a pet. David refused. The only reason he'd give was a mumble. Do you know what he said? 'I'd probably kill it'!"

Tessa did give Sophie a kitten, whose coat pattern made him look like he was wearing a tiny black suit. Sophie named him

Mignon. When Joseph came to meet the little creature, David was in his room reading again.

While Sophie was absorbed with her furry playmate, Tessa whispered to Joseph: "What worries me most is the way the children behave toward each other. I know they were very young when I last saw them together, but I remember David being so protective and indulgent with Sophie, and her adoring him. Now, they actually leave rooms to avoid each other. I don't understand it."

"Perhaps they remind one another of their grief," Joseph suggested. "Or they're simply growing into a young woman and a young man."

THE CHILDREN HAD BEEN IN CHARLESTON less than a month when one of the Stratford slaves came to fetch Joseph from the Bishop's residence late in the evening. Master David had hurt himself, the messenger explained. Joseph's father was attending a birth outside the city, so one of his doctor friends had seen to the boy.

Joseph found Tessa pacing the lower hall, clearly distraught. First, she apologized for calling him there. "I know you say the early Mass. But David won't talk to me! He won't tell me why he did it! He wouldn't say a word to the doctor, and Edward is still at his club. I thought maybe David would talk to you: you're a Priest, and his family…"

"Tessa." Joseph caught her by the shoulders so she stopped pacing. "It's all right. I'm glad you called me. David won't tell you why he did *what?*"

Tessa stared down at her palms, cradling her handkerchief. "I heard Sophie screaming, so I ran upstairs. I found David *attacking* the mirror on his dressing table. He'd struck the glass with his hairbrush—it has a strong silver back. I pried that away from him, but he started pounding the larger shards with his palm. He sliced his hand open, and I had to drag him out of the room to make him stop."

Joseph swallowed. "Did he hurt you?"

"Not intentionally. But he terrified me. He terrified Sophie too."

Tessa began to sob. "I looked after so many nieces and nephews in Ireland. I thought I could do this. I thought…"

Every instinct in Joseph's body shouted at him to embrace her. He might have justified it in daylight, but Tessa was wearing a dressing gown. He settled on caressing her upper arms through their patterned wool sleeves. "I'm here. It will be all right. This isn't about you."

She stepped back as if he'd slapped her. "You're right: I called you here for David, not me."

Joseph grasped her shoulders again. "I meant: This is not your fault, Tessa."

She nodded, but he didn't think she believed him.

Joseph followed her eyes to the stairs. Light trickled down to them from the third floor. "Was David crying, or angry?"

"Both."

"Did he give you *any* explanation?"

"Yes, but it made no sense. All he said was: 'I didn't like what I saw!' I told him he was a handsome little boy! Why would he say such a thing?"

Joseph climbed the stairs slowly. As soon as he reached the third-floor hall, Sophie darted from her room and threw her arms around him.

Mindful of the oil in his lamp, Joseph placed a hand on her head. "I'll make things better, *ma petite*—I promise."

When his niece pulled back, she stared up at him with such a haunted expression, her mouth trembling, as if she longed to say something but feared to.

Joseph frowned. "Sophie? What—"

Before he could finish, she ran back into her chamber, snatching up Mignon.

Joseph moved to follow her. Then he saw the slave standing silently in his nephew's doorway. The man must be there to ensure David did no further harm to himself. Sophie would have to wait.

In the light of a fire and another lamp, the boy sat on the edge of his bed, hunched over his bandaged hand. He wore a night-shirt with a dark blue dressing gown fastened over it. David did not raise his eyes at Joseph's approach; he only stared at the floor beneath his dangling feet.

The rug was missing, the floorboards swept clean of shattered glass. Atop David's marble-topped bureau, the oval frame of his dressing mirror sat strangely empty. Where there should have been a reflection, there was only blue wallpaper.

Joseph set down his lamp and glanced to the slave standing at attention. "Would you leave us, please?"

The negro obeyed.

A desk stood near one of the windows. Joseph pulled over the chair and sat down across from his nephew. Still David did not look up. Joseph waited perhaps two minutes before he spoke, hoping the silence would inspire confession. It didn't. At last, Joseph settled on how to begin. "Would you hit your sister, David?"

Without raising his head, the boy glared at him, as if this question were so ridiculous it did not deserve an answer.

"Would you hurt your sister?"

"Of course I wouldn't!" It sounded like David's teeth were clenched.

"Would you hurt Tessa?"

"No!"

"Then you mustn't hurt yourself either, David. When you do, you hurt your sister *and* Tessa, because they care about you. You hurt me—and most of all, you hurt God." Joseph leaned forward to take David's hands gently in his own. "God gave you these hands, David. He gave them to you so you can fasten buttons and turn book pages and a thousand other things you haven't even tried yet: so you can create music from piano keys and plant rose bushes and…"

"I want to do this." David raised his bandaged hand a little. "I want to learn how to stitch up wounds and cut out tumors like Grandpa. How to save people."

"That's wonderful, David. Your grandfather will be delighted to make you his apprentice." Joseph stroked David's wrists with his thumbs. "But you cannot practice medicine unless you take care of the gifts God gave you. Do you understand?"

Slowly, the boy nodded.

Joseph released David's hands and looked back to the empty frame. "You told Tessa you didn't like what you saw in the mirror. What did you mean by that?"

"Nothing."

"*David.*"

The boy closed his eyes. "Everybody keeps calling me a hero!"

"You *are* a hero, David. You saved your sister's life."

"We were only alone for *one day*."

"I imagine that was the most difficult day—and night—of your life. You must have been terrified. A grown man would have been. But in spite of your fear, you chose the right path."

His nephew made a sound halfway between a scoff and a choke.

"You could have stayed at Independence Rock and waited in vain for help to come to you. You could have tried to follow the other wagons and become lost. You could have shot at those Indians the moment you saw them—they would have attacked you in kind. You could have been prideful and tried to cross the Platte on your own. Instead, you made all the right choices, David. I don't think one boy in a hundred could have done what you did."

His nephew did not reply, but his breathing was becoming ragged.

Joseph knelt and looked up into the boy's anguished face. "There was nothing you could have done to save your father or your mother or your brother. Is that what's troubling you?"

David pulled up his legs and crawled away from Joseph using his one good hand. He thumped down from the bed, ran to the nearest window, and wrested aside one of the blue curtains.

"David?"

"I can't…breathe…"

Joseph crossed to the window and helped him lift the lower sash. David fisted his good hand and raised it. For a moment, Joseph feared he'd break this glass too. But the boy only leaned his arm and his forehead against the panes, sucking in the night air as if he'd been drowning.

Was David remembering his father's death? Joseph recalled

Tessa's mention of nightmares. Perhaps Joseph had been wrong to remind the boy. But Joseph knew what guilt looked like. He'd encountered it many times: a child who was certain he'd caused his parent's death through some misdeed.

"David?" Joseph asked as the January cold seeped into them. "What is it you think you did wrong?"

"Everybody also says how much I remind them of you," his nephew muttered. "But I'm nothing like you. You're perfect, and I'm…"

"I am *far* from perfect, David. I sin every day, in thought if not in word or deed. We *all* stumble. We all need God's grace." He touched David's shoulder through the quilted dressing-gown. "Do you need to make a Confession?"

Still leaning against the window, heedless of the cold, the boy shook his head. "I made one in Missouri, after we got back."

"The Priest gave you Absolution, and you did your Penance?"

"I…" Sobs broke up his words. "I hated my brother. For a couple hours, I hated him—I *wanted* him to die, because I thought: 'If it weren't for him, everything would be different. Mama would still be alive…' And then—" His nephew's tears splashed on the window-sill. "How can I ever be sorry enough for something like that?"

Joseph shivered at the winter air pouring through the window. "Selfish thoughts are a grave sin, but they cannot end someone's life, David. You repented, and that is what matters. Through the Sacrament of Penance we are forgiven forever, no matter what sins we have committed. We need never think of those sins again. They have been washed 'whiter than snow.'" Joseph rubbed his arms to fend off the chill.

His nephew leaned back from the window. He wiped his eyes and his nose on the sleeve of his dressing gown, then struggled to close the window with one hand. Joseph helped him. David did not turn his head; but in their reflection, the boy met his eyes at last.

It was almost like looking back at his own younger self. Eerie, yet somehow comforting. Like all Priests, Joseph would die without issue; and yet… He smiled. "When people say you remind them of me, I think they mean we look alike. Is that so terrible?"

He'd meant it in jest, hoping for a smile in return. Instead, David dropped his gaze again. In the silence, his undamaged hand crept upwards to tug the thick black curls at the nape of his neck, nervously, perhaps unconsciously.

Finally, Joseph understood. No wonder the boy had used a hairbrush to destroy his dressing glass. Joseph remembered how critically he'd examined himself, those first weeks after Ninon's revelation. Seminary had been a refuge in more ways than one: it had no mirrors.

Joseph strode to the bedchamber door and closed it, then returned to his nephew. He clasped his hands in front of him. He must do this carefully. "David, how much do you know about your great-grandmother? My father's mother?"

"All of it. Mama told me, before she died. I know we're... That my great-grandmother was a..." The boy finished in a whisper: "Slave." His eyes pleaded with Joseph to deny it. When Joseph only nodded, David looked away again. "Sophie doesn't know."

Seven was too young, Joseph decided. Ten had been too young. "Perhaps we should wait and tell her when she is older?"

David nodded.

"You see yourself differently now? You don't recognize yourself?"

Another nod.

Joseph sighed. "This is our cross to bear, David. As you grow older, you will have to decide how cautious you wish to be. Whom you wish to entrust with our secret. Whether or in what circumstances you will marry."

David looked toward the hall. "There are so many negroes here..."

"Your conduct toward them should be that of a gentleman and a Christian—the same way you should treat all men: with the respect due them as children of God. That includes the person you see in the mirror, David. This may not be the form we would have chosen for ourselves, but it is the form God chose to give us.

Remember, vanity is a mortal sin." Joseph glanced again at his own reflection in the window panes. "In a way, God has blessed us. There have been saints who *prayed* for ugliness, so that no one would desire them and they could offer themselves completely to God. For now, I urge you to remember the advice Saint Paul gave to the Corinthians: However humble, our bodies are the temples of the Holy Ghost. Will you promise me, David, not to harm yourself again?"

Timidly, the boy met his gaze. "Yes, Father."

"I will ask one final thing of you, David. You must apologize to Tessa and your sister."

His nephew followed him into the hall. Sophie was hovering near her threshold. Joseph led her by the hand down the stairs. They found Tessa in the parlor.

David murmured: "I'm sorry I destroyed the mirror. I'm sorry I frightened you. Can you forgive me?"

"Of course we do!" Tessa knelt down to him and clasped his good hand. "But why—"

Joseph cleared his throat. "It's best to put it behind us."

Tessa frowned at him.

Joseph knew she wanted an explanation for the boy's behavior. He couldn't give her one.

She looked back to David. "It wasn't because you're unhappy here?" Tessa hesitated. "If you want to live with your grandfather instead... Please understand: I want you to stay, but if you're lonely or uncomfortable..."

David shook his head. "I'm not— I want them back, but it's not *your* fault. I want to stay."

"*I* like it here," Sophie put in, clutching Mignon. Tessa smiled with relief and hugged girl and kitten both.

"Now, what did you want to say to me earlier, *ma petite?*" Joseph asked his niece.

Sophie glanced at David, then lowered her eyes. "Um... I..." When she found her words, they came in a rush. "God says we should honor our father and mother. Is it a sin if I love Aunt Tessa as much as I loved Mama?"

Joseph laughed. "Love is *never* a sin," he assured Sophie. "And Tessa is your foster-mother, so the Commandment applies to her as well. You *should* love and honor Tessa. And Mr. Stratford." Edward had not given the children permission to use his Christian name. "Does that answer your question?"

Sophie nodded. Mignon was squirming, so she set him down and ran to find his feather toy.

David asked permission to retire to his chamber. Joseph and Tessa granted it simultaneously.

As they watched him climb the stairs, Tessa murmured: "'Love is never a sin.' What a beautiful sentiment."

"*Love* is never a sin," Joseph qualified. "*Lust* always is."

"Of course," she whispered, and turned away.

PART VI
LAMENTATIONS

1842-1843

CHARLESTON

But though He cause grief, yet will He have compassion
according to the multitude of His mercies.

— Lamentations 3:32

CHAPTER 37

Fifteen years have I been with him, ten of them were years of happiness. I enjoyed his confidence, to me he unbosomed his cares, we lay down at the same time, we arose at the same... I alone am desolate, tho' all are afflicted.
— Father Richard Baker, 1842 letter

To see death approaching made it no easier. Since Rome, Joseph had watched Bishop England's vitality ebbing away. This last year had been worst of all. His Lordship drove himself to exhaustion. He led retreats for the clergy, the laity, the Sisters of Mercy. He made another tour of his diocese. He crossed the Atlantic again to raise funds and recruit Priests and nuns.

He also made another visit to Philadelphia to assist at an episcopal consecration. Castalio accompanied his master as he had on so many other journeys; but this one was different. Bishop England allowed Castalio to disappear. Philadelphia had long been a haven for runaway slaves.

Everywhere His Lordship travelled, Catholics and Protestants alike clamored to hear him speak. They would crowd into the churches and halls till many had to be turned away. He could not refuse any opportunity to bring souls to God. Even in his fatigue, he was transcendent. *Was this what it was like to witness Christ preaching His Sermon on the Mount?* his listeners wondered. Certainly that was Joseph's reaction.

In December, Bishop England had returned to Charleston in a state of collapse. At first, it seemed he would rally as he had so many times before. He was barely fifty-five years old. Surely God would not take him so soon. Now and again during Advent, His Lordship managed to celebrate Mass or preach in the cathedral. But his once-vibrant body was now stooped, his once-resounding voice now hoarse.

Soon after Christmas, Bishop England became unable to rise from his bed. For three long months, his diocese waited anxiously for either his recovery or the grace of a happy death. Not only the Catholic churches but also Protestant congregations and the Synagogue offered prayers for him.

By Holy Week, they abandoned their last hopes. His Lordship's principal physician consulted with Joseph's father and other doctors, but nothing more could be done. Bishop England's affliction was complex, though it most resembled dysentery. That the holiest man Joseph had ever known should be felled by refractory bowels seemed a ridiculous injustice.

Through Father Lynch, His Lordship dictated his wishes to the Archbishop: Father Baker should be his successor. Joseph often returned from his duties to hear the younger Irishman conversing with their Bishop in low voices. His Lordship left his friend a great burden, but Father Baker knew its weight: he had served as Vicar General for years now during the Bishop's travels.

His Lordship called the seminarians and the Sisters to his bedside in turn. He spoke of his own sister, Joanna. Stranger's fever had taken her fifteen years before, yet in these final days, the memory of her goodness returned to him. "I should have been a better man—a better Priest—if she had remained here to guide me," Bishop England lamented.

Every evening before he retired, Joseph knelt to kiss His Lordship's episcopal ring. Such power had flowed through those fingers once—the power that had made Joseph a Priest. It was painful now to see that skeletal hand, that sunken face. *This will be me*, Joseph thought selfishly on the day he turned thirty. He knew he would not serve in Charleston forever. In another thirty years, he too would succumb to exhaustion; he too would die alone, thousands of miles from his family.

"So much I have attempted over these two decades has ended in failure," Bishop England observed, when Father Baker had gone. "The mission to Haiti, the school for black children… When my cathedral was first erected, it was simply pitiful. Now, it is dilapidated. This very building is falling apart." He glanced to the stained ceiling. Though His Lordship's face remained white as death, his eyes brightened then, and he managed a smile. "But I look at you, Joseph, and I know I have done one thing right: I have enabled an uncertain boy to become a capable Priest—and a teacher of Priests." Weakly, Bishop England squeezed Joseph's hand. "You are a credit to your race, son—living proof that through the grace of God, anything is possible."

Joseph could only nod.

In April, all the Priests from the cathedral, St. Mary's, and St. Patrick's gathered to celebrate a Solemn High Mass for their Bishop. Afterwards, they processed across the Biblical garden to his bedchamber in order to offer him the Last Sacraments. One final time, Father Baker helped His Lordship vest in his episcopal robes.

Propped against pillows, Bishop England addressed them: "Tell my people that I love them… Be with them, be of them, win them to God. Guide and instruct them. Watch as having to render an account of their souls, that you may do it with joy and not grief. … Remember me, I beseech you, in your devotions…"

Joseph and his fellow Priests promised to obey. As they knelt around the episcopal bed, many of them were weeping. Their Bishop blessed each of them one last time.

Before dawn the next morning, his great soul went to God. His

Lordship's final word on Earth began in a moan and ended in a gurgling cry. It was: "Mercy!"

All across the city, bells tolled the news of Bishop England's passing. Businesses remained closed that day, and courts did not meet. Even the ships in the harbor hung their flags at half-mast. Theirs was a missionary Church in a hostile land; such an honor was unprecedented. They laid His Lordship to rest beneath his episcopal chair in their sad little cathedral.

His beloved sister Joanna was reinterred beside him. "Now," Father Baker murmured over them that evening, "they may commingle their dust in death as they did their hearts in life." There was a strange catch to his voice, as if he envied them. "They only await the blast of the Archangel's trumpet, at which they are to spring forth from their lowly bed, and hand in hand go forth to glory. May you and I meet them there."

"Amen," Joseph whispered.

CHAPTER 38

The mortality among foreigners during the summer months at Charleston is incredibly great. He, whose veins glowed but yesterday with health, shall today be undergoing the agonies of the damned.

— John Davis, *Travels of Four Years and a Half in the United States of America, 1798-1802*

Sometimes, as Joseph made his parish visits, he would cut through Longitude Lane between Church Street and East Bay. For much of the way, the fine old brick wall draped with climbing Noisettes was all that separated him from Tessa's garden. And then, for a moment, nothing separated them—only the narrow gate and its claire-voie half-hidden by petals. He might have curled his fingers through the opening and touched someone standing on the other side. The delicate tracery of the wrought iron reminded Joseph of the rose windows he'd seen in French cathedrals. Here, there was no stained glass, yet the claire-voie framed splashes of color nonetheless: glimpses of Tessa's flowers.

No properly bred Charleston lady dirtied her hands, just as no properly bred Charleston gentleman peered into a lady's garden.

But Tessa was Irish; she loved the land. He was French—and she'd invited him to look. She wanted that sliver of garden to be beautiful.

"It's like a glimpse into Paradise," Joseph assured her. "Like the Garden of Eden."

"There's even a fig tree!" Tessa laughed. "Should I plant a pomegranate?"

David inhabited the garden only if he had a book in hand; but just as Tessa had hoped, Sophie played there often. In May, Joseph was passing the garden gate when he heard his niece giggling on the other side. He paused to peek through the claire-voie. If he leaned in, he could just see the statue of the Blessed Virgin, crowned now with blossoms as they'd done at the cathedral. Nearby, Tessa was trimming the thorns from roses and then handing each flower to Sophie, who tucked them into another crown.

"If 'tis not for you..." Tessa mused aloud, "is it for your brother?"

Joseph's niece shook her head and giggled again. "He'd look silly!" Sophie finished the crown and held it up proudly. "This one is for *you*, Aunt Tessa!"

She smiled as bright as the sunshine. Tessa removed her bonnet and bowed her head so the little girl could crown her.

Joseph smiled too, before he went on his way. To anyone else peering through the claire-voie—though he hoped no one did— Tessa and Sophie might have been mother and daughter. They *were* mother and daughter.

WHEN JOSEPH VISITED his niece and nephew on the Feast of the Most Holy Trinity, Sophie met him breathlessly at the front gate on Church Street. "Uncle Joseph! I'm going to have a baby brother after all!" Sophie grabbed one of his hands and towed him toward the piazza steps.

"Is that so?" Joseph stammered. He'd been secretly relieved that Tessa and her husband no longer shared a bedchamber. But apparently, their two separate countries still merged on occasion.

At the top of the steps, Sophie nodded eagerly. "Aunt Tessa told us this morning. Grandpa thinks he'll be born around Christmas—just like baby Jesus!"

Reclining on a chaise-longue, Tessa smiled nervously. "It might be a baby *sister* instead."

"That would be even better!" the girl declared.

After Sophie darted off again, Tessa murmured: "Or it might not remain with us at all..." She kept her eyes on her bodice. "I didn't want to tell the children—not yet. But they could see I was ill. And I keep thinking: 'This is the seventh. Perhaps he—or she—will be lucky.' Perhaps Our Lord will allow me this miracle." She looked up to Joseph. "I've been clinging to that verse in the Psalms: 'He causeth the barren woman to be a joyful mother of children.' The morning sickness has been worse than with any of the others. Your father says that's actually a *good* sign. In all other ways, my health has been *better* since we came to Church Street. Your father speculated that it might have been something about the old house, that... He is hopeful. Cautious, but hopeful."

"Aren't you a seventh child yourself?" Joseph remembered.

Tessa nodded. "The Irish would say that the seventh child of a seventh child is destined for great things. That he or she will be a healer."

"You know we Priests do not subscribe to superstition," Joseph smiled. "But this child *will* be blessed: I can promise you that." He himself blessed it immediately.

ON THE FEAST OF THE ASSUMPTION, as Pharaoh admitted Joseph to the Stratfords' entry hall, their greetings were interrupted by quarrelling on the second floor. The butler appeared uneasy, and the harsh words plummeting down to them made communication impossible. Finally, Pharaoh simply bowed and retreated. Joseph supposed he should wait on the piazza. He turned back to the door.

Above him, Edward demanded: "Do you expect me to predict the future now?"

"This is August and we are in Charleston! There is a risk *every* year!" Compared to her husband's, Tessa's voice was hushed, but every bit as passionate. "I said it months ago: 'We should take David and Sophie to your sister's in Greenville till fever season has passed'!"

Joseph's hand paused on the doorknob, and he held his breath.

"And then you admitted you were with child again!" Edward shouted. "You know what the mountain roads are like! Are you *trying* to kill this baby?"

Even a floor away, Joseph heard Tessa's sharp intake of breath. "How can you ask me that?"

"Because you seem to care more about a dead man's children than you do about mine!"

"David and Sophie are our responsibility now! And you don't seem to care about them at all!"

Edward sounded like he was speaking through clenched teeth. "After everything I have done for those brats—"

"Throwing money at David and Sophie is not the same as being a father to them!"

For a moment, Edward only fumed incoherently. "They were born in Charleston! They're supposed to be protected from stranger's fever!"

"Only if they have a mild case and survive it!"

"Maybe that's what this is!"

A door slammed, and then the house went eerily quiet. Only Tessa's sobbing drifted down to him. Finally a small thump drew Joseph's attention to the parlor. Mignon appeared on the threshold and mewed up at him, as if he were asking: *Is it safe to come out now?* In the next moment, Joseph realized David had been sitting in the parlor a few yards away all this time. The boy must have heard everything. Joseph stepped toward his nephew.

David kept his eyes on Mignon. "Sophie is sick," the boy explained. "We've already sent for Grandpa."

"Stranger's fever?" Joseph whispered.

"Aunt Tessa thinks so."

Joseph closed his eyes in dread. But perhaps in this one instance, the children's black blood would be a boon: far more negroes than whites survived the onslaught of this disease.

Over his niece, Joseph prayed:

> "O God...extend Thy hand upon this girl who is afflicted at this tender age; and being restored to health, may she reach maturity, and ceaselessly render Thee a service of gratitude and fidelity..."

JOSEPH'S FATHER CONFIRMED THEIR WORST FEARS. He administered quinine and rhubarb. Still Sophie's skin took on the jaundice that gave stranger's fever its other name: yellow fever, the scourge of port cities from Philadelphia to Havana. To prevent another epidemic, Charleston's militia dragged their cannons through the streets, firing off gunpowder to drive the miasma from the air.

No one knew what caused stranger's fever (animal or vegetable putrefaction? some combination of heat and humidity?) but most scientists were convinced the disease was not contagious. Decades ago, a doctor had attempted repeatedly to infect himself without success. So Tessa defied her husband: despite her advancing pregnancy, she remained at Sophie's bedside throughout that awful week. Every day, she assisted Hannah in bathing the girl's body with the coolest water they could find.

In her delirium, Sophie murmured: "But I want to be a big sister..." and "We can't *leave* him! He's our brother!" For a while, this puzzled Joseph—was she speaking of baby Ian?—but finally he dismissed it. Joseph knew many children could not accept the finality of death.

Even he struggled to do so, as the fever abated and then returned without mercy. At last Sophie coughed up the black vomit that meant she'd reached the crisis: the girl would either recover or...

Joseph anointed his niece, but she was too ill to receive Viaticum or make a final Confession. She was all of eight years old. Surely no mortal sins lay upon such a young soul.

"I cannot bear to watch her suffering like this," Tessa wept. She fisted a hand against her rounding bodice. "I thought it was agony to lose my babies. But I never *knew* them—not like I've known Sophie. They never embraced me. They never called out to me. This is worse." Tessa turned away from Joseph, shaking her head. "I never should have adopted David and Sophie. My reasons weren't pure. I should have known this would happen. I am like poison, and—"

"You are balm, Tessa, not poison." Joseph allowed himself to caress her face, but only for an instant. "I've seen the difference you've made in the children's lives these past months—especially Sophie's. Her fate is in God's hands, not yours. It always has been. *He* will decide whether to take her."

H℮ TOOK HER.

Joseph prayed over his niece's coffin:

> "God, Who art the Lover of holy purity, Thou hast now in Thy great mercy called the soul of this child to the Kingdom of Heaven. Deign, likewise, to dispense Thy mercy to us, so that we too may possess happiness without end…"

In the seven years of his Priesthood, Joseph had celebrated the Rites of Burial for hundreds of children. None had been as difficult as Sophie. She had survived so much. Two thousand miles from her parents' graves, she had found contentment and a second chance, only to fall like this, barely a year later… Saint Paul's words rang in Joseph's head: *"How incomprehensible are His judgments!"*

The Lazare tomb would stand empty no longer. In the wall of the mausoleum, beneath the cenotaph for her parents and baby brother, Sophie's coffin looked tiny inside its crypt. David stood staring at it for so long, Joseph feared he never intended to leave. His father urged Tessa and Hélène to retire from the August heat, so Joseph remained alone with his nephew.

When he touched the boy's shoulder, David muttered: "It was all for nothing. I did it for nothing! I should have just stayed at Independence Rock and let us all die together!"

"David!" Joseph turned the boy away from his sister's coffin and knelt before him on the floor of the mausoleum. "Your bravery wasn't 'for nothing'! I cannot tell you how much it meant to us—to every member of your family and to Tessa—to have known Sophie, even for a little while. Her faith and resilience were shining examples to the rest of us." He grasped his nephew's limp arms. "Most of all, David, you got *yourself* to safety. You have a bright future here! You can go to medical school and save the lives of thousands of people like you saved Sophie's."

His nephew scoffed. "For thirteen whole months?"

"Every one of those days is a gift, David. We must not say that Sophie was 'only eight' when she died. We must say your sister had eight long years full of adventures and love, and now she has gone ahead of us to Heaven where she will never know pain or sadness again. She is with your mother and father and baby Ian—with the God Who made her and loves her more than any of us ever could."

David glared at him. "What's the use of becoming a doctor, then? Why don't we all just stop eating and go to Heaven, if it's so wonderful?"

"Because Our Lord has placed each of us on this Earth for a reason, David. Only He knows when we have fulfilled our mission and are ready to go to Him."

"What about babies who die?" David challenged. "What is *their* mission?"

For a moment, Joseph averted his eyes. "I know the death of an infant is hard to accept. But God's ways are not our ways. Someday, we will understand. For now, we must trust that He will make all things beautiful in their time."

THE DAY AFTER SOPHIE'S FUNERAL, Tessa felt her baby quicken. Never before had she carried a child so long. Soon Joseph's father heard its heartbeat through his stethoscope. Everything seemed *normal.* They still prayed fervently.

CHAPTER 39

There is no experience of a physician more trying than cases of flooding. ... In a moment [they] change a scene of rejoicing and happiness into one fraught with danger and filled with horror.

— Augustus Gardner, "A Treatise on Uterine Hemorrhage in all its forms" (1855)

"When I first told David I was with child," Tessa had confided to Joseph, "he was terrified. It was as if I'd told him I was dying." Yet in the wake of Sophie's passing, the boy grew closer to his foster-mother. Joseph's father had confined Tessa to her bed in these final months of pregnancy—he was worried about pains in her abdomen. When Joseph visited, he usually found his nephew seated at Tessa's bedside, reading to her from Cooper or Irving, even Austen. If she slept during the day, David would bring his schoolwork into the room and watch over her so that Hannah could attend to other duties.

When Joseph praised his nephew's attentiveness, the boy answered simply: "She needs me." Even at eleven, David must understand that Edward was poor company. (Joseph had heard Tessa's husband reading Dickens to her once. Edward might as well have been reciting the plantation's account books.) Hélène would have liked to sit with her friend every day; but she needed rest herself. And Tessa's mother was an ocean away.

Joseph visited as often as he could. Since Tessa could no longer come to the cathedral, Father Baker gave Joseph permission to celebrate Mass in her home. David assisted him. His Latin was as good as Joseph's. He thought it a pity that his nephew did not wish to serve at the altar in a more formal capacity.

If Edward was out, Joseph would play Tessa's piano afterwards, so the music would drift up the spiral stairs to her bedchamber. Mostly Schumann, Chopin, and Liszt; but as they entered Advent, Joseph played French carols as well. These were the baby's favorite, Tessa said.

David would help by turning the pages and occasionally joining in the singing. Usually his nephew was so timid, Joseph doubted Tessa could hear him at all. But when they sang "Un flambeau, Jeannette, Isabelle," the boy cried out "Ah! Que la Mère est belle!" with such enthusiasm, Tessa's laughter left no doubt that she'd heard.

The mother certainly *was* beautiful. Tessa was still in mourning for Sophie; she was bedridden; and the greatest trial of her life loomed closer every day. Yet Joseph always found Tessa smiling. More than three years had passed since the dark day she'd cut off her hair. Her plait fell nearly to her waist now, looking golden against the black of her dressing gown.

Following one of his little concerts, Tessa whispered to Joseph: "Don't tell your father, but your medicine is better even than his."

Joseph chuckled.

"'Tis right, that Priests are called 'Physicians of the Soul.' But to me, you are far more, Father." Tessa dropped her eyes to her tray. She picked up a spoon and stirred her tea rather vigorously. "In ancient Ireland, a trusted Priest was called a 'soul-friend.' 'Tis a lovely expression, don't you think?"

Joseph nodded. *Soul-friend*, he repeated in his head. *Soul-friend. This relationship does not involve bodies at all.* Yet his palm longed to feel the child stirring inside her; his ears ached for one more word from her lips; even his nose yearned to bury itself in her neck and inhale her perspiration and her new perfume. It was gardenia, exotic and beloved at once. He'd thought the pull strong before, but the sight of Tessa *increasing* did something else to him entirely—her gravity was becoming inescapable.

Even that thought proved his wickedness. Tessa was not Potiphar's wife; she did not seek to entrap him. Her tenderness toward him was that of a sister for a brother—nothing more. Tessa was as innocent as the babe she carried. This unholy desire was his alone.

TESSA'S PAINS BEGAN not on Christmas Eve but on the morning of Epiphany. Joseph wished he could install himself on a prie-Dieu in the Stratfords' parlor immediately, so that he could entreat God every moment for her safety and that of her child. But as a Priest, his time was not his own.

Now more than ever before, Joseph's work overwhelmed him. Technically, he remained a curate, but Father Baker had authorized him to perform most of the duties of a pastor, while Father Baker performed most of the duties of a Bishop—without the dignity, authority, or grace of that title. Nearly a year after Bishop England's death, their diocese remained widowed. Archbishop Eccleston had barred Father Baker's appointment to the episcopate, and no one else had been found yet. Perhaps it was Father Baker's relative youth impeding his advancement (he was thirty-six), his delicate health (the curse of malaria), or the rumor that he and Bishop England—

Calumny. Joseph refused to believe it.

Moreover, Epiphany was a holy day of obligation. They celebrated not only the Magi recognizing the Christ Child but also Christ's Baptism and His first miracle. During the High Mass, Joseph announced all the moveable feasts for the coming year. Afterward, he hurried through the parish, blessing as many homes as he could.

Since Tessa was confined to her bedchamber, David and Edward provided the responses in their house. The boy did so solemnly, Tessa's husband reluctantly. Joseph concluded the prayers in the entry hall:

> "O Lord, bless this home, that in it there may be *health*, chastity, self-conquest, humility, goodness, mildness, obedience to Thy commandments, and thanksgiving to God the Father, Son, and Holy Spirit."

Then Joseph blessed each room. As he approached Tessa's bedchamber, Joseph heard her moaning and his father noting the spacing of her contractions. The door was ajar, but Joseph peered cautiously inside. Propped against a mound of pillows, Tessa was decently covered by her dressing gown and the sheets. Hélène sat beside her, holding her friend's hand.

"It's perfectly safe," Joseph's father assured them as he pulled the door wider. "She'll be in the first stage of labor for hours yet."

Tessa greeted Joseph, Edward, and David with a valiant smile. Even in pain, she was radiant.

Joseph sprinkled Epiphany water and swung his thurible, filling the bedchamber with the fragrance of myrrh. "Lord, bless this room where we both rest and labor"—he glanced at Tessa and returned her smile—"and let us dwell here together in peace."

Before he proceeded to the next room, Tessa called in a wavering voice: "You'll come back, Father? After Vespers?"

Joseph nodded. "I promise."

Finally, he took a piece of blessed chalk and wrote above the front door

$$18 \, C + M + B \, 43$$

so that the three Magi, the Saints Caspar, Melchior, and Balthasar, would watch over this home in the coming year of 1843 —today, most of all.

Joseph had blessed the Stratfords' home last year as well; but he'd noticed that the chalk above the door disappeared shortly thereafter. Edward had ordered one of the slaves to wipe it away,

Tessa told Joseph—her husband had not wanted his Protestant friends to laugh at him. Joseph could not help but wonder if Sophie had paid the penalty for this impiety.

Throughout that long day, Joseph's thoughts remained with Tessa. Between blessing other homes and visiting other invalids, he prayed for her in every spare moment. Night had settled before he was able to keep his promise to return.

Even with the windows shut tight against the cold, Joseph heard Tessa screaming from Church Street. He knew this was how it must be—that he himself had come into the world through such agony. As God had promised Eve in punishment for her sin: "I will multiply thy sorrows: in pain shalt thou bring forth children."

Still Tessa's cries unsettled his soul. Saint Augustine had written of the Blessed Virgin: "She conceived without carnal pleasure and therefore gave birth without pain." If only that principle applied to all women.

Joseph set down his portmanteau in the entry hall—he saw with relief that his blessing remained above the door—and Pharaoh took his overcoat. Joseph left the pyx hanging around his neck in its pouch, because it contained the Body of Christ. Since he'd come from other sick calls, Joseph had brought everything necessary for the Last Sacraments; but he prayed he would need none of it here.

Liam and David waited in the parlor, trying to play chess. Edward sat pondering a glass of whiskey. Mignon was curled up by the fire, but his ear twitched at another cry from the floor above.

Joseph looked back to David. The memory of his mother's death must be pressing down on him with every scream. Joseph laid a hand on his nephew's shoulder. "David, let me take you to your grandmother's."

The boy shook his head.

"I already offered," Liam explained.

"I should be here," David murmured, "if Aunt Tessa..."

Joseph knelt on the prie-Dieu and led them in prayers. At least, he led his brother-in-law and nephew. Edward took up *The Spirit of the Times*, a newspaper about horse racing and fox hunting.

Joseph invoked the Blessed Virgin; Saint Teresa; and Saint

Margaret, patroness of women in labor. He begged the intercession of Saint Anne, who had thought herself barren only to become the mother of Our Lady herself. Saint Elizabeth too seemed appropriate. Tessa was hardly elderly—she was but twenty-six. Nonetheless, this day had a lifetime of loss and hope behind it. This child was still a miracle.

At a sudden assault on the windows, Joseph started. The jalousies and shutters were closed, but Edward paced out to the piazza and back. "It's sleet," he reported.

Joseph remembered his parting from Father Baker earlier that evening. *"Come and fetch me, if Mrs. Stratford requires the Last Sacraments,"* he'd told Joseph. And then he'd sneezed. Joseph suspected Father Baker was coming down with another cold.

Tessa would not need her confessor, Joseph assured himself. She would bear a healthy baby, and she would live to see it grow and thrive—

A scream louder and longer than any of the others arrested all his thoughts. A terrifying silence followed. Sleet was still flinging itself at the windows; surely it was only that they could hear nothing above the clamor of the storm. Surely in Tessa's bedchamber, the baby was crying out indignantly and everyone was rejoicing.

The long hand on the mantle clock crept around the face. Ten minutes. Twenty. *Forty.* Still no perceivable sounds trickled down to them. A slave added wood to the fire, then changed out the lamp in the hall. Edward poured himself more whiskey and offered some to Liam, who accepted. David hid his face in his hands, and he began rocking.

At a noise in the entrance hall, Joseph leapt to his feet—even as a maid darted past the parlor into the fury of the storm. Joseph stood gaping through the open door. The young negress had been carrying a washstand pitcher. When she hurried back up the piazza steps, the pitcher was full of ice pellets she must have gathered from the ground. The maid shoved the door closed and did not pause till Joseph blocked her path. "Please—will you tell us what's happening?"

The negress glanced up, hesitated, then replied: "It's a little girl."

The parlor's occupants must have been listening; behind him, Joseph heard Edward groan. He distracted Joseph just long enough that the maid was able to slip past him. Joseph's mind overflowed with questions. Why did they need the ice? Why had the negress not mentioned Tessa? Did her silence mean Tessa was in danger? That she was already—

When it came to it, the maid had not even assured them that Tessa's daughter was healthy. Joseph's father knew to call on him the instant he feared for the child's life, didn't he? Or had this child been born dead like all the others? Was the ice to preserve its body?

Above him, another scream rent the silence. Tessa was still alive. For how long? Birth did not end the peril to mother or child. Cathy and Ian's deaths had been proof of that.

Joseph did not make it back to the parlor. He fell to his knees right there in the hall. In staying closer to Tessa, nearly beneath her, he felt as if his prayers might be more effective. *Spare her, Lord,* he pleaded. *Spare her daughter...*

Was that the protesting voice of the newborn, or only his imagination playing tricks on him?

He repeated the Blessing of an Expectant Mother: "Preserve Thy handmaid as she pleads for the life of her child... Let Thy gentle hand, like that of a skilled physician, aid her delivery..."

Joseph did not know how long he crouched there. It felt as though the storms inside and without had been raging for hours before heavy footsteps finally descended the stairs. He looked up to see his father.

In the flickering light of the lamp he carried, his father looked ghastly. He had washed his arms—they were still damp—but his rolled sleeves remained blood-stained. Framed by hair that had never looked more grey, his face was as weary as a corpse. Edward, Liam, and David heard his footsteps and came into the hall. Joseph's father leaned against the stair rail for support. His eyes skimmed over each of them and alighted on the floor-cloth. "I am optimistic about the child. She is small, but strong."

Liam hesitated, then asked for the rest of them: "And Tessa?"

Joseph's father raised his eyes again, but they settled nowhere. "She's still in the third stage of labor," he said as if it were an apology. "Her condition is precarious. I cannot *tear* the placenta away without risking another hemorrhage and syncope; but—" He glanced at his grandson and stopped. "I have done everything within my power. She has regained consciousness, at least." He noticed the pyx around Joseph's neck. "Do you have what you need to administer the Last Rites?"

Joseph remained kneeling, as if rising were capitulation—an acknowledgement that the end had truly come. He struggled to swallow his dread. "I brought the Blessed Sacrament and the holy oil; but we need Father Baker..." Joseph looked toward the window behind the staircase. Sleet was still rattling the shutters. The seminary was seven streets away, and it must be nearly midnight.

"There isn't time, son."

David made a muffled sound of distress. His face crumpled, and Joseph knew his nephew was trying not to cry. Liam put his arm around the boy's shoulders as silent tears descended his own cheeks. Edward disappeared into the parlor, but his sob carried out to them.

With effort, Joseph rose. He promised his brother-in-law and nephew: "After Tessa makes her Confession, I'll summon you and Mr. Stratford for the rest of the Rites." Numbly Joseph gathered his portmanteau and followed his father up the stairs. He paused partway to whisper: "Is she still in pain?"

His father nodded. "More than you or I will ever know. I've given her as much laudanum as I dare, but she insisted I keep her awake."

Hannah was helping Hélène stagger into the spare bedroom. His sister's eyes were already bloodshot, and her nose was leaking. She gripped Joseph's hand. "If there are prayers you were saving for me, Joseph—*please*, say them for her."

Tessa's gardenia perfume reached him before he entered her bedchamber. He suspected Hélène had sprayed it to disguise the room's less pleasant smells. The tangs of blood and something even more elemental saturated the warm air. Other odors met him too:

vinegar, the pine logs in the fireplace, and rose water. The maid he'd seen earlier was gathering sheets from the floor—sheets more red than white.

Bolstered by pillows, Tessa lay on her left side, her back near the edge of the four-poster bed with its gathered green curtains. Her plait was tidy; someone must have rebraided it. Tessa's long legs seemed to be drawn up beneath the fresh sheet, which barely reached her waist. Her left arm was stretched out across the mattress, her head tilted downwards. She wore only a chemise, and as Joseph rounded the bed, he realized its buttons were undone— Tessa's newborn daughter lay not in her cradle but curled against her mother's bare breast.

Joseph looked away, but not quickly enough. They might have *warned* him. He set down his portmanteau and busied himself with clearing the small table he used for an altar.

His father followed him into the bedchamber. "Can I help you with anything, Joseph?"

He nodded at the table. "We'll need to bring this into Tessa's sight line." Estimating this required Joseph to glance back at her.

Tessa's right arm cradled her daughter, her fingers caressing the small bald head. "She fussed and fussed, until they returned her to me," Tessa explained. Her voice was hoarse, breathless with wonder, and weighted with grief. "She wasn't satisfied while a scrap of linen separated us; but the moment she touched my skin, she calmed."

Joseph's father smiled, but worry pinched the corners of his eyes. "She knows her mother." He helped Joseph move the table. "Do you need anything else?"

"No; thank you." Joseph opened the little wall cabinet that contained Tessa's altar furniture, the pieces he used when he said Mass here.

Tessa tried to say something else, but it became a cough instead. Her daughter whimpered at the disturbance. "I am sorry, *a chuisle mo chroí*," Tessa soothed. "I will try very hard not to cough or scream anymore."

Joseph's father reached for the water pitcher at the bedside, but Joseph said: "Wait." Quickly he retrieved the bottle of holy water from his portmanteau and poured some into the gilded spoon-cup from Tessa's cabinet.

His father squinted at the holy water with suspicion. "How fresh is that?"

"We blessed it last night at the Vigil." Which his father would know, if he ever came to anything but morning Mass. Joseph leaned over the bed to give Tessa the holy water, holding the gilded cup in one hand and supporting her head with the other.

She drank every drop. "Thank you, Father," she whispered, before Joseph lowered her head back to the pillow. Her skin was nearly as pale as the linen.

Still frowning, Joseph's father crossed around the bed, crouched, and peered beneath the sheet with Joseph right there. As if this were not disconcerting enough, he spoke to them while in this position. "You must call me the moment you see or sense any change."

Joseph turned back to the cabinet and began preparing the altar. He spread a white cloth on the table, set the pyx atop it, and genu-flected to the Body of Christ.

When he glanced toward the bed again, his father had replaced the sheet and was bending to kiss Tessa's temple. "Please, *ma belle*, try not to move." When had his father started addressing Tessa with terms of endearment? His tone was exactly the one he used with Hélène.

Tessa disobeyed him almost immediately. Her daughter was stir-ring and making small unhappy noises. Tessa turned her head toward Joseph's father to ask: "Is she hungry, do you think?"

"Let's see." Without either permission or warning, Joseph's father leaned over Tessa and grabbed her breast.

At least, this seemed to be what he was doing. Joseph saw it only out of the corner of his eye while he lit the altar candles.

"*There* we are," his father declared. "That didn't take her long at all." He leaned back. "This may even help you with the final contraction." Pitching his voice a little louder, he returned his atten-tion to Joseph. "You'll need to watch Clare—make sure she doesn't become smothered or tangled."

"Of course," Joseph stammered. He didn't think he could

refuse, even though watching the baby also meant watching Tessa's breast.

"I'll be just outside." His father closed the door behind him.

Joseph was alone with Tessa and her daughter. All he wanted to do was admire them, this perfect tableau of Madonna and child. He thought he understood a glimmer of what his patron saint had felt, two thousand years ago inside that Bethlehem cave, as he watched over the beloved child who would never be his and the beloved woman he could never have. He had a duty to perform; that was all. A duty that had nothing whatsoever to do with breasts.

Joseph busied himself vesting. He drew his soutane over his clothes and began fastening the thirty-three buttons. Even now, he should be reciting the prayers he'd intoned at a hundred death-beds; but to someone who understood only snatches, the Latin sounded so cold. In their last moments together, he could not treat Tessa like a stranger. Instead, Joseph asked: "You named her Clare?"

"Do you like it? I thought about naming her Sophie…"

The idea made him smile; but he supposed it was best not to repeat the past. Tessa's daughter should be her own person. *Clare* would honor not only a remarkable saint but also the Irish county of Tessa's birth. Yet the name was not obviously Irish, so it should meet with her husband's approval. Surely Edward would not deny Tessa this final wish. "Clare is perfect." Joseph fastened the lowest button on his soutane and looked over at the nursing child. "She's perfect."

"She's worth everything." Then Tessa's beautiful face tightened in anguish. "Except what I am doing to David. I brought him here to *shield* him from death…"

"We'll look after him." Joseph slipped his surplice over his head.

"Promise me you will look after Clare, too? You will baptize her as soon as possible? And teach her the catechism and the names of all the plants in your Biblical garden—and you will sing for her? At least once?"

Joseph had to chuckle, so he did not weep. He kissed the cross at the center of his violet stole and draped it around his neck.

"I want Clare to know you; I want…"

Joseph came to the edge of the bed and tried to smile. "I will gladly be her 'soul-friend.'" When he offered Tessa her crucifix, she stared up at him with such heart-breaking longing. Then Tessa closed her eyes and kissed Christ's broken body.

Joseph was sinning in thought again. He gazed down at Tessa's newborn daughter nursing so contentedly, and he thought: *Why NOW, Lord? Have You no mercy?* Tessa's only living child would never know her remarkable mother. After her miscarriages, Tessa would have welcomed an escape from this vale of tears. Now, she would leave behind two children who needed her desperately. David was already so angry at God.

Determinedly, Joseph returned Tessa's crucifix to the altar. He poured holy water into the aspersorium from Tessa's cabinet, then took up the aspergillum and prayed: "Purge me with hyssop, Lord, and I shall be clean: wash me, and I shall be whiter than snow." First he sprinkled Tessa with holy water, then he blessed each corner of the bed and each wall. All the while, he continued the Psalm: "Let me hear joy and gladness; that the bones which Thou hast crushed may rejoice…"

Finally, Joseph brought a chair to the bedside. He would have preferred to sit with his back to Tessa, so he might concentrate on her sins instead of committing new ones himself. The delicate, undone buttons at the front of her chemise drew his gaze as if they were lodestones. The buttons shimmered in the firelight; they must be mother-of-pearl. But if he faced away from Tessa, he could not watch Clare.

Tessa closed her eyes. "I confess to almighty God and to you, Father, that I have sinned exceedingly, in thought, word, and deed." Her right arm still cradled her daughter. Tessa tried to make a fist with her left hand, but the fingers trembled.

He could see she was weakening. Joseph rose, took her wrist, and helped Tessa fold her arm across her chest till her loose fist made contact just above her right breast, the one still concealed by her chemise. He struck her gently, once for each accusation.

She switched to Latin: "*Mea culpa, mea culpa, mea máxima culpa.*" Joseph released her wrist, but she left it there against her breast. She was weeping now, her tears flowing into the pillow. "I have dreaded this moment, Father, and longed for it… You are the only man to whom I *can* truly confess—yet in your presence, I cannot repent."

Frowning, Joseph settled back on his chair.

Tessa dragged her left hand up to cover her eyes. "I have been lying to you, Father, since the day we met—each and every time we have spoken, I have lied by omission. You know I entered my marriage with a guilty conscience. But I have concealed from you *why* I cannot love my husband. Long before I met Edward, my heart was full of someone else: *his* face, *his* voice, *his* tastes; the quickness of his mind and the depth of his compassion."

Every muscle in Joseph's body tightened like the strings of a piano. She couldn't mean—

"I knew that even if I remained free, this man could never be mine," Tessa sobbed behind her hand. "His vocation means he belongs to everyone. I know 'tis depravity to want him only for myself, that feeling what I do for him is not only mortal sin—'tis sacrilege. To touch him as I long to would be a desecration. But even knowing my last chance for repentance is slipping away, I can feel no remorse. I have *tried*."

The dam burst. Joseph let his own tears splash to the floor.

"All I want is to tell him what a solace he has been to me these seven years—how I have cherished every moment in his presence— how much I love him. He must despise me for it; but I can feel no other way." Tessa's hand slipped down the pillow, and her tormented eyes met his. "Forgive me, Father! I know God never will; I know I am damned; but please, Father…" Tessa reached out to him across the bed. "I need *your* forgiveness, before— I think I can bear anything, even Hell, if…"

Joseph shook his head vehemently. "No, Tessa…" He didn't need to forgive her. The opposite was true, because the sin was *his*, far more than hers.

Before he could speak, Tessa clenched her eyes shut and drew in a sharp breath. She'd seen only that he was shaking his head. She'd heard only the word *"No."* She thought he was refusing to forgive her.

Then Tessa clutched the pillow with her free hand and moaned. Joseph stood up in alarm. This pain was as much physical as spiritual: from between her legs, a bright crimson bloom was staining the sheets with terrifying rapidity. "Tessa?"

"Joseph?" his father called from the hall. "What's happening in there? Is Tessa worse?"

"She's bleeding!" Joseph shouted.

His father flung open the door, and he and Hannah rushed inside. He went to his patient, and Hannah gathered up Clare, who started wailing.

Joseph made the Sign of the Cross and muttered the prayer without once taking a breath: "I absolve thee from all censures and from thy sins, in the name of the Father, the Son, and the Holy Spirit—Amen." Tessa was screaming; he knew she didn't hear him. She'd also said she did not repent. If that were true, the Absolution wasn't valid. But he had to try.

Joseph snatched up the Body of Christ and retreated into the hall with his portmanteau. Hélène hurried past him into Tessa's bedchamber, as did the maid he'd seen earlier, who pushed the door shut behind her. Joseph heard his father barking commands, but his own heart was pounding in his ears, so he understood little.

In a daze, he descended the stairs. Liam and David were standing in the hall. They stared up at him, begging for a word of hope. Joseph opened his mouth, but nothing came out.

David frowned, then narrowed his eyes at Joseph as if it were his fault that Tessa was worse—as if being a Priest meant Joseph could call down miracles whenever he wished. The boy paced to the front door and yanked it open. Cold hit them like a tidal wave, but David plunged into it and disappeared outside.

"At least the storm is over," Liam told Joseph as he grabbed his overcoat and David's from the rack. "I'll go after him. He's my nephew too."

With shaking hands, Joseph restored the pyx to its pouch and hung it back around his neck. He took off his violet stole—the color of repentance. For an eternity, he knelt before his portmanteau, staring down at his white stole—the color of purity and resurrection. The color of those who died blameless. But if Tessa died now…

Joseph shut the portmanteau. When he peered into the parlor, he saw Edward slumped over the chess table, queens and pawns scattered everywhere. His face was hidden in his crooked arm, his other hand still clutching an empty glass.

So a few minutes later, when Joseph's father descended the stairs again, only Joseph was present to hear the news. "She's delivered the placenta—all of it. Her uterus has finally contracted. I *believe* the danger has passed."

Joseph exhaled with relief. But he knew this only postponed the reckoning. The truth remained: he, who was supposed to lead Tessa to Heaven, was dragging her to Hell. Joseph strode to his overcoat and shoved his arms inside.

"You're not leaving?" his father demanded like an accusation.

"I can do no more good here." Joseph ignored his father's protests and fled—into the merciless embrace of the icy, dimly lit streets. If he'd broken his neck, it would have been divine justice. He slipped several times but fell only once.

In the end, he made it relatively intact to his little room in the Bishop's residence where there was no longer a Bishop—where there was no longer even a Priest worthy of the name. Shivering with cold and foreboding, Joseph sank to his knees on the floor.

Tessa was going to live. And she loved him.

CHAPTER 40

"It must be inconvenient to be made of flesh," said the Scarecrow, thoughtfully...
— L. Frank Baum, *The Wonderful Wizard of Oz* (1900)

Joseph peeled off his overcoat, surplice, soutane, and clothes. He lit a fire in the hearth and crawled into his cold bed. He knew he would have to celebrate Mass in six hours, but he could only lie there, staring at the enormous crack in the ceiling. So he banked the fire, donned fresh clothes and his overcoat, and crossed the frozen Biblical garden. Ice glazed the branches of each bush and tree, white gilding a dark core.

The holy water had frozen in the font, but the altar lamp greeted him: God was here. When Joseph genuflected, the pang in his knees reminded him of his fall on Church Street. His breath created a cloud in the sanctuary like an odorless incense. He returned the pyx to the Tabernacle and kissed the cold altar.

Finally, he lowered himself onto the floor until he was prostrate before God and above Bishop England's tomb. *Help me to feel for Tessa only what you felt for your sister,* he begged the holiest man he'd ever known. Surely Bishop England was already a saint in Heaven, where he could easily catch the ear of their Lord. Joseph wanted only to be a good Priest. How could God refuse such a prayer?

Seven years ago, on this very spot, Joseph had accepted the burden of the Priesthood. His vow of celibacy was implicit and not explicit, but he'd understood the price of Ordination. At least, he'd thought he understood. "Be careful to mortify your members concerning all vices and lusts," Bishop England had commanded, and Joseph had promised to obey.

Flattened against this frigid floor, his members felt sufficiently mortified. They might even freeze and fall off, if he remained here long enough. He might contract pneumonia, and all his problems would be solved. His lungs convulsed in a bitter laugh before he returned to his prayers: *Help Tessa to feel nothing more for me than she feels for Liam. Help her to desire her husband instead.*

Less than six years ago, on this same spot, Joseph had blessed Tessa's marriage to Edward. "Plighted to one husband, may she fly from forbidden intimacies," Joseph had intoned. "May Holy Matrimony become for her a yoke of peace and love…"

God had not been listening.

Of course He had been listening. God had never promised them happiness in this life—He had promised the opposite. They must discover His will and fulfill it. Only then would they find true peace, true love.

God's will was that Joseph and Tessa part. They were each other's proximate occasion of sin. Nearness endangered both their souls. If Tessa had died tonight, she would have been damned, because of Joseph. But with distance between them, she would forget about him. Eventually, she would repent of her sin.

Joseph must leave Charleston. He had been able to minister in his family's own parish for seven years—not one Priest in a thousand was so fortunate. He would ask Father Baker to station him in North Carolina.

But the thought of exiling himself to that wilderness, with no company but his horse… Never again to sit at his parents' table, hear Hélène's laughter, watch his mother smile, or inhale Tessa's perfume…

You are an alter Christus—another Christ, Joseph reminded himself. *Did Christ yearn for His mother's smile or the scent of a lover? He knew His purpose and did not depart from it. Remember what Christ suffered for the sins you are committing right now.*

Joseph slid his folded arms from beneath his forehead till his nose flattened against the cold floor. He welcomed the discomfort. He stretched his arms to either side of him and imagined the Roman lash biting into his own back.

Remember Saint Paul's words to the Galatians: "with Christ I am nailed to the cross... Not I, but Christ liveth in me..." Joseph Lazare ceased to exist seven years ago. You are only Father Lazare now. Only God's instrument, a vessel for the Holy Spirit. Your body is nothing more than a despicable prison.

Joseph fisted his hands so tightly that his blunt fingernails dug into his palms. He imagined iron spikes being driven through his hands and his feet. He shuddered.

It is an honor and a privilege to suffer, to become more like Christ. If you are cold, if you are lonely, offer it up as a Penance.

Joseph didn't need Tessa or his family. God was sufficient. Again Joseph prayed with Saint Ignatius: "Lord, grant me only Thy love and Thy grace—with these I am rich enough and desire nothing more."

I desire nothing more...

I desire nothing...

I desire...

Hot tears mingled with the snot trickling from his nose. Perhaps he needn't leave immediately. Tessa was recovering from a difficult childbirth. It would be months yet before either of them would be tempted to *act* on this desire.

But his wicked mind discarded the months in an instant. His fantasy carried him perhaps a year into the future. He saw Clare toddling through Tessa's garden—bronze ringlets bobbing, her mother in miniature. She was bringing him a camellia blossom. Edward had vanished from the face of the Earth. When Tessa's daughter fell into Joseph's arms, giggling, she called him not "Father" but "Papa." Then Clare was slumbering in her crib, and he and Tessa were...

. . .

"FATHER?"

Joseph's head snapped up, and he winced. His altar server was kneeling beside him, worry wrinkling his young face. Weak light seeped through the cathedral windows and set the boy's red hair aglow like a halo.

Joseph must have fallen asleep on the floor. His fists had loosened, but his arms were still splayed as though they were nailed to a cross. Slowly, painfully, Joseph drew them beneath him. Every muscle in his body ached, as if he were a corpse trying to come back to life. "I'm sorry, Thomas." Even his voice needed thawing. "Is it time for Mass?"

"N-Nearly, Father."

With considerable difficulty, Joseph pushed and pulled himself to his feet, which felt like blocks of ice. He could barely wiggle his toes. When his knees remembered his fall, they nearly buckled; he had to catch himself on a pew and Thomas's shoulder. What must the boy think of him? Joseph's face must bear the impression of the floor, and a trail of snot had crusted beneath his nostrils.

Joseph dug in his overcoat for his handkerchief. His skin was chapped and half his knuckles had cracked open. He might have lost his anointed hands to the cold.

The memory of his dream brought heat to his face. Joseph tried very hard not to dwell one more moment on what he'd imagined doing to Tessa, or what he'd imagined her doing to him. He'd been awake when the fantasy began; he had consented. And as Saint Finnian had written in his Penitential: *"It is the same sin though it be in his head and not in his body…"*

Joseph couldn't celebrate Mass with mortal sins blackening his soul—sins he'd committed on the very floor of the cathedral, while lying on top of Bishop England and his sister. Joseph should run to St. Mary's and find his confessor.

Then he heard murmuring at the back of the sanctuary. Joseph looked to see the Sansonnet sisters arriving for Mass. Bundled as they were against the cold, they noticed him immediately and began chattering. Joseph grimaced and turned away. The Sansonnets feigned piety; but they cared more about other people's sins than their own.

Joseph did his best not to limp, though he felt like a cripple. "Is there still ice outside?" he asked Thomas in a whisper.

"Everywhere, Father."

Joseph knew he couldn't reach St. Mary's with any kind of speed. He couldn't postpone the Mass either. His parishioners had duties of their own. Some of them were slaves who might be punished if they returned later than expected.

He would have to confess to Father Baker. "I need a few minutes," Joseph told Thomas. "You can light the altar candles and lay out the vestments."

"We're still in Epiphany?" the boy asked. It was his first week assisting Joseph.

"Yes. White vestments until the end of the Octave—we won't change back to green till the fourteenth." Joseph gave the Sansonnet sisters a wide berth and reached the seminary as fast as he could.

The moment he stepped inside, he heard Father Baker coughing. Joseph's heart sank. He should have known such cold would be deleterious to a system already weakened by malaria. Perhaps this illness was not as bad as it sounded?

When Joseph called through the door, Mrs. O'Brien bade him enter. The sight—and smell—of the miserable figure retching into a chamber pot gave Joseph his answer. Father Baker wiped his mouth with a handkerchief and smiled apologetically at the housekeeper as he held out the pot. His arms trembled.

Mrs. O'Brien clapped on the lid and told Joseph: "Can't keep anything down, poor lad."

Joseph tried to swallow his own distress. Father Baker already had a cross to bear; he didn't need the weight of Joseph's sins—let alone Joseph begging to leave Charleston. That would have to wait.

Joseph realized their housekeeper was speaking to him again: "As for *your* breakfast, Father Lazare, I was thinking—"

"Please, Mrs. O'Brien," Joseph interrupted. He remembered Saint Finnian's Penance for a cleric who'd committed adultery in his head. "If you'd prepare only a slice of dry toast and some hot water instead of coffee, I'd be very grateful—the same for dinner and supper."

The housekeeper frowned at him.

"I'm— I'll be fasting for the next forty days."

"If that is your wish, Father." Still the housekeeper left grumbling.

"I hope you will allow yourself a *little* more than bread and water." Father Baker blew his nose. "The last thing we need is *both* of us too weak to perform our duties."

Reluctantly, Joseph yielded to the wisdom of his superior. He could still abstain from meat and any foods that gave him pleasure.

"How is Mrs. Stratford?"

"She and her daughter are recovering." Joseph prayed that was still true.

"God be praised."

Joseph shuddered involuntarily.

"Did you come to ask me something?"

"Only the state of your health," Joseph lied.

Father Baker coughed again. "Rather poor, at the moment. But 'this too shall pass.'"

"I'll ask our parishioners to remember you in their prayers."

The clock on the mantle said four minutes till seven. Before he returned to the cathedral, Joseph knelt in an empty classroom to murmur the Act of Contrition. He could do that, at least. "...I firmly resolve, with the help of Thy grace, to confess my sins, to do Penance, and to amend my life—*to avoid the proximate occasions of sin.* Amen."

To postpone the Mass now would invite the sin of scandal by revealing publicly the state of his soul—to the Sansonnet sisters, who would ensure that the whole parish was whispering about him by nightfall. The Sacrament would remain valid in spite of his sinfulness.

Mrs. O'Brien's granddaughter had brought warm ablution water to the cathedral. As he cleansed his raw hands and as Thomas handed him each vestment, Joseph uttered the prayers he'd recited every morning of his Priesthood: "Give virtue to my hands, O Lord, that every stain may be wiped away, that I may be enabled to serve Thee without defilement of mind or body..."

But even Thomas reminded him of Tessa. This was the red-haired boy she'd sung to sleep the day Joseph had met her, seven years before. Seven long years he might have explored every inch of Tessa's body...

Joseph bound the white cord tight around his waist, pleading: "Gird me, O Lord, with the cincture of purity, and extinguish in my heart the fire of lust..."

At last, Thomas helped him cover the other vestments with the white-and-gold chasuble, as Joseph prayed: "O Lord, Who hast said: 'My yoke is easy and My burden is light,' make me able to bear it..."

He and Thomas entered the sanctuary and began the Mass. With chapped lips, Joseph kissed the altar and then the Gospel. When he took up the Host, Thomas rang the bell thrice. Joseph struck his chest so hard that his knuckles split open anew, repeating with each blow: "Lord, I am not worthy that Thou shouldst enter under my roof; but say the word, and my soul shall be healed." He was sick. Tessa was sick, and only God's medicine could cure them.

JOSEPH THANKED GOD for his dry toast and hot water. Then he picked his way through the icy streets to St. Mary's to unburden his soul. His confessor closed the door of the presbytery library and invited Joseph to sit by the hearth.

For a moment, Joseph only stared into the little Hell of the fire-place. "The woman about whom I have spoken before..."

His confessor sighed in disappointment.

Joseph shielded his eyes with his hand. "I have learned that she feels for me what I feel for her."

"When a sin is shared, it is not mitigated, Joseph—it is compounded."

"I know. But I find that this revelation... It is as if there was a door behind which I had shoved all my lust. While I thought I was alone in it, I only glimpsed these desires through the cracks. But now that I know she would welcome my touch, the door has not only swung open—it has been ripped from its hinges. I don't know how to close it again."

"Your mistake was to leave a door at all. You must build a *wall*, Joseph. Impenetrable. There can be no going back. That part of us is dead."

"I know," said Joseph's voice, while his mind, his heart, and his body continued to rebel.

IT WAS SATURDAY, so Joseph returned to the cathedral to don the violet stole himself. While he waited in the cold confessional, he tried to read his breviary. But the words kept blurring. He squeezed his eyes shut. This proved unwise. Visions lurked in the darkness, and fatigue still stalked him. Tomorrow, Joseph decided, he would allow himself coffee. In spite of the cold and the gnawing inside his belly, he nearly fell asleep in the booth.

A penitent roused him: an old woman. Her sins were petty next to his. After he assigned a Penance and granted her Absolution, Joseph repeated words he'd said many times before. Now, he was begging: "And say a prayer for me?"

THE DAYS THAT FOLLOWED WERE NO EASIER. He continued his fast and total abstinence from meat. On Monday, for the first time in years, Joseph did not join his family for dinner. He refused everything his parishioners offered during visits, though the smells alone made him salivate. He ate so sparingly, his stomach rumbled at him incessantly. At first, the pain distracted him from missing Tessa. Then he remembered that she had suffered such hunger the first nineteen years of her life—and the pain made him feel closer to her.

Why did it have to be *January*? He was frantic to flee to Sullivan's Island and plunge into the sea, to work these desires out of his stubborn flesh by fighting the waves. But swimming now would be akin to suicide. He couldn't even garden; the ground was still frozen.

Instead, he took the first opportunity to visit an invalid who lived miles outside the city. Joseph urged Prince faster and yet faster, as if he could escape from his own thoughts.

He worried about Tessa constantly. Surely his father would have sent word if she or her daughter were in danger again. Joseph had seen his mother, sister, brother-in-law, and nephew at Sunday Mass, though he'd been careful to catch no one's eye. They would have sought him out if something had changed.

Was Tessa thinking about *him*?

If he went on like this, he would have no choice but to mortify his flesh in earnest. His confessor suggested it. Joseph had not punished himself in that way for years, but he still owned a discipline. He dug it out of his bureau and laid it on top, praying the mere sight of the scourge would chase away his dreams.

It didn't work. The next morning, he woke certain he could smell Tessa's perfume. Knowing she waited a few streets away and forcing himself not to go to her—that was an agony greater than any lash.

CHAPTER 41

There is no heresy or no philosophy which is so abhorrent to my church as a human being…
— James Joyce, 1902 letter

On Friday afternoon, his father appeared in the cathedral sacristy, glaring like some avenging angel. Perhaps a fallen one. "It's been a *week*, Joseph. Every day when I visit her, Tessa asks about you. What am I to tell her?"

Joseph returned his attention to the vestments he'd been inspecting for mold and insect damage, even though that was the sacristan's job. Joseph had found himself with a few spare minutes before Vespers; and he knew if he did not fill them with work, he would spend the time day-dreaming about Tessa. "Father Baker has been convalescing. I have been occupied with his duties as well as—"

"Are Tessa and Clare not also your parishioners? According to your Church"—he jammed a finger at Joseph in accusation—"she has buried six children—*six*—without hope of ever seeing them again because they didn't have water sprinkled over their heads." He fluttered his fingers in a mockery of Baptism. "Naturally Tessa is eager to secure eternal happiness for her one living child. Yet you—their Priest—are behaving as though Tessa and her daughter no longer exist."

Joseph felt as if his father had stabbed him, but he could not allow the man to see this. "You said Clare was healthy."

"I am not a prophet, Joseph. From one day to the next, anything might happen—you know that. If you'd had an ounce of sympathy, you would have baptized Clare the night she was born in her mother's presence."

"The short form is only to be used in danger of death; at all other times, the solemn rite must—"

His father slammed his hand on the vestment cabinet. "Shut your Ritual and *be a Priest*, Joseph! Tessa nearly died! She is still bedridden! You make sick calls every day. Why haven't you visited her?"

Joseph closed the sacristy door so that no one in the sanctuary could hear them. Before he turned back, he asked: "She's recovering, isn't she?"

"Physically. But have you thought about the gaping wound you left in her *soul*?"

"I think about Tessa's soul every day—every minute! It is *why* I must stay away. I cannot be her Priest any longer. We are nothing but a temptation to each other!" Joseph realized he'd been speaking as though his father were privy to his private sins—and to Tessa's. Joseph narrowed his eyes. The man was completely unperturbed by what should have been a revelation. He only stood there with his arms crossed over his chest. "But how could you know..." Joseph's mouth fell open. "You were listening outside Tessa's bedchamber. You heard her Confession!"

"I had to stay close enough to hear you calling for help."

"You violated a Sacrament!"

"I didn't hear anything Hélène, Liam, Hannah, and I hadn't figured out ages ago." His father gave a short laugh. "We've been watching the two of you for *years*, wondering how long it would take before one of you *finally* admitted it."

Liam knew Joseph lusted after his sister?

His father added with a sigh: "For a bright man, Joseph, you can be incredibly dim."

"Fine," Joseph spluttered. "We've admitted—"

"*She* admitted it. *You* did no such thing. You left her believing that she is depraved for the unpardonable sin of *loving you*." With every word, Joseph felt he was shrinking, as his father seemed to loom taller and taller. "You have watched that woman suffer for nearly *six years*. You chained her till death do they part to a callous fool who cares nothing for the mind or the heart inside that beautiful body. You have seen her lose six children for all eternity, not to mention Sophie. You have heard her blame herself for every one of these tragedies. After all of that, the man she loves and respects most in the world, who *should* be her refuge and her defender—what does he do? He damns her and he abandons her."

"I didn't damn her!"

"You didn't forgive her."

"I was interrupted! I was going to say that—"

"Don't tell *me*, Joseph—tell *her*."

Joseph threw up his hands. "What would that accomplish? It doesn't matter how I feel! We cannot—"

"It matters a great deal to Tessa."

"There can be *nothing* between us! Do I need to list the impediments?"

"You Priests do love your litanies."

Joseph clenched his teeth. The truth was, he'd been chanting these impediments in his head for days, as if they were a blessing to keep him away from her. "*That* is the foremost impediment: I am a Priest. Forever. That means I am celibate."

"Not for the first *thousand years* of Church history it didn't," his father muttered.

Joseph ignored him. "Through the Sacrament of Holy Orders, I have been *changed*, not unlike the Host in that Tabernacle." He gestured beyond the sacristy door toward the altar. "To behave as if I were only a man—"

His father descended on him and gripped Joseph's head between his hands, pressing his fingers so hard into Joseph's skin that it hurt.

His voice was so calm now, it was frightening. "You still feel like flesh and blood to me."

Joseph broke free of him. "Even if I weren't a Priest, Tessa is married to another man!"

"Edward has had half a decade to get it right. He's become more selfish, not less. You should have been there when I explained that there won't be any more children. Instead of grieving with Tessa, Edward accuses her. He does not say the words: 'This is all your fault. You have failed me.' He doesn't even look at her—but that's the accusation. Instead of comforting her, he literally turns away from her. Don't you make the same mistake, Joseph. Don't turn your back on the best thing that has ever happened to you."

"The fact remains: Edward is her husband. Even if we were godless, the laws of South Carolina do not permit divorce any more than the Church does."

Joseph's father crossed his arms again. "Are you finished?"

"Hardly!" He was only halfway through his impediments. "Tessa is white, and I am colored."

"Disgusting," his father mocked. "Unthinkable."

"Any contact between us would also be incestuous!"

"*What?*" At least he'd wiped that smirk off his father's face.

"My sister is married to her brother. Husband and wife become one flesh. Tessa and I are now related by affinity. The Church forbids—"

"Didn't the Church allow Jean-Baptiste de Caradeux to marry his own niece?"

Joseph recognized the name of another émigré from Saint-Domingue. "Caradeux obtained a dispensation."

"Meaning: he paid off the Pope."

"He— I think I have made my point. Tessa and I are impossible. The further apart we are, the better for us both." He turned from his father with what he hoped was finality and pulled another vestment from its drawer.

"You're planning to run away permanently," his father realized. "You're going to leave Charleston."

Joseph answered with silence.

"Have you asked Father Baker yet?"

"I am waiting till he is back on his feet."

"Surely he will want you to finish the seminary term?"

"Probably."

"Then you can stay until your sister's surgery."

Slowly Joseph set down the maniple. "It's come to that?"

His father nodded gravely. "Two weeks ago, the tumors started paining her. She didn't even tell me; she wanted to see Tessa through her confinement. Hélène's pains are intermittent, but Dr. Mortimer and I agree that the time has come to act. We will insert a trocar first and examine the tissues. That will determine our next course—whether we can remove the tumors only, or if we must amputate the breast."

"How soon?"

"There's a new opera coming next month that Hélène wants to see. She's persuaded us to wait until the day after that. She wants to have 'one last thing' to look forward to, before... Your sister is terrified, Joseph."

"I will stay until she has recovered." Or until...

"In the meantime, son, you owe Tessa an apology and an explanation—at the least. Think what this is like for *her*—what she endures every day in that house, living with that petty tyrant, under the thumb of that atrocious father-in-law. Sneered at by the ladies of Charleston who think her beneath them. Separated forever from her parents. Trying to be a mother to someone else's adolescent —*your* nephew. Tessa is drowning, and she needs something to cling to."

Joseph looked away. "She has Clare now."

"That is like saying: 'Tessa has arms! Why should she need legs?'"

This made Joseph start thinking about Tessa's legs. He'd never seen them, of course, but he'd seen enough to imagine—

"You look terrible, by the way. Doesn't Mrs. O'Brien feed you anymore?"

Joseph turned back to the drawer of vestments without answering. "I will be happy to baptize Clare as soon as she can be brought to the cathedral."

His father sighed. "We'll bring her tomorrow."

TESSA'S LITTLE DAUGHTER stared up at him in trepidation. Joseph smiled at Clare and tried to treat her like the thousand other babies he'd baptized, but this was impossible.

Tessa was still confined to her bed, as were most mothers at their child's Baptism. Hélène gave the responses, and Liam held their goddaughter. Beside them stood Joseph's father, David, and Edward.

Joseph instructed Clare: "Thou shalt love the Lord thy God with thy whole heart, thy whole soul, and thy whole mind..." A fitting admonishment for himself. Gently, he blew thrice into the little face.

Tessa's daughter blinked at him but did not turn away. Since the cold spell was lingering and they were outside, she probably appreciated the warmth of his breath.

Joseph exorcised the salt Thomas held for him, then placed a tiny piece of it into the girl's mouth. "Clare, receive the salt of wisdom..." Tessa's daughter bunched up her face and whimpered. She did not seem to like the taste of wisdom. Few children did.

Joseph placed his hand on the girl's head and blessed her. Finally he draped the end of his violet stole over Clare and led everyone into the cathedral. All the while, he read from the Ritual.

When their little procession stopped, Joseph exorcised the girl: "I expel thee, every unclean spirit... Depart from this handwork of God, Clare..." Joseph touched the pad of his thumb to his tongue and transferred his saliva to each of Clare's ears, then her tiny nostrils. "Be thou opened unto the odor of sweetness... Clare, dost thou renounce Satan?"

Hélène replied for her goddaughter: "I do renounce him."

The little girl began struggling against her godfather's chest. Liam soothed her.

"And all his allurements?"

"I do renounce them."

Next Joseph dipped his thumb into holy oil and anointed Clare's breast and back. She kept fussing and looking around as if her mother might be hiding nearby. It was a challenge to wipe away the oil.

Joseph exchanged his violet stole for a white one. At the baptismal font, he continued Clare's interrogation. After Hélène answered each question properly on her goddaughter's behalf, Joseph poured holy water over the girl's head three times in the form of a cross. "Clare, *ego te baptízo…*" He said all the words; but only God heard the rest of them, because they were drowned out by the girl's wails. Joseph had held the silver ladle in his hand for a few moments in an attempt to warm the water, but there was ice around the edges of the font. Joseph completed the Sacrament as best he could while the indignant voice of Tessa's daughter bounced off the walls.

At last, he presented Hélène with a lit candle and admonished Clare: "Safeguard thy Baptism by a blameless life…"

Liam replaced his goddaughter's frilly cap and promised her: "You'll see your mother again in a few minutes, *a pheata*." He handed the girl to her father. Edward held his daughter at arm's length as though she were something dirty. Clare screamed louder than ever.

Hélène lingered with Joseph while he inscribed Clare's name, her sponsors' names, her parents' names, and his name into the baptismal register. His sister's eyes remained on the candle. "Tessa said that last autumn, you promised to graft one of her camellias. The one that isn't blooming?"

Joseph sighed. He'd forgotten. He dipped his pen nib into the inkwell, which he'd stored in his pocket to keep it from freezing. "I suppose I did."

"Shouldn't you do that before it gets any warmer?"

Joseph wished she'd let him concentrate. He might spell something wrong.

"Or the two won't unite properly?"

"Yes," Joseph answered irritably. He'd left an inkblot in the middle of Edward's name.

"So you'll come?"

"Yes!"

Clare's cries faded to whines, then stopped altogether. Joseph glanced to the back of the sanctuary and saw that his father was cradling her now. He cooed at the little girl with all the affection of a grandfather.

CHAPTER 42

What it slays is the disease of the soul, and by slaying this it restores and invigorates the soul's true life. ...such personal expiations [are] very pleasing to God.

— "Mortification," *Catholic Encyclopedia* (1911)

Father Baker was well again, but still Joseph hesitated to ask him about North Carolina. How could he abandon his pastor now, when they remained without a Bishop? Joseph taught more classes at the seminary than any of the other Priests. He also directed the cathedral's choir. He could do more good here than in exile. Even his confessor agreed that this was a difficult time for their diocese. Joseph must avoid his proximate occasion of sin; but if at all possible, he should remain in his current post until they had a new Bishop.

Another worry plagued Joseph: Wouldn't he have to admit to his pastor the *reason* he needed to leave Charleston? He suspected Father Baker would not be as forgiving as his confessor. His pastor was so austere and assiduous. Father Baker allowed himself no pleasures—no friends even, except their late Bishop. He would think Joseph weak. He *was* weak. He was not fit to be a Priest. Father

Baker might have him excommunicated. Joseph would be damned in the next life and forbidden to exercise his vocation in this one, and he still wouldn't have Tessa.

Joseph supposed his father was right in one respect: he owed Tessa an apology and an explanation. But surely these could be transmitted by letter. If he saw her again—she looking at all recuperated, he knowing how she felt about him—he feared he might throw himself upon her.

Joseph quarrelled with himself about how much to include in this letter. Perhaps he *should* tell Tessa he dreamt about her every night. Perhaps he should even tell her his father had been born a slave. Perhaps he should appall Tessa purposefully, so she would understand that he wasn't worth a moment of her attention, let alone affection. But the thought of Tessa recoiling from him...

He continued to fast and abstain, consuming only one meal a day and no meat, fish, eggs, cheese, or butter. This discipline had little effect except to render him irritable and distracted. More than once, his stomach gurgled in the middle of a Sacrament.

Hélène begged him to join them for dinner again. Joseph felt he could not refuse, when these might be his sister's final weeks on Earth. He went for the conversation. When May brought the first course, he had to admit he was fasting.

Even his mother, so ascetic herself, frowned at him in worry. 'I *thought* you looked thin,' she signed.

Joseph's father interrogated him about the duration of this "starvation" and exactly what he *was* eating.

"I fast much of the year: for Advent and Lent..." Joseph argued. "So does every obedient Catholic."

"Not like this." His father railed against the practice of mortification in general: good health like Joseph's was a blessing and how dare he take it for granted by endangering it. "How is a *dead* Priest of use to anybody?"

"I'm not trying to kill myself!" Joseph shouted back.

"No, because *that* would be a sin!" his father mocked.

"My confessor knows about my fast. He applauds it."

"Your confessor is not a doctor!"

Joseph stood up and threw down his napkin. "He is a Physician of the Soul! That is the only kind I need!"

Since the scent of the oyster soup was making him light-headed anyway, Joseph left the house. He took refuge in the stable. Prince did not criticize him.

Hélène and Liam soon found him. "Your Penance..." his sister said gingerly. "It's because of Tessa, isn't it?"

Joseph didn't answer. He kept brushing his horse.

"She's every bit as miserable without *you*. If you could find a way to..." In the corner of his vision, Joseph saw Hélène take Liam's hand. "You have our blessing, Joseph."

He glanced at them cautiously, his eyes alighting on Tessa's brother, or at least on his shoulder. He couldn't meet Liam's eyes. "Surely *you* cannot wish me to..."

Tessa's brother had no trouble staring at Joseph. "If you hurt her, I'll break every bone in your body—Priestly or not."

Hélène continued the thought quickly, as though they'd rehearsed this. "But the thing is: you're hurting Tessa right now."

Liam cleared his throat. "I trust you, Father—Joseph. I know you'll find a line and you won't cross it. But please: don't leave it like this."

Hélène also reminded him about Tessa's camellia: "The roots are strong, but it's barely blooming. You *promised* you'd help."

Joseph realized the longer he waited, the more likely it was Tessa would be well enough to rise from her bed. Already a month had passed since Clare's birth. If he hurried, he could tend to her camellia without seeing Tessa at all.

Joseph did not waste a minute. He took scions from his mother's garden and his own tools. The Stratfords' gardener let him in the front gate, but Joseph insisted that Tessa not be disturbed. Edward was at the plantation, and David was at school.

In this little pocket of garden around the camellia, a hedge of sweet olive shielded him from the house, while a hedge of sweet myrtle shielded him from the work yard. Joseph said a quick prayer of thanksgiving for evergreen leaves.

They would not be alone for long. With the sun streaming down on his back, it felt nearly like spring. Already the daphne and violets had opened their fragrant blossoms. Before he set to work on the camellia, Joseph doffed his coat and laid it on an iron bench in the Mary Garden. The bench was painted sea-green, so that its legs seemed to blend into the maidenhair ferns.

Joseph rolled up his sleeves and pulled on his gloves. He trimmed Tessa's camellia until only two inches showed above the ground. He knelt before his patient and created a cleft in the stock. The rest he found easier to do with bare hands. One of the scions was going dry, so Joseph placed the end in his mouth to moisten it before insertion.

Then he felt a nudge against his buttocks. He nearly leapt out of his skin, till he realized it was Mignon come out to greet him. Joseph smiled and scratched under the cat's chin. He was rewarded with a purr.

While Mignon continued to rub against him, Joseph sat back to assess the graft. The scions nestled comfortably in the cleft of the stock. He told the cat: "As long as you don't chew on it, I think that will do well." It never ceased to amaze him, how two distinct organisms could so quickly become one. "I know it looks rather improbable at the moment, but you'll see. In a few months, this bush will be thriving. Come next winter, it will be *blooming*."

"Thanks to you."

Joseph tensed. He willed himself not to turn around. He directed his gaze to Tessa's statue of Mary. Her eyes looking Heavenward, the Blessed Virgin held her hands open in welcome, while she crushed the Serpent beneath her bare feet. Even in his death throes, the Serpent clutched the forbidden fruit in his teeth.

"Is it safe, for you to be out here?"

"Your father said 'tis all right for me to walk a little now."

That wasn't what Joseph meant.

"Clare is asleep, and Hannah is watching her." The source of Tessa's voice lowered; she must have sat on the iron bench behind him, next to his coat. "Your father has been so kind. He must have scores of patients, but he's visited me nearly every day this past month." There was gratitude in her tone, but no censure for Joseph.

"And Hélène brings me books. The latest one was about the Language of Flowers. Do you know it?"

"I've heard of it." He understood that it was used chiefly by lovers who wished to send each other secret messages in blossoms. Mignon went off to stalk a robin, and Joseph returned to his work. He tied moss around the graft to keep it damp.

"Would you care to guess what camellias mean in the Language of Flowers?"

Joseph placed a glass dome over the union, so that moisture would collect inside. "'Hope,' perhaps? Because they bloom in winter?" Tessa had been wearing a camellia in her hair when he'd met her.

"My destiny is in your hands."

Joseph's throat closed. "Pardon?"

"Camellias mean: 'my destiny is in your hands.' Hélène's book even lists parts of plants that aren't flowers—it has myrrh."

When they could obtain it, Joseph added myrrh to his thurible. He'd never forget the first time he'd watched the heat reach it: myrrh bloomed when it burned.

"Myrrh means 'gladness.' I'll think of that, every time you spread incense."

He'd think of it every time he looked at her. He'd decided long ago that Tessa's hair was the color of myrrh by firelight. In ancient times, myrrh had been as valuable as gold, used in medicines and perfumes. Myrrh had anointed Christ's crucified body, and it featured prominently in the Canticles. Solomon spoke of his lover's breasts as—

This was precisely why he could not be near her. He forced himself to concentrate on the camellia. He placed a canvas cover on the dome.

Behind him, Tessa's voice dropped nearly to a whisper: "It can't ever be like it was, can it?"

Joseph didn't answer. He took up handfuls of soil to spread around the edge of the canvas as an anchor.

"I understand, why you cannot bear to look at me, Father." Her words were breathless with anguish. "You must have realized why I adopted David and Sophie—not the only reason, but chief amongst them: so I could be nearer to you. You know why God took my own children: because, every time, I wished they were yours. I do not know how long He will let me have Clare…" Tessa wept audibly. "I must disgust you."

"You could *never* disgust me, Tessa." Still on his knees, he allowed himself to turn, so he could see her at the edge of his vision. She was caressing his coat as if it were something precious. "I—disgust myself," Joseph muttered. "Somehow, *I* led you into this sin; you must have sensed how I feel about you, and you only responded."

Tessa's hand stilled on his coat, and she sniffled. "How *you* feel about *me*?" she echoed timidly.

"I have sinned against you every day for more than seven years." Joseph closed his eyes, because she must be wearing a single thin petticoat beneath that lavender skirt—he could see clearly the bend of her legs. If he pressed down through the fabric, mightn't he trace the glorious sweep of her thighs? "Even now, in this very moment, I am sinning against you."

Her voice became stronger yet more tremulous. "Are you saying…you love me too?"

He shook his head, gripping the soil beneath him to anchor him in his blindness. "This is sin, Tessa; it is *lust*, and we must—"

"*Joseph.*" If he'd not already been on his knees, he would have collapsed at the sound—at once declaration, plea, and endearment. She came to him in the darkness. He felt her kneeling beside him the instant before her fingers caressed his cheek—gentle as petals and shattering as an earthquake. "This is not *lust*."

Perhaps not for her. Tessa's thumb hovered dangerously close to his lips. Eyes still closed, he lifted his hand and found her wrist. He meant to pull it away, but his arm refused to obey him. "Then…I was wrong, when I told Sophie that love is never a sin." Slowly, painfully, Joseph allowed himself to gaze upon the beautiful woman before him. Tears stained Tessa's cheeks, but her eyes shone; they resembled nothing more than halos in stained glass. He swallowed. "Do you understand, Tessa? We can never touch like this, ever again." Even as he swore it, he brought his other hand from the earth and slid his fingers along her slender neck into her silken hair. "We can never *speak* like this again."

New tears overflowed from those luminous eyes, spilling down her cheeks and her neck till they reached his wrist, warm and wet against his skin. Her fingers stroked his face desperately.

When she brushed his lips, he finally gathered the strength to wrench away from her, standing violently and turning his back. "At seminary, they warned us: '*Always* keep a piece of furniture between yourself and any woman.' And *never* be alone with one!" He jammed his fingers into his hair and pulled. "But I didn't listen!"

Behind him, Tessa was sobbing. He had been a fool to come here. At the edge of his vision, he watched Tessa stagger to her feet. He almost stepped back to help her—but then he saw the black streaks he'd left on her wrist and neck. Filth from his fingers marring her alabaster flesh. As soon as he saw the marks, Tessa whirled away from him, still unsteady but with enough fortitude left to flee.

All he wanted was for her to come back. All he wanted was to hear his name on her lips again.

CHAPTER 43

The true priest immolates himself on the altar of duty... His whole life is a perpetual sacrifice...
— James Cardinal Gibbons, *The Ambassador of Christ* (1896)

I f he was going to remain in Charleston until Hélène's surgery, he must find a mortification that would drive Tessa from his mind. On the advice of his confessor, Joseph resorted to the discipline. As Pope Clement XIII had written: "we cannot avoid God's punishment in any other way than by punishing ourselves."

At first, taking the discipline did not help at all. The throbbing of his back forced him to sleep on his stomach, which his rebellious flesh found arousing if he shifted even an inch. *Don't let me feel this,* he pleaded over and over. *I don't want this pleasure; please God, take it away from me...*

He begged his patron to help him: *Guardian of virgins, holy father Joseph, look mercifully upon my infirmity...* Saint Joseph, who had slept chastely beside his beautiful young wife—Blessed Mary, ever virgin —who had never once defiled her with his touch.

You must follow his example, Joseph told himself. *That is the only way to a happy death. Gnash your teeth now or in the hereafter.* As Saint Paul had written, as Joseph's confessor reminded him: "'present your bodies a living sacrifice, holy, pleasing unto God.' We please Him only if we keep ourselves pure, Joseph—reserved for Him alone, like the unblemished lambs of Passover. Remember how God accepted Abel's sacrifice but rejected Cain's, because *he* tried to offer God second best? Our God 'is a jealous God'—He will not accept tainted meat on His altar."

Think of your own Confirmation name, Joseph told himself. *Think of your Great-Granduncle Denis. He gave up his* LIFE *for his faith. Surely you can give up a woman!*

But this is not "a woman"—this is Tessa!

Joseph began sleeping on the floor. He scourged his thighs instead of his back, and these welts proved more effective. Compared to an eternity in Hell, the pain was minor; but it lingered as a constant reminder of his sinfulness and the path he must follow to salvation.

Joseph envied all the Priests who did not have this hot African blood surging through their veins, and thereby committed yet another mortal sin. They seemed indelibly intertwined, envy and lust. Sometimes he added anger toward Edward—that he had had the audacity to be born, that he should treat Tessa like a possession, a brood-mare, a disappointment. Edward was unworthy even to kiss her feet.

But lust was always the strongest. As he struggled to become master of his flesh and his thoughts, Joseph practiced all the tricks they'd taught him in seminary: *Imagine her as an old woman.* He meditated on the wisdom of Petrus Cantor:

> Consider that the most lovely woman has come into being from a foul-smelling drop of semen; then consider her midpoint, how she is a container of filth; and after that consider her end, when she will be food for worms.

Joseph's wickedness always found some rebuttal: *But while Tessa IS young and soft, beautiful and breathing; while she IS clothed in ephemeral, magnificent flesh...*

When he thought such things, he would be forced to take his discipline again. *She is not yours*, he reminded himself with each blow. *She has never been yours. She will never be yours.*

JOSEPH COMPLETED THE FORTIETH DAY of his fast and ended it, since that hunger had done nothing to quell his hunger for Tessa. He had less than two weeks' reprieve before the Lenten fast. He joined his family for dinner again.

Hélène informed him: "Tessa is ready to be churched."

Joseph did not raise his eyes from his slice of ham, which he was trying not to devour whole like a ravenous wolf. "Then she should ask Father Baker."

"She wants *you*, Joseph."

Rather too forcefully, he cut another piece of meat. Fortunately, he did not crack the plate.

"If you won't do it for *her*, Joseph—do it for me?"

HE DECIDED HE COULD MANAGE THIS ONE LAST RITE for Tessa. The Blessing of a Mother after Childbirth was simple, and he'd done it hundreds of times. Joseph resolved not to speak a word of English. He would use the Latin as a shield. If Tessa did not understand, Thomas could translate.

Hélène accompanied Tessa to the cathedral grounds. This *must* be important to his sister: Joseph knew she ventured out as little as possible now. No alteration could keep her corset from pressing painfully against the distended flesh of her diseased breast. The largest tumor was nearly the size of a hen's egg.

His sister sat on one of the stone benches in the Biblical garden, cradling Clare but watching him. Her stare seemed a warning.

At the edge of the garden, Tessa knelt with a lit candle, her head covered in a white lace mantilla. The veil was distressingly similar to the one she'd worn as a bride.

Aided by Thomas, who held the aspersorium, Joseph sprinkled Tessa with holy water. In the language of the Church, he declared:

"This woman shall receive." Joseph read the opening Psalm, then offered Tessa one end of his white stole. Humbly, she grasped it and rose. He led her into the cathedral. "Enter the temple of God," Joseph commanded, "adore the Son of the Blessed Virgin Mary, Who hath given thee fruitfulness of offspring."

Tessa obeyed. She knelt at the altar. Thomas followed, and Hélène sat with Clare in one of the back pews.

Joseph forced himself not to look at Tessa as he prayed through the tightness in his throat: "Lord, have mercy on us." Joseph murmured the Pater Noster until he reached the end, when he pronounced forcefully: "And lead us not into temptation."

Even in Latin, he knew Tessa understood. Her head bowed more deeply, as though beneath the weight of shame.

"Save thy handmaid, O Lord... Grant that after this life she together with her offspring may merit the joys of everlasting bliss..." Joseph sprinkled Tessa with holy water a final time and intoned as a farewell: "May the peace of almighty God come upon thee, and remain for all time."

"Amen," replied Thomas, oblivious.

Joseph could feel his sister scowling at him from the back pew.

PART VII
CONSUMMATION

1843

SOUTH CAROLINA

Each sought to allay, not his own sufferings,
but those of the one he loved.

— Pierre Abélard,
The Story of My Misfortunes (1132)

CHAPTER 44

She recognized all the intoxication and the anguishes of which she
herself had nearly died. The voice of the woman singing seemed
to be but the echo of her own consciousness...
— Gustave Flaubert, *Madame Bovary* (1856)

The eve of Hélène's surgery finally arrived, the night they
would attend *Lucia di Lammermoor*. His sister pleaded with
Joseph to accompany her, their father, and Liam to the opera—a
tale of star-crossed lovers. "You can translate the Italian for us!"

"You've read Scott's novel," Joseph pointed out. "That's in
English."

"The opera changes things!"

"And how would you know that?"

"I've read the English libretto," Hélène admitted. "But we might
lose our place!"

In truth, Joseph was eager to experience another opera. In the
seven years of his Priesthood, Joseph's superiors had permitted him
a handful of concerts, so he'd heard a few precious arias. These
merely whetted his appetite for feasts he would never enjoy.

Following her own theatrical adventures, Hélène would often

purchase the score, and she and Liam would attempt to recreate the duets at their father's piano. Bellini, Rossini, and Mozart were not mangled; but Joseph knew these renditions were poor echoes of the original. His sister thought the more delight she took in an opera, the more likely he would be to join her the next time. Joseph knew better: the more he longed for this entertainment, the more of a sin it was.

The temptation was always there. The New Theatre was impossible to miss: it was on Meeting Street and twice the size of the cathedral. Joseph passed it often during parish calls. He would pause to read the playbills and sigh with envy. The theatre resembled a pagan temple: wide marble steps rose to an arcade, which supported a portico, four fluted Ionic columns, and a pediment.

Only ticket-holders could access the portico. Once, Hélène had been taking the air with Liam when she spotted Joseph lingering below. (He'd been trying to catch a few strains of music through the open windows.) His sister had hollered and waved at him, making Joseph go crimson. The uncertainty of her future had lowered Hélène's inhibitions more than ever. His sister could never have endured marriage to a man like Edward; but Joseph had heard Liam laughing.

Surely, after so many years of denial, when this might be Joseph's last chance to share an opera with his sister, he could make an exception. Donizetti had composed Joseph's first opera; it seemed fitting that he should be the creator of Joseph's final one. When Joseph asked Father Baker about *Lucia di Lammermoor*, his pastor looked disappointed—he never allowed himself such pleasures—but he gave Joseph permission to go.

AT THE LAST MINUTE, Liam sent a note that he was finishing a legal brief and would join them as soon as he could. The news did not dampen Hélène's spirits for long. She'd been conserving her strength, and God was merciful: her pains were mild today. The mere thought of the opera was enough to rally her. May had helped Hélène fashion a new undergarment that was only a distant relation to a corset, and she would conceal her altered bodice with her cloak. His sister refused all talk of a carriage—the theatre was only three streets away.

Joseph tried not to gape as he, his sister, and their father passed up the marble stairs, through the arcade, and into the vestibule of the grand building. They had no need to pause at the ticket office, since their father had bartered a box from a wealthy patient.

Hélène was leaning heavily on their father now. Joseph stopped ogling the light fixtures and realized the walk had exhausted her. They'd nearly reached the end of the corridor (their box was on the far right) when his sister told them she had to rest. She braced a gloved hand against the wall and panted.

"You go ahead, Joseph," their father instructed, nodding toward the door of the last box.

"I'll wait."

"It's only a spell. She's had them before. You've been on your feet all day. I insist."

Reluctantly, Joseph obeyed. He was as eager to sit down as he was to see the interior of the theatre. When he opened the door and stepped through it, however, he realized the box was already occupied. Hoping the woman had not sensed him, Joseph retreated quickly—and someone slammed the door in his face. He frowned and grabbed the handle. It turned, but something seemed to be *blocking* the door. "Father? Ellie?"

In reply, Joseph heard what sounded like a titter, followed by two distinct male chuckles. One of the men was his father. He could have sworn the other was Liam.

Joseph glanced over his shoulder to the other occupant of the box. "I'm terribly sorry; there seems to—"

As the woman turned around, he caught her gardenia perfume. *Tessa.* She gasped.

Behind her, his father peered around the edge of the next box. "We're over here. But *you two* are staying there. Have a wonderful evening." His father grinned and disappeared.

Joseph gaped. He tried the door again. "They've jammed it shut!" Where were the theatre attendants? Had his father bribed them?! The man was fifty-three years old and behaving like a schoolboy pulling pranks.

Tessa was laughing now.

Joseph whirled on her. "Did you know about this?"

"I knew Hélène asked to use Edward's box. I thought it was strange when Liam escorted me to this one and then disappeared 'for refreshments.' I didn't know you'd be here. And I certainly didn't know they were planning this entrapment."

"This is ridiculous!" Joseph cried through the wall of the box.

"If you get peckish, we'll bring you something during intermission," Liam called.

Hélène giggled again. That she was not as ill as she'd pretended was a small comfort.

Joseph groaned and leaned against the door.

"You might as well sit down." Tessa turned back to face the stage.

The only furniture in the box was a single scarlet sofa. Joseph peered nervously past Tessa, across the wide theatre to the two boxes opposite theirs. One was occupied by a sedate elderly couple. The other held a group of young men who had clearly taken an interest in his family's antics. Joseph didn't recognize any of them— they must not be Catholics. Still he glared at the theatre's forty-eight lamp chandelier and longed for darkness to cover him. "Someone will see us," he hissed.

"'Tis too late now to change that." Tessa kept her eyes on her libretto, but he could hear her smiling. "We shall simply have to behave ourselves."

Three hours was a long time to stand. His thighs still throbbed from last night. He contemplated sitting on the floor, but that *would* look suspicious. The only box *beside* them was the one occupied by his father, Hélène, and Liam, Joseph assured himself. Perhaps a handful of the audience could *see* him and Tessa together; but at this distance, amidst the cacophony of conversations, no one could *hear* them. He must try to act as though this were *not* an adulterous rendez-vous.

Joseph hung his overcoat and hat next to Tessa's cloak at the back of the box. Finally he came to perch on the far corner of the sofa. Still, he nearly brushed her wide skirt—a cascade of embroidered gold that shimmered in the lamplight. It reminded him of a gown he'd seen on a statue of the Virgin in Rome.

Tessa did not turn or raise her eyes; and still she made it impossible to breathe. Her perfume surrounded him like an embrace. Only elegant gloves sheathed most of her slender arms. Her throat and shoulders were bare. He'd never seen her shoulders before. They were as white and smooth and round as—

Joseph forced his eyes to the interior of the theatre: the dome and the classical paintings inside; the proscenium with its ornamented frieze and gilded pilasters; the pastoral scene on the drop curtain; the men in the orchestra lighting the candles on the music stands—but of course his thoughts remained on Tessa's bare flesh. Surely no other woman on Earth had such exquisite hollows above her collarbones. He wondered how they might taste if he kissed them.

She was a nursing mother! Yet even this fact did not deter him. It only made him more curious.

Christ had proclaimed in the Gospel of Saint Matthew: *"I say to you, that whosoever shall look on a woman to lust after her, hath already committed adultery in his heart."* Perhaps the rest of the audience could not see the sins being committed inside this box, but appearances were deceiving. He and Tessa might as well be naked on the floor.

Joseph swallowed and recalled as a Penance: "This is Edward's box?"

"Our captors are in Edward's box," Tessa corrected with a smile. Then she sobered and lowered her voice. "I feel him between us, just the same. But he was happy to let me come with someone else. When Edward brings me to the theatre, he is usually asleep by the second act—or he goes out to the saloon and doesn't return till the end."

"He leaves you here alone?"

"I don't mind. I can lose myself in the story." She abided by their unspoken agreement; she pretended to watch the musicians tuning their instruments. "Edward does love me, in his way. It's only…he doesn't really *see* me. He—and his father—thought I was someone else, someone they could mold. Heaven knows I have tried to please Edward, to be what he wants. But when I defy him or disappoint him, even in the smallest way, he is *puzzled*, like a man who has bought a gosling and waits and waits for it to turn into a swan. It cannot, no matter how hard it tries."

But she *was* a swan. Didn't Edward ever tell her that? She was a *phoenix*.

Tessa returned her eyes to her libretto. "Have you ever heard of a Teltown Marriage?"

"No."

"For centuries, they were contracted at the ring-fort on the River Blackwater in Ireland. Some say Teltown Marriages *still* happen there. After a year and a day, if the new couple were unhappy, they would return to the ring-fort. They would stand with their backs to each other and simply walk away."

Such was the commitment of pagans. "You have a daughter now," Joseph reminded her.

"*I* have a daughter, yes. Edward treats Clare like some kind of changeling."

Joseph's breath caught. Did Tessa's husband suspect she loved someone else? Perhaps the man was not his wife's intellectual equal, but neither was he an idiot. Did Edward know it was Joseph? Did Edward think Clare was—

Tessa's voice cut into Joseph's thoughts: "At least my father-in-law is fond of her. He has deigned to accept a female as Edward's heir. So my husband has what he wants after all: his family's plantation."

Was that why Edward kept silent?

Joseph was spared any further speculation, because the conductor was taking his place. Applause and then a hush rippled through the audience, though someone below them was still cracking nuts. The curtain rose on a woodland glade, and the Prelude began. Joseph closed his eyes and tried to enjoy the music. It began in a soft, ominous larghetto. Muffled timpani and horns underscored the lament of oboes and clarinets. He settled back against the sofa. Mindful of the welts on his thighs, his left hand rested on the arm, his right on the seat beside him.

Then Joseph felt a tickle, a brush. His eyelids flew open. Tessa was slipping her slender fingers between those of his own gloved hand. He dared not look down, or he would only draw *more* attention. "What are you doing?" he hissed.

"Shh!" Tessa chastised, though the sound lilted; it was half laughter. Joseph did not need to glance at her to know Tessa was grinning.

His hand twitched. Even through the kid of their gloves, the warmth of her shot straight to his galloping heart. He knew he should pull away, but he couldn't. Instead, he started—she did too—at a sudden, deafening dissonance of cymbals and strings in the Prelude, like a thunderbolt of doom.

"Look at the people across from us," Tessa soothed. "I can't see any lower than their chests."

Joseph's eyes leapt to the boxes across the stage. She was right. Surely the reverse was true, and no one could see what was happening on the seat of this sofa. Still he wished they were watching a magic lantern show instead of an opera. The chandelier blazing like broad daylight was entirely inappropriate for misty Scotland. Even if it did allow Tessa to read her libretto.

The huntsmen's chorus was lost on him. The tenors and basses might as well have been singing Chinese. Eight years Joseph had waited to attend another opera, and Donizetti's genius washed in one ear and straight out the other. Every one of Joseph's senses was keyed only to Tessa. He felt only her hand in his. He heard only her breaths. He smelled only her perfume—so heady he could almost taste it. He saw not the burly men of the chorus but only the memory of her beauty.

The baritone entered. Joseph willed himself to concentrate. Enrico Ashton, the heroine's ruthless brother, sang of his rage against Lucia for daring to love the wrong man. The Ashtons were supposed to loathe the Ravenswoods!

Italian was easier to understand spoken than *bel canto*. Joseph caught most of it, but he allowed himself glimpses of Tessa's libretto, which had the Italian and English side by side. She moved the pamphlet to the edge of her skirt, turning each page faithfully with the hand that did not anchor his.

Enrico vowed vengeance against the lovers. Only Italians could make annihilation sound beautiful. In English, it was: "with your blood I will quench the impious flame which consumes you!"

Enrico and his men stalked off. The glissade of a harp announced that the heroine was coming. And Tessa withdrew her hand. The muscles of Joseph's arm tensed to recapture her. He managed, barely, to restrain himself. He should be thankful that she had tired of her wickedness.

Below them, the soprano had a pretty face and a lovely voice; but she could not hold a candle to Tessa.

Then, Joseph felt a flicker at his wrist, followed by a tug at the fingertips of his glove. Tessa had unbuttoned it. She was pulling it off! As soon as his hand was bare, she slid her own naked flesh against his. Joseph nearly fainted. He'd tied his choker far too tightly.

It was her left hand, but she was not wearing her wedding ring. Tessa's daring did not stop there. She kept their fingers locked; but as the heroine sang of her ecstasy, Tessa canted her hand from his just enough to stroke his palm with her thumb. She chose the lines "He brings light to my days, and solace to my suffering..." As if she were underlining the words on his flesh.

Joseph remembered the claim of his Roman confessor, that forbidden fruit was more delicious in the mind than in the mouth. But if Tessa could do *this* to him by touching only his hand...

"It seems that when I am near him, Heaven opens for me..." Tessa told him with Lucia's voice.

If they went on like this, Heaven would *close* to them.

The tenor, Edgardo Ravenswood, appeared and told his beloved that he must go into exile. Lucia implored Edgardo to forget his feud against her brother, while he argued in glorious counterpoint.

"Renounce all other passions!" she pleaded as only a soprano could. Tessa traced the words into Joseph's flesh: "The holiest of all vows is love!" Her voice became lower, impossible to deny, like the beating of a steady heart: "Yield to me! Yield to love!"

At last Edgardo's voice harmonized with Lucia's. The couple exchanged secret vows, in spite of all the reasons why their love was doomed. "God hears us," Edgardo declared. "A loving heart is both church and altar."

The couple promised: "Death alone shall end our love." They poured out the agony of their parting in an exquisite duet, each syllable stretching out to bridge the growing distance between them. Donizetti had surpassed himself. Joseph felt their heartbreak as if it were his own.

Tessa kept her hand fast in his, through the last soaring notes and the explosion of applause. The singers bowed, and conversations started up below them. Tessa remained facing the stage. "Do you remember"—her voice was just loud enough for him to hear— "during my wedding Mass, how you began to say the vows using your own name?"

"*I, Joseph Lazare, take thee, Teresa Conley,*" he'd said. "How could I forget?"

"While you were blushing and everyone else was laughing, under my breath I said *my* vow back to you, before I ever exchanged vows with Edward." Joseph realized she was cradling his stolen glove in her other hand. "So one might say that *you* are my true husband, and that I am unfaithful only when I am with Edward."

This was not an opera. "Even if you were widowed tonight, I can never stop being a Priest, Tessa. I don't mean I *will* not; I mean I *cannot*. I *can* be suspended; I can be forbidden to exercise my Office; I can even be excommunicated. But in the eyes of the Church, in the eyes of God, I have been irreversibly *changed*. I will remain 'a Priest forever.'"

Almost imperceptibly, without meeting his eyes, Tessa turned her head to him. "Whatever you can give me, Joseph, I will accept it gladly." She stroked his palm with her thumb again.

He swallowed, staring down at their clasped hands. "On the day I was ordained, when you kissed my palms, you weren't doing it for the indulgences, were you?"

"I needed every one of them."

Somehow, Joseph withdrew from her and stood. Not only his hand but his entire body felt bereft, as if a part of him had been amputated. This proximity deceived him into believing the impossible: that they were already one.

Perhaps their captors had relented. Joseph tried the door again. It still wouldn't budge. His sister must have heard the rattling, because she giggled.

"What if one of us has to use the necessary?!" Joseph cried.

Whispers, sniggers, and then a gale of laughter from the other box. Even Tessa was amused. Joseph turned to see that his father was holding a spittoon around the wall that separated them. "Will this do?"

After the jokers had recovered, Liam called: "Seriously, Tessa— I'm going to stretch my legs. Do you need anything?"

Before she answered, she turned her eyes to Joseph. "Only a longer opera." Her smile was warm and sad at once.

His sister asked: "Was it worth the wait, Joseph?"

Mutely, he nodded.

"He says *Yes*," Tessa informed Hélène. Tessa stood, her gold dress glistening. She still grasped Joseph's right glove. She moved closer to the next box. "This evening was supposed to be about *you*, Ellie. Are you enjoying it?"

"Very much." Then Hélène sighed. "Although, I would be enjoying it more if the 'Scotsmen' were wearing kilts…"

Tessa laughed like a harp. Joseph's father laughed like a kettledrum.

Joseph did not laugh at all. He remained at the back of the box with his overcoat and Tessa's cloak. He busied himself unknotting his choker, so that he could retie it more loosely. Then again, if he passed out, his father would *have* to open the door.

Tessa leaned against the wall of the box, distressingly close to him. She did not offer to return his pilfered glove, and her own arm remained scandalously bare.

He paused with the ends of his choker hanging down his chest.

Still he avoided her eyes. "I am sorry I've not looked in on Clare—or on David."

She stared down at his glove. "I understand."

"They are well?"

"They are."

Joseph continued his blind toilette. "How is David adjusting to the change?"

"Sometimes, he almost seems happy." Yet she was frowning. "He treats Clare with such affection and solicitousness; but beneath it… I've woken in the middle of the night to find David standing over her cradle, staring down at Clare with such a worried expression on his face. 'I wanted to make sure she was all right,' he will say, even though he knows Hannah and I are both there to watch over her. And last week, when I asked David if he wanted to hold Clare, he shook his head at once—as if the thought terrified him. 'I might drop her!' he cried. He actually ran from the room."

Joseph finished with his choker. "I think most boys—most *men*—find babies disconcerting. They're so fragile and unpredictable. I'm sure it will be different when Clare is older."

At the edge of his vision, Tessa smiled and nodded.

Her every movement excited her scent. He thought it also wafted from the folds of her cloak. Gardenia encircled him—overwhelming yet not nearly enough. He asked without thinking: "In the Language of Flowers, do you know what gardenias mean?"

"The first book Hélène gave me said 'purity.' But the second book said 'ecstasy.' So, I suppose 'tis both."

He closed his eyes. He remembered Bernini's statue of Saint Teresa in ecstasy.

Scattered applause told them the intermission entertainment had ended—some sort of acrobats. When he and Tessa settled back on the sofa, Joseph was careful to keep his hands beyond her reach. Finally, she relinquished his glove onto the seat between them. As he covered his hand again, she replaced her own long glove. They sat like two strangers, although they shared her libretto.

Joseph ventured another glance at the boxes across from them. The young men had lost interest in them. The elderly couple leaned close to each other. For a moment, the woman looked up; and Joseph thought she smiled at him and Tessa. But from this distance, it was difficult to tell.

In Act II, Enrico revealed his villainy. By seizing Edgardo's letters and forging one in their place, he convinced his sister that her beloved had abandoned her. Enrico also claimed that his life was in danger, now that the Ashtons' allies had fallen from power. He would be executed if they did not secure the protection of Lord Arturo—Lucia must marry him instead. The Ashtons' chaplain, the bass Raimondo, also urged the distraught young woman to accept this new husband: "You are offering yourself, Lucia, as a victim for your family's good."

Heartbroken and trembling, Lucia signed the marriage contract. "I have sealed my doom," she predicted.

As soon as she released the pen, Edgardo burst into the castle. Lucia fainted and was revived. After a stunning sextet, Raimondo showed the marriage contract to Edgardo. "Forget this fatal love," the minister counselled. "She belongs to another." Edgardo denounced Lucia and wished he were dead.

At the second intermission, their captors asked again if Joseph and Tessa needed anything. He did not humor them with a response; but Tessa answered. Joseph's father passed her two coupes of champagne around the side of the box. For a while, Joseph and Tessa chatted awkwardly about the qualities of the score and singers. All along, he sensed that the music was not what concerned Tessa.

Finally, she blurted: "I don't understand why Lucia didn't tear up the marriage contract the moment Edgardo returned. 'Tis a piece of paper—nothing more."

Joseph stared into his champagne. "She made a promise. She *should* take that seriously."

"But she was coerced! If she'd known her beloved was waiting for her, longing for her as she was for him—"

"She believed her brother's future depended on her marrying the other man."

For a moment, Tessa fell silent. Finally, she murmured: "No

matter what it meant for his career, *my* brother told me *not* to marry Edward. Liam knew, even then…" She set down her champagne coupe and paced to the back of their little prison. "I think I would be fond of Edward, if he were a neighbor—or if we could live as brother and sister the way some of the married saints have. 'Tis only because he…" She broke off, her left hand braced in a fist, her right hand gripping her forearm, as if she were steeling herself. "The truth is, I am grateful when Edward leaves me alone. He's kept his distance for nearly a year now, because of Clare; but I know 'tis only a matter of time. I feel it, like the Sword of Damocles. Even the *scent* of him—his sweat and the Florida water he uses after he shaves—I can hardly bear it. He can be across a room, and I still feel as though he is suffocating me. 'Tis all I can do not to retch."

Joseph closed his eyes in shame. All these nights, as he'd imagined Tessa in his bed, Joseph had told himself he had her consent. But he'd only twisted her words to serve his own depravity.

In her Confession, she'd said she longed to touch him, which he'd promptly interpreted in the vilest way possible. He understood now: she'd meant caressing his face as she'd done beside the camellia, or his hand as she had a few minutes before. For her, that had not been a promise of something more but a consummation in itself. Perhaps her own dreams extended to a chaste kiss or a clothed embrace—but not *coition*!

She'd spoken of wishing her children were also his—but this did not mean she desired the act that made children possible. How could she, when it had caused her nothing but pain? The weight and invasion of another sweating male body must be the last thing she wanted.

Joseph had always known his sin was greater than hers, but now his true selfishness raked its claws across his heart. For weeks, he'd been violating her in his head, just as his father had violated his mother. If Tessa knew how Joseph had been aching to rip open that golden dress, his proximity would repulse her more than her husband's. Tessa thought she was safe with Joseph. She had every right to expect it. Surely it was one of the reasons she'd fallen in love with a Priest—because she knew he would never ask *that* of her.

A burst of applause signalled the end of the second intermission. Tessa returned to Joseph's side. She *was* safe with him, he vowed silently.

The opera resumed. The guests celebrated Lucia's wedding to Arturo. Then the chaplain Raimondo appeared, bearing terrible tidings. Lucia had gone mad. When her unwanted husband tried to claim his marital rights, she had killed him with his own dagger.

Lucia staggered on stage, her hair loose, her husband's blood smeared across her white night-dress. She did not see it; she seemed unaware of what she'd done. In her madness, Lucia's arias were particularly breathtaking. Yet Joseph noticed that Tessa turned her face away from the stage and even the libretto; she failed to turn the page after the cadenza.

In flights of coloratura, Lucia imagined she was marrying her beloved: "At last I am yours, at last you are mine; God has given you to me! Every pleasure, every joy I shall share with you!" Finally, she collapsed.

After the soprano took her bows, the wedding party hurried off stage. Set dressers shoved fake gravestones into view. At the tombs of his ancestors, Edgardo poured out his grief. From the chorus, he learned that Lucia had never stopped loving him; but now she was dead. He resolved to join her: before Raimondo could stop him, Edgardo stabbed himself. As he lay dying, he continued to sing of Lucia's "beautiful, loving soul," in a melody more sublime than any music Joseph had ever heard.

At the edge of his vision, Joseph saw a flash of white. It was Tessa's handkerchief. She was weeping.

Without a moment's hesitation, he reached for her. Of his own free will, he joined his hand with hers. Tessa gripped it as if he were a life-raft and smiled at him through her tears.

"I am coming to you!" cried Edgardo on the stage. "Though we were divided on Earth, God will unite us in Heaven!"

While the deep voices of Raimondo and the chorus remained Earth-bound, Edgardo's tenor seemed to soar to his beloved. The other men pleaded for the suicide's soul: "God, forgive such a sin!" They were the final words of the opera.

As the cast luxuriated in the applause, without releasing Joseph's hand, Tessa dabbed her eyes and blew her nose. She smiled apologetically. "I knew how it would end, and yet…"

If she'd come with Edward tonight, Tessa would be alone right now. Joseph offered her his own handkerchief as well. She was not *quite* so beautiful with a reddened nose and a lapful of snotty linen. Yet he wanted to be nowhere else but beside her.

Maybe, just maybe, they could do this, he thought. Now that he understood the limits of Tessa's desire, surely he could restrain himself. He must, or he would lose her. The affection between them was still a sin; but free from physical violation, it was less grave. If they schooled themselves, their sins might even become venial and not mortal. They'd acknowledged how they felt and that they could do nothing about it. They would simply continue on as they had for the last seven years.

Tessa squeezed his hand. "You know, you have a divine voice yourself, Joseph. 'Tis not only your sister and I who think so. Many of the other women in our parish have said what a *joy* 'tis to hear you chant a High Mass. You might have been an opera star yourself."

He glanced down at Edgardo and Enrico taking their bows. "Tenors get all the hero *rôles*. A baritone is either the villain; a buffoon; or some forgettable supporting part. I wanted all eyes to be on me, so I had no choice but to become a Priest."

Tessa laughed as he had hoped, but she argued: "There are baritone heroes!"

"In serious opera? Name one."

Tessa's forehead bunched up in thought. "Don Giovanni."

"A Hell-bound libertine?" Joseph chuckled. "You are proving my point."

It took them a minute to realize the door was open at last. Their erstwhile captors stood watching him and Tessa with self-satisfied smiles. Joseph wasn't sure whether to shake them or kiss them. All he knew for certain was: he never wanted to let go of Tessa.

CHAPTER 45

O, but they say the tongues of dying men
Enforce attention like deep harmony:
Where words are scarce, they are seldom
  spent in vain,
For they breathe truth that breathe their
  words in pain.
— William Shakespeare, *Richard II* (1597)

Tessa's brother escorted her home—or at least, to Edward's home. She was eager to reunite with Clare.

Hélène linked her arm through Joseph's and asked if he might stop at their parents' house. "Papa says it's no use my trying to stay awake tonight, in the hopes that I'll be able to sleep through the surgery tomorrow. It will wake me." She drew in a deep breath. "On the contrary, if I am not rested, the shock may be more severe. I know I shall rest easier if my favorite Priest blesses my dreams."

Joseph had never felt less like a Priest than he did tonight; but his sister needed him. Their father told them he wanted to look in on a patient, so Joseph and Hélène walked back to Archdale Street alone.

"Papa and Liam may have helped with the execution," his sister informed Joseph, her chin elevated proudly, "but trapping you and Tessa together was *my* idea."

Joseph chuckled, then sighed.

"We had to do *something*. And I owe it to Tessa, don't I? To try and correct my selfishness six years ago."

"You mean when you encouraged her to marry Edward."

Hélène nodded.

"Tessa made that decision, not you."

"She made it to please Liam and me, even more than Edward."

"She doesn't blame you, Ellie."

"I know. She laid down her life for us willingly."

Joseph opened their parents' gate. A light shone in the parlor. He wondered if their mother or May had waited up for them. But his sister steered him to their Mary Garden. A gibbous moon showed the way: the paths of crushed oyster-shell and the statue of the Virgin seemed to glow.

"Holy Mother," Hélène prayed as they knelt, "if I am spared tomorrow, I promise to be different—better. I will be selfless, like your Son and like Tessa. I will think first how I might help others." She crossed herself and stood. "I've been pondering that a great deal these past weeks. How I might behave more like Christ. How I might manifest my thankfulness for my recovery."

"Yes?"

"Do you realize, Joseph, that it's been nearly *eighteen years* since we learned about our grandmother in Haiti? And I have done *nothing* about it except write her letters. In this very city, thousands of people who share our blood suffer every day." His sister looked behind them toward the gold glow of the parlor, then toward the dark slave quarters. "I sit here in my cozy little house, enjoying the labor of three of those people, and simply accept it as my right." Hélène nodded decisively. "If I survive tomorrow, I will do it no longer."

Joseph frowned. "What do you mean?"

"We must *act*, Joseph! We must strike the blows we can! Perhaps we cannot kill the dragon, but we can rescue dozens, perhaps hundreds, from its jaws!"

"What in the world are you talking about, Ellie?"

"You could hide them at the Bishop's house, or in the sacristy! No one would think to look there!"

"Look for…"

"Fugitive slaves!"

For the first time, Joseph felt the chill in the air. "That is madness, Ellie."

His sister pouted. "I was hoping you'd help me. *I* can hardly ask discreet questions of sea captains; but *you* could pretend—"

"We could be forced to compensate the slaves' masters for their value. I don't have that kind of money, and neither do you. We could be thrown in jail. To say nothing of the scandal!"

"What would our suffering be to the suffering that slaves endure every day, Joseph?"

"The law would probably pass over you entirely and punish Father. Or Liam!"

"I am sure *they* will understand." Even by moonlight, he knew Hélène was scowling. "I only have to learn how to do it *right*, so we won't be caught. But even May and Henry and Agathe say they don't know very much. It's all so secretive. It *has* to be. 'Conductors' and 'passengers' communicate in code. They use—"

"This isn't a children's game, Ellie."

She lifted her chin defiantly. "'To him therefore who knoweth to do good, and doth it not, to him it is sin.' You said that in a homily less than a month ago."

He'd been quoting the Epistle of Saint James. He'd been speaking about Works of Mercy, but…

The moon passed behind a bank of clouds then, and his sister was lost to him. In the darkness, Joseph proceeded as best he could. "Interfering with God's plan is not 'doing good,' Ellie. Must I explain this again? Suffering is *necessary*. It is the only way we become worthy to enter God's presence. But suffering is wasted if we rebel against it. If we really wish to help the slaves, we must teach them to accept—"

"Master Joseph? Miss Ellie?"

Joseph turned toward the light on the piazza. May was lifting a lamp, trying in vain to illuminate the distance between them.

"It's us," his sister sighed.

"I told your mama I heard your voices." As May spoke, the moon emerged again. "Did you enjoy the opera?"

"Yes—but I am *quite* ready to be out of these clothes." Hélène stamped toward the house but tossed over her shoulder to Joseph: "Don't you *dare* leave yet!"

He still needed to bless her sleep. Joseph shed his hat and coat, then waited in the upper hall while May helped his sister disrobe. Hélène left the door wide open so she could continue spinning her plans to liberate half the slaves of Charleston.

When their mother saw Joseph's expression, she frowned too. In explanation, he signed a half-truth: Hélène wanted to do more to evangelize the city's colored population. Their mother looked as skeptical as Joseph about Hélène's chances for success, but she bid them both good-night.

His sister invited him to enter her dressing room. She wore a white wrapper now. May was still undoing her coiffure. Joseph flung himself in the easy chair.

"I did find out a few signals," Hélène prattled on. "A station master might put a light in a certain window to let potential passengers know it's safe to enter. That gave me an idea for you and Tessa. You know Edward doesn't spend *every* night at their house on Church Street? Sometimes, he stays at the plantation."

Joseph's eyes widened in horror and fixed on May. She continued to comb out Hélène's hair, as if her mistress frequently discussed adultery in her presence. "May, would you leave us please?"

His sister opened her mouth to object, but Joseph planted both feet on the floor and silenced her with a glare.

After May obeyed him, Hélène burst out: "I can hardly talk about you and Tessa with Mama! To her, you're a Priest first and her son second." His sister snatched up her comb and attacked a remaining tangle. "I can hardly talk about anything with Mama—

not because she is deaf, but because she weighs *everything* for its propriety in the eyes of God."

"As should you!"

"Our mother worries that our garden is too beautiful, that she derives too much pleasure from the *flowers*! She thinks embracing her children is sinful gratification! It's May who lets me sob on her shoulder."

"You needn't have told her *my* sins! This is how gossip starts, Ellie!"

She tossed aside her comb and stood. "As I was saying: You could spend the whole night with Tessa and never risk discovery, if only you knew when Edward was away—if only you had a signal. So a few—"

"The Stratfords also have slaves," Joseph pointed out as he gripped the chair arms. "Do you really think they won't notice?"

Hélène paced to her washstand and poured water into the basin. "They're already accustomed to you visiting. They won't—"

"Not at night!"

"Edward's valet always travels with him," his sister argued while she splashed water on her face. "The only other slave who sleeps in the house is Hannah, whom Tessa trusts with her life—just like I trust May."

Hannah might be genuinely fond of Tessa. But the negress knew her future depended on the goodwill of her master, not her mistress. "Someone else sleeps in that house, Ellie: our eleven-year-old nephew."

"A legitimate excuse for you to be visiting!" For a moment, a towel muffled Hélène's voice. "And David's bedchamber is on the other side of the upper floor! He won't even know you're there." She took up the lamp and strode from the room, across the hall toward her bedchamber.

Joseph could either follow—or remain alone in darkness.

"If David does discover the truth, I think he's old enough to understand. *He* doesn't like Ed—"

"David shouldn't have to 'understand'!"

"Will you please stop interrupting me? *You* may have decades left, but *I* don't! I am trying to explain about the signal." With a small clatter of metal and glass, she set down the lamp on the table at her bedside. "A few days ago, I bought Tessa a new lamp." Hélène motioned to hers, though it was a plain thing that had been in their family for years. Joseph supposed she was inviting him to imagine the other lamp. "It's japanned in gilt and this beautiful Parisian blue—the very color of your eyes. Mine, too." His sister smiled. "So you see, even if I don't survive tomorrow, it'll be like I'm guiding you. All you have to do is look for the blue lamp."

Joseph sighed in exasperation. He braced his forearm against one of the bedposts, leaned his forehead against it, and closed his eyes.

Hélène reached out to clasp his free hand. "Liam has made me unspeakably happy these past two years—happier than I ever imagined I could be. I want that for Tessa—for you."

Joseph did not open his eyes. He was, after all, leaning against the bed where Liam had made his sister unspeakably happy. "It's impossible, Ellie."

"*Everything* is possible—while we have breath in our bodies." At the end of every phrase, she squeezed his hand, as if she were tugging him away from something—or toward something. "Joseph, have you learned nothing from Cathy and Perry, from Sophie, from me? When we open our eyes each morning, we never know if we shall live to see the sun set."

Finally Joseph looked down at her, though he did not move his arm from the bedpost. When had his right hand become a fist?

"'The grave's a fine and private place—but none, I think, do there embrace.'"

"'Carpe diem' is for pagans."

"It is for *mortals*."

"Our souls are *immortal*, Ellie—we must think of them. Only our bodies are mortal."

She dropped her eyes to her right breast. "Yes. They are." She grimaced and released his hand. She kneaded her flesh through her night-clothes, as if the tumors were paining her again.

After he had prayed for her, his sister plucked a small box from the table at her bedside. "I got you a present. Since I might not be here for your birthday."

Joseph undid the green ribbon and lifted the lid. Nestled in a little bed of rose silk was an iron key, polished till it shone in the lamplight.

"Would you care to guess what that opens?"

He looked up warily. "Tessa's garden gate?"

Hélène nodded, grinning. "The one on Longitude Lane. It's perfect! You don't even have to climb a balcony."

She knew he'd recognize the allusion. Before his Ordination to the Subdiaconate, his sister had persuaded Joseph to accompany her to the play. "Ellie, you *do* remember how *Romeo and Juliet* ends?"

"If Romeo had been wiser, it could have ended happily."

"Romeo and Juliet were married to *each other*." Joseph replaced the lid. "You know I can't accept this, Ellie." He extended the box to her, but his sister crossed her arms and refused to take it back. So Joseph set the box on the table again and coiled the green ribbon atop it like a serpent. Then he lit a second lamp to see him down the stairs. "You should also know that counselling another to sin is itself a sin. Please try to muster some contrition before your Confession tomorrow."

Hélène pouted, then rubbed above her breast again.

"Good night, Ellie."

As he passed into the hall, his sister called after him: "Tessa's breasts are perfect, by the way!"

Joseph nearly dropped the lamp.

CHAPTER 46

To perform the operation, the surgeon should therefore be steadfast and not allow himself to become disconcerted by the cries of the patient.
— Lorenz Heister, "Of Cancer of the Breasts" (1718)

The next morning, Joseph offered Mass for his sister. Then he returned to his family's home with Father Baker. When they reached the gate, a sign greeted them:

SURGERY TODAY.
PLEASE DO NOT SUMMON THE POLICE.

Joseph grimaced. He peered up through the balustrade to watch his father and Henry carrying part of their dining table onto the third-floor piazza. Surely Dr. Mortimer did not intend to operate in *public*?

Joseph found Tessa on the first-floor piazza, cradling Clare on the joggling board. She did not see them at once, so intent was she on her daughter. On such a day, this beautiful idyll of mother and child was a welcome distraction; but Joseph reminded himself not to smile—Father Baker stood beside him.

Tessa rose and bowed her head in greeting, as the stomping and scraping continued above them.

"My father and Dr. Mortimer cannot mean to do this on the *piazza*?" Joseph inquired.

"They plan to use a screen," Tessa explained. "Your father says the piazza has better light than anywhere *inside* the house." Then she looked away. "And Dr. Mortimer said it will be easier to clean."

Joseph invited Tessa to sit again.

She told Father Baker: "Mrs. Conley is in her bedchamber."

He went up to hear Hélène's Confession.

Considering his sister's behavior last night, Joseph imagined the Confession would be a lengthy one. He could not sit *beside* Tessa on the joggling board—they might be thrown together—so he pulled over a chair.

Tessa asked her wide-eyed daughter: "Clare, do you remember Father Joseph?"

"I hope not," he chuckled. "She slept through your churching, so the last time she saw me, I put salt in her mouth and poured cold water on her head."

If Clare recalled the incident, she proved forgiving. When Joseph offered his forefinger, the little girl grasped it with her tiny, perfect fingers. For someone so small, Clare was wonderfully strong. Her mouth was a rosebud, and even the two tiny moles on her left cheek became her. Joseph sang her a French verse, and Clare's eyes widened attentively.

"David is here too," Tessa told him. "He insisted on coming."

Joseph should start behaving like a Priest. He climbed the stairs to find Hélène's bedchamber door closed. Dr. Mortimer and Dr. Michaels (the assistant surgeon) were carrying the easy chair from her dressing room onto the piazza.

The men positioned the chair atop a canvas floor cloth. Reassembled across the piazza's width, the dining table was set with a terrifying assortment of blades. They might have been plucked from a butcher's shop. The surgeons even wore bloodstained aprons. Joseph shuddered.

His mother paced past him, clutching her rosary.

He caught her attention. 'Do you really think this is punishment for Hélène's sins?'

His mother frowned, confusion in every line of her face. 'How can a Priest ask that?' She averted her eyes. 'I only wonder that God has not struck me instead.'

Dr. Mortimer had warned them that, if the cancer had spread beyond Hélène's breast, he would have to cut away her axillary glands and pectoral muscle as well. She might lose the use of her right arm and her ability to sign. That would punish Joseph's mother after all. There were so few people left with whom she could converse.

Joseph turned to his nephew, who stood at one end of the dining table caressing a tall wooden case. David called to Joseph's father, who was adding a Chinese screen to the strange assemblage of furniture. "May I set up the microscope, Grandfather?"

"If you're careful, David."

"I will be." Reverently the boy undid the latch.

Joseph asked: "Are you certain you wish to be here, son?"

David nodded as he withdrew the microscope from its case. "I want to be a surgeon, not a physician. Physicians only advise people. Surgeons *fix* them."

If Joseph's father was insulted, he did not defend himself. He only asked Joseph to anchor one end of the folding screen so he could pull it open.

David muttered: "They won't let me watch."

"Three men staring at my daughter's breast are quite enough," Joseph's father reasoned with his usual misplaced levity.

"But I don't care that it's her breast!" the boy persisted. "After Dr. Mortimer removes it, *then* may I—"

"David." His grandfather's face was grave now. "Try and see this from your aunt's perspective."

Chastened, if still disappointed, the boy dropped his gaze. "Yes, sir."

"Whether you become a physician or a surgeon, you must think of your patient, not only her disease."

Father Baker called Joseph into Hélène's bedchamber to assist with Viaticum and Extreme Unction. Liam, Tessa, and Joseph's mother joined them for the prayers, with Clare offering her own cooing accompaniment. Following the last "Amen," Father Baker gave Joseph leave to remain with his family as long as they needed him, then departed.

Hannah appeared from somewhere to ask: "Should I take Clare now, Miss Tessa?" Joseph supposed the surgeons did not want any sudden noises startling them while they had knives in their hands.

"Let me kiss her first, for luck." Hélène leaned over her goddaughter's bassinet and smiled. "After all, little one, you are a living miracle. An answered prayer. The seventh child of a seventh child."

Clare sucked her thumb with great importance.

Joseph crossed back out to the piazza to bless the operating theatre. A sheet was draped over the easy chair now, and two smaller chairs were set beside it. He knew Liam and Tessa would brave the bloody business. Someone must restrain Hélène's arms.

Dr. Mortimer was concealing the last of his blades by laying a towel over them—to hide them from his patient, Joseph imagined. The surgeon hesitated. "Should I have left the instruments uncovered for you?"

Joseph tried to smile. "Thank you, but no. God can see them, even if I can't." He motioned toward the easy chair. "Why seated and not reclining?"

"Supine patients are less likely to faint," Dr. Mortimer explained, "and that is the best bulwark we have against pain."

"Surely you will give her laudanum?"

"Opiates are beneficial only in small doses. In large ones, they induce severe vomiting. A small dose is useless against this kind of pain. But too deep or too protracted a syncope is also dangerous. If your sister does faint, your father will be monitoring her pulse very carefully. We may be forced to revive her before we can continue."

"So your choices…"

"Are between the Devil and the deep sea. I believe that's why we need *you.*" Dr. Mortimer left Joseph to the blessing.

At last Liam led Hélène onto the piazza. She was trembling. She wore pink slippers and a white wrapper. She embraced her husband, her friend, and her father in turn, as if drawing strength from each of them. Her mother too, though she offered only a stiff pat on her daughter's back. When Hélène embraced May, both women had tears in their eyes.

Dr. Michaels leaned over the edge of the piazza. "We're ready for the hot water!" he called.

Finally, Hélène slid her arms around Joseph. He pulled her close, as if he could press his chrism into her. He blessed her one final time, then kissed her forehead for good measure.

Hélène sank into the chair. Their father knelt before her as if she were an enthroned queen, only to bind her ankles to the chair legs. She squeezed her eyes shut.

Joseph could not help but recall the last time he'd seen his father restrain an innocent woman. He'd been standing on this very piazza, that terrible night he'd glimpsed his father raping his mother.

Dr. Mortimer pulled protectors over his shirtsleeves. "Remember, Mrs. Conley: we wound but to heal."

Hélène nodded. Liam and Tessa settled uneasily on either side of her. Behind them, the cheery, fragrant blossoms of the yellow jessamine twining up the piazza columns seemed a frame for a romantic interlude, not a surgery.

Henry brought the hot water. Joseph, his mother, his nephew, and May crossed around the Chinese screen to the other end of the piazza. David took up the book he'd left on a chair, while Joseph and his mother knelt on prie-Dieus, May close beside them.

As he prayed, Joseph's ears strained for every sound on the other side of the screen. Liam and Tessa murmured encouragement while the doctors murmured to each other.

"We'll need samples of *both* tumors," Dr. Mortimer said clearly.

Hélène sucked in her breath. The first puncture, Joseph imagined. There were footfalls and a long pause, followed by male whispers. Joseph caught only scattered words that held little meaning for him: "colloid," "encephaloid," "muco-serous"—and then, unmistakably, "cancer juice."

Sloshing in the water basin. Footfalls. Dr. Mortimer spoke distinctly again, as if instructing Dr. Michaels: "The situation of the smaller tumor…"

Another sound from Hélène, halfway between a whimper and cry. Footfalls to the table and microscope again. Murmurs, increasing in volume. The doctors conferred with animation. David looked up from his reading. A glance at the distressing illustration told Joseph it was a medical text, not a prayer book.

Finally, his father stepped around the edge of the screen. He exhaled—and smiled. His hands followed his words so Joseph's mother would understand too: "The matter is not cancerous. Not in either growth."

"You mean…" came Hélène's feeble voice.

"We will remove the tumors only," Dr. Mortimer affirmed.

Joseph released his breath and praised God for this mercy. His mother wept her thanksgiving, while May shouted hers.

Even as they celebrated, Joseph's father returned to the other side of the screen. The worst of the surgery was yet to come. Dr. Mortimer promised: "We'll be as quick as we can, Mrs. Conley."

Still she cried out and sobbed. Her breaths became more and more ragged.

Liam's voice broke through her pain: "I bet you cannot recite our sonnet anymore."

"Of course I can!" she yelled at him.

"Prove it to me then, Ellie."

Her rendition would never have won an oratory prize. The words were as jagged as her breaths, climbing and falling with a meter entirely separate from Shakespeare's. The pagan verses invaded Joseph's prayers even still, desperate and defiant:

"Let me not to the marriage of true minds
Admit impediments. Love is not love
Which alters when it alteration finds,
Or bends with the remover to remove:
O no; it is an ever-fixèd mark,
That looks on tempests, and is never…"

That was as far as she got before she fainted. Practicality replaced poetry. Joseph's father informed them that Hélène's pulse remained strong, but could Liam please fetch the smelling-salts, to have them at hand? Liam must have hesitated to leave Hélène's side; after a moment, Tessa offered: "I'll get them." Joseph heard her flit to the table.

An instrument clattered in a basin. Dr. Mortimer assured them: "We're nearly finished." Yet several more minutes passed before they called Joseph, his mother, his nephew, and May around the screen again. "Everything went as planned," the surgeon declared. "There will be a scar, but I kept it as small as I could."

Hélène sat slumped in the easy chair, her head resting against one wing. Her right shoulder and arm were bare, and clean bandages encircled the right side of her chest. Joseph tried not to look at the bloody linen surrounding her. Their father untied her ankles and roused her with the smelling-salts.

Hélène sucked in a panicked breath. "Papa?"

"It's over, *ma poulette*. It's all over."

Her eyes darted to each of them, as if for confirmation.

"Welcome back," Joseph and Tessa said almost in unison, then blushed.

"You were magnificent, Ellie," Liam told her. "As brave as any man would have been."

"How is the pain now?" Joseph's father asked. "Would you like a little laudanum?"

She nodded without hesitation.

Gently, Liam carried her to their bedchamber.

In addition to the abandoned instruments streaked with gore, beside the operating chair lay a porcelain bowl covered with a towel.

David watched with interest as Dr. Mortimer transferred the bowl to the dining table, setting it down next to the microscope.

The surgeon offered: "Perhaps we might dissect the tumors together, Mr. Lazare?"

The boy leapt to his side. "Yes, sir!"

Joseph grimaced and followed his sister.

CHAPTER 47

And it makes no difference how honorable may be the cause of a man's insanity. ... It is disgraceful to love another man's wife at all, or one's own too much. ... The wise man should love his wife reasonably, not emotionally. ... Nothing is more sordid than to make love to your wife as you would to an adulteress.
— Saint Jerome, *Against Jovinianus* (393)

When Joseph came to visit his sister the following afternoon, he passed Tessa and her daughter in the entry hall.

"She's asleep," Tessa whispered.

"Clare, or Hélène?"

Tessa laughed quietly. "Both, in fact."

Joseph knew he shouldn't disturb his sister's rest. He would have to find something—or someone—to occupy him till Hélène woke. Except Tessa was glancing at the door. He lowered his voice even further. "Can you stay?"

Her beautiful features tightened in apology. "That would be unwise." Tessa looked down at her slumbering daughter. "I'm afraid we're on our last diaper."

He chuckled. So much for a tête-à-tête. Yet Joseph realized he and Tessa could communicate volumes even without words—now that they were speaking the same language.

I should like nothing more in all the world than to sit with you for the rest of the afternoon, Tessa's luminous bronze eyes told him. She checked the stairs for observers and squeezed his hand, to make certain he'd understood.

This was enough, Joseph told himself. The caress of their eyes; the embrace of their hands; the marriage of their minds. This was all he wanted, all she wanted. They had no need of midnight meetings in the light of Hélène's blue lamp.

In Tessa's absence, he wandered the garden, where the jonquils were already wilting. He pulled up a few weeds. He talked to Prince, who tossed his head and whinnied his displeasure when he realized Joseph wasn't there for a ride. Finally, Joseph found himself on the threshold of his father's office.

Joseph had meant to walk past it up the stairs; but the door was open, and he noticed a new painting. It hung between the Holy Family with the nursing Christ Child and Saint Denis reclaiming his severed head. The new painting was a *Noli Me Tangere*—Do Not Touch Me—representing Christ's reunion with Mary Magdalene after His resurrection. Joseph had seen many *Noli Me Tangeres* in Rome, but none quite like this.

Christ was nearly nude, wearing only a shroud knotted around His neck like a cape and another bunch of linen around His loins like a diaper. He gripped a hoe—in Saint John's account, Mary Magdalene had mistaken the risen Christ for a gardener. Having realized her error, she knelt at His feet, reaching out to Him in wonder. He denied her, His posture expressing the words of the Gospel: "Do not touch Me, for I am not yet ascended to My Father."

This artist was certainly a master, but Joseph found the composition oddly sensual. True, in holy art, the Magdalene was usually voluptuous and always surrounded by her luxurious hair. Sometimes, her breasts were bare—or she appeared as she did here, in robes of scarlet, to represent her former life of sin. But somehow, the combination of these elements and Christ's near nudity, when

His exposed flesh bore none of the marks of His crucifixion... The landscape behind the couple was simply pastoral, with no hint of the empty sepulchre.

Most of all *where* the Magdalene seemed to be looking—and reaching—disconcerted Joseph: the shadowed center of Christ's flawless flesh, barely concealed by loose linen... Christ was bundling up His shroud to protect Himself, His hips retreating from the Magdalene even as His upper body leant toward her. He seemed to be wielding the hoe as a weapon.

Joseph supposed these elements were the reasons his father had chosen this painting. Or perhaps the bronze color of the Magdalene's hair had simply sent Joseph's thoughts spiraling into sin, and his own wickedness was distorting an innocent painting. Surely the Magdalene only sought to confirm that her eyes did not deceive her, that Christ was real and not a ghost.

And yet...a few verses later, He was inviting Saint Thomas to "bring hither thy hand, and put it into My side." Christ let His male disciples touch Him. Why had He refused her?

"The connection between them is almost palpable, isn't it?"

Joseph started. His father had joined him.

His father's gaze remained on the painting. "Do you think He'll give in any time soon?"

Joseph narrowed his eyes. "You cannot be suggesting that Christ and Mary Magdalene—"

"An attractive young man and an attractive young woman, who care deeply about one another and about the same things—why shouldn't they delight in each other's bodies as well as each other's company?" Then his father looked away and sighed. "No. If God had ever truly loved a woman, He would have done something about childbirth."

"Do you hold *nothing* sacred?"

"On the contrary, Joseph. *Life* is sacred. What Hélène and Liam have—what you and Tessa could have—*that* is sacred. These are divine gifts, fleeting and precious." His father rounded his desk and opened a drawer. "Tessa is what I have always wanted for you. I certainly wish things had happened in a different order." His father shrugged. "But 'the course of true love never did run smooth.'" He found whatever treatise he'd been seeking. "Tessa will improve you, if you let her. She will make you a better Priest, just as your mother has made me a better doctor."

Joseph scoffed. He couldn't help himself, though the convulsion was painful in its bitterness.

"What was that?"

"Nothing," Joseph muttered.

"Are you impugning my character as a doctor or your mother's character as a wife?"

"Neither."

"Then why—"

"I am questioning your character as a husband!" Joseph was nearly thirty-one years old. He could do this. He could confront this monster at last. "I am laughing at the absurdity of *you* giving anyone advice about love!"

"I am as qualified as the next—"

"'Absurd' isn't strong enough. It is *ludicrous—obscene.* I know your *other* secret, Father: the way you've abused my mother—the way you're still abusing her, for all I know."

"'Abused' her? What in Heaven's name are you talking about, Joseph?"

"I *saw* you, the night the kitchen burned."

Across the desk, his father squinted at him in confusion. "You were thirteen years old when the kitchen burned."

"It was hardly something I can forget."

"You can't forget the kitchen...?"

"My mother! Bound to her bed! While you..."

Realization dawned at last, and his father collapsed into his chair. But instead of bowing his head in shame, the man *laughed*: a full-throated, deep-belly guffaw. "Oh, Joseph. All these years, you've thought... No wonder you despise me."

"I don't despise you. I—pray for you."

"Let me explain, son."

"I know what I saw!"

"What you saw was one small piece of a whole, Joseph. Before you leap to any more erroneous conclusions, sit down and let me explain how your mother and I reached such a compromise."

"Compromise"? Joseph refused to sit. He only scowled at his father across the desk.

His father inhaled a deep breath and began. "At the Institute for Deaf-Mutes in Paris, your mother was effectively raised by Priests and nuns—celibates and ascetics who knew little of sexual pleasure and flagellated themselves for what they did feel. You know the teaching of your Church: that all sexual pleasure is sin—that even husbands and wives sin if they come together for the 'wrong' reasons or engage in 'forbidden' acts. The only behavior the Church condones is penile-vaginal penetration for the purpose of conceiving children. But for the wife, that act in isolation is painful at worst and tolerable at best. She needs more. But desiring more, asking for more, is a mortal sin. In her terror of eternal damnation, she must actively refuse her husband if he tries to give her pleasure in other ways. If he merely seeks to prepare her body to accept his, she must push him away, because this preparation is pleasurable, and therefore sinful. The wife becomes nothing more than a passive vessel, the husband nothing more than a dispenser of semen. That isn't the way God designed us, Joseph. He gave us everything we need at the tips of our fingers and tongues—and He intended us to use it all! But the Church keeps its head in the sand and goes on enforcing ridiculous rules so husbands and wives will be as miserable as celibates. Your mother refused to relinquish these rules, these fears of sin and damnation, no matter how I reasoned or pleaded. What was I to do? At last I remembered that a person cannot sin unless she *consents* to the sin. I realized this was the answer. If I—ostensibly—took away your mother's capacity to consent, I could take all the 'sin' on myself."

"But you're not removing her consent 'ostensibly'; you're actually removing it!"

"You think I haven't been vigilant every moment for her welfare?"

"You can't have been! Mama was in pain! She was moaning and biting her lip!"

His father covered his face with his hand and muttered: "This would be so much easier if you weren't a virgin."

"That does not make me an idiot!"

"In this, it does. Coming is incredibly intense, Joseph." His father frowned. "Have you not even—"

"No!" Not while he was awake, at least.

"Well, you feel as if you're about to explode—and then you do."

That hardly sounded pleasurable.

"It isn't for nothing that some doctors refer to the sexual climax as a 'paroxysm,' or that the French call it 'the little death.' In the throes of passion, women—and men—make all sorts of strange faces and noises."

"Mama was *weeping*!"

"Apparently that isn't uncommon." His father shrugged. "It's another kind of release, I think. Your mother wept just yesterday when she learned Hélène's tumors were benign—tears not of pain or grief but relief and *joy*."

Joseph turned away from him, back toward the *Noli Me Tangere*. He didn't believe anything his father said. The man had always been a liar.

"I love your mother, Joseph. I would sooner die than hurt her."

He glared at his father again. "Yet you defy her wishes."

"Her *Church's* wishes that she experience no pleasure whatsoever? Absolutely."

"You cannot know it is pleasure and not pain she feels when—"

"A man knows when a woman is responding to him, Joseph. Certainly a doctor does. When she is aroused, a woman's body *changes* as profoundly as a man's. There are physical signs. One of them is aptly described by another euphemism for the female climax: 'to melt.'"

Joseph didn't have to listen to this obscenity. Yet he feared that if he attempted to move, he might shatter. It wasn't possible, that something he'd *known* for eighteen long years could be—

"When I untie the stockings from her wrists, your mother turns *toward* me, not away." His father sat back in his chair and smiled. "You are welcome to confirm all this with her. Although I would recommend bringing smelling-salts. One of you is likely to faint from embarrassment."

Joseph managed to leave his father's office without shattering or fainting; but when he reached the empty hall, he stood with his arm braced against the staircase banister for a very long time. His heart was racing and his breaths were labored, as though he'd just escaped a burning building. If this was true—if his father had done such a thing to his mother not because he was a monster who couldn't control himself but because...

Joseph's understanding of his father was so deeply rooted in that moment, in what he thought he'd seen. If he'd been wrong about that... Might not Joseph's own capacity for restraint, for tenderness, be sufficient—

He was still a Priest, Joseph reminded himself. He still had a dozen sick calls to make. He must conclude this one.

Joseph didn't have to ask anyone if Hélène was awake now; her excited voice drifted down the stairs. In the upper hall, her words became clear. She was planning her future with her husband. "I think my body was too distracted before. I'm certain I'll be able to conceive now. It simply wasn't the right time yet."

"You just get well first," Liam told her. "We have all the time in the world."

CHAPTER 48

So far well; but four days after the operation…a blush of red told
the secret…
— Dr. John Brown, "Rab and His Friends" (1859)

Joseph visited his sister again the next day. Hélène was strangely
sedate—her wound ached—but she remained cheerful. On his
way down the stairs, Joseph caught Tessa on the first landing.
He peered toward the entry hall. "Is anyone behind you?"

"No…"

He grasped Tessa's left hand, the one that did not hold her slumbering daughter. He pulled them up the half-flight of stairs into the
empty bedchamber. The curtains were drawn, so only the palest
light sifted into the room. Joseph closed the door. Most recently, this
had been his grandmother's bedchamber; but until he left for seminary, and for a week after he returned, it had been his.

"Joseph?" Tessa inquired from the darkness, a lilt of amusement
in her voice.

He pulled open the curtains that faced the piazza.

Behind him, still holding her daughter in the crook of her arm,
Tessa caressed one of the pillows. "I slept in your bed, my first

Christmas in Charleston." Her voice was nearly a whisper. "I was certain I could still feel you here—*smell* you here. It was agony and ecstasy at once."

She was making him forget his purpose. In his thoughts, Joseph travelled farther into the past, toward another bed. He'd crawled through this very window, the night he'd seen his mother bound to her bedposts. "Tessa, if I ask you a question, will you promise to tell me the truth?"

"Of course."

Joseph remained at the window, bracing a hand against the frame. "Even if you think it might offend me?"

"Even then."

He turned his head to her. "What is your opinion of my father?"

Tessa blinked at him. Her shoulders drooped and she looked away. Had she thought he'd brought her into this room for another reason? She laid Clare (still asleep) on the bed and gazed down at her in the half-light. "Your father is a remarkable physician and an even better man."

Joseph turned his whole body now, though he did not move from the window. "But has he ever... When he's—examined you, has he made you uncomfortable?"

"*Childbirth* is uncomfortable. That is hardly your father's fault."

Joseph advanced a step. "I mean...*uneasy*. Has he ever touched you when or where he needn't have?"

Tessa gaped at him. "Never!"

Joseph turned away again.

Tessa came to stand beside him. "Joseph, your father is one of the kindest, most solicitous men I have ever met. I hope he continues practicing until he is ninety, because I want no one else attending my daughter or my grandchildren. Now, will you tell *me* the truth about why you asked such a question?"

Joseph planted his fists on the window-sill. "When I was a boy, I saw something that made me certain my father was abusing my mother. But I think now...that I may have been mistaken."

"You must have been." Tessa slipped her hand around Joseph's wrist in reassurance. "Your father doesn't have a cruel bone in his body, Joseph—any more than you do. I know you disagree about a great many things; but at heart, you and he are very much alike. You are gentlemen to the bottom of your souls." Tessa saw Joseph wasn't ready to leave the window yet, so she took up her daughter and went to Hélène.

JOSEPH REALIZED he did not need to speak to his mother. He needed only to watch her with his father—without prejudice, for the first time in eighteen years. The way she darted down the stairs when he returned home. The way she took his coat with such tenderness. The way she smiled at him. Not even a saint would delight in the presence of a man who had violated her.

His father was not a monster. He was simply a man. His mother was not a victim. She was simply a woman.

When Joseph returned to his father's office, he found him standing before the great cabinet of medicines, taking stock of his pharmacopeia.

Joseph waited on the threshold until his father lowered his note-pad and turned. Joseph could not meet his eyes. "Regarding my mother…" Joseph advanced only a step. "Forgive me, Father."

His father came to meet him and reached out to touch Joseph's face. "Of course I forgive you. You were a child. I wish you had come to me then, but I am grateful you have come now." Then, he smirked. "Before I grant you Absolution, however, I must impose a Penance. Your mother mentioned you will be travelling to Columbia next month?"

Joseph nodded. "To deliver a monstrance to St. Peter's."

"You will return to us afterward?"

Joseph averted his eyes. "At least until we have a new Bishop." He hadn't made up his mind about whether to leave Charleston after that. He knew remaining in Tessa's proximity was playing with fire.

"While you are in Lexington District, I want you to meet some-one: Father James Wallace. He's my age, an Irishman by birth.

When we met, he was serving here in Charleston. You were eight years old, I think, when he left."

The name sounded a distant bell in Joseph's memory. "Is he the Father Wallace who was a mathematics professor at South Carolina College?" Joseph remembered another Priest talking about it several years ago at a diocesan convention: how a new, anti-Catholic college president had dismissed Father Wallace from his post of fourteen years.

"That's him. He's also a skilled astronomer. Like many of your kind, he is quite brilliant. James was trained as a Jesuit, but he withdrew from the Society so he could remain in Columbia."

A former Jesuit was rare indeed. This Priest was a rebel. No wonder Joseph's father liked him. Why should Father Wallace wish to remain in South Carolina, when so many Irish Priests fled its climate at the first opportunity? At least he and Joseph would have something to talk about.

BY MORNING, Father Wallace and Columbia seemed as distant as the stars.

On the fourth day after Hélène's surgery, Joseph's mother appeared before Mass. Her eyes were bloodshot. 'Are you still praying for your sister?'

'Of course.'

His mother's hands trembled as she signed. 'She is worse.'

Joseph came home as soon as he could. He raced up the stairs to hear Liam begging his father: "What can we do?"

"Manage her fever…beyond that, we can only wait."

They could pray.

Their mother was doing just that, while May bathed Hélène's forehead. Her breaths were rapid, and their father said her pulse was as well. He explained: "The wound showed signs of inflammation last night."

"Why didn't you send for me?" Joseph demanded.

"It's not unusual after surgery. A fever like this is also common; but preceded by chills…" Their father looked back to her. "Your sister is a fighter, Joseph—we all know that. None of this means she won't recover." But Joseph could hear in his father's voice that he'd not even convinced himself.

This was exactly what had happened to Joseph's grandfather. Just when it seemed the danger had passed...

No! His sister was younger and stronger. She would survive this.

HÉLÈNE'S MIND WANDERED. She whispered instructions to fugitives as if she were already aiding the Underground Railroad. She murmured phrases from Shakespeare and hummed bars from operas. Liam tried to engage her by reciting the next line of the speech or the aria. Much of the time, she seemed unaware of anyone's presence. She appeared to be conversing with another Liam, another May, another Tessa from months before.

Other times, Hélène clung to the present so long, they began to hope. She and Liam recreated their favorite poems. But these lucid intervals became shorter and shorter, more and more precious.

Joseph could not remain with her all day; other parishioners needed him. On his third visit, one of the candles guttered, and Hélène murmured: "'Put out the light, and then put out the light.'"

Joseph frowned and looked to Tessa.

"It's from *Othello*." She did not have a chance to explain.

"Hélène means 'light'; did you know that?" His sister gripped Tessa's hand as if this were a matter of utmost importance. "'Clare' does too! One's Greek, and the other one's Latin. I forget which is which... I don't mean Clare is going to die next, Tessa! I mean the *opposite*: that I am 'passing the torch' to her! I know she can't even *talk* yet, but Clare will be your best friend, you'll see!" Tears spilled from Hélène's eyes. "Oh, I wish I could be there! But you'll tell her about her godmother, won't you? I haven't fulfilled my duties very well, I know..." She sat up suddenly, as if she'd found the solution. "I'll come back as a *fairy* godmother, and make all her dreams come true! Clare will be happy, Tessa, I know she will—she'll find *her* prince! Maybe even two, who'll fight to win her hand, and she'll have a hard time deciding..."

Tessa stroked Hélène's arm, trying to calm her, even as she smiled at Joseph. "One prince is quite enough."

ALL OF THEM HAD TO SLEEP SOME TIME, if only in anguished snatches. Tessa and Joseph were alone with Hélène again when his sister squeezed his hand and gasped:

> "Oh, night that guided me!
> Oh, night more lovely than the dawn!
> Oh, night that joined
> Beloved with lover!"

Tessa blushed. "Ellie, you must save that for Liam."

But Joseph recognized the words. "It isn't— That is to say: It *is* a love poem; but it's the Soul speaking to God. It's a stanza from 'The Dark Night of the Soul,' by Saint John of the Cross."

For a moment, Tessa only stared at him, as if she didn't quite believe it. "Oh."

THE NEXT MORNING, at the gate, Joseph passed Dr. Mortimer leaving. The man's face told him everything. At first, Joseph thought it meant he was already too late. Then the surgeon murmured: "She's still with us."

For how much longer?

Joseph entered the hall to find his father attacking the newel post at the bottom of the stairs. He slammed his palm against the wood again and again till it must have hurt. "Damn, damn, damn, damn, *damn!*"

Joseph's mother stood beside his father. She glanced at Joseph, then touched his father's shoulder and offered: 'At a time like this, we must remember our blessings.'

'*What* blessings?'

She hesitated. 'God spared our home during the fire…'

'What is a pile of wood and brick beside our daughter's life,

Anne?' He glared at the portrait of Christ on the wall. 'Take the house!' He stopped signing and started shouting. "Do you hear me, you bastard? Take the damn house! Just leave me my girl..." He sank to his knees on the floor. Joseph had never seen his father sob before.

His mother tried to comfort him, but she told Joseph: 'He's given up hope.'

Hélène had too. Joseph climbed the stairs to hear her pleading with her husband. She spoke no longer of Shakespeare or fairy godmothers, only reality. "Don't you see? That's why God didn't give us children—so you could start again."

"I can't," Liam insisted, his breaths as labored as hers.

"But I am saying I want you to!" Hélène's tears belied her words. "Heaven will be a *little* awkward, yes; I cannot pretend I won't be a tiny bit jealous. But the last thing I want is for you to spend the rest of your life mourning me!"

Liam saw Joseph on the threshold. "Tell her, Joseph," he begged. "Tell her you only love once. That everything else is meaningless."

Joseph opened his mouth to argue. He'd been taught these answers so long ago. He'd taught them so often himself: *This is why you must never love a created thing more than the Creator. Only God is deathless. Only He will never fail you.*

Yet his sister's own childish words invaded his thoughts:

"I do love Our Lord—but I can't hug Him!"

"The grave's a fine and private place..."

Joseph could only cover his face and turn away. In that moment, he didn't care about God's will or even His love. It was weak and it was wicked; but he wanted his sister to stay.

When their father dragged himself back up the stairs, Hélène smiled at him. "I know you did everything you could, Papa."

His face crumpled again.

"You did the best thing you could have done: you let me marry Liam."

Their father wiped angrily at his tears and glanced at Joseph before he answered: "My child asked me for bread. I was not about to give her a stone."

ONE MORE TIME, Hélène pressed the key to Tessa's garden into Joseph's palm. His sister's eyes blazed like blue flames. "You have fasted for so long, Joseph…"

To soothe her, he accepted the little box. But at the first opportunity, Joseph slipped across the hall to Hélène's dressing room, where he tucked the key into a drawer in her wardrobe.

He must direct her thoughts *away* from sin. This was his last chance. "Dearest sister…" Joseph prayed before she left them, words that might have been written for this moment alone and had never been more painful to pronounce:

"Freed from the fetters of this body, mayest thou return to thy Maker, Who formed thee from the slime of the Earth. … May Christ place thee in the ever-verdant gardens of His Paradise… Lord, be not mindful of her former transgressions and excesses which passion and desire did engender. … Blessed Joseph, patron of the dying, I commend to thee the soul of this handmaid Hélène, suffering the throes of her last agony…"

The agony passed. The end came as gently as sunset. Such a simple change: a final breath, a stilling of that vibrant heart. But Hélène's sun would never rise again. Not on this side of the grave.

JOSEPH CELEBRATED THE LONG RITE OF BURIAL like some kind of automaton, as if he were one of the mechanical figures on his grandfather's clocks. When it was over and he had unvested, he returned to his father's house. He climbed to the third floor and stared into his sister's bedchamber as if all of it might have been a mistake.

But of course the bed was empty. His parents were downstairs accepting condolences. Liam had announced his intention to drink himself unconscious, and Joseph did not doubt it.

Perhaps Tessa had seen him go upstairs. Somehow, she appeared at his side and took his hand. That was when the tears began. Within a few moments, he could barely see her.

"I'm here," she said simply.

In his blindness, Joseph let her lead him away from Hélène's chamber, down the stairs and into his old room. Tessa pushed the door closed and pulled him into her arms. Even this was not enough. His legs shuddered beneath the weight of his grief, and Tessa swayed with him. As powerless as wheat before a scythe, they fell onto his old bed.

He clutched her so tightly he could feel not only the softness of her throat but also the stiffness of her corset and petticoats through his own garments. Her skirts were a hindrance; but as much as they let him, without thought of propriety or violation, even his legs clung to hers, like a vine climbing desperately towards the light. She didn't resist him. When he felt wetness on his forehead, he knew she was weeping too. But Tessa held him more than he held her.

In time, the storm calmed, as all storms must. He found he could breathe again, albeit with difficulty. He loosened his grip on her, though he did not let her go. He pulled back just enough to see her beautiful face taking shape in the dimness. Only gauzy white curtains covered the windows.

Her fingers sunk into his hair, Tessa's thumb stroked his forehead as if he were a child. The comfort suffused him like sunlight. With every caress, her own tearful eyes communicated her thoughts: *I know. I understand.*

Joseph didn't. Why should the loss of Hélène wound him more deeply than Sophie's passing? The only answer he could find was *regret.* He'd chastised his sister because he loved her, because he didn't want to spend eternity without her—had she understood that?

"If my Ordination granted me one miracle," he whispered hoarsely, "if I could raise *one* person from the dead as Christ raised Lazarus…"

Tessa tried to smile.

For a moment, Joseph closed his eyes to chastise *himself*. "I'm sorry. I shouldn't say that. You've lost so much."

"I still have you."

He avoided her eyes now, looking past her to the windows.

Tessa's thumb stilled on his forehead. "Your father said you were planning to leave Charleston?"

The morning after Epiphany, and so many times since, he'd "firmly resolved to avoid the proximate occasions of sin"…

"Might you reconsider?"

"It is the wisest course." He withdrew from her and sat up. She followed him, her petticoats rustling. His arms and legs ached to enfold her again. His hands actually twitched. He fisted them in determination. "I suppose Hélène explained why she gave you the blue lamp."

"Yes." Tessa's smile was brighter now. "Did she give you the garden key?"

"She tried. I left it in her wardrobe." Gazing at Tessa was dangerous, so he stared at his fists instead.

"I wish *I* could come to you. I wish there were a better place…"

Where? At the Bishop's residence, in the shadow of the cathedral? Here, where his *mother* might see? Joseph shuddered at the thought of Tessa flitting unprotected through the dark streets.

"We needn't do anything more than this, Joseph." She took one of his hands, uncurled his fingers, and laced hers between them. "Edward stays at the plantation for two or three days at a time; I could put out the blue lamp during the day, and you could visit in the morning or afternoon…"

Was that really what he wanted: afternoon teas with her, half an hour in the parlor or garden—when one of her slaves might interrupt them at any moment? He wanted *this*: a time and place where they might be truly alone, where they might belong only to each other, when they might speak without censure and embrace without fear of discovery. But such a refuge would always be tenuous. Even if they never unfastened a single button, anyone who caught them together would assume they were committing adultery. Joseph *would be* committing it, in his heart. "I need…"

"I need *you*, even if you don't need me."

"I need time." It was not entirely a lie. Tomorrow was Ash Wednesday. He kept staring at their joined hands. Whatever *this* might become, Joseph knew one thing for certain: he could not begin it during Lent. "Give me until Easter?"

He felt Tessa's hand tremble in his—whether from disappointment or anticipation, he couldn't say. "If 'tis safe before then, I'll still light our blue lamp, so you'll know what to look for. 'Tis a double-burner Argand lamp. It will be on the second floor, in the right-most window."

Behind the house, from the direction of the slave quarters, a baby began to cry. When Tessa drew in a sharp breath and turned toward the sound, he realized it must be her daughter.

"Clare is another reason I cannot come to you." Tessa smiled an apology. "So the decision must be yours." She squeezed his hand and left him.

He curled up on the bed again, basking in her warmth as long as he could.

CHAPTER 49

Rev. James Wallace…moved to Lexington District, within a few miles of the city, and devoted his declining years to meditation and prayer…

— Father J. J. O'Connell, *Catholicity in the Carolinas and Georgia* (1879)

Joseph held the aspersorium while Father Baker blessed the ashes with holy water. His pastor dipped his thumb into the damp black dust to make a cross on his own forehead, and then on Joseph's. Finally, they offered this symbol of Penance to each of their parishioners. Over and over, they admonished: "Remember, man, that thou art dust, and unto dust thou shalt return."

They echoed God's words to Adam after his Fall. The ashes were supposed to remind them all to repent before it was too late. For a Christian who died in a state of grace, death was not something to fear. On the contrary, saints like Teresa of Ávila longed for death, because it meant they would finally be united with their divine Beloved. But Joseph could not help but think of his sister, alone in her tomb—or his brother-in-law, alone in their bed.

The ashes had stained Joseph's fingers black and worked their way beneath his nails long before Tessa approached the altar. Her eyes flitted up to his for only a moment. But a moment was all it took. Just as the crucifix was veiled for Lent, Christ vanished from Joseph's mind.

As he felt that black cross on his forehead, as he placed that symbol of death upon Tessa's soft flesh and he recited those ominous words, Joseph longed for another kind of union—while he and Tessa still had breath in their bodies. Eight weeks ago, he'd almost lost her to childbirth. A few days from now, on his journey to Columbia, Prince might stumble and throw him; Joseph might break his neck before he ever knew the taste of her skin. Thanks to his father's carnal catechism (imprinted in his mind as surely as Priesthood was imprinted in his soul), Joseph knew there were ways he could make Tessa "unspeakably happy" without hurting her.

Every one of which was a mortal sin. As a Penance, he tried to reread the "Meditation upon Death" from *The Imitation of Christ*. "In every deed and thought, order thyself as if thou wert to die this day," counselled Thomas à Kempis. "When it is morning, reflect that thou may not see evening…" Before her surgery, Hélène had said nearly the same thing, but she'd argued for an entirely different purpose—not that Joseph should prepare his soul to meet God, but that he should seize Tessa while he could. "Now the time is most precious," agreed Kempis. "While thou hast time, lay up for thyself undying riches."

The only riches Joseph cared about were the gold rings in Tessa's eyes, the ruby curtains of her lips, the pearls of her teeth, the ivory of her throat…

He was writing another chapter of the Canticles, apparently. At least he hadn't compared her hair to a flock of goats.

A NOBLE BENEFACTRESS IN EUROPE had sent their diocese two monstrances. Even without the Real Presence inside them, these vessels were dazzling: rays of gold radiating from a center inlaid with jewels. Their benefactress wished one monstrance to remain in the cathedral and the other to grace St. Peter's Church in

Columbia, since it was dedicated to her late husband's patron saint. Father Baker had decided not to entrust such an important delivery to the postal service.

Besides, the Priest who made the journey could visit the Catholic families between Charleston and Columbia, families who enjoyed the consolation of the Sacraments only a few times a year. Joseph had volunteered because he had Prince. He also saw it as a trial: how might he and his horse adapt to permanent mission work?

Prince seemed eager to stretch his legs in earnest. With the monstrance wrapped up securely, they travelled through Colleton District, south of the railroad. Joseph spent each night and morning with the scattered members of his flock, baptizing infants, hearing Confessions, and celebrating Mass. He even blessed a Marriage. Work only a Priest could do.

Yet every moment in-between, Joseph prayed—and dreamt—about Tessa. Might not God grant him this solace? If Joseph was gentle, might not Tessa grant him more than a clothed embrace?

Fortunately, Joseph had brought along *Dignity and Duties of the Priest* by Alphonsus Liguori. The saint devoted whole chapters to "The Sin of Incontinence, or The Necessity of Purity in the Priest." He reminded Joseph: "the unchaste priest not only brings himself to perdition, but he also causes the damnation of many others." He confirmed the wisdom of Joseph's first instinct when he'd learned Tessa loved him: to flee at once from his occasion of sin. "In this warfare cowards, they that avoid dangerous occasions, gain the victory."

Joseph's course was clear. He must leave Charleston permanently. He must turn his back on the best thing that had ever happened to him, because it was also the worst thing that had ever happened to him. If he truly cared about Tessa's welfare or about his other parishioners, he could not delay any longer. As soon as he returned from Columbia, he would speak to Father Baker.

But whatever strange bed he inhabited, Tessa always found him. Sometimes she only sang to him or stroked his hair. Sometimes she was as wanton as Delilah. That night, she began by whispering in his ear: *"I need you."* The truth was: he needed her as much as she needed him. Whatever she could give him, he would accept it gladly. But he dreamt of union.

The following afternoon, Joseph and his horse took refuge from a thunderstorm in a barn. As lightning streaked the sky, Joseph returned to Alphonsus, who often cited the wisdom of other saints:

> In the revelations of St. Bridget we read that an unchaste priest was killed by a thunder bolt; and it was found that the lightning had reduced to ashes only the indelicate members, as if to show that it was principally for incontinence that God had inflicted this chastisement upon him.

Joseph flinched.

HE DELIVERED THE MONSTRANCE SAFELY to St. Peter's. Then he followed his map and his father's directions to the home of Father Wallace. The farmstead stood in a handsome setting near the edge of a forest—though the house seemed unnecessarily large. Joseph's father had told him the Priest had made wise investments and now owned considerable property in and around Columbia. Father Wallace likely had his mastery of mathematics to thank for that.

As Joseph approached, he heard what sounded like a Paganini caprice drifting down through one of the windows. So Father Wallace was a violinist. Joseph had assumed his father wished him to meet this Priest because Father Wallace had broken his vow of obedience by leaving the Jesuits. But perhaps their shared love of music had some bearing on this visit, too. When Joseph had asked his father's reasons, he'd been frustratingly vague: "You'll understand once you're there."

Half mesmerized by the music, Joseph pulled Prince to a stop, dismounted, and tied his lead rope to the fence around the kitchen garden. When Joseph climbed the porch stairs and knocked on the front door, the violinist did not stop. But a patter of footsteps punctuated the notes, and the door swung open to reveal a mulatto boy of about seven.

"Good afternoon!" the boy cried.

Joseph frowned. "G-Good afternoon."

"Are you Father Lazarus?"

"If you mean 'Father Lazare,' I am."

The boy scrunched up his nose. "I 'membered wrong! Your pa wrote us you were coming."

"I'm...looking for Father Wallace?"

"You're in the right place," called a woman's voice. Joseph turned to see a negress approaching from the kitchen. She wiped her hands on her apron, then shielded her eyes from the afternoon sunlight. "He hasn't returned from his mission to the Fairfield District yet. We expect him for supper. You'll join us, won't you? And spend the night with us?"

"I— Yes, thank you."

The negress (Joseph guessed her to be forty) was close enough now to see the mulatto boy standing in the doorway, and she turned to him. "James, would you run upstairs and ask your brother to take care of Father Lazare's horse and put his bags in the spare room?"

"I can do it, Mama!" young James insisted.

The negress smiled indulgently. "Why don't you *help* George?"

James pouted but ran to obey.

Joseph had known Father Wallace must have a housekeeper. But it was unusual for such a woman to bring her children into a Priest's household. Their noise was hardly conducive to meditation and prayer: James clomped up the stairs and shouted to his brother. The violin ceased.

"Are you thirsty, Father?" the negress asked him. "I have some switchel ready. James says it's the best restorative after a day in the saddle."

"Thank you." Still Joseph scowled. By "James," he assumed she meant Father Wallace, not her young son. Did Father Wallace know she referred to him by his Christian name in his absence?

"I hope you don't mind following me to the kitchen? I have supper going." The negress turned before Joseph even responded.

In the kitchen, she offered him a chair and poured him a mug of switchel, which had the perfect amount of ginger. "I'm sorry,

Father; I realize I haven't introduced myself. My name is Sarah. Your father's letter wasn't clear—but judging by your reactions, he didn't tell you about me?"

That sounded ominous. "No…"

Sarah seemed uncomfortable too. She rearranged the fire. "I wish James were here to do this with me," she sighed. "But I know I cannot leave you in suspense." She crouched down and gave her Dutch oven a quarter-turn. "Twenty-two, nearly twenty-three years ago, James purchased me from a plantation outside Charleston."

She was a slave. That was hardly surprising.

"Six years later, I gave birth to our first son."

Despite the sudden dryness in his throat, Joseph lowered his mug to the table. *This* was meant to inform Joseph's decision about Tessa? A man who forced himself on his slave so often there were *children*? Wallace was not only her master, he was her *Priest*; she'd had no choice but to submit. Joseph kept his eyes on the ginger water. "You must despise him."

Sarah had been reaching toward one of the herb bundles hanging from the rafters. She paused. "'Despise him'?" she echoed in confusion.

"Wallace—not your son." The ability of violated women to love the products of their violation was one of God's miracles.

Sarah laughed. "James did not force me! I understand how you could think that, viewing us from a distance. But it isn't true." She smiled and plucked down a sprig of rosemary. "What happened between me and James was a slow, gentle thing—and *I* began it, not him."

Joseph frowned. Twenty-three years ago, she'd been seventeen? eighteen? "But when he purchased you, he must have done it with the *intention* of…"

"He purchased me to *save* me, Father." Sarah used a hook to swing her cooking crane out of the fire. "Me and the man I was with then, Marcus, we'd tried to run, even though we knew what would happen if they caught us: first our master whipped us, and then he sold us. Master had meant to sell me and Marcus *both* 'down the river.' But James came to say Mass at our plantation that day.

He understood what 'down the river' meant, especially for a woman."

Joseph did too: in New Orleans, she would have been auctioned as a "fancy girl"—or worked to death in the cane fields.

Sarah added her rosemary to the pot. "The college in Columbia already wanted James to be their mathematics professor, and he needed a housekeeper. So he asked my master if *he* could buy me. I'd still be separated from Marcus and my mother, James argued—wasn't that punishment enough? It was your father who lent him the money he needed—your father who cared for my back till I was well enough to travel." Sarah returned the pot to the fire. "At first, I *did* despise James, like I despised all white men. I thought about running again. I even thought about killing myself. I assumed what you did: that he wanted me for more than cooking and cleaning." She took up a pile of radishes fresh from the garden and crossed to her sink. She had a hand pump right there in the kitchen. "But James saw how frightened and unhappy I was. He started doing these little things for me, never expecting anything in return. Big things too: he taught me my letters. Through a Priest friend of his, I was able to write to my mother. James missed his mother too, you see. As the years passed, we got to know everything about each other—until it wasn't enough. We couldn't say what we wanted to say with words anymore."

Joseph stood and stared out the open window toward the sinking sun. "He is still a Priest; he had no right to—"

"The Church says we cannot marry; the law says he cannot free me; the neighbors say our union is 'unnatural.' But none of that matters, Father. Once you close the door behind you, there is no white or black, master or slave, Priest or parishioner. There is only a man and a woman—two bodies and two souls who need each other. Slavery took my body away from me, but James gave it back to me. He saved my soul, too—not by being a good Priest, but by being a good man."

A boyish shout drew Joseph's attention to the road. He saw a bespectacled white man approaching, riding alongside a young colored man of perhaps seventeen. As her youngest son ran out to greet the riders, Sarah joined Joseph at the window. "That's Andrew, our eldest. He's apprenticed to a bricklayer in Columbia. It's not often now I have him and James *both* home for supper!" She poured another mug of switchel and hurried outside.

Joseph remained at the window, watching their reunion, wishing he hadn't agreed to spend the night.

Wallace gulped half the switchel while he caressed Sarah's back. "Thank you, princess." Her name was Hebrew for princess, Joseph remembered. "How are you today?"

"*I* am well." Without breaking their embrace, Sarah glanced back to Joseph. "I am not so sure about Father Lazare. I have been trying to explain our family to him."

"Ah!" Wallace peered through the window. He'd not let go of Sarah. "It's quite safe to come out, son! If God were going to strike me down with a thunderbolt, He would have done it a long time ago!"

Joseph sighed and emerged from the kitchen.

Wallace gazed around him with obvious pride. Little James was still hanging about his parents, while Andrew and George were leading the horses into the barn. "On the contrary, God has blessed me with three handsome sons." Wallace stroked the frizzly head of his namesake, then looked back to Joseph. "And *you* are certainly the image of your father. Since he and I are of an age, I hope you will allow me to call you Joseph? You are welcome to call me James."

Reluctantly, Joseph nodded.

Sarah asked the younger James to set the table, then returned to her kitchen.

Wallace—even in his head, Joseph could not use his Christian name—kept smiling at Joseph. He motioned him toward the porch. "I am sure you have questions. Begin!"

Joseph avoided his eyes. "What in Heaven's name do you tell your confessor?"

"The truth."

"But he *cannot* absolve you…"

"My confessor does not believe I am 'living in mortal sin' any more than I do. He was also in love once. Still is. She's the reason they sent him across the Atlantic."

"And your superior?"

"He knows." Wallace shrugged. "He pretends not to. There is only *one* sin our Church cannot bear: the sin of scandal. You and I are hardly unique, Joseph. There are more of us than you realize. How many Priests are there in Charleston now?"

"Six."

"Mark my words, Joseph: two, probably three of those men have, had, or will have a mistress. And I would wager all six of them have been in love."

Impossible. Yet Joseph had to force himself not to speculate about his fellow Priests. Father O'Neil? Father Burke?

"The Church turns a blind eye because it has no other choice. If it excommunicated every Priest with a 'concubine,' it would lose half its clergy." Wallace seated himself on the porch, and Joseph settled uneasily beside him. "If the Church had any sense, it would return to its roots and allow us to take wives openly. Saint Peter— the only Pope chosen by Christ—was married! This cult of celibacy not only torments us Priests—it devastates the women and children we leave behind. I have been very fortunate, to remain with my family. Most Priests are moved from parish to parish to parish, *especially* if they've 'fallen.' That only encourages them to flit like honeybees from woman to woman, seeking the sympathy and encouragement they could have found in a wife. We are with our parishioners during the most painful periods of their lives: Confessions and sick calls and Last Rites... The work of a Priest is physically, spiritually, and emotionally exhausting. We pour ourselves out again and again until we are empty. We must find someone to fill us up again, or we collapse."

"*God* fills us."

"He does—but He cannot fill us completely."

That was heresy.

"The Priests who will not allow themselves to turn to a woman often find solace in a bottle. Others choose..." Wallace averted his eyes and did not finish.

Joseph suspected he knew what the man was implying, and he was grateful to let the alternative lie. "Do your *parishioners* know about Sarah and your sons?"

"Some of them do."

"And they tolerate it?" Isolated as they were, Joseph supposed Wallace's parishioners had no other choice.

"Those who object do so because of Sarah's color. If she were white, it would be easier. We wouldn't have to worry about our boys' futures. No matter how much property I acquire, I cannot will it to my sons—because South Carolina considers *them* property. Your father didn't mention—the woman you love, she is white?"

"Yes. She is also married."

"I am sorry. *That* is a problem not even a mathematician can solve for you."

At least the man did not stoop to condoning adultery—or murder.

"I can tell you this, Joseph: If you truly love this woman, if she truly loves you, and you turn away from her, she will haunt you for the rest of your life. You will *always* be empty. *Carnal* intercourse is the easiest way to still that longing inside you, but it is not the only way. Perhaps together, you and she can manage to be soul-mates without mingling your flesh. The path is narrow indeed, but others have found it before you: there are many precedents amongst our saints. Think of Saint Clare and Saint Francis of Assisi, or Saint Teresa and Saint John of the Cross."

Sarah approached then, carrying a salad she'd made with the radishes. "We're almost ready."

Wallace opened the door for her, then called toward the barn: "Andrew! George! Come help your mother!"

The Priest's sons obeyed their father promptly. The Church considered such children a special class of bastards, born "from a damned union." The warnings of Saint Alphonsus rang through Joseph's mind: *"In a word, the Church regards as a monster the priest that does not lead a life of chastity."*

The monster passed him carrying a plate of cornbread.

They sat down to supper. Wallace blessed the meal. Andrew

began telling his mother and brothers about his day. Joseph had little appetite.

Wallace noticed. "If I might venture a guess, Joseph: you're imagining everlasting hellfire?"

Joseph didn't need to answer.

"Remember, Joseph: it is not the Church that will decide who is saved and who is damned. Only God can do that." He gazed at his concubine. "What I feel for Sarah, what she feels for me, it is *love*. I cannot believe that offends God. What Saint Paul talks about in his First Epistle to the Corinthians, how we are nothing without love— the Church has forgotten that. It has become a 'sounding brass' and puffed itself up with rules that have little to do with God and everything to do with control. That's what celibacy is about. The Church tries to terrify us into submission; it claims we endanger our ministry and forfeit our souls if we fulfill the needs God Himself instilled in us. One day, Joseph, all the false trappings will fall away, and only the perfection of God will remain. If we are wise, if we listen to Him alone, we can glimpse that perfection here on Earth. 'He that loveth not, knoweth not God: for God is love.'"

That was the First Epistle of John.

"I know what you've been taught: that if a man loves a woman, 'his heart is divided,' that only 'he who is free from the conjugal bonds' can belong to God." Wallace was quoting Saint Alphonsus. "But before I knew Sarah, my heart was considerably more divided than it is now. I was in far greater bondage to lust than I am to love. I spent hours and *hours* battling my attraction to women, punishing myself. Now, all of that wasted energy is fulfilled with Sarah or redirected into my ministry. My feelings for her strengthen me instead of exhausting me. I am a better Priest *because* of my family, not in spite of them. Being a husband to Sarah has made me a wiser confessor. Being a father to my sons has made me a wiser pastor. I was lost, alone in the darkness. But I have found my guiding stars."

After supper, George and Andrew played their violins. Already rubbing his eyes, James crawled into his father's lap. Afterward, when Sarah tried to dislodge him, James clung to his father's neck and murmured drowsy protests.

Wallace whispered: "Let him stay. I'll carry him upstairs. Very soon, he'll consider this unmanly and he won't let either of us close enough to kiss him. 'Now the time is most precious.' Just hand me my breviary, would you, my love?"

Sarah smiled and relented, kissing both of them while she still could.

With his youngest child slumbering in his lap, Wallace read the Divine Office for the day—keeping one promise he'd made at Ordination, at least.

Seven and a half years ago, if Joseph had married Tessa instead of Holy Mother Church, they might have had a son like James.

Joseph's bedchamber shared a wall with Wallace and Sarah's room. Fortunately, as far as he could tell, they managed to restrain themselves that night. Perhaps they'd relinquished each other for Lent. He heard only companionable murmurs and once, muffled laughter.

THE NEXT MORNING WAS SUNDAY. Joseph suspected Wallace did *not* have permission from his superior to celebrate Mass in his home; but he did it anyway. He asked Joseph to assist. After silently begging God's pardon, Joseph conceded.

As he fastened his amice, Wallace observed: "I see I have not yet convinced you. Allow me to play Devil's Advocate, then. Even if I *were* in a state of mortal sin, remember that every Sacrament I administer remains valid. We have the authority of Saint Thomas Aquinas on that."

They had the authority of Saint Alphonsus and Saint Teresa as well—though both of them shivered in terror for the soul of any Priest who so offended God. *"We defile the body of Christ whenever we approach the altar unworthily,"* wrote Alphonsus. The mere violet of Lent did not seem sufficient Penance. They should be wearing sackcloth.

Wallace interrupted: "We're not *meant* to be sinless, Joseph. In his Epistle to the Hebrews, Saint Paul talks about how 'every priest...can have compassion on them that are ignorant and that err: because he himself is beset with weakness.' And surely you are familiar with the *felix culpa* paradox?"

The "happy fault," the "blessed fall," depending on how you translated the Latin. Reluctantly, Joseph nodded. Saint Augustine, Saint Ambrose, and Saint Francis de Sales all discussed it. Each Easter eve, in every Catholic church across the world, a Deacon or Priest sang the paradox aloud:

> O truly necessary sin of Adam, which has
> been blotted out by the death of Christ!
> O *felix culpa*, which has merited so great a
> Redeemer!

"Indulge me, please," Wallace urged. "Pretend I am one of your students: Why did God place the Tree of Knowledge in Paradise? Didn't He know Adam would eat the forbidden fruit?"

Joseph stared down at his stole. Like most of his vestments, it had a cross embroidered at its center. Against the violet of Penance, the golden cross was particularly striking. "Of course God knew. But if mankind had never fallen, Christ would never have died for us; and if Christ had never died for us, we would never have understood the depth of God's grace and His love."

"In the words of Saint Thomas Aquinas: 'God allows evils to happen in order to bring a greater good therefrom.'" Wallace donned his chasuble. "Purity is not perfection, Joseph."

AFTER THEY HAD BROKEN THEIR FAST, Wallace and his eldest son saddled Prince. When his things were packed and Joseph had mounted, Wallace patted the horse's neck and smiled up at him. "I cannot tell you *how* or *when*, in your situation or in mine; but I can tell you this, Joseph: 'Sin is necessary, but all shall be well, and all shall be well, and all manner of thing shall be well.'"

Joseph thought he'd heard those words before, or part of them. He did not remember *"Sin is necessary."* "Who are you quoting now?"

"God"—Wallace grinned—"by way of Mother Juliana of

Norwich. She was a fourteenth-century anchorite and mystic." He held up his index finger. "Grant me one minute longer." Wallace dashed up the porch steps and disappeared into the house. When he emerged again, he carried a slender, leather-bound volume. Wallace handed it up to Joseph, who opened the cover and read: *Sixteen Revelations of Divine Love: Shewed to a Devout Servant of our Lord*. "'All shall be well' is part of Juliana's Thirteenth Revelation."

Thirteen seemed appropriate.

"Keep it, please. Something to remember us by."

As if Joseph could ever forget.

CHAPTER 50

I and my bosom must debate awhile…
— William Shakespeare, *Henry V* (1600)

Joseph returned to Charleston differently than he had come, so he could minister to other parishioners. The way these people greeted him, the way they honored him—as if he were an angel, or Christ in their midst… They thought Joseph holy and pure; they thought he desired only God. How could he ever bless them with hands that had groped a woman's breast?

Saint Alphonsus had much to say on the matter:

The priest who, while he is defiled with sins against chastity, pronounces the words of consecration, spits in the face of Jesus Christ; and in receiving the sacred body and blood into his polluted mouth, he casts them into the foulest mire… Such priests are worse than Judas… How horrible to see a priest that should send forth in every direction the light and odor of purity, become sordid, fetid, and polluted with sins of the flesh…

And yet…these were abstractions. Was *Tessa* sordid, fetid, or polluted? Was *her* perfect mouth a foul mire? How then could touching her defile him? Surely God understood that Joseph wished only to honor Him, only to venerate the beauty He had created?

Joseph closed *Dignity and Duties of the Priest* and opened Juliana of Norwich's *Revelations*. In many ways, she reminded him of Saint Teresa; yet Juliana was different from any theologian Joseph had ever read. The God who had spoken to her would never condemn an unbaptized child to Hell.

Juliana wrote:

> I saw verily that Our Lord was never wrath, nor ever shall be: for He is God, He is good, He is truth, and He is peace... His love excuseth us, and of His great courtesy He doth away all our blame, and beholdeth us with compassion and pity... I shall do right naught but sin, and my sin shall not hinder His goodness working...

BEFORE HE ENTERED CHARLESTON, Joseph paused at St. Patrick's Churchyard to visit Hélène. He stood inside the Lazare mausoleum and placed his palm on the cool limestone that held his sister's name and her body, but not her spirit. "I'll never forget you, Ellie," he whispered. "I couldn't even if I tried." He prayed her sojourn in Purgatory would be brief. "If you're already in Heaven, will *you* pray for *me*, sister?" If he followed her advice, if he accepted her gifts— the lamp and the key—it would be almost like she was still with him.

He knew now that he would remain in Charleston as long as he could. Their next Bishop might very well make Joseph a mission Priest; but these two weeks on the road had proven he would be a poor one. He would yearn not only for Tessa, his mother, even his father's company—Joseph would miss the ocean, his garden, and his library too.

Joseph would miss returning to his own bed every night, however humble that bed. The night before his sister's surgery, he'd stopped sleeping on the floor and stopped using the discipline. He'd decided Hélène deserved more than a pale shadow of her brother. He did not resume these mortifications now. His head was clearer without them.

Furthermore, despite Prince's smooth action, Joseph had developed saddle sores on his journey. They were worse than any wound from the discipline. He refused to remove his trousers and drawers for his father, but Joseph described the sores. While trying not to chuckle, his father mixed him a balm that proved blissfully effective.

Joseph tried to find out more about Juliana of Norwich; but she had largely been lost to history. The Church had not canonized or beatified Juliana, but neither had it condemned her.

Joseph longed to wrap himself in the promise Christ had made her: that whatever choices Joseph made, whatever sins he committed, God would forgive him; God would forgive Tessa; and all would be well. Joseph wanted so much to believe those words were divine revelation. But in the Gospel of John, Christ commanded the adulteress: "Go, and sin no more." How could the same God have said "Sin is necessary"? And yet…Christ forgave the adulteress when no one else would. He made the Pharisees see they were *all* sinners.

JOSEPH HAD BEEN NEGLECTING both the Biblical garden and his parents' garden. He took up his tools again. Tessa was often visiting his mother. She must understand how isolated his mother was, especially since losing Hélène. On this side of the Atlantic, only a handful of people knew his mother's language; but Tessa was one of them. This kindness made Joseph love her all the more.

He was careful not to linger near Tessa. He would smile at her in passing, but he was determined not to touch her or speak to her again till he had made his decision. Tessa had the perfect way to reply without saying a word. When she was certain only Joseph could see, she pressed both hands to her heart. She was signing: *I love you.*

Joseph retreated to his father's empty office—not to stare at the Blessed Virgin's bare breast or at Mary Magdalene reaching for the half-naked Christ but to meditate on the painting that had been here the longest: Saint Denis picking up his own severed, haloed head. This third-century martyr had lent his name to Joseph's great-granduncle Denis, who perished during the Terror, and to Joseph himself at his Confirmation. His great-granduncle's presence at an Ancien Régime salon had inspired the famous exchange between the Cardinal de Polignac and the Marquise de Deffand. When he was a child, Joseph's great-grandmother Marguerite had passed the story on to him.

First, Cardinal de Polignac had described Saint Denis's martyrdom: even after pagans beheaded him, Denis remained undeterred. He was a Bishop, and his work was not yet complete. His decapitated body stood up and reclaimed his head, which preached a homily as he walked. Denis refused to die until he'd finished this homily. By that time, he'd carried his head an entire league.

"Some say it was *two* leagues!" Cardinal de Polignac had exclaimed.

"The distance doesn't matter," the Marquise de Deffand had observed. "It is the first step that is difficult."

JOSEPH FORCED HIMSELF to finish rereading *Dignity and Duties of the Priest*. "Let us tremble: we are flesh," admitted Saint Alphonsus. He related:

> Blessed Jordan severely reproved one of his religious for having, without any bad motive, once taken a woman by the hand. The religious said in answer that she was a saint. But, replied the holy man: "The rain is good, and the earth also, but mix them together and they become mire."

No, Joseph thought, as he watered the soil around his pomegranate tree and admired the scarlet buds. *Mix rain and earth together, and they become LIFE and BEAUTY.*

As long as there was not *too much* rain. That was the key. Even Father Wallace had assumed Joseph and Tessa would not fully consummate their union. *"You'll find a line and you won't cross it,"* Liam had said. Joseph would never ask Tessa for more than she wished to give him. He would *take* nothing at all.

On the Feast of Saint Joseph, the day he completed his thirty-first year, he returned to his father's house and climbed the stairs to his sister's dressing chamber. He opened the drawer of her wardrobe and found the key to Tessa's garden still nestled inside, like a seed awaiting planting. Joseph searched Hélène's jewelry-box for a long silver chain. He threaded the key onto it and fastened the chain around his neck. He undid his choker and tucked the key beneath his shirt. No one else would know the key was there. But he would know.

HE RESISTED THE TEMPTATION to try the key in advance; yet throughout Passiontide, Joseph haunted the corner of Church Street and Longitude Lane, watching for the blue lamp. He would not answer till after Lent, but he wanted the assurance that Tessa would still welcome him.

On Good Friday, Joseph finally saw the lamp in the right-most window on the second floor, just as she had promised. Even across the front garden and through the wrought iron fence, the double-burner lamp shone like a beacon. Calling him into her bedchamber.

Joseph could not answer it—not on Good Friday, even if this was his last chance. It might well be. Surely Tessa's husband would return from Stratford-on-Ashley tomorrow. His appearances at the cathedral were erratic, but he'd always managed Christmas and Easter. After that, Edward might remain in Charleston till the fall. It was already the middle of April, and planters never spent summers at their plantations—the risk of fever was too great. By fall, they might have a new Bishop, who might send Joseph to a faraway parish. He might never see Tessa again.

Apprehension descended instead of sleep. Joseph's total fast made waiting no easier. He would consume nothing but Christ until after Easter Mass. At Lauds the next morning, his breviary directed him to pray Psalm 62: *"For thee my soul hath thirsted; for thee my flesh, O how many ways!"* Joseph wondered if King David had meant those words only for God, or for Bathsheba, too.

For reasons that were not entirely clear to Joseph, over the centuries the timing of the Easter Vigil had shifted to earlier and yet earlier on Holy Saturday. Once, the long rite had begun late in the evening and reached its climax at midnight Easter morning. Now, they lit the Paschal Candle and celebrated Christ's nighttime resurrection when the sun had barely risen *Saturday* morning. This was the greatest moment of the Christian year; by the end of the Mass, it would be Easter, liturgically. But most of Joseph's congregation waited till Sunday morning to celebrate. Only the truly faithful gathered in the Biblical garden for the Easter Vigil.

Tessa was amongst them. Even before her Confession to him, he'd been careful not to look her way during Mass. But his eyes were starving for the sight of her even more than his stomach was aching from his fast. It took Father Baker a few moments to kindle the New Fire with a flint. While they waited, Joseph allowed himself a glance at Tessa.

She wore a simple white cotton dress, adorned only with pleats. She made it breathtaking. Framed by her mantilla, her own eyes remained intent on Father Baker; she did not look to Joseph. She held her hands just below the point of her bodice, yet they were not clasped in prayer. In fact, her small motions seemed out of place. Tessa had extended the first two fingers of her right hand. Again and again, she pressed them into her cupped left hand and rotated her extended fingers as if she were turning a key.

For a moment, Joseph forgot to breathe. Beneath his clothes, the key to Tessa's garden felt as if it were burning his chest. His mother was standing behind Tessa; she couldn't see Tessa's hands. The sign was for him. *Safe!* Tessa's hands cried. Or perhaps she meant the pantomime more literally: *Use the key!* Either way, it was an invitation. Edward must have remained at the plantation. But how could she know he wouldn't return before nightfall?

Joseph dared not risk confirmation. He dared not look back at Tessa. His part of the Easter Vigil rite had come. He discarded his violet vestments of Penance, melancholy, and sacrifice. In their place, he donned white vestments of purity and joy—light breaking through the darkness. If he'd looked down to see their key glowing bright through the linen and silk, he would not have been surprised.

They processed into the cathedral. Joseph genuflected and prayed: "May the Lord be in my heart and in my lips…" Joseph clasped his hands before him and sang for joy. But it was Tessa in his heart and in his lips, as much as God.

"Ex-ul-tet…" the hymn began: *Rejoice…* Joseph let the ancient words flow through him: the plainchant whose beauty belied its name. This was an aria to surpass Mozart and Donizetti, all the more elaborate for its lack of accompaniment. Lifted by jubilation and weighted with yearning, every syllable rose and fell, dipping and turning like the incense that billowed around him. For a quarter of an hour, he stopped time. For more than a thousand years, men of God had chanted the Exultet on this day.

Before celibacy became compulsory, how many of those men had been husbands? Ever since, how many had sung these words to a beloved hidden in the crowd? Even now, Father Wallace must be chanting the Exultet to Sarah.

"O truly necessary sin…" Joseph sang. "O truly blessed night… The sacredness of this night dispels wickedness, washes away sin, restores innocence to the fallen, and joy to those in sorrow…"

After Joseph bowed his head and the last note died away, the twelve lessons began. The first reading was from Genesis: "And God said: Let there be light. And God saw the light that it was good…" With his eyes, Joseph saw the Paschal Candle; but in his mind, he saw Tessa's blue lamp.

When Joseph laid Christ's Body on Tessa's tongue, she closed her mouth so quickly, her lips brushed his fingers—like a tiny Baptism. The memory of her warmth remained with him beyond the last "Amen."

As soon as he'd unvested, Joseph longed to run after her. But it wasn't even noon yet. Tessa's slaves would be in the house. He must wait the ten excruciating hours till sunset.

He blessed the homes he hadn't blessed on Epiphany. He returned to the cathedral and heard the Confessions of parishioners who planned to receive the Eucharist at the Easter Mass. It was only mid-April, and already the closeness of the booth felt oppressive. He did not visit his own confessor. Joseph knew what the man would say.

By late afternoon, Joseph was exhausted. He must conserve his strength, or he would faint before he even caught sight of Tessa again. He allowed himself a little water, since this was permitted during the forty-hour fast.

Before he lay down, he knelt by his bed and prayed for a sign. The key felt like a millstone around his neck. Was he truly about to do this: skulk into another man's home to ogle his wife? On *Holy Saturday*? It wasn't too late. He could still decide not to go to her.

Somehow Joseph managed to rest; but he did not dream. He rose only to kneel in prayer again. *"O God, be merciful to me, a sinner." Above all, be merciful to Tessa. I am her Priest; her soul is in my care. If this is mortal sin, let the punishment fall on me alone. Give me a sign that whatever I do,* SHE *will be saved...*

I do not pray as Saint Augustine did in his wicked youth: "Grant me chastity and continency, but not yet." Instead I beg You: Grant me chastity and continency—and Tessa. Grant me the strength to live without the touch of her flesh, but do not ask me to live without the sound of her voice and the sight of her face.

The sun was setting; but David would still be awake. Joseph must wait an hour or two longer. This was his last chance to think things through, to make the right choice once and for all.

He browsed the books in the library downstairs. Inscribed on these pages, there were a thousand reasons to remain in this sanctuary, to turn his back on Tessa. He'd read and recited the arguments so many times, they rattled around in his head—admonishing him, condemning him. *"It is necessary, above all things, to abstain from looking at women, and still more from looking at them a second time. ... Our intercourse with women should be passing, and as if we were in flight."*

Joseph noticed that someone had left a pink ribbon in one of the books. It was Saint Teresa's *Interior Castle*—his own copy, though he hadn't read it since seminary. He'd lent it to Tessa and later to Hélène. He opened to the page with the ribbon. Someone had underlined: "it is not so essential to *think* much as to *love* much; do, then, whatever most arouses you to love."

Joseph released his breath. Saint Teresa was speaking of loving *God*; but Joseph had asked for a sign. Writing in someone else's book, the pink ribbon—these were traces of his sister, surely. She was guiding him even now, his Hélène—his light. Joseph closed his eyes, then the book, and pressed it against the key still nestled close to his heart. "I hear you, Ellie."

He wondered if his sister had read Juliana of Norwich. Hélène would have liked her. Perhaps they were conversing even now.

CHAPTER 51

Thou art…a locked garden, a fountain
  sealed up.
Thy plants are a paradise of pomegranates…
— Canticle of Canticles 4:12-13

Joseph left the theological library and the Biblical garden behind him. He tried to progress nonchalantly toward Church Street, as if he were out for an evening stroll. But the nearer he came to Tessa, the faster each step followed the last. By the time he reached Meeting Street, he was racing. Anyone who recognized him would think he was rushing to a deathbed. The truth was quite the opposite.

Yet he felt as if he were a skiff careening around breakers, as if this mad dash could end in no way but splinters. Then, on the corner of Longitude Lane, he found his bearings at last. The blue lamp was shining for him, like a lighthouse in the midst of a storm.

Before turning into the alley, he gripped the Stratfords' wrought iron fence to steady himself. He remained light-headed from his fast, and sweat was collecting around his waist. He doffed his wool hat, unbuttoned his wool coat, and panted. Only April, and already so warm. This was Charleston, after all.

In the next moment, he noticed the ghoulish shadows the fence cast on the sidewalk and across his own body. He saw the *chevaux-de-frise* that guarded Tessa's house as if for the first time: the spikes meant to protect the inhabitants' lives, their valuables, and the virtue of their women. To impale lustful negroes.

Joseph's throat tightened with guilt for sins not yet committed—and so many which already had been. Beyond Edward, beyond even God, there remained this: Joseph's deception of the woman he claimed to love. This was the barrier he'd not yet overcome: the amalgamation of his blood. He'd pushed it aside and refused to think about it at all, because he was terrified it would outweigh everything else. *"For what communion hath light with darkness?"* Before he put his colored hands on Tessa's alabaster flesh, he must tell her the truth about his family. But when he did, these midnight meetings might cease before they began. Tessa might never again love him as anything but a brother.

Suddenly, he was literally cast into darkness: the blue lamp disappeared from the window. Joseph's heart nearly stopped. Tessa couldn't know what he was thinking. And Edward couldn't have returned home; the carriageway entered the lot a few feet from where Joseph stood. Perhaps Tessa had grown tired of waiting.

Joseph had asked for a sign. This was it. He'd missed his chance.

Then the twin lights of the blue lamp appeared on the piazza and floated into the garden, toward the far gate. Tessa had seen him. She was coming out to meet him—but not here, where anyone could see. She was flying to their secret door.

Joseph released his breath. He replaced his hat and fled from the shadows of the *chevaux-de-frise*. He followed the scent of the Noisettes to their wall. The flagstones of Longitude Lane stretched out before him like twin paths, illuminated *just enough* by the full moon and the street lamps at each end. Deserted, but for him and the roses.

First the white Lamarques greeted him, crisp and luminous in the pale light. Then the sweeter, muskier scent of the Jaune Desprez, luscious as pineapple with heads the color of flesh—unless you were a negro. And finally, from inside Tessa's garden, the fragrance of gardenias.

She was waiting for him on the other side of her gate, holding their blue lamp. For a moment, she only grinned at him through the claire-voie. "You saw," she whispered. "You understood. You *came*."

He did not even need the key; she'd already unlocked her gate for him. One last time, he glanced right and left to ensure they were alone. As Tessa opened the door, Joseph stared down at the line where stone became grass. He thought of Saint Denis; and then he stepped over the threshold into Tessa's garden.

As soon as he was inside, she clasped his hand. Joseph looked for the myrtle hedge—as if it might have vanished since February, exposing them to the slave quarters. But the myrtle kept their secrets.

"You needn't worry about the slaves seeing the light," Tessa told him in a low voice. "They know I come out to my garden at night sometimes: to inhale the moonflowers or to pray." She looked not to her statue of the Blessed Virgin but to her Arbor Vitae, the tallest tree in her garden. "*This* is my cathedral, too."

She *was* descended from Druids who worshipped trees.

Tessa had changed her attire since the Vigil Mass; she was in glorious dishabille. If he'd been able to see as much through the claire-voie, Joseph might have thought twice about joining her. Tessa wore a wrapper of vivid blue edged in gold, the same colors as their lamp. A wide print bordered each hem, featuring scarlet flowers that resembled nothing so much as pomegranate blossoms.

Joseph sided with the scholars who believed the Tree of Knowledge was a pomegranate, the forbidden fruit of Paradise. But other scholars argued that the Tree of *Life* was a pomegranate.

Tessa had buttoned the pomegranate wrapper only to the gold sash at her waist; below, the openwork embroidery of her white petticoat peeked through. At least the shape of the bodice proved she'd not yet shed her corset. She still wore pearl earrings too. Neither had she let down her hair, her plait done up simply in the way that resembled a Renaissance halo.

The grass muffled their footsteps as he allowed Tessa to lead him within sight of the white piazza. Then, sweat rolled down his spine again, and he stopped. She turned, frowning at him in the light of the blue lamp.

Joseph looked back in the direction of the slave quarters. He couldn't meet her eyes. He recalled Jefferson's treatise on the differences between negroes and whites. Negroes *"secrete more by the glands of the skin,"* that great man of science claimed, *"which gives them a very strong and disagreeable odour."*

Joseph swallowed. "Tessa…there is something you do not know about me."

She seemed to hesitate. "Yes?"

"When my father was born, he was a slave. His mother was a slave. I have African blood, Tessa."

Of all the reactions he'd imagined, Joseph had not anticipated this. When he managed to look back at her, Tessa's eyes were crinkled up, and she was grinning. "You finally told me."

For a moment, Joseph only blinked at her. At last he realized: "Hélène told you."

"*Years* ago."

Joseph almost laughed. Of course Hélène had ignored his advice. "Y-You never said anything."

"Neither did you. I knew you'd tell me when you were ready."

"It doesn't bother you?"

"Do you think less of *me* because my parents are poor?"

"It's hardly the same."

"Isn't it?" She caressed his palm with her thumb, as she'd done at the opera. Then she tugged on his hand again.

Caught in her tide, he washed up the steps of the piazza and into the entry hall. The only sound was the tall case clock, ticking loudly in the darkness. The spiral staircase loomed above them, the familiar become suddenly foreign.

"David?" Joseph whispered to Tessa.

"He blew out his lamp an hour ago. Clare is also asleep. I just gave her to Hannah. She'll stay with her in the nursery." Tessa led him to the first step.

Joseph hesitated. He hadn't expected her to be out of her dress already. "Surely it would be wiser to remain in the parlor..."

"Only if you wish to arouse the suspicions of my neighbors. They are accustomed to me sitting up at night reading or with Clare —but I do it in my bedchamber."

Joseph gulped and followed her up the stairs. He half expected one of the steps to shriek in accusation beneath his feet; but they were as silent as tombstones. Still he glanced above them in worry, as if he might find David's young face peering down at them. When he and Tessa reached the second floor, Joseph saw the glow beneath the door of the nursery, nothing more. Her husband's room was dark.

Tessa led him into her bedchamber, closing the door quietly behind them. Still it clicked with finality. In spite of himself, Joseph's attention went immediately to the bed. Two pillows lay atop the smooth counterpane, the green brocade bed-curtains drawn open. Across the room, Tessa's méridienne was emerald too. In vestments, green was the color of ordinary time. *This* was anything but ordinary.

Tessa closed the inner jalousie shutters of the left-most window. Then she plucked off his hat and set it down next to their lamp, on the table he'd used so many times as an altar. Fortunately the sick call cabinet was shut tight. While he was thinking about the crucifix tucked inside, Joseph realized Tessa had undone the sash of her wrapper and was beginning to undo the buttons.

"Don't—" He choked on the word.

She peered up at him through her lashes. "I refuse to wear this corset a minute longer."

Did she think he was made of stone? While Tessa unbuttoned her wrapper, Joseph stared determinedly at their lamp. He'd not yet had a chance to examine the fine French craftsmanship. Above the two burners, the oil reservoir took the shape of a fountain. Two exotic, golden birds perched on its edge. They had crests and luxuriant tails; he thought perhaps they were phoenixes.

Tessa's voice broke into his thoughts: "I cannot do this by myself. I can either ask Hannah—and probably wake Clare—or..."

She'd peeled off her blue wrapper now. The neckline of her chemise was low, exposing her gorgeous collarbones. This chemise had no buttons, only a delicate line of embroidery just beneath a gathered draw-string. Her corset was quilted white on white, patterned simply but beautifully with flowers. Joseph had seen his mother and sisters' corsets when they weren't wearing them; he knew such garments laced down the back. But on the front of this corset, laces fastened together each gusset as well, so that they might be opened. This must be a nursing corset, he realized. The knowledge retarded his lust only briefly.

"Will you help me?"

Slowly, Joseph nodded. Tessa turned her back and motioned first to the draw-string of her petticoat, which covered her corset where it extended below her waist. Joseph tried not to let his hands tremble. He undid the string, and the petticoat slid to the floor, pooling at their feet like a fallen white rose.

There was another petticoat beneath the first, this one of dove-grey and fastened by a single button at the waist. When this too had fallen, Tessa's legs remained concealed by her chemise, and further obscured by the drawers underneath. Nevertheless, his eyes riveted below the line of her corset, trying shamelessly to discern the shape of her buttocks.

But Tessa twisted her hand behind her to direct him to the end of her corset laces. He undid the knot and tugged the laces through each eyelet. As he learned the rhythm, Joseph pulled faster and faster. The laces made a slight hissing noise till at last he tossed them aside like a snake.

"Thank you!" With a sigh, Tessa withdrew her arms from the straps and discarded the corset onto the nearest piece of furniture. It was her prie-Dieu. As she turned to him, her chemise slipped off one shoulder. At least this distracted him from finding her breasts through the linen. "*You* can't wish to remain as you are either?" Tessa inquired. "'Tis too warm."

It was true: he was more damp with sweat now than he'd been on the street.

Tessa peered appraisingly at his choker, the badge of his Priesthood. She slid the tip of her thumb beneath one of the folds. "Will you show me…?"

Joseph reached under the layers of silk and withdrew the knot. Tessa undid it with something like glee, the edge of her lower lip caught between her teeth. She tossed one end of the neckerchief over his shoulder, then the other, tugging and unlooping till he was free of it. Finally, she draped his choker over her corset on the prie-Dieu. Their shed clothing, already in union.

She helped him shrug off his coat and threw that over the back of her méridienne, on top of her wrapper. Tessa dispatched his waistcoat nearly as quickly. But when she reached for his braces, he managed to stop her, capturing her hands in his. "That's enough."

She frowned, her eyes sliding down the length of his body. "Your boots, though—you'll want to remove those." She kicked off her slippers and directed him to sit on her méridienne. She knelt before him and bent her myrrh-brown head to the task.

While she popped open each button, he focused his gaze on her shimmering hair, so that he would not stare inside her gaping chemise. As she slid off the second short boot, Joseph stammered: "Would you— Would you let down your hair?"

Tessa smiled up at him and inched closer. He'd splayed his legs a bit, to give her access to the rows of buttons on the inside of his boots; now, Tessa inserted herself between his knees before he could stop her. Head bowed, she took one of his startled hands and placed it beneath her halo of braids. "The first pin is right…*here.*" She helped him extract it, and the long bronze plait began to unravel.

After seven and a half years of waiting, finally his fingers were plunging into those silken strands, unfurling each plait like a banner —so enraptured that she was squeezing his knee before he'd realized her hand was there. She'd braced her other hand against the edge of the méridienne, so her arm was grazing his other leg. His trousers were broadcloth; but never had they seemed so thin. With every dropped hairpin, he seemed to release more of her perfume; he was drowning in her scent and her softness and he never wanted to come up for air.

Tessa's own nose brushed his shirt. "I love the way you smell: of myrrh…"

"You smell of gardenias." Purity and ecstasy.

She tilted her face to him now, her bronze hair spilling over her shoulders. "Do you like it?"

"Very much." What he liked—what he adored—was the scent of gardenias mingled with *her*: perspiration and something else he could not even name. He longed to taste her. Only his fingers lapped the pomegranate blush of her cheek; only his thumb licked at the corner of her luscious mouth. But she was more masterpiece than meal. His hand plunged down the soft column of her neck, across the exquisite workmanship of her collarbone, all the way to that bare alabaster shoulder.

And then he saw his hand against her skin, how it was several shades darker. He wore gloves so often; he could not blame that darkness on the sun.

"What are you thinking?" Tessa whispered.

"It would be different, wouldn't it, if I looked more like my Haitian grandmother? If I were the color of pitch and my features were African?"

She squeezed his knee again. "I would love you if you were *green.*"

He looked behind her, to her wall mirror, which reflected only his curly head. "But not if I were black." Why did it even matter to him, when his skin *wasn't* black? When she shouldn't love him in the first place? Yet it mattered more than anything in the world.

"I want to say it wouldn't make any difference at all. But I cannot truly answer that question." Tessa stroked her thumb beneath his lower lip. "I have grown very, very fond of your person, exactly as it is."

Joseph did not smile back.

Tessa knew he wasn't satisfied. She rested her hand on his upper thigh and closed her eyes. "I shall try to imagine it. When I first came to Charleston, everything here was so new and strange, frightening even—the negroes most of all. But the longer I know them, the more beautiful they become to me. *That* is the truth." She opened her eyes again—shining like hot myrrh in the lamplight. "I think it only would have taken me a little longer to fall in love with you." She twined her fingers into the tight curls at his brow. "You are black *and* beautiful, my beloved."

This time, he smiled back. She'd changed the verse; originally, it was: *I am black BUT beautiful.* He finally understood the importance of "and." He no longer felt fractured. He felt whole and truly colored for the first time in his life. He felt newly baptized, blessed to the bottom of his soul, because this woman loved him. "You've read the Canticles."

"They are quite…inspirational." Tessa caught her lower lip between her teeth again. "Now, will you come to bed, my love?"

What *exactly* did she mean by that?

She took his hand in hers and sprang to her feet, lithe and agile as a doe. Somehow, they managed not to stumble over their shoes as she towed him across the bedroom—though her petti-coats hindered him temporarily, making Tessa giggle and Joseph blush.

When she reached the end of the bed, Tessa released him, only to draw up the skirt of her chemise and climb onto the counter-pane. Joseph tried not to stare at her legs, sheathed only in translu-cent stockings, one of them exposed all the way to her knee. He tried even harder not to watch how her breasts moved beneath her chemise as she slid backwards on the bed and then lounged on her elbow against one of the large pillows.

Tessa held out her hand to him. "Come here."

What on Earth did she expect from him? Did she really believe seeing her like this would do nothing to him, that they could cuddle chastely like children? His only consolation was this: his member remained in a state of shock so profound that it seemed to be cower-ing, terrified rather than elated by its luck.

He chose to lie down on the far side of the bed, where he could gaze at her without touching her. Tessa did not approach him, but she did turn toward him. Her head on the pillow, she tucked her hands under her neck, so that her bent arms blocked her breasts, which was a mercy. But most of her hair had ended up either beneath her or behind her. Only a few precious tendrils lay between them on the counterpane.

Tessa saw him looking, and she knew him as well as he knew himself. She pulled the gold-brown tresses from beneath her and flung them above her head. Her hair settled on the pillows like the rays of a monstrance. "Better?"

"Yes," he laughed. "Even better."

"I have a favorite part of you, too—a *new* favorite part."

"Oh?"

"'Tis right"—she extended her arm across the space between them till her fingertip tapped the bulge in his throat—"here."

Joseph frowned. "My Adam's apple?"

"There it goes again! I love watching it move! This is the first time I've ever seen it—your choker always hides it. 'Tis so deliciously *masculine*."

"You have one too, you know."

"I do *not*! What a terrible thing to say!" She crossed her arms over her breasts and looked away from him, with only coy glances back. "Your inexperience with women is showing, sir. I'm not sure I can forgive you."

"*Everyone* has an Adam's apple!" Joseph protested, lifting on one elbow. "It's nothing but cartilage protecting your larynx—your vocal cords. Yours is harder to find than mine, but it's there. My father taught us about it years ago." His sisters had been delighted by the secret, but Joseph had never imagined *he* would need to know such a thing.

Tessa pouted, still unwilling to believe him.

"I'll show you." He slipped his hand to the place where her neck became her shoulder and rested his thumb at the center of her throat. "Tilt back your head?"

Tessa obeyed, though it might have been a gesture of affront. Gently but firmly, Joseph pressed down his thumb near the base of her throat, seeking the hidden ridge beneath the surface. Her eyes narrowed.

"Am I hurting you?"

"I trust you, Joseph."

He'd *almost* found the place; he'd felt it move just then. "Sing something for me."

Tessa smiled wickedly and obliged: "O-O-O-O ve-re be-a-ta nox…" She pulled out the "O" just as he'd done that morning, so it took up nearly as many notes as "vere beata nox." Her tiny perfect apple leapt and vibrated beneath his finger with every transcendent syllable: *O truly blessed night…*

"Did you feel that?" Joseph asked excitedly.

Tessa only grinned at him.

"It's right here." He tapped her hidden apple with his thumb. "Right…" The next instant, he'd leaned closer, and his lips had replaced his finger.

He didn't know what possessed him to do it. Without the participation of his mind, his body chose for him.

Every time he celebrated a Sacrament, he kissed the cross on his vestments. In the course of every Mass, he kissed the altar that held the bone of a saint and the Body of Christ. For three decades, he'd kissed the rings of Bishops, the hands of Priests, and the feet of Popes. He honored them with his kisses; he acknowledged his unworthiness and their right to his veneration; he told them they were precious to him.

But nothing and no one he'd ever felt beneath his lips had responded like this. Tessa moaned his name, and the well of her beautiful voice trembled against his mouth. She grasped the front of his shirt and the key with it, but she did not ask him to stop.

One kiss was not nearly enough, so he did it again and then again. He wanted to praise every inch of her. He wanted to trail kisses down her throat, lick the perspiration from her collarbones, and discover her glorious breasts. But she was nursing; he would embarrass her. So with a sigh of his own, he skimmed his mouth upward instead, deepening his kisses, lingering, tasting the sweet salt of her skin and the musk of gardenias. He must be leaving a sheen on her flesh, but he didn't care. Four months before, hadn't he blessed her daughter with wetness from his mouth?

He reached the underside of her jaw, let his teeth brush her skin, felt her quivering against him as her pulse grew quicker and quicker, and still he did not stop. One hand gripping that bare shoulder, the other lost in her hair, he kissed toward her ear, up to the edge of her cheek, hesitated. Her mouth was so near now, but the way he wanted to kiss her there might appall her, and he'd no real notion how to do it. Perhaps he should continue upward instead, kiss the lids of her luminous eyes... But Tessa was turning, deciding for him, panting warm at the corner of his lips, at their center, her open mouth—

Then all at once she was jerking away from him, sitting up. Startled, bereft, Joseph's eyes blinked open, but he saw only the white pillow and the ends of her hair. He'd asked too much of her, too soon. He never should have grasped her shoulder; she must have felt trapped. Her moans had been discomfort, not pleasure.

In the next moment, he understood. Tessa called out her daughter's name, and Clare's wail reached them from the other side of the hall.

"I'm coming, *a chuisle!*" Tessa cried. But before she dashed from the room, for one brief second she caressed Joseph's shoulder. "I'm sorry."

Joseph hesitated. He wanted to go after her, but Hannah would be there too.

Hannah knew everything already.

In her haste, Tessa left the doors open. Across the hall, he heard Hannah telling her mistress: "I'm sorry; I tried to calm her. But she wanted *you.*"

Joseph wondered if Clare's wailing had woken David. He supposed his nephew was used to such sounds by now. Still, Joseph must be careful not to make any loud noises himself; he did not wish to alert the boy to his presence, especially not in his current state of undress. Even when Tessa had sung for him, they'd been careful to keep their voices low. Joseph rose from the bed and gently pushed the door closed.

He supposed David would become aware of his visits eventually, but Joseph was not eager to face the boy. *"I think he's old enough to understand,"* Hélène had said. That much was probably true: David had left his childhood beside Independence Rock. Joseph's sister had also implied that their nephew disliked Edward as much as they did. But neither was David reconciled to God. The knowledge that his spiritual advisor was fondling his foster-mother would hardly restore the boy's faith.

Joseph had done a great deal more fondling than he'd intended for their first night together—less than he'd wanted, but more than he'd intended. Tessa's willingness to fondle *him* was simultaneously exhilarating and unsettling. It frightened him, how easily he surrendered to it, how quickly and completely his body snatched control from his mind. If he waited for Tessa to return to this bedchamber, they were sure to do more.

One of their guardian angels must have woken Clare as a warning. Joseph should not have needed such divine intervention. He should have been more careful. He *would be* more careful. He would prove to himself that he could stop. Right now.

Right *now.*

He closed his eyes and steeled himself.

He returned to the méridienne and pulled his boots back on. He retrieved his waistcoat and rebuttoned it, then his coat. His choker had slithered to the floor under the prie-Dieu, and he nearly forgot it.

He crossed the hall as quietly as he could. In the nursery, Tessa's maid stood with her back to the door, but she turned at Joseph's approach and smiled a greeting. "Hannah…" he began. He stared down at his hat, uncertain how to proceed. Finally, he said simply: "Thank you."

She understood. Hannah looked to the easy chair, where Tessa was singing softly in Irish to her daughter. "I know what it's like to be separated from someone you love. Tessa does all she can for me —I'll do all I can for her."

Joseph remained at the threshold. Clare was content now that Tessa had pulled open the neck of her chemise. The baby's eager mouth concealed Tessa's nipple, but not the white swell of her breast. No: not truly white, any more than he was truly black. Tessa sat in shadow, but he could still see it: her skin was closer to peach flushed with pink, like the Jaune Desprez.

Barely three years ago, Tessa had longed for death to end her grief. Now, she was pulsing with life, blooming with love before his very eyes, as fresh and new as her daughter—and a thousand times more beautiful than the Virgin in his father's painting.

In the portrait, Joseph the saint averted his eyes to his prayer book. Joseph the boy had fled to the confessional. Now, Joseph the man lingered and smiled.

When Tessa looked up at him, she saw he was dressed. Her rose mouth turned downward. "Won't you stay?"

Reluctantly, Joseph shook his head. "Not tonight." Tomorrow was a rather important Mass.

"But you'll come back to me, another night?"

"I will."

They were the words of the Marriage vow. *I, Joseph Lazare, take thee, Teresa Conley, for my unlawful wife, to have and to hold, from this day forward, for better or worse...*

THE END of *Necessary Sins*.
But the Lazare Family Saga is just beginning…

If you enjoyed this novel, please help other readers discover it by leaving an honest review, even a short one, on Amazon, Goodreads, and/or BookBub. I'd be thrilled if you'd mention *Necessary Sins* on social media too. Word of mouth, literal or virtual, makes an enormous difference to an indie author like me. Thank you so much!

Do you want to know what happens next between Joseph and Tessa? What's really haunting David? Who Clare will grow up to be? The rest of the Lazare Family Saga is now available for Kindle, in paperback, and in hardcover, starting with Book Two, *Lost Saints*.

For a Lazare Family Tree, visit my website:
https://elizabethbellauthor.com/faq/

For my private Facebook group:
https://www.facebook.com/groups/LazareFamilySaga/

AUTHOR'S NOTE

While all of my central characters are fictional, they interact with many people who really lived. To the best of my ability, I have portrayed these figures as the historical record reveals them, inventing as little as possible. In some cases, I have adapted their actual words into my text, such as John Horry's chilling statement to his enslaver or Father Baker's farewell over the tomb of Bishop England. The following is a list of these historical figures.

Médéric-Louis-Elie Moreau de Saint-Méry, who left the most complete record of Saint-Domingue; **Dr. Charles Arthaud**; **Jean-Baptiste de Caradeux**, who married his nineteen-year-old niece when he was forty-two; and the **Gallifet** family. **Makandal, Vincent Ogé, Toussaint Louverture,** and Haitian **President Jean-Pierre Boyer**.

"Father of the Deaf" **Abbé Charles-Michel de l'Épée** and **Dr. Jean-Marc-Gaspard Itard**. Swiss scientist and inventor **Ami Argand**.

Denmark Vesey; **Jemmy Clement**; **Elias Horry** and his coachman, **John**. Postmaster **Alfred Huger**.

Horticulturist **Philippe Noisette**, **Celestine**, and their children. Botanist and physician **Carolus Linnaeus**. Diplomat **Joel Poinsett**, for whom the poinsettia is named. English landscape architect **Lancelot "Capability" Brown**.

Schoolmistress **Ann Marsan Talvande**. Since Mary Chesnut's novel *Two Years* is semi-autobiographical, her character "**Monkey**" is likely based on a real person; historian Elisabeth Muhlenfeld found "a young free black female under ten years in age" listed in the Talvande household in the 1830 census (*Two Novels by Mary Chesnut*, 2002).

Most of the priests, with the exception of Joseph himself and Fathers Laroche and Verchese. I named the latter in homage to Father Ralph de Bricassart's mentor in Colleen McCullough's *The Thorn Birds* (1977). **Archbishop Ambrose Maréchal**; **Bishop John England** (as well as his sister, **Joanna Monica England**); **Father John McEncroe**; and **Father Richard Swinton Baker** are all taken from life—although there is no evidence the latter ever wore a corset.

Bishop England did ordain the mixed-race **George Paddington** in Port-au-Prince, Haiti. He also banished a mixed-race nun from Charleston. The Bishop's ownership of an enslaved man is based on the 1830 Federal Census and the Bishop's mention of "**Castalio**" in a May 4, 1831 letter reprinted in the May 14 *United States Catholic Miscellany*. History does not tell us how Bishop England acquired Castalio or what became of him after 1831; these are my invention. My gratitude goes to Professor David C. R. Heisser, who put the pieces together and brought Castalio to my attention via his article "Bishop Lynch's People" in *The South Carolina Historical Magazine* 102.3 (2001).

Father James Wallace's priesthood, professorship, investment acumen, and general brilliance are described in Father Jeremiah Joseph O'Connell's *Catholicity in the Carolinas and Georgia* (1879) and Father Peter Guilday's *The Life and Times of John England* (1927). That Wallace "was the father by a colored woman whom he owned of three sons—**Andrew**, **George**, and **James**" is documented in Julian A. Selby's *Memorabilia and Anecdotal Reminiscences of Columbia, S. C.* (1905). I discovered the Wallaces through John Hammond Moore's *Columbia and Richland County* (1993).

All the writers, composers, artists, and saints I mention are historical, such as **Saint Teresa of Ávila**, **Julian(a) of Norwich**, **Gian Lorenzo Bernini** and **Gaetano Donizetti**. I took a bit of poetic license by having *Lucia di Lammermoor* (written in 1835) performed in Charleston a few months before its recorded debut in the United States, although the French version had been performed in New Orleans in 1841.

"Absence is to love as wind is to fire…" is from Count Roger de Bussy-Rabutin's *Histoire amoureuse des Gaules* (1665). The lyrics of the ballad "I'd Offer Thee This Hand of Mine" were penned by Bransford Vawter of Lynchburg, Virginia, who would die of consumption at the age of twenty-three in 1838. "The grave's a fine and private place" is a line from Andrew Marvell's poem "To His Coy Mistress," written about 1651.

All the clocks in Gérard Saint-Clair's shop are based on real 18th- and 19th-century timepieces. In his office, René has copies of Joos van Cleve's *The Holy Family* (1515-20) and Titian's *Noli Me Tangere* (circa 1514), both now held by The National Gallery in London. Léon Bonnat's *Martyrdom of St. Denis* (1885), a mural in the Panthéon in Paris, inspired the third painting.

My characters use several foreign terms of endearment, some of which translate into English better than others. They are all equivalent to "sweetheart" or "my dear." Haitian Creole: *trezò mwen* (my treasure). French: *ma petite* (my little one), *ma poulette* (my chicken), *ma minette* (my pussycat), and *ma belle* (my beautiful one). Irish: *a pheata* (my pet) and *a chuisle mo chroí* (pulse of my heart). For a more extensive glossary and bibliography, please visit my website: https://elizabethbellauthor.com/

About half of my period sources capitalize priest and the sacraments. To indicate Catholic reverence for them, I decided to maintain the capitalization. Conversely, the word Negro is lowercase because it would not have been capitalized at this time. The word octoon would later become octoroon.

I find third-person limited point of view the richest and most rewarding way to explore the past and understand it, but this presents challenges akin to an unreliable narrator since I am forced to reflect the era's prejudices. If any of my readers have been hurt by my inclusion of the n-word, I apologize sincerely. My intention is historical accuracy and nothing more. Where this word appears, I am quoting or reflecting 19th-century sources.

ACKNOWLEDGMENTS

Everyone who ever told me I was a writer made this book possible. Your faith in my work, even and especially when I doubted myself, means more to me than you will ever know or I can ever express. Your words of encouragement were like life-saving blood transfusions. I am particularly grateful to my first supporters: Kristy Calhoun, Kristin Holstun, and Amy Weatherman. And to the first readers of the Lazare Family Saga, who gave me fantastic feedback all along the way: Christina Campbell, Mary Overton (who always knew it was a series), and Lillian Rouly.

My beta readers for their invaluable comments: Maron Anrow, Susan Bainwol, Ida Bostian, Hilary Brown, Mary Liles Eicher, Anna Ferrell, Juliette Godot, Elizabeth Huhn, Tara Mills, Kristen Stappenbeck, and Tammi Truax. Anaid, Christian, and Khaiyah, readers at The Spun Yarn. The ladies of the First Fridays workshop, especially Tess Allen, P. J. Devlin, Taehee Kim, Brie Spencer, and Norah Vawter.

My editor, the fabulous Jessica Cale. The eagle-eyed Susie Murphy, for catching all those stubborn typos. Any remaining errors are entirely *mea culpa*.

My professors in the Johnston Center for Integrative Studies at the University of Redlands, especially Patricia Geary and Tim Powers. My professors in the Masters of Creative Writing program at George Mason University, especially Richard Bausch, Courtney Brkic, Alan Cheuse, Stephen Goodwin, Susan Shreve, and Mary Kay Zuravleff. Ann Weisgarber, my support at a critical moment.

When I was eight years old, my parents, John and Lynne Becker, took me to visit Charleston, South Carolina. I fell in love, and I knew I had to set a story there. My mother introduced me to John Jakes's *North and South* (1982), Alex Haley's *Roots* (1976), and Colleen McCullough's *The Thorn Birds* (1977). With these inspirations, I soon had the foundation and scaffolding of my own saga. My mother is also an excellent proofreader.

I am grateful to the authors of every book I consulted along the way, especially the seminarians, priests, and priests' lovers who shared their stories. Paul Hendrickson's *Seminary: A Search* (1983) and Gordon Thomas's *Desire and Denial* (1986) were particularly illuminating.

James M. O'Toole's *Passing for White: Race, Religion, and the Healy Family* (2002) was also indispensable in my understanding of Joseph. Brothers James, Patrick, and Sherwood Healy were the first Catholic priests of African ancestry to serve in the United States. Born slaves, one became a Bishop, another the President of Georgetown University. As far as we can tell, all three men turned their backs on their African heritage.

The prayers and rites I use come from several sources, especially: Bishop John England's *Translation of the Form for Conferring Orders in the Roman Catholic Church* (1830); England's *Roman Missal* (1843); Philip T. Weller's *The Roman Ritual in Latin and English* (1950); *The Ordination of a Subdeacon, a Deacon, a Priest* (1959); and the website *Fish Eaters: The Whys and Hows of Traditional Catholicism*, http://www.fisheaters.com/

Sharon Dean Walker, who so generously shared her time and research materials on the Diocese of Charleston. What I did with that information is entirely my own responsibility! Father Alejandro Tobón, for singing such a gorgeous Exultet, and prozars who posted the video on YouTube: https://youtu.be/nP_5YxIAV2E

The historical interpreters at Colonial Williamsburg, especially Mary Carter. Barbara Doyle at Middleton Place and Rikki Davenport at Drayton Hall for answering my random transportation questions. The tour guides and curators of every historic home, museum, and Catholic site I've ever visited. This project has been in progress for so many years, I have lost track of most of your names;

but if you ever spoke or wrote to me, please know that I deeply appreciate your contribution.

Thomas Hardy's *Tess of the D'Urbervilles* (1891) not only provided the epigraph for Part II but also inspired its title. Hardy's subtitle for *Tess* is "A Pure Woman, Faithfully Presented." I took the title of Part III, "The Man that Was a Thing," from another nineteenth-century novelist: this was Harriet Beecher Stowe's original subtitle for *Uncle Tom's Cabin* (1852).

But my greatest debts are to the late Colleen McCullough and to Richard Chamberlain, who first convinced me that a priest remains a man; that stories are more satisfying on a grand scale; and that "the best is only bought at the cost of great pain." The Lazare Family Saga essentially began as a *Thorn Birds* homage a quarter century ago. I hope you, dearest reader, will go on to discover how Father Ralph, Meggie, Fee, and Dane echo through the next three books in my series: *Lost Saints, Native Stranger,* and *Sweet Medicine.*

ABOUT THE AUTHOR

Elizabeth Bell has been writing stories since the second grade. At the age of fourteen, she chose a pen name and vowed to become a published author.

That same year, Elizabeth began The Lazare Family Saga. New generations and forgotten corners of history kept demanding attention, and the saga became four epic novels. After three decades of research and revision, Elizabeth decided she'd done them justice.

The first book of The Lazare Family Saga, *Necessary Sins*, was a Finalist in the Foreword Indies Book of the Year Awards. The second and third books, *Lost Saints* and *Native Stranger*, were Editors' Choices in the *Historical Novels Review*.

Upon earning her MFA in Creative Writing at George Mason University, Elizabeth realized she would have to return her two hundred library books. Instead, she cleverly found a job in the university library, where she works to this day.

Elizabeth loves hearing from readers and chatting about writing and history. Visit her on social media or her website:

https://elizabethbellauthor.com/

CPSIA information can be obtained
at www.ICGtesting.com
Printed in the USA
LVHW101539190522
719219LV00003B/77